Help us Rate this book...
Put your initials on the
left side and your rating
on the right side.
  1 = Didn't care for
  2 = It was O.K.
  3 = It was <u>great</u>

	Rating
mc	1 2 ③
mc	1 2 ③
LR	1 2 ③
	1 2 3
	1 2 3
	1 2 3
	1 2 3
	1 2 3
	1 2 3
	1 2 3
	1 2 3
	1 2 3
	1 2 3
	1 2 3
	1 2 3

DATE DUE

APR 1 9 2013		
MAY 1 0 2013		
MAY 1 9 2018		
JUN 1 2 2018		
JUN 2 5 2018		
JUL 5 2013		
AUG 2 7 2018		
SEP 0 5 2018		
JUL 0 2 2019		
JUL 2 9 2019		
		PRINTED IN U.S.A.

WHAT THE
Bishop Saw

Center Point
Large Print

Also by Vannetta Chapman and available from
Center Point Large Print:

Deep Shadows
Joshua's Mission
Raging Storm
Sarah's Orphans
Light of Dawn

**This Large Print Book carries the
Seal of Approval of N.A.V.H.**

WHAT THE
Bishop Saw

Vannetta Chapman

CENTER POINT LARGE PRINT
THORNDIKE, MAINE

This Center Point Large Print edition is published in
the year 2018 by arrangement with Harvest House Publishers.

This is a work of fiction. Names, characters, places,
and incidents are products of the author's imagination
or are used fictitiously. Any resemblance to actual persons,
living or dead, is entirely coincidental.

The text of this Large Print edition is unabridged. In other
aspects, this book may vary from the original edition.
Printed in the United States of America on permanent paper.
Set in 16-point Times New Roman type.

ISBN: 978-1-68324-717-3

Library of Congress Cataloging-in-Publication Data

Names: Chapman, Vannetta, author.
Title: What the bishop saw / Vannetta Chapman.
Description: Center Point Large Print edition. | Thorndike, Maine :
    Center Point Large Print, 2018. | Series: The Amish bishop mysteries
Identifiers: LCCN 2017057566 | ISBN 9781683247173
    (hardcover : alk. paper)
Subjects: LCSH: Amish—Fiction. | Clergy—Fiction. | Murder—
    Investigation—Fiction. | Large type books. | BISAC: FICTION /
    Christian / Suspense. | FICTION / Christian / Romance. | GSAFD:
    Christian fiction. | Mystery fiction.
Classification: LCC PS3603.H3744 W48 2018 | DDC 813/.—dc23
LC record available at https://lccn.loc.gov/2017057566

For My Friday Morning Prayer Breakfast Group

Acknowledgments

This book is dedicated to my Friday Morning Prayer Breakfast Group. Ladies, you cannot possibly know how much I look forward to that weekly hour together—high-carb food, good friends, plenty of laughter, and the sweet offering of prayer.

I'd like to thank the awesome staff at Harvest House. You all make the sometimes perilous job of writing a real pleasure. Gratitude to my agent, Steve Laube, who answers emails promptly and succinctly. As usual, I owe a giant debt of gratitude to my pre-readers Kristy Kreymer and Janet Murphy. You two ladies have eagle-sharp eyes and a good ear for how a sentence should sound. I also appreciate Patti Gallagher's input and her patience in answering my many questions about the Monte Vista, Colorado, area.

My family continues to support me through this journey. I wouldn't even attempt to do such a thing as write a novel without them. I love you guys.

I also would like to express my appreciation to my readers, who impatiently wait for the next book, devour it in a single day, and then email me asking when the next one will be available. You all are awesome!

And finally, "Always giving thanks to God the Father for everything, in the name of our Lord Jesus Christ" (Ephesians 5:20).

Each of you should use whatever gift you have received to serve others, as faithful stewards of God's grace in its various forms.

1 PETER 4:10

Of all the senses, sight must be the most delightful.

HELEN KELLER

Prologue

Goshen, Indiana

Henry Lapp needed an escape.

He sat at the kitchen table, his chin propped on his hands, staring out the window at his brothers and sister. That was where he should be, in the field, playing ball. One glance at his mother told him that was not going to happen, which didn't stop him from arguing about it. At twelve years old, he'd learned parents could sometimes be persuaded if one nagged with determination.

"I promise not to bat."

"Absolutely not."

"I'll stand in the outfield. No one ever gets a ball to the outfield."

"It's not going to happen. And baseball. I never want to see you playing baseball again. It's not up for discussion, Henry."

"And yet we are discussing it, *ya*? So maybe there's a possibility." He offered his crooked smile, the one that always made her laugh, but it did nothing to diminish the worry lines around his mother's eyes.

"You've been home three days, Henry. Only three days after . . . what? Three weeks in the hospital?"

He gingerly touched the side of his head. The stitches were gone. As for the three weeks, he remembered very little of that time since he'd spent much of it in a medically induced coma.

His mother sat down beside him and waited until he turned his gaze from the window to look at her. "You almost died, Henry. Your *dat* and I sat by your hospital bed, not knowing if you would wake up."

"I'm better now."

"And we praise *Gotte* for that every night, but you will follow the doctor's orders. She said for you to take it easy for a few weeks."

"Weeks?"

"Getting sick is easy. Getting well is the trick."

"Not a *gut* time for proverbs, *Mamm*."

"The best time for a proverb is when you think you don't need one."

"But I'm bored."

"How about you write your *mammi*?"

"I did that yesterday. Besides, writing feels like school, and it's summertime."

"I'll have dinner ready in an hour. Until then, you can draw her a picture." She stood and turned back to the stove, and he knew the discussion was over.

At least he'd given it his best try. He fetched a large sheet of construction paper and a pencil from the supply his mother kept near the table for school projects. He paused to consider what he should draw. *Mammi* was always asking about their church dinners. She missed the folks in Goshen since moving to Illinois to help one of his *onkels*. He would draw the picnic they'd had the day before. He bent over the sheet of paper and set to work.

And then his father was coming in the back door asking about dinner, and his brothers were trooping in the front talking about the baseball game, and his little sister was standing beside him.

"Look what Henry drew, *Mamm*. I can see me! And I can see my doll too."

"That's great, honey. Now wash your hands."

Henry pushed the sheet of paper away and rubbed his eyes. Suddenly he felt tired, as if he'd been clutching the pencil for hours. How long had he been drawing? Before he could work out the answer to that question, his three brothers stepped behind his chair.

"Whoa."

"That's a little spooky."

"*Mamm*, you'd better come look at this."

Henry wasn't entirely sure what they were talking about, but then his father reached over him and pulled the sheet of paper closer. Henry glanced down to see what looked like a photograph. Every person, every facial expression, every leaf looked real down to the smallest detail.

"Boys, take your sister outside." Henry's siblings left, and his father sat down next to him as his mother joined them. Her face paled when she looked at the drawing.

"You did this?" His father was still staring at what he'd drawn.

"*Ya.* I guess."

"How—"

"I don't know. *Mamm* told me to draw, so I did."

"But this . . . you shouldn't be able to do this."

Henry touched the paper, and that was when he noticed that perhaps he'd been a little too detailed. A husband was berating his wife about something, his face wreathed in a mask of anger. Two boys were fighting over a volleyball. Henry could imagine the unkind words they were saying by the expressions on their faces. A teenage boy stood next to a tree with a girl, no doubt thinking they couldn't be seen. In the drawing he was kissing her, one hand touching her face and the other hand resting on her hip. The look on their faces was one of complete happiness.

Anger and sadness and love. They weren't merely words. They were played out over every inch of the sheet of paper.

"I didn't mean to draw those things." Henry picked up his pencil, flipped it over, and frantically began erasing.

His father slipped his drawing off the table as his

mamm pulled the pencil out of his grasp. "Perhaps you should go rest," she murmured.

Henry had made it to the sitting room when he noticed his shoes were untied. He squatted to tie them, not intending to eavesdrop.

"This is from the brain injury," his father said. "It has to be."

"I don't understand. How could being hit in the head by a baseball cause . . . cause this?"

"Remember? The doctor said he could lose things—abilities, balance, whatever. And that he could gain things too."

"This? He gained this?"

"Maybe."

"And he drew it from his memory?"

"How else?"

"What do we do about it?" his mother asked.

"We'll speak to the bishop, and we'll pray."

"It will frighten people if they see this. No one wants their actions, their every emotion recorded." She paused, and Henry knew she was looking at the angry expressions, not the joyful ones.

"It's a gift," his father said, though his voice sounded anything but certain.

"It could be," his mother agreed. "Or perhaps it's a curse."

One

Fifty-two years later
San Luis Valley, Colorado
May 1

The smell of fire woke Henry Lapp from a sound sleep.

He stumbled out of his bed and hurried toward the window he'd left cracked open. A red glow on the horizon confirmed he wasn't dreaming. Throwing on his clothes and shoes, heavy black coat, and Plain hat, he made it out the front door in less than five minutes.

Should he take the time to hitch up Oreo? Or would it be quicker to walk?

Before he could decide, he heard the distant clatter of hooves. Jogging to the street, he raised a hand as Abe Graber's mare trotted around the bend in the road. Abe pulled to a stop and Henry hopped into the buggy.

"Where's the fire?"

"Vernon's house."

"Anyone hurt?"

Abe yanked off his hat, pushed the hair out of his eyes and plopped the hat back on again. "*Ya*, probably so. Word is Vernon was home. It doesn't look *gut*."

Henry didn't bother asking Abe more questions. He was surprised the man knew as much as he did, but then the Amish grapevine was efficient and reliable. If they said Vernon had been home at the time of the fire, then more than likely he had been.

Henry spent the remainder of the ride praying for Vernon's soul and staring out at the darkness of the Colorado night, offset only by the glow of the half moon. The weather had warmed recently, but temperatures were still quite chilly at night. Perhaps a fire in the stove had sparked, igniting something lying close by.

"Talk to him lately?" Abe asked.

"Yesterday. I went by to see him after church. He didn't stay for luncheon."

"Not unusual—for Vernon."

"True, but I was concerned."

"So did everything seem okay . . . when you visited him?"

"As much as it could with Vernon." Henry didn't explain.

He knew he didn't have to.

Two

Henry could hear the crackle of the flames from where they tied the mare, next to several other buggies and well away from Vernon's house. The horse snorted and stomped her foot, and then she began to crop at the grass. Henry and Abe hurried toward the side of the house, where the bulk of the activity was taking place. It wasn't easy going. They had to skirt around a dilapidated chicken coop, weave their way through rusted farm equipment, dodge several chickens, and then pick a path through piles of broken garden pots.

Emergency personnel hadn't taken such a careful route. The fire truck had crushed a pile of bicycle parts and what looked to Henry like a motor scooter.

The house itself was ablaze, a sight that stirred an ache deep in Henry's heart.

Firefighters, risking their lives, were trying to keep the fire from spreading to either of the barns.

A homestead—gone.

A life—abruptly ended.

Because he didn't see Vernon anywhere, he feared that was the truth. But then every life was complete. Isn't that what Abe had preached recently? Every life was complete. Henry believed it to be so. The Bible said as much in the book of Job. *A man's days are numbered. You know the number of his months. He cannot live longer than the time You have set.*

It was difficult to understand at times, but it was true. God determined the length of a person's life. As the bishop for their small Amish community, Henry presided over funerals, celebrated births, and led his flock. He would guide them through this.

He suddenly became aware of the firemen, all of them volunteer, rushing away from the building.

"It's coming down!" Sam Beiler hollered. Sam had been on the volunteer crew for nearly ten years now, since he'd been baptized into the church at nineteen.

The smoke rolled away from the building— black and thick, like the worst of clouds descending over the San Juan Mountains. Henry couldn't see those mountains in the dim light of the moon, but he could see the smoke thanks to the firefighters' lights set up around the scene.

The crowd of onlookers stepped back, though they'd been huddled safely behind the line set by the fire captain. There was a collective gasp as the roof collapsed, sending out sparks. The fire roared, and as Henry instinctively held up his arm and felt the heat of the flames through his coat, he understood in his heart that Vernon could not have survived. Nothing could survive such an inferno.

The fire blazed hotter and brighter, grabbing at the timbers and greedily consuming them. The smoke that had been rolling out toward them turned up and evaporated into the inkiness of the night. The house groaned. Walls fell. Windows burst, showering glass onto the lawn.

Another fifteen minutes and the worst of it was over. The firemen again set to work with their ladders and hoses. Within the next hour, they had reduced the blaze to a few manageable hot spots.

The men from Henry's congregation as well as a few *Englischers* offered to help, but the fire captain sent them home. As they were slowly dispersing, Captain Warren Johnson scanned the crowd. When he saw the bishop, he waved him over.

"Terrible thing," Henry said.

"It is." Warren Johnson still wore his heavy firefighting uniform, but he'd pulled off his gloves and now swiped a giant hand over his face. The man was over six feet and built like an ox.

"Vernon?"

"Pulled him out within five minutes of getting here. I'm sorry, Henry. He didn't make it."

It was then that Henry noticed the ambulance parked on the far side of the fire truck. Its lights were off, but the bay doors were open. He stepped to the left and saw a body on a stretcher, covered with a sheet.

"Paramedics decided to stay in case one of my men needed them."

"I hope no one else was hurt."

"No, though your guy Sam . . . " Johnson shook his head. "The man doesn't know the meaning of the word danger."

"I'd be surprised to hear he was careless."

"Not at all. It's only that he throws himself into fighting a fire. He insisted on being the one to go in after Vernon. He brought out his body."

Henry didn't know what to say to that. He'd known Sam Beiler since he was a young lad. The man was as generous and dedicated as a person could be. When Henry had talked to him about the dangers of firefighting, he'd smiled and said, "It's my way of serving others, Henry."

Chief Johnson barked some orders at a group of men, and then he turned his attention back to the bishop. "The reason I called you over is because I want to show you something."

Henry nodded, and Johnson led him around to the front of the house. The fire had done less damage to this portion of the dwelling, though everything was wet and covered with ash and soot.

"Watch your step," Johnson warned.

They stopped at the window to the right of the front door, their feet crunching against shattered glass.

Henry could see through to the sitting room and the charred destruction beyond.

"I'm not sure what I'm looking at," he admitted.

"The window."

"Looks like it exploded, same as the others."

"Yeah, when the heat built up, it did." Johnson shone his flashlight on the floor inside the home. "Shattered glass blows out, as you no doubt noticed when we walked around the house."

"But there's glass on the inside."

"Exactly. That's my point."

Maybe it was fatigue catching up with him, or perhaps the smoke had messed with his reasoning abilities. "I guess I'm not seeing what's important here."

"This is where it started."

"The fire?"

"Someone threw an incendiary device through this window, Henry. This fire wasn't an accident. Someone started it. I have no doubt the arson team will find a homemade explosive of some sort. The person threw it through this window, busting the glass. The device slid across the room, came into contact with a couch or something flammable, and *whoosh*. The entire house went up in smoke and flames."

Henry turned to study Johnson, to see if the man was serious, but he wasn't known to joke around, especially at a fire. And the expression on his face was grim, determined.

"You think this was arson?"

"I do." The captain refocused the beam of his flashlight on the glass inside the front window. "Can't say if they meant to kill Vernon or only wanted to scare him. Whether the homicide was intentional or not, it looks like we have a crime on our hands."

"Hard to imagine."

"I'd like you to think about it and try to come up with a list of names for me."

"What names?"

"People who would want to kill Vernon Frey."

Three

Emma Fisher walked with her granddaughter in the early morning sunshine. The San Luis Valley stretched out around them—broad and flat and dry. Situated at an elevation of 7664 feet, their rainfall amounted to a whopping seven inches a year. The Sangre de Cristo Mountains rose to the east. The San Juan Mountains towered to the west. Both were capped with snow, though there hadn't been any on the ground in the valley since the month before.

"So he . . . died?" Katie Ann asked. She had turned sixteen the previous summer, was finished with school, and could ask more questions than the average three-year-old. She was blond and pretty and still growing into her arms and legs.

"He did." Emma swiped at strands of her hair that insisted on escaping from her *kapp*. At sixty, she was slightly plumper and a bit grayer than she'd ever imagined she would be. Neither bothered her much, but the arthritis in her knees did. She considered the dry mountain air a blessing—it seemed to ease the ache in her bones. By noon she barely noticed it.

"From the fire?"

"*Ya.*"

"That would be terrible."

"It would be indeed."

Katie Ann switched the bucket of cleaning supplies to her left arm and slipped her right hand into her grandmother's. It reminded Emma of when she was a little girl.

"I don't want something like that to ever happen to you."

"You don't need to worry yourself about such, Katie Ann."

"Because *Gotte* will take care of us."

"He will."

"But He didn't take care of Vernon Frey."

"Every person's life is complete when the Lord calls them home."

"Your reasoning goes round and round, *Mammi*. It reminds me of the math problems Teacher gave us."

"Does it now?"

"See? Instead of denying it, you only smile at me."

"I'll admit some things are hard to understand."

"That's the truth."

They'd reached the corner of Henry Lapp's property. Katie Ann released her hand and ran forward to greet Oreo, Henry's black-and-white buggy mare. Emma wasn't a bit surprised when the girl pulled a slice of apple from her pocket and fed it to the horse.

"I thought you'd eaten that for breakfast."

"I ate the rest." Katie Ann rubbed Oreo along

her nose and then hurried to catch up with Emma.

"Why do we clean Henry's house each week?"

"You know why. He's widowed and has no family here."

"Why doesn't he marry again?"

"I suppose the Lord hasn't seen fit to send him a wife."

"Maybe he could just meet one the way normal people do."

"Maybe he will."

"I'm not marrying until I'm old, like thirty."

"Is that so?"

"You can laugh, but it's true. I want to see the world first. Experience some stuff."

"Sure you can postpone your plans long enough to help me with the bishop's cleaning?"

"Of course. Henry always lets me ride Oreo when we're done."

Henry was standing on the porch waiting for them by the time they'd crossed the front yard. Emma thought he was a nice-looking man—his hair was brown going to gray and had a bit of a curl in it. His beard had turned nearly white in the last year, something he found amusing. "It's as if I'm getting old from my chin up." Laugh lines fanned out from eyes that were a warm brown. In his midsixties, he'd watched his weight, or maybe he had a naturally fast metabolism. He didn't have the large belly many men his age did, even farmers who spent their time laboring in the fields. It came from eating too many carbohydrates. Henry was mostly at the mercy of his congregation's casseroles, though he claimed he could fry an egg or make a sandwich as well as anyone.

"Morning, Emma."

"Morning."

"Katie Ann."

"Morning, Henry. I fed Oreo an apple slice. She's looking full of energy today."

Henry rubbed a hand up and down his jawline, as if he were puzzled. "I suppose I should take her out more often. Haven't needed to use the buggy as much lately because I've been working in my woodshop more."

"I can ride her for you. That will settle her down."

"A fine idea."

"Thanks, Henry." Katie Ann hurried inside, her step light and energetic. She'd have the sheets off the bed and in the washer before Emma started on the kitchen.

"The energy of *youngies* is a mystery to me."

Henry smiled, held the door open, and then followed Emma inside.

She insisted he get out from underfoot. "I know you have orders to fill in your workshop."

"Now that you mention it . . ." With a smile and a wink, he was gone.

Back in Goshen, Henry had made furniture

27

from pine, oak, and cherrywood. Now he created smaller pieces.

When their group first moved to Colorado, they'd all had adjustments to make.

Neighbors were different. Farming was different. Hobbies often generated more income than crops.

Henry had begun scouring the area for run-down barns. There were plenty of those. Most of the time, the owners were happy to have some of the lumber hauled off. Occasionally Henry would pay a small fee for the wood. He took it into his work-shop, sanded it, oiled it, put a finish on it, and hammered it into picture frames, shelves, and birdhouses. Downtown Monte Vista was an art haven, and several of the stores were happy to carry Henry's creations.

For the next two hours, Emma and Katie Ann swept and mopped, cleaned the kitchen and the bathroom, washed bedding, and attempted to banish the dust that seemed to return as soon as it was wiped away. Henry kept a clean house. Emma almost laughed out loud, thinking of her George and what his house would have looked like if she'd gone first. The man was a marvel in the field but rather helpless on the domestic front. He'd passed four years earlier, and she still found herself surprised and occasionally bereft to wake and discover herself alone in their queen-sized bed.

She didn't speak to Henry about the fire until

the housework was done. Katie Ann, excused from the last of it, had enjoyed her ride and led Oreo back into the barn to give her a thorough brushing. Emma and Henry sat at the kitchen table, enjoying the last of the coffee and a midmorning snack.

"She's a *gut* girl," Henry said, pushing the plate of oatmeal cookies toward her.

"These look like the work of Ruth Schwartz."

Henry hid his smile behind his coffee mug. "*Ya.* She gave them to me after our church luncheon."

"You would think the widows in our church would have given up on turning your head, Henry Lapp."

"You're suggesting I'm too old?"

"I'm suggesting you're too stubborn. You're set in your ways, and we both know it."

"Hard to turn down a plate of cookies." Henry reached for another.

Emma shrugged and chose one from the plate. "Now tell me about the fire."

Four

"He wants you to make a list?" Emma had been leaning forward during Henry's brief recital of Sunday night's events. Now she sat back, her hands folded in her lap, and stared at him incredulously.

"*Ya.*"

"Where would you begin?"

"Unfortunately, starting the list wasn't a problem. The real issue came when I realized I was jotting down the names of nearly everyone I know."

"You're saying we could all be murderers?" Emma's voice squeaked as she reached for another cookie.

"Of course not. Captain Johnson asked for a list of names that included anyone who would *want* to kill Vernon. That doesn't mean I think they'd do it."

"I see your problem."

"The man wasn't well liked."

"And yet he was a member of our community. He was Plain." Emma tapped the table. "Each person agrees to abide by the rules of the *Ordnung*. We all do—Vernon Frey as well as those who disagreed with him. We are Amish. We turn the other cheek."

"The doctrine of nonresistance is strong in our faith and our culture. I'll agree with you there, but you know as well as I do . . . it doesn't make us perfect."

"I never said—"

"Plain folk have tempers, same as anyone else."

"Of course we do."

"We're human, Emma. We make mistakes. Whoever did this could be a member of our community."

"Or it could have been an *Englischer*." Emma stood, refilled her coffee mug, and waved the pot toward Henry, who shook his head. "Vernon was known to pick a fight over the smallest things—in a passive, nonresistant way, of course."

"It's true." Henry rested his forearms on the table and frowned into his cup. "I spoke to Vernon many times about his attitude toward others. In fact, Clyde and I met with him last month, and I stopped by again recently."

"Clyde told me he visited, although he didn't share any particulars." When George died, that left the district with only one other minister— Abe Graber. The congregation had nominated a half dozen of the married men from their midst, but no one was surprised when the lot fell to her son, Clyde.

"*Gotte* is using your family," Henry had said to her more than once. She'd wanted to laugh.

She'd never imagined herself as a minister's wife, and now she was a widow and the mother of a minister. *Gotte* had a sense of humor indeed, as her family was far from perfect. They cared, though. She never doubted how much they cared for one another.

She refocused her attention on Henry. "You did your best, I'm sure."

"The *Ordnung* does not allow us to discipline a member because he has a sour disposition."

"Nor should it."

"And yet if it did, if I had, perhaps Vernon would be alive today."

"Don't go blaming yourself for this, Henry." Emma stood again, cleaned off their dishes, rinsed the mugs and put them in the drain, and covered the cookies with a clean kitchen towel. "You make the list, exactly as Warren Johnson asked. He's a *gut* man, and he'll know where to take the investigation from there. If your list is several pages long and includes every name in Monte Vista, then so be it."

"I suppose, though I hate to cast suspicion on innocent people."

"When was the last time you saw Vernon?" Emma picked up a dish towel and swiped at the already clean counter.

"Sunday afternoon."

"Did you notice anything that seemed out of place or suspicious?"

"Not that I can remember."

Emma put the dish towel on a hook and turned to look directly at Henry. Her next question wasn't one he would be comfortable with, but it was important that she ask.

"Have you tried . . ." She mimicked drawing on paper.

Henry shook his head, met her gaze for a second, and then glanced away.

"When will the funeral be?"

"Depends on when the morgue can release the body. Vernon had no family in the area. He had a few cousins back east. I stopped at the phone shack on the way home early this morning and called the bishops in Lancaster. Both expressed their condolences but were sure the families would not be able to make it out to attend the funeral. His relatives are older, older even than Vernon was, and not in *gut* health."

The back screen door banged against its frame, and they heard the sound of Katie Ann stomping dirt off her shoes. Emma began gathering the cleaning supplies they'd brought. She didn't want to speak of such things in front of the teenager. Her granddaughter was impressionable, not to mention unsettled enough about the fire.

Henry was standing with his back against the counter, arms crossed, with a smile playing on the corner of his lips. "*Danki*, Emma."

"For the cleaning?" She made a *pshaw* sound that reminded her of her mother.

"Not just the cleaning. You can't know how much it helps to be able to talk to someone . . . person to person, not bishop to congregant."

Emma would have told him he was welcome and assured him he could speak to anyone in their community in the same way. But she didn't say either of those things because Katie Ann walked into the room talking of horses and spring and the fact that Henry had a litter of newborn kittens in his barn.

"Do I?"

"Well, *ya*. They're in the back corner stall, in a box with a blanket . . ." She glanced at Emma and then again at Henry. "Oh. That's a joke. You knew already."

"I might have heard a meow or two."

"And you took the blanket out."

"It was old and torn."

"That explains why there's a bowl of cat food for the mother, and some water as well."

Instead of defending himself, Henry offered her a cookie.

As they walked home, Katie Ann collected a bouquet from the wildflowers blooming in the ditch, though she had a difficult time finding many. Much of the ditch was planted with asparagus, which was common in the area and grew well in the May weather. The temperature had risen to a pleasant sixty degrees or so.

Emma's thoughts returned to Vernon's death, Warren Johnson's opinion that the fire had been intentionally set, and Henry's list. They rounded the corner on their own property, a scant fifty-two acres—hardly large enough to make a living out of, even if they had sufficient rain to do so. When they'd arrived thirteen years earlier, they'd had such a different vision, thinking they could overcome the environment with hard work and dedication.

The land had humbled them in more than one way, but they'd endured. Now the flat acreage seemed like home. Her husband had been happy here, and her son had assured her he was content to stay. She was grateful. She would have gone back east if he'd asked, but she preferred the valley, rimmed in by the mountains. It was an oasis of sorts.

Katie Ann hurried ahead of her, up the steps of the front porch and into the house to tell her mother about the horse and the kittens and the flowers.

But Emma didn't go inside right away.

She sat down on one of the porch rockers and thought about what Henry had said, about being able to talk to her person to person. It occurred to Emma that Henry probably missed her husband nearly as much as she did. George had been a simple man, and he had often sat where she was now—on the porch with their bishop, talking of fishing and farming and their life in the San Luis Valley.

And what would he think of the bishop's list? Most likely he would have laughed and admitted that his own name could have been added there. Not that George would hurt a horsefly, let alone a man. Which was the heart of the problem. Vernon Frey had a way of bringing out the worst in folks, and apparently he had paid for that with his life.

Five

Henry had hoped the afternoon would pass peacefully.

He'd just spent an hour in the woodshop, working on three birdhouses. As he sanded the weathered wood, he thought of Emma's question. He had not tried to draw the details of his visit to Vernon's. What good would it do? What could he possibly have seen? And he wasn't comfortable with his ability, his *gift*. Unless it became absolutely necessary, he would not pursue answers from that direction.

He pushed the thought from his mind, finished his projects, and made his way inside for lunch. He enjoyed a turkey sandwich, made from the fresh bread Franey Graber had brought by. Emma had laughed about the widows who pursued Henry with a surprising determination.

Ruth Schwartz had lost her husband the year before. She was a kind woman but a real talker. No, Henry couldn't see himself marrying someone who wouldn't allow quiet to seep into a room for even a moment. She did make fabulous desserts, though. In fact, Henry had spoken to her about opening a bakery, and she was considering doing so. It would certainly help her family financially.

Franey Graber wasn't a widow, not in the legal sense of the word, though people still thought of her as such. Henry had heard the kids calling her Frowning Franey, and though he wanted to reprimand them and would have if it had been said directly to him, he understood why they called her that. He'd rarely seen her smile. She was Abe's sister-in-law. Abe and Alvin were brothers. Since her divorce, Franey survived off Abe's benevolence. She'd shared with Henry more than once that she had nothing to be happy about. She was another of the women who had showed a dogged interest in him. He wasn't blind. He understood what the deluge of fresh bread and biscuits meant. Franey wasn't one to talk much, but often when she did her words had a biting edge to them.

He could remember when Franey was a sweet, young newlywed back in Goshen. The move to Colorado had proven too much for her husband, but instead of suggesting they join another community in a different state, Alvin had moved over to Alamosa, fallen in love with an *Englisch* woman, and served Franey with divorce papers. Under their *Ordnung* there was no such thing as divorce, but Franey had signed the papers because Alvin wasn't asking for divorce from the Amish church. In *Englisch* courts, divorce was common. Franey was not eligible to remarry per the *Ordnung*, but he supposed she was lonely and perhaps that was why she brought fresh baked goods to his door at least twice a week. The entire episode with Alvin had left her bitter. Who wouldn't be? But it hadn't affected her bread baking ability. Perhaps she should go into business with Ruth. Why hadn't he thought of that earlier?

He found an old envelope next to the pile of junk mail he'd meant to throw away and proceeded to jot down the list of tasks he needed to accomplish for the week.

Speak to Franey about bakery
Visit Rebecca Yoder
Counsel with Albert again
Pick up more scrap lumber
Purchase seeds for garden

He hesitated, stared out the window for a moment, and prayed for wisdom in all things concerning his congregation. He petitioned the Lord to direct his path and supply his words. Finally, he again picked up the pencil and wrote . . .

Call meeting of elders

Satisfied with the list, he walked back to the table and set it under his salt shaker. Reaching for another one of the oatmeal cookies, his thoughts turned again to the widows. The third woman who regularly brought him food—casseroles, in this case—was Nancy Kline. Henry bit into his sandwich and stared out the window. There was absolutely nothing wrong with Nancy Kline.

Well, truthfully there was nothing wrong with any of them. They simply were the way they were. Nancy was a kind, pleasant, patient woman, and even Henry, who had little experience in such things, would call her good looking.

No, the problem with the women wasn't the women themselves. It was Henry.

He'd lived alone for more than twenty years. He still missed Claire, but now he could smile at the memories. She'd been a joy, a real blessing in his life. He wished they'd had children, wished she was still with him, but it was not to be. Unlike Job, he wouldn't question God, though he certainly had in the first few years without her. It was true that some nights he found himself lonely, wishing he was surrounded by the noise and energy of grandchildren. But more often he found himself relieved when he returned home from some event, happy to step into his quiet, orderly world.

What was it Emma had said? *You're too stubborn. You're set in your ways, and we both know it.* Emma Fisher was tough stuff. She called things as she saw them, and she always did so with a smile on her lips and a kindness in her voice. And she was right. He was stubborn and set in his ways. Perhaps that wasn't such a sin.

He had finished the cookie, drained his glass of milk, and was looking forward to an hour of reading, when there was a knock at the front door.

He was surprised he hadn't heard anyone drive up. That's what came of daydreaming about widows.

He opened the door to find Sheriff Roy Grayson standing there in full uniform. Beside him was a woman Henry had never seen before.

"Afternoon, Henry."

"Sheriff."

"This is Meg Allen. She's the arson investigator sent over from County."

Sheriff Grayson was in his forties, balding, tall, and thin. He'd always been respectful to Henry, though their paths had crossed relatively few times and never more than casually. The woman beside him had bright red hair, cut short. She was Henry's height, which was tall for a woman and muscular in ways most Amish women weren't. She looked to be quite young.

As if reading his thoughts, Grayson said, "Meg is one of the best arson investigators in the state. We're lucky to have her on this."

"Would you like to come inside?"

"That might be better."

They settled in the sitting room—Allen and Grayson on the couch. Henry took the rocker.

Henry waited. He wasn't one to jump into a conversation.

"Meg wanted to ask you some questions, and

41

she wanted to see the list, the one Warren Johnson asked you to compile."

"I expected that Warren might come by to pick it up."

"He turned his report over to us because this is a criminal matter now. I'll be in charge, working in conjunction with Meg. Do you have the list?"

"*Ya.* I've spent a fair amount of time working on it," Henry admitted.

"May I see it?"

"Of course, but before we get to that, are you certain this was a case of arson?"

Allen glanced at Grayson, who nodded once.

"Yes," she said. "We're sure."

"How sure?" When she glared at him, Henry said calmly, "Are you reasonably sure, as in it isn't likely that an accident caused the fire? Or are you completely sure? Have you found evidence that can't be refuted?"

"I'm not accustomed to sharing the details of an ongoing investigation, a barely begun investigation, with friends of the deceased—"

"Now, hang on, Meg." Grayson sat forward, his forearms resting on his knees, and clasped his hands together. "Henry is the bishop for this group of folks. We've had no trouble in all the years—"

"Thirteen."

"In the thirteen years they've been here." Grayson scrubbed a hand across his face. "And we are asking him to give us a list of names that probably includes more than a few of the people in his church."

"Is that what this is about? Clergy privilege? It doesn't apply here. Not in a case of felony murder. Regardless, I don't see it. Unless you counseled an individual, specifically about his or her propensity to start fires."

Henry shook his head.

"Or unless the person has confessed to you, which I have to say would be a record confession since it's been only twelve hours since the fire and subsequent death of Mr. Frey."

"*Nein*. I haven't received a confession."

"Then I'd like to see the list."

"And I'd like to know why you're certain this is arson. I'm aware of the broken glass inside the room and Captain Johnson's suspicions, but a person can't be convicted on those two things alone. Is there even a small possibility this was an accident? Certainly it wouldn't be the first time a person has been careless with a fire or a candle or a lantern." Allen began shaking her head, but Henry felt duty bound to continue. "Maybe Vernon left the oven on or the burner lit. Once a family in Goshen left a dish towel too near a burner, and the whole house went up in flames. Real tragedy."

Her reply was curt, choppy, and to the point. "We found evidence of three Molotov cocktails."

43

"Bottle-based improvised incendiary devices," Grayson offered, sitting back. "Whoever did this had done their research. They knew what type of bottle worked best—to be efficient the bottle must be breakable. A heavy glass, like an old Coke bottle, wouldn't work well."

"And you found proof of this?"

Allen picked up the explanation. "We're waiting for results from the lab, but from the fire pattern and the speed at which the blaze grew, yes. Both Captain Johnson and I are quite certain. In all likelihood, our perpetrator used a mixture of petrol and motor oil. The cloth wick could have been soaked in alcohol or kerosene."

When Henry still hesitated, Allen leaned forward again. "We found evidence of at least three of these devices. This wasn't someone who was angry and hoped to scare Mr. Frey. This was someone bound and determined to kill him. Based on my experience, once a person kills via arson, they can't stop. Instead, they become obsessed with a driving compulsion to do so again."

"We're looking at felony arson, Henry. Damages certainly exceeded five hundred dollars. Frey's death means there will also be a charge of felony murder. That's the same as first-degree murder, and Meg is right. The statutory privilege between patient and physician, and hence clergy privilege, does not apply. Whoever did this is looking at one of two sentences—death or life without the possibility of parole."

Henry had heard enough. He wouldn't have withheld the list, but he wanted to be sure the *Englisch* authorities knew what they were doing. The last thing he needed was a new recruit looking for trouble to pad his or her résumé. A world of difference lay between an accidental fire and arson.

But Allen seemed convinced. The woman was pushy and somewhat arrogant, but she appeared to know what she was talking about. More importantly, Grayson trusted her.

Henry walked into the kitchen, pulled a pad of paper from the drawer where he'd stored it, and tore off the top sheet. Walking back into the sitting room, he handed it to the investigator.

She studied it top to bottom, glanced at him, and then she went over it again.

Beside each name, Henry had listed the person's association to Vernon.

Finally, she handed the paper to Grayson, who had been reading over her shoulder, and said, "Maybe you could explain to me why Mr. Frey had so many enemies."

Six

He passed the Monte Vista Sheriff's cruiser as it pulled out of the bishop's lane.

So they were interviewing Henry Lapp. Well, they wouldn't learn anything there.

He'd been extremely careful and was sure he'd left no evidence pointing to himself. The bottles, if they hadn't been destroyed, would provide no fingerprints. Roy Grayson could bring in as many outside investigators as he wanted. They would find nothing, and they certainly wouldn't catch him.

What bothered him was not the authorities. What bothered him—irked him, actually—was that they might get in the way. He had a plan—a specific schedule. He had five targets in mind, and he knew in what order he wanted to hit them. He would exact his revenge. These people had been responsible for destroying his life, and he would make them pay. He refused to be derailed by a group of amateurs. Once he was finished, they could do whatever they wanted. He didn't plan to stick around for that.

His mind skittered off in a dozen directions. He could play this out in countless possible ways given the investigation and what he'd read in the paper about "investigative procedures." But he could tell from the article that the authorities were clueless. It would take them a while to even come up with a list of suspects, and he could be finished by then.

He thought of his mother and father and brother. He thought of all that had happened to them, all the tragedy they had endured. Once again, he vowed in his heart to fulfill the promise he'd made to his brother.

Soon he would strike again, and he'd continue to do so until he accomplished what he'd set out to do.

Vernon Frey was only the beginning.

Seven

Emma helped her daughter-in-law, Rachel, put together dinner—a baked chicken, mashed potatoes, green beans, biscuits, and salad. There had been a time when Emma worried her son might starve after marrying Rachel. The girl had been raised Mennonite, and with her sights set on college to become a literature professor, she barely knew how to make toast. But all of that was twenty years earlier, and now Rachel was a fine cook, though she still tended to take peeks at whatever book she was reading while she cooked—which had occasionally resulted in a burned meal.

"Mmm. Smells *gut*. *Mamm* must have finished her book." Silas slid into his seat and smiled at his mother. He was the oldest, having recently turned seventeen, and felt he had the right to tease his mother now that he was no longer in school.

Katie Ann followed the year after.

The two younger boys had been born later. Thomas had recently turned ten, and Stephen was nine. They'd each been a pleasant surprise to the entire family. Rachel was a fine mother to the four children, and the family was constantly bustling and busy.

Emma had only had the one child—Clyde. They were the odd family of three in a community where families usually had eight to ten children. She'd always been close to her only son. When Clyde and Rachel expressed an interest in moving to Colorado, leaving their established community in Goshen, Indiana, Emma and George had readily agreed to pull up roots and go with them.

Rachel finished setting the food on the table and sat down, each person paused for a moment of silent prayer, and then Clyde said, "Amen." A flurry of activity commenced. Emma loved the sounds of serving platters being passed, silverware scraping against plates, the boys jostling for the largest biscuit. To her, mealtimes encompassed the most basic moments of family life. She thought of Vernon Frey, eating alone all his days. Why had he never married? Why had he moved west? What had gone so terribly wrong with his life that it ended in such a drastic fashion?

"Everyone on the construction crew was talking about the fire today," Silas said, his words garbled by a mouthful of potatoes. He'd recently taken a job in town working on the building of a large new discount store.

"It's a real tragedy, for sure and for certain." Rachel jumped up from the table to get the butter from the refrigerator. The appliance was small and gas operated. There had been talk within their district of converting to solar power, but it was still being discussed by the church elders.

"They say someone did it on purpose."

Emma glanced at her son. Clyde didn't seem perturbed by the statement. He wasn't one for shielding the children from bad news.

"That's stupid," Stephen said.

"It's smart if you ask me." Thomas studiously cut his piece of chicken with a fork and knife. The boys preferred fried chicken, which they could pick up and eat. They weren't as keen on baked chicken, which required the use of silverware.

"Nothing smart about killing a man," Clyde said.

"Oh, I don't mean that. I mean if you did it, and if there was a fire, then any evidence would be burned up." Thomas twirled his hand in the air, mimicking smoke spiraling away.

"There's always evidence, though." Silas reached for another piece of chicken. "Guys on the construction site say whoever did it wrote with red paint on the wall—one of the walls that didn't burn."

"Why would somebody do that?" Katie Ann asked.

"I don't know. A warning maybe?"

"There was no message scrawled on the wall," Emma said.

Everyone stopped to stare at her.

"What? I spoke with Henry this morning after

50

we'd done our cleaning. There was no note of any sort, though the authorities do suspect it was a case of arson, and that the person who set the fire did so in order to kill Vernon."

"Why would someone kill another person?" Katie Ann used her fork to push her potatoes back and forth across the plate. "I can't imagine a reason to do such a thing."

"Greed," Silas said. "Most sin is from greed. Don't you agree, *Dat*?"

"I suppose much of it is."

"Maybe he made someone angry."

"He made everyone angry."

"Could be a person was robbing him, and then he set the fire to cover up the robbery."

"Not much there to steal, not that I could see when we had church there last."

"Revenge, that's a *gut* motive."

"But revenge for what?"

"Money."

"Same thing as greed, I suppose. I don't think he had much of that."

"Jealousy?"

"Can't see what he would have to be jealous of."

The topic was volleyed back and forth between the children until Clyde brought up the subject of their upcoming crops and water conservation. Vernon was temporarily forgotten. But after Rachel, Emma, and Katie Ann had cleaned up

51

the kitchen, the adults slipped out onto the front porch to the rockers. Silas had cleaned up and left on an errand, which Emma supposed meant he was courting. Well, that was what seventeen-year-old boys were supposed to do. Stephen and Thomas were practicing for the next softball game with a ball and bat. Katie Ann headed to the barn to brush down the workhorses, though the boys had no doubt already done that.

"Any excuse to spend time with a horse is a *gut* excuse to our Katie Ann." Clyde reached out and squeezed Rachel's hand. The look that passed between them brought a smile to Emma's heart. What could make a mother more content than seeing her son happily married?

"I can't say I liked that conversation at dinner," Rachel said.

"Best to let them work through the topic and be done with it. Otherwise, we'll find them speaking of it in whispers every time we come around a corner."

"It's not a subject that's likely to go away until the authorities find the killer." Emma pulled a knitting project from her bag. The long days allowed enough light to work on it for the next hour, and she'd much rather do so outside while she enjoyed the setting sun casting colors across the sky.

"Henry had no idea who it might have been?"

Emma told them about the list.

"It included *Englisch* and Amish?" Clyde stood, walked to the porch steps, and stared out at a beautiful sunset complete with purple, rose, and gold light splaying across his land. With a sigh, he turned toward them. "That's surprising."

"It is, but I suppose he wanted to be thorough. I don't think he believes any Amish person did such a thing."

"I heard Henry had been to visit Vernon the afternoon before." Rachel held a book in her lap, but she didn't open it.

"*Ya*, he said as much."

"If he was there in the home, then he might remember seeing something. Perhaps the killer had been to visit earlier."

"He says he doesn't."

They were all quiet for a moment. Clyde finally asked, "Has he tried drawing whatever he saw?"

"*Nein.*"

"It's been years since Henry used his gift." Rachel drummed her fingers against the cover of her book. "Who knows if he even still has it?"

"I imagine he would be relieved to find that he didn't." Emma focused on the yarn and knitting needles, attempting to push back her memories of those dark days.

"The last time was before we left Indiana, right?" Clyde glanced from his mother to his wife and back again.

"*Ya*, and I have no doubt that incident played

a large part in Henry's decision to join this community."

"People weren't fair to him." Rachel opened her book, but she didn't look down at the page. "They seemed almost afraid of him, as if he was some sort of freak or something. It's always caused me to feel a little protective of Henry, which I know is silly. He's twenty years older and my bishop to boot."

"That's a *gut* way to put it," Clyde said. "We do feel protective."

Emma tugged again on the yarn. "That situation was heartbreaking from start to finish. Henry and your father had been to counsel the girl the night before she ran away. She'd refused to come down to the sitting room, so they'd gone upstairs to her bedroom. Which is why Henry saw what he did."

"Only he didn't know what he'd seen. Not until later. Not until he'd drawn it." Rachel shut the book again, keeping her finger in the spot where she'd intended to read. "I've never understood how it works."

"Henry doesn't understand himself, or so he told me." Clyde sat back down in his rocker with a sigh. "It's a blessing and a curse."

"What was the name of that expert they brought in? The trial had been going on for a few days and then Mr. . . . "

"Malinowski," Rachel said.

"Right. He called it acquired savant syndrome."

54

"Another doctor called it accidental savant."

"First time I'd heard either term." Clyde studied her, and Emma knew he was falling back into the memories of those terrible days.

"I can't remember how he described it, the gift Henry has. Something about the conscious mind . . . I don't know. The *Englisch* can explain away the beauty of a sunset with their science and experts." Emma realized she'd dropped a stitch. She pulled out the knitting needles and set to unraveling what she'd done.

Clyde grunted in agreement. "I was in court that day. Malinowski testified that Henry's conscious mind worked the same as ours, but his unconscious mind was able to remember anything he'd seen down to the smallest detail."

"When he draws it." Rachel's voice dropped, as if what they were speaking of was a secret.

It wasn't a secret. Henry made sure every family in the community moving west knew about his ability, and he'd made sure the small group already in Colorado was aware as well. He didn't want anyone regretting the fact that they'd joined in with him.

"That's why officials thought Henry had some-thing to do with the girl's disappearance, but of course he didn't." As the memories cascaded forward, Emma felt anew the pain of that time. She'd spent many an hour on her knees for their bishop and for their community.

"My *mamm* was so concerned," Rachel admitted. "She believed in Henry's innocence. We all did. But she still worried. I'd get up in the middle of the night and find her sitting in the family room, an open Bible in her lap and a cold cup of coffee untouched next to her."

"But he was proved innocent," Emma said. She didn't want her mind to drift back to the man who had been found guilty, the man the girl had been texting. Fortunately, he was convicted and sentenced to prison.

"It's little wonder Henry is hesitant to use his gift in this situation," Clyde said.

"But what if that's the only way we can know what happened to Vernon?" Emma picked up her needles and began knitting again. The yarn was a pale yellow, and she planned to trim it in a soft green. It would make a nice blanket for the next baby expected in their congregation.

"Give the *Englisch* process time to work. Perhaps with their technology they can solve this crime without the help of our bishop."

Eight

Henry was up early the next morning and had Oreo hitched to the buggy by seven o'clock. He went by the homes of his church elders, but he didn't stop—opting instead to leave a note in their mailboxes. The notes said he'd like for them to meet at his place after dinner that evening.

He was in town by the time the stores opened. At the lumberyard, he spoke with the manager, who was happy for him to take more scrap lumber. A young man loaded it into the back of his buggy.

Next, he dropped off the woodworking items he had completed. The owner of Monte Vista Art paid him for what he'd sold and assured him there was room for more if he had a chance to make it. "The birdhouses are selling especially well."

Henry thanked the man and stopped by the bank to cash the check. Then he realized he should visit the morgue and check on when Vernon's body would be released. The coroner explained that the autopsy had been limited because of the damage to Vernon's body. They would notify the local mortuary, which would be able to transfer the remains out to his home whenever the bishop was ready for them.

Which left Henry with the task of deciding when to have the funeral. They could wait a few days, but what would be the point? Best to put this behind them as quickly as possible. The funeral could be sooner if a plain casket could be made quickly. At his next stop, the town's mortician assured him a few were in stock. "I'll have the boys bring one to your place when they deliver the body."

"I'll need time to notify everyone, have the grave dug, and a marker made."

"Day after tomorrow?"

"*Ya*. That would work. We can have the funeral on Thursday. *Danki*."

Finally Henry directed Oreo down the road and to the hardware store, which fortunately had parking for buggies in the shade. He hoped to be in and out in a few minutes. He only needed to purchase seeds for his vegetable garden. Yes, he still planted a garden, though the families in his church insisted on providing most of his meals. But he felt it would be wrong to rely on the charity of others. He wasn't so old that he couldn't work in a vegetable plot. His own father had done so well into his eighties.

It was while waiting in line to check out that he heard Sam might be in trouble.

"Wouldn't be the first time," a woman with bleached-blond hair was saying to the clerk. "Remember that terrible explosion in Texas?

It was in a town called West. I remember that because I thought it was west Texas where my sister lives, but it's actually located in central Texas. The town's name is West."

The clerk feigned interest as he rang up her purchases, and the woman continued talking—oblivious to the fact that Henry was standing behind her.

"I never could understand how one of those Amish people could be allowed to serve as a volunteer firefighter. Aren't they kind of, you know, slow?"

The clerk raised an eyebrow and glanced at Henry.

The woman turned, had the decency to blush, but continued with her story. "Anyway, the explosion in West was set by a volunteer firefighter. He was never actually convicted of setting it, but everyone knew he did. So it wouldn't be the first time. That's all I'm saying."

Henry waited patiently to check out, accepted the clerk's apology though the woman's ramblings weren't his fault, went back out to his buggy, and studied the list he'd written on the back of the envelope. Next was visiting Rebecca Yoder. She was the most senior member of their community. Clucking to Oreo, he set off down the road and made it to the Yoder place in under twenty minutes. The sun was shining brightly, and the scenery was spectacular. If he hadn't been preoccupied by Vernon's murder, he would have been able to appreciate another beautiful Colorado day.

Mary Yoder was standing on the front porch by the time he tied up Oreo to the hitching rail.

"Is everything all right, Henry?"

"Oh, yes. I wanted to visit with Rebecca, is all."

"Her birthday's this summer." Mary Yoder led him out to the screened back porch, where Rebecca sat near a window in the sun. "Chester is in the fields, but I can call him in if you like."

"No need. I'll be staying only a few minutes."

"Then I'll be in the kitchen. Let me know if you need anything."

Rebecca Yoder looked every bit of her ninety-two years. Though she had plenty of children back in Indiana, she'd chosen to move to Colorado with her youngest son ten years earlier. The doctors, even then, had known how crippling her arthritis would be. They'd suggested that the dry air would be a benefit to her, and at first it had been. But for the last few years her condition had worsened.

As he approached her chair, he studied this dear woman.

Her hands were sitting on top of the armrests—thin, veined, twisted. She'd lost several inches in height and her posture was somewhat stooped. The *kapp* pinned carefully to her head revealed only wisps of white hair, and he could see quite a bit of scalp. Rebecca Yoder reminded him of an infant, and his thoughts drifted to a baby girl whose mother had used Karo syrup to keep the toddler's *kapp* in place. The mother had worried the child would never grow hair, but she'd ended up with abundant blond tresses.

"Bishop! It's *gut* to see you." Rebecca's smile revealed missing teeth, reinforcing Henry's thoughts of infants.

"We missed you at church on Sunday. I wanted to stop by and see how you are."

"The Lord is *gut*. I'm alive." Blue eyes danced with good humor. It humbled him, visiting with Rebecca. Her attitude reminded him of the many blessings in life.

He sat across from her. On the table next to her chair was a jar of cream made from goat's milk. All of the *grandkinner* in Indiana sent gifts to their *mammi*, and several had managed to come and visit over the years.

"May I?" He nodded toward the jar.

Rebecca raised her right arm. "These old hands have served me faithfully many years, but now . . . they seem to have a mind of their own."

Henry opened the jar, removed a dollop of the cream, and began to rub it into her right hand.

They spoke of spring, the upcoming marriage of her grandchild, and a great-grandchild who had been born the previous week. Henry moved

61

his chair to the other side of Rebecca's and went to work on her left hand, careful to rub the cream in gently, to massage and stretch the joints as the health aid had shown them. "How can I pray for you this week, Rebecca?"

"That I might be useful." Her smile was nearly constant, but now she met his gaze and the corners of her mouth dropped and her lower lip trembled a bit. "Surely there is a way I can still be useful. *Gotte* has kept me here, *ya*? And if so, then for a reason."

He clasped both her hands in his. "Let's pray."

Their heads bowed, nearly touching, Henry searched for the words to comfort her. "May Your hand be on Your servant, Rebecca, Holy Father. May You use her this day. Bring to her mind those who need prayer. Bring to her lips words for those who want encouragement. And bring to her heart a certainty of Your purpose in her life, as we know You are all-knowing, all-giving, and all-loving. It is in the name of Your Son, Christ Jesus, that we pray. Amen."

Though tears had trekked down her cheeks, Rebecca's smile was once again firmly in place. Henry returned the jar of cream to the side table, picked up his hat, and was about to leave when she said, "I will pray for you as well, Henry. This terrible thing with the fire, I will pray that *Gotte* uses you to restore peace to our community."

Then the back screen door slammed shut, and

twin girls who were seven years old ran into the room, intent on showing their *mammi* flowers they had found in the field.

Henry looked back to see Rebecca exclaiming over the dandelions, her promise to pray for him ringing in his ears. As he left, he told Mary the funeral would be Thursday. She promised to help spread the word.

His next stop was to visit and counsel young Albert Bontrager, who admitted he'd been riding a battery-charged bike.

"It gets me to town much faster. You should try it, Henry."

"And yet faster isn't always better."

Albert pulled off his hat, ran a hand through sandy hair, and replaced it. "I have to admit it's more fun, though."

"Indeed. Perhaps you could keep using the bike, but leave off the power until I have a chance to discuss it with the elders."

"*Ya.* I can do that."

"And be careful out on the roads. Word is that you were racing one of the buggies."

"Uphill." Albert laughed. "The horse still won in spite of the battery."

The lad loved new gadgets. He always had. It seemed that Henry had these discussions with him at least once a month. Fortunately, Albert was easy to correct. It wasn't that he was intent on going against their *Ordnung.* It was more that he saw technology as mostly good and couldn't imagine how using it would be bad.

"The funeral for Vernon will be Thursday," Henry said as he was leaving. "It'll be at my place. Will you pass the word on to your parents?"

"Sure. We'll be there."

"*Danki*, Albert."

Elmer and Grace Bontrager had moved to the area with the first wave of Amish folk, five years before Henry and the families from Goshen arrived. They had six children and lived in a farmhouse that could use an expansion. They were good people—strong in their faith and quick to help someone else. He'd counseled with them several times about Albert, suggesting they give the boy space and time to figure out who he was and what he planned to do with his life.

Henry wasn't sure battery-operated bicycles were bad, but he wasn't prepared to approve that change yet. Adjustments in the *Ordnung* were best accomplished one item at a time and slowly. First things first, and at tonight's meeting with his elders, they needed to discuss something far more important than what new technology to allow. They needed to discuss the fire, Vernon's death, a possible killer among them, and the involvement of *Englisch* authorities.

Motorized bikes would have to wait.

His mind already on the last errand of the day,

64

added after he'd first begun his list, he wondered what he could possibly say to Sam Beiler. Sam had risked his life to save Vernon, but he'd been too late according to Captain Johnson. And now rumors were swirling that Sam had somehow been involved with causing the tragedy. Henry didn't know what he could say to ease the lad's burdens, but perhaps it would be enough for him to listen.

Nine

Sam was in one of his fields, clearing chico brush that had managed to pop up during the winter. He pulled the team to the side and climbed down from his wagon when he saw Henry's buggy.

"*Gut* timing. I could use a break."

They settled onto two lawn chairs next to an old tree stump, where a jug of water and two cups had been placed. Sam filled one of the cups with water and offered it to Henry.

"*Nein*. I had enough coffee this morning to float me away. How's the clearing going?"

"Well enough, I suppose. I was only sixteen when we moved here, but I can still remember Indiana dirt. It was rich and black, and I'd never seen chico brush."

"Thinking of moving back?"

"Not on your life. Mom and Pop love it here, and so do I."

Sam's parents were good people. Abigail and Daniel had tried a community in Texas years before, and then they had moved back to Goshen when the Texas land proved too hard to farm without the benefit of tractors and irrigation. Probably that was why young Sam referred to them as Mom and Pop rather than the traditional *Mamm* and *Dat*.

"Except for the chico bush."

"Except for that."

Henry studied the mountains on the horizon, the occasional white cloud that spotted the vast blue sky, and the forty acres Sam was attempting to farm. The horses seemed content to crop on weeds, but Henry knew Sam needed to finish his clearing.

"Heard a woman talking at the dry goods store this morning," he said.

"About me?"

"And the fire."

Sam drained his cup and set it back on top of the water jug. "Sheriff Grayson and Meg Allen came to see me last night."

"They came to my house as well."

"I doubt they interviewed the other volunteers on the fire crew, but for some reason she was interested in me."

"How did it go?"

"She struck me as overbearing, but I suppose you might need to be if you dealt with arsonists every day."

"It's hard for me to imagine enough of those incidents to constitute a full-time job."

"Seven people a day die in the United States because of home fires."

"I suppose each of those has to be investigated."

"Sure they do." Sam leaned forward, stretching the muscles in his back. He was a man in the prime of his life, nearly six feet tall, healthy, with unkempt brown hair in need of a cut, and a farmer's tan where his shirtsleeves were rolled up. "Most are caused by cooking equipment, smoking, or heating apparatus."

"But some are arson."

"*Ya*. Eleven percent of residential fires. And that number goes up to twenty-seven percent in commercial fires."

"What did Grayson and Allen want? Why did they single you out for questioning?"

"They'd heard I'd been to Vernon's place the night before. I'd driven my parents' buggy over, and I suppose some neighbor noticed it. You know how the *Englischers* to the south disliked him. They watched the place with binoculars, if you were to believe Vernon."

"Visiting a man isn't a crime."

"True enough, but we argued—loudly enough that I imagine they heard." Sam shook his head, as if the memory still puzzled him. "I went over to talk to him about a plow he'd sold me. The first time I used it, the thing broke. It had been welded, but the job was shoddy and didn't last through the first row."

"And what did Vernon say?"

"Not much. Pointed to that old sign he had."

" 'All Merchandise Sold As Is.' "

"Exactly."

"More than once I talked to him about that,"

68

Henry admitted. "I reminded him honesty is an important aspect of our life, and that leaving out information is the same as lying."

"He never told me the plow was welded. I wouldn't have bought it if I'd known. I thought I'd looked over it closely, but I was in a hurry that day. When I went to see him about it, I was willing to take a portion of the blame."

"You wanted your money back."

"Some of it. I was willing to return his broken plow. Maybe he could have fixed it properly."

"So you argued."

"We did. I'm not proud that I lost my temper. You know how hard it is to make a living here, Henry. It's difficult enough with the short growing season and lack of rain, and then there are the *Englischers* who think we're trying to steal their jobs."

"You don't sound happy here."

Sam laughed ruefully and resettled his straw hat on his head. "I am. It's only that any conversation that centers around Vernon gets my suspenders twisted. Not that I would have wished the man dead."

"Is that what Allen accused you of?"

"Not exactly, but she didn't give me a T-shirt proclaiming my innocence either. She said they'd look into my story and be back if they had more questions."

"I'm on your side, Sam. My job as bishop is to

help and guide you. If there's anything you need, you let me know."

"I will."

Henry had nearly reached his buggy when he turned back toward Sam. He hadn't moved from the lawn chair. He was sitting there, staring out at the scrubby forty acres he'd purchased the year before. He still lived with his parents, but he had high hopes of making the acreage productive and then maybe building his own place. He'd shared those dreams with Henry.

"The funeral will be on Thursday," he called out.

Sam raised a hand to indicate he'd heard, and then he went back to staring out at his fields.

Ten

Henry's church leadership consisted of three men. Abe Graber was a minister and therefore preacher. Clyde Fisher, Emma's son, shared those same responsibilities with Abe. Leroy Kauffmann was their deacon, and he handled the collection of offerings as well as disbursements to missions and benevolence funds. In many communities, the deacon was sent to remind wayward members of their transgressions and explain any confusion about the *Ordnung*, their daily rules for living. But Henry preferred to take that last task upon himself.

Henry was the bishop. As such, he oversaw the other three and shared preaching duties with Abe and Clyde. He visited families after births, presided over funerals, and called any necessary meetings. He shepherded his flock, and though he had served as a minister for many years in Goshen, he found the role of bishop to be particularly to his liking. The truth of the matter was that he liked people. He enjoyed visiting with elders in the communities, such as Rebecca. He liked talking with young men like Sam, guiding them through the difficult early years of adulthood. He found a special satisfaction in welcoming new members into the faith, baptizing them into a life of Christian servitude, and preparing them through classes for what lay ahead.

Abe arrived after dinner with the bench wagon. He and Clyde unloaded the benches, stacked them on the front porch, and then set to pulling out Henry's furniture and placing it in the barn. While they were attending to that, Leroy Kauffman drove down the lane. Leroy was a small man, slight in build and short with a ring of hair around his head and a shiny bald spot across the top. Everyone had been pleased when he'd been selected as their deacon. Leroy would have been an accountant if he was an *Englischer*. He was good with figures and had no problem asking people to donate when there was a need. A practical man, he had managed to be prosperous even in the valley, where farming was a trial.

Once they had everything situated, Henry motioned toward the kitchen. All three of the men had put in a long day in the field, and Henry himself had been up and running about since before daylight.

"I'll keep this meeting as brief as possible. Vernon's body will be delivered first thing Thursday morning. We'll have the visitation here beginning at ten, accompany the casket to the cemetery at noon, and finally return here for a meal." It was the standard way they did such things, and when he'd stopped by to see Clyde and Emma after visiting Sam, they both had agreed that the time schedule was do-able.

"My oldest boy can help with the horses and buggies," Clyde said.

"And so can mine." Abe pushed up his glasses and looked around the room. "The women have contacted all the families in our congregation."

"My mother will come early to help lay out the body," Clyde added. "Are you sure the county examiner will release it in time?"

"He said he could release it earlier, but I thought we needed an extra day to prepare. It'll be a closed casket. Leroy, can you arrange to have the grave dug?"

" 'Course."

"Clyde, I'd like you to speak with Elmer Bontrager. Make sure he can have the grave marker ready in time."

"I stopped by earlier today, and he'd already started working on it. Thursday will be no problem."

Henry cleared his throat, hesitating, but if he couldn't trust his own elders, they had bigger problems than a murder. "I realize Vernon wasn't well liked, but he was a member of our community. I would like for everyone to show up. It's a sign of respect. It's the right thing to do."

"The congregation is aware of your feelings, Henry," Leroy said. "We have a *gut* group here. Folks will turn out."

Abe sat back and crossed his arms. He was only forty-five, which made him almost twenty years younger than his bishop. He had dark hair, wore glasses, and had bushy eyebrows. With seven children at home plus the burden of his sister-in-law, Franey, he struggled as much as any of them to make ends meet. He'd been worried about that when the lot had fallen on him to be one of their preachers. Henry had counseled with him several times, and it seemed that Abe had found a good balance between his calling and his work. He was committed to their community and had said often enough that he planned to stay in Colorado.

Henry thought that might have something to do with his love of fly-fishing, which he did anytime he had a chance. Abe was a good preacher and a good addition to their community.

Now he cleared his throat and asked what was on his mind. "Is it true what they're saying? That it was arson? And is that what we're meeting about tonight?"

"*Ya* to both of your questions."

"So someone wanted Vernon dead."

"Apparently."

"How could anyone do such a thing?"

"We both know evil exists in this world." When Abe nodded, Henry added, "And men who are misguided. It's not for us to judge which this might be."

"But it is our duty to keep our community safe," Clyde said.

"*Gotte* keeps our community safe."

Clyde didn't respond to that. He was the youngest of them. He'd been raised with a deep and abiding faith, but he was fairly new to the position of minister and church elder. Perhaps in part because his father had been an elder, he felt the responsibility keenly, and sometimes he questioned whether he would be able to rise to the occasion. He stared at the table now, reminding Henry of a younger man, perhaps reminding him of himself.

"Times like this are hard," Henry admitted. "It's difficult to understand how *Gotte* can allow such things to happen."

Abe spread his hands out on the table, palms down. "A man can die many ways. Fire has to be one of the worst."

Henry nodded in agreement. "But this life is brief, Abe. And our death? It happens in a mere blink of time. Read Revelation 21, John 14, and the fifth chapter of Second Corinthians. We have these promises and more. They all remind us of the next life, which is eternal."

"I've read them before."

"At times we need to be reminded." Henry thought of that bleak time back in Goshen, of the missing young girl and her parents' wailing, and he prayed that such a time was not upon them again. "We can all stand to be reminded."

They spoke for a few more minutes about the funeral, finally deciding Abe would speak for a few moments after the time of viewing and Clyde would lead them in prayer before the lunch. Henry would speak at the gravesite, and Leroy would write letters to Vernon's family in Indiana.

It wasn't until they were walking out to the buggies that they returned to the subject of Vernon's killer.

"Should we be worried about protecting our families?" Abe stood with one hand on the side of his buggy. "What I'm asking is, in your opinion, Henry, do you think this killer had a vendetta against Vernon? Or is he angry with our community?"

"*Nein*. You shouldn't be worried. Be anxious for nothing." Henry smiled and patted Abe on the back. "That said, there's been no indication that this person had any animosity toward our community in general. No one else has been threatened or approached in any way, as far as I know."

Abe, Clyde, and Leroy all nodded their heads.

"Of course, we should be vigilant until the person is caught."

"You think he will be?" Always the practical man, Leroy. "I suspect there was little evidence. Could be that he gets away with . . . well, with murder."

"Every man will be judged by *Gotte*, but the *Englischers* seem intent on catching the guilty person."

"*Mamm* told me about your list," Clyde said.

Henry explained to the others what he'd done. No one seemed surprised or offended.

"*Ya*, Vernon was a difficult man to like," Abe said.

Leroy stared out into the darkness that had fallen while they met. "I would still be surprised if it was an Amish person."

"As would I." Henry stood in the yard, raising a hand in goodbye as each of his elders drove off into the night. Long after the sound of the horses' *clip-clop* faded away, he stood there, staring up at the Milky Way, searching for the words to pray for his congregation. But God already understood what was in his heart. Wasn't that what Scripture promised? Perhaps it was enough for him to stand there, empty his mind of the troubles of this world, and fill his heart with the wonders of God's grace and provision.

⊷══◑◑══⊷

Word spread easily among the families of their community, and the women arrived at Henry's late the next afternoon—Emma and Katie Ann, the three widows, and Abe's wife, Susan. They scrubbed the floors, washed the windows until they shone, and placed the dining room table in the middle of the sitting room with the leaves put in it. Finally, they fetched the benches and set them around the perimeter of the front hall, sitting room, and dining room. The remainder were lined up across the front porch. Henry's one-story house was small by Amish family standards, but it was still large enough for such a gathering.

Ruth was packing up her cleaning supplies and talking to Franey about what food they would bring. Emma, Katie Ann, and Susan walked to the front door, but Nancy held back. "Do you need anything, Henry?"

"Only help getting word out about the funeral. I realize we're doing this rather quickly, but I think it's better this way."

"We can do that," Nancy assured him. "Anything else?"

"*Nein*, but *danki* for asking."

Henry could tell Emma saw Nancy looking for an excuse to stay longer. She glanced away, trying to hide a smile, and suddenly Henry found himself fighting the urge to laugh himself. Even in the midst of tragedy, there were things to smile about. Though technically widowed, he was like a crusty old bachelor and had done nothing to deserve the women's attention. Yet life was full of little surprises, and people had to embrace joy whenever and however they could.

As the women drove their buggies back down

his lane, he thought of how life insisted on moving forward, even in the midst of tragedy. *Youngies* continued to court. Grown men worked toward a better future. And widows? Well, they adjusted to their new life and sometimes sought companionship. It was the natural way of things, as Solomon reminded them in Ecclesiastes. *What has been will be again, what has been done will be done again; there is nothing new under the sun.*

Ecclesiastes might be a good place to find something to say at the gravesite.

Henry walked inside, found his Bible, and made his way to the back porch to study and pray.

Eleven

Cloudy, damp, dismal days were rare in the San Luis Valley, but the day of Vernon Frey's funeral was exactly that. Silas hitched up the buggy and drove his grandmother and sister to the bishop's house. Clyde was busy attending to the morning chores, and Rachel was frosting a cake.

"You won't be in trouble for taking off from the job site?" Emma asked her grandson.

"*Nein*. The boss says I always get there early and stay late. He's also hired Plain folk before, so he knows funerals are important to us."

"I wish I had a boss," Katie Ann said to no one in particular. She was sitting in the back seat and unhappy that she'd be spending the day at the funeral rather than working outside caring for the horses.

"You sort of have a job with me," Emma reminded her. "And you're a real help."

"But I'd like a real boss."

"*Mammi* seems bossy enough to me," Silas said, laughing, and soon Emma and even Katie Ann joined in. Maybe it was the stress of the day, but it felt good to have a moment of light-heartedness before they stepped into the bishop's house.

Silas dropped them off at the door.

"Remember to help your mother with your brothers."

Silas promised to make sure Stephen and Thomas were dressed properly. They'd been known to get dirty between the house and the buggy, or wear their straw hats instead of their black ones, or carry marbles in their pockets, which they always managed to click together at the most inopportune time.

"Don't worry, *Mammi*. I know all of their tricks."

Emma and Katie Ann started up the front steps, the teen carrying a box holding plates of sliced meat and cheese to be added to the luncheon table.

"Maybe I can help park buggies," Katie Ann said. "I'd be more use outside than I would in the kitchen."

"You're a huge help in the kitchen." Emma smiled at her granddaughter and reminded herself to be patient. Their community was small, and Katie Ann had attended relatively few funerals. No doubt that, along with the unusual circumstances surrounding Vernon's death, had her on edge.

Henry walked in from the back porch. "*Gut* morning."

"And to you, Henry." Emma looked at Katie Ann, but she was staring at the plain wood casket, which had been placed on the table.

Normally they would dress the body in white clothes, a symbol of the person's new heavenly life. But because of the state of Vernon's body, this wasn't possible. It was a troubling thought, but Emma was sure Henry had covered Vernon's remains with the pristine white cloth she'd provided the day before. It was a small gesture, but it was something.

"Could you do without Katie Ann for a few minutes?" Henry asked. "Those kittens are growing fast. Nancy's *grandkinner* are already out in the barn, and we could use Katie Ann's help in picking out some names."

A smile broke across Katie Ann's face, though it disappeared when she glanced again at the casket. Fidgeting with her *kapp* strings, she said in a low voice, "*Ya*. I'd love to see them. If it's . . . if it's okay, that is."

Henry assured her it was. She handed her grandmother the box, and then she and Henry walked out the back door together.

Though it was still an hour before the visitation was set to begin, Nancy, Ruth, and Franey were already in the kitchen.

"You three must have cooked all night," Emma said.

"In spite of my arthritis." Franey had brought a half-dozen loaves of fresh bread, a platter of biscuits, and two pans of corn bread.

Nancy hurried over to help Emma with the box she was carrying. "I brought a spaghetti casserole and a chicken one. What did you bring?"

"Sliced ham and a cheese platter."

"I have two cakes and three pies," Ruth said. "I was thinking lemon, but then that seemed too happy a thing to bring to a funeral, so I decided on chocolate for one and carrot for the other. Do you think that's all right? And then the pies. Well, there were so many options, but I made a banana cream for church just a few days ago. I decided on red raspberry cream since they had raspberries at the grocery store in town. I prefer fresh. Don't you?"

Ruth continued to talk as she set out plates, silverware, and glasses. At some point Emma's attention drifted back to Vernon, and then without even realizing it she'd walked into the sitting room. She found herself standing beside the closed coffin and staring down at it.

"Did you know him well?" Nancy asked.

Emma nearly jumped out of her apron.

"Sorry. I thought you heard me walk in after you."

"No worries. I'm too jittery. Actually, I'm not sure what's wrong with me. I feel a little off."

"I suppose we all do."

They stood there a minute, both staring down at the plain pine coffin. Same as everyone who was Amish would one day have.

"In answer to your question, no. I didn't know him well. Which is a real shame because we've lived here thirteen years. After so long a time, you would think I could tell you something about him, but I can't."

"He didn't seem to let anyone close."

"Perhaps, or perhaps I didn't try hard enough." She turned and offered Nancy a weak smile. "Now we'll never know."

Nancy nodded, and then she stepped closer and lowered her voice. "I heard the person who did this could be Amish."

"I doubt that."

"The investigator and the sheriff went to see Sam Beiler."

"They also came to see Henry, but no one is accusing him of such a thing."

"I'm not accusing Sam. I'm worried about him. I'm worried that he's somehow mixed up in this."

Emma attempted to count to ten, made it to three, and said, "Think before you speak, but don't speak all you think."

"My *mamm* used to quote that one too. But Emma, this isn't gossip. My grandson, Nathan, was coming back from town that night . . . the night Vernon was killed."

"At two in the morning?"

"He's courting Abe's girl. You remember how it is. They lost track of time." Nancy stared at the casket, and then she turned her attention back to Emma. "He saw Sam at the phone shack, the one close to Vernon's place."

"That proves nothing."

"I agree, but according to what was in the paper this morning, the emergency call was placed from that phone shack."

"Sam Beiler . . . " Emma lowered her voice. "Sam Beiler did not kill Vernon. I've known Sam since he was born, since our time in Goshen, and so have you."

"I'm not saying he did, but it's not for us to decide, is it? The *Englischers* will find out, and if he's guilty, then they'll arrest Sam."

"Did Nathan tell the police?"

"*Nein.* And since they haven't asked, we're letting that be. But if they do ask, he'll have to speak the truth."

"All right. I'll talk to Sam when he gets here."

Nancy turned back to the kitchen but stopped when Emma reached for her arm and pulled her closer.

"I'm sorry for being short with you."

Nancy patted her hand. Emma looked down, saw Nancy's hand upon her own, and suddenly realized how closely their lives were intertwined— everyone in an Amish community. They were more than neighbors but less than family. They were a group of believers bound by faith and history.

The sound of buggies approaching ended their conversation.

But as Emma helped with the last-minute preparations in the kitchen, she couldn't help glancing up every few moments, hoping to catch a glimpse of Sam.

Twelve

The viewing went well, even if it was a bit more somber than usual. Each family paid their respects, pausing a few moments in front of the closed coffin to offer a prayer. Henry's home was full to overflowing, and though the weather was dour, the rain held off.

Abe preached using some of the scriptures Henry had suggested he read. His tone was cautionary, reminding them that no one knew their appointed hour, but it was also hopeful. He quoted verse after verse that described their heavenly home. He traced the promise of life with their heavenly Father from the Old Testament, through the Gospels, and ended with Revelation. They sang hymns, offered prayers, and finally carried the casket to the bench buggy, which had been draped with black cloth.

Henry's buggy, with Oreo hitched and waiting patiently, had been chalked with a number one. The bench buggy with the casket would be second. Everyone else would fall in behind it.

Henry led the procession to Leroy Kauffmann's place. Leroy had the largest acreage and had donated a corner of the land for use as a cemetery. Henry had been there many times. He'd buried the young and the old. He'd buried some who had been sick for years and some who had fallen ill suddenly. He'd even buried one family that was killed in a buggy accident by a speeding and inebriated *Englischer*.

Today the *Englischers* were respectful, pulling to the side of the road and allowing the long line of buggies to pass. The grave had been dug by hand the night before. As they approached, Henry saw the mound of fresh dirt next to the hole. His heart ached for Vernon, and he prayed for God's forgiveness, wishing he'd done more to minister to the man while he was alive.

Once everyone had gathered around the grave, Henry opened his Bible and began to read from the third chapter of Ecclesiastes. " 'There is a time for everything, and a season for every activity under the heavens: a time to be born and a time to die, a time to plant and a time to uproot.' "

Several of the women dabbed at their eyes with handkerchiefs.

Henry had not dreamed of being a bishop. Given the other challenges in his life, it had never even crossed his mind. When his name had been submitted, he was certain God would choose another, but the lot had fallen on him. That had been so many years ago. He could never have envisioned the journey that would bring him to the San Luis Valley. His voice carried out across the group, confident and even. He'd learned long ago that he could have such confidence because the words he shared were the Lord's, not his. God's words were eternal. They were the one true, certain thing in this life.

" 'A time to kill and a time to heal, a time to tear down and a time to build, a time to weep and a time to laugh, a time to mourn and a time to dance.' "

He hadn't known what to say to his congregation. He had been at a complete loss for how to minister to them during this terrible tragedy. They were familiar with death. But murder? That was something he'd hoped to never encounter again.

Someone coughed, and Henry realized he'd stopped reading. They were waiting for him to finish the words of wisdom written so long ago by King Solomon.

" 'A time to scatter stones and a time to gather them.' " The rain began to fall softly around them.

" 'A time to embrace and a time to refrain from embracing.' "

He'd explained Vernon's unexpected death to Katie Ann and the other children when they were in the barn, or he'd tried to. *Just as this cat had no idea when she would give birth, so we have no idea when our time will come to die. But* Gotte *knows, and we can trust Him.* He glanced up now and caught Katie Ann staring at him, her hand in her mother's.

" 'A time to search and a time to give up, a time to keep and a time to throw away.' "

He nodded to the pallbearers, who lowered the coffin and then began to shovel soil into the grave as he finished the reading.

" 'A time to tear and a time to mend, a time to be silent and a time to speak.' "

Young Nathan Kline had been staring at his shoes, but now, Henry noticed, he jerked his head up.

" 'A time to love and a time to hate, a time for war and a time for peace.' "

Then Henry led them in praying that Vernon Frey had claimed his heavenly reward, that their community would find peace, and that this would be a time for their members to love one another and a time for their hearts to mend.

Before leaving, he glanced again at the headstone and read the words simply and plainly engraved there.

Vernon Frey
3-14-1954
5-1-2016
62 years, 1 month, 18 days

Which pretty much summed up Vernon's life. They would all be remembered by their deeds, their kindness to one another, and the roots of love they left behind. Vernon's life on this earth was over.

All that was left was to find his killer.

Thirteen

The trouble didn't begin until after the funeral service. Emma was standing in the food line, pulling away an empty bowl that had held green bean casserole and replacing it with a full dish of sweet potatoes. She was preoccupied, wondering why she hadn't seen Sam, when she caught the first stirrings of gossip.

"Vernon paid no consideration to whether he was legally right or wrong." Leroy shook his head as if he couldn't understand such an attitude. "He basically did as he pleased."

"You can't know that," Lewis Glick said. Lewis was the newest addition to their community. He kept to himself generally, so it surprised Emma that he would be talking to Leroy about anything other than the weather.

"Sure can. Saw the property pins myself. He had stuff scattered across his property line in three directions. The only thing that could stop Vernon was the road."

"It did seem like he'd accumulated quite a bit of . . . merchandise."

"Junk. It was junk, plain and simple, and the neighbors were tired of it."

The two men spoke in low voices, and Emma

wouldn't have heard if Nathan hadn't held up the line waiting for more fresh bread. The men glanced up and realized she was standing there listening. They smiled weakly before moving silently on down the line.

"Something wrong?" Ruth asked.

"*Nein*. Nothing at all." The last thing she needed was to get Ruth started talking about Vernon's supposed misdeeds. The woman was a hard worker, but she didn't have much of a filter for what not to say and where not to say it. She'd once mentioned seeing Henry's underthings hanging on the line and needing to show him how to use bleach. Fortunately she'd only said it to other women, but that was because they were at a sew-in and no men were in the room.

Emma hurried back to the stove to check on what dishes remained to be set out.

And that was when the trouble worsened.

Susan and Franey were standing at the kitchen sink. Because Abe was a minister, Susan held an important place in their community. Plus there was the fact that Henry was widowed and had no wife to help him in ministering to their group. It fell on Susan—as well as Rachel with Emma's help—to put together meals for those who were sick, make sure weddings were well attended, and coordinate gifts for new babies.

Abe and his brother, Alvin, were as different as night and day in personality, though the brothers bore a strong resemblance physically. Emma knew Abe occasionally hired a driver to take him over to Alamosa to see his brother, perhaps hoping to draw him back into the fold. But Alvin had remarried, and Emma didn't think he'd be returning to their Plain life. If he did, he'd have to leave the second wife and reclaim the first. She'd never heard of such a thing happening.

Susan was a sweet, kind woman, but apparently she'd been tested to her limits by Franey's whining.

"Don't pretend you cared overmuch for Vernon." Susan was already washing dishes—the empty casserole bowls. She plunged her hands into the soapy water, causing suds to fly.

"Of course I cared for him." Franey sniffed, a habit she sorely needed to lose. It was as if she always smelled something terrible. It caused a person to question their own hygiene.

"You are terrified of being alone."

Franey snatched a dish from the drain and turned it round and round, drying it with the dish towel that had been draped over her shoulder. "That's not true."

"It is, and I don't understand it when we are happy to have you living with us."

"*Ya*, you're quite kind to give shelter to the

poor abandoned Amish woman. I'm sure you're thrilled to have me there."

"You need to stop this."

"There's nothing to stop!"

Franey's voice was rising, and her eyes had widened in embarrassment, but Susan seemed not to notice.

"The man hasn't been in the ground more than an hour. This day is not about you."

"Did I say it was?"

"It's about Vernon and doing right by members of our community." Now Susan was aggressively washing dishes and tossing them into the side drain.

All of the women working in the kitchen, which was pretty much all of the women in their community, stopped and stared. It was impossible not to hear the argument, but no one knew what to do.

Emma stepped forward. "Perhaps I could help you with the dishes."

"So now I can't do dishes either?" Franey snatched a dish from the rinse water and tossed it back at Susan. "You didn't clean this one properly."

Susan appeared not to hear her. "You took meals to Vernon when he plainly told you to stop. Why? Because you don't listen to others."

"He never said that."

"He did say as much, and I was there the last

time he brought your casserole dish back."

Franey's cheeks blossomed into two bright red spots.

"Your situation is something you must learn to accept, Franey. Stop harassing the men in our community, and for heaven's sake stop bringing food to Henry when he does not need or want it."

"I'm not surprised you're speaking hatefully to me."

"I'm speaking plainly."

"Cruel. That's what you are." Franey put her hand into the rinse water, and after that everything happened very quickly.

Franey scooped up a handful of rinse water and tossed it at her sister-in-law.

Susan stepped back, mouth open, and bumped into Nancy, who was carrying one of her raspberry cream pies. She stumbled, nearly dropped the pie, caught it, and then she bumped into Emma. The pie went flying like a goose at Christmas, and it did not land on Franey. There might have been some poetic justice if it had. Instead, it splattered across the front of Susan's clothes, leaving a trail of red and white on her black apron.

Several women rushed forward to help Susan.

Franey stomped out of the room.

And Nancy looked as if she didn't know whether to laugh or cry.

"There's another pie," Emma assured her.

She hurried back to Henry's refrigerator to pull out the second pie. She'd opened the door, grateful for the bit of cool air that drifted out, and that was when they all heard the scream of the fire engine.

Fourteen

Henry insisted they continue the meal. "I'll send Nathan to the phone shack to find out what's happened."

The rain that had begun falling at the graveside service had stopped, but certainly the ground would be damp enough to prevent any fire from spreading. The day had remained overcast and gloomy, and Henry had trouble envisioning how anything could be burning. Perhaps it had been a medical emergency. But Nathan returned from the phone shack to say there had, indeed, been a fire.

"It's at the JSW construction site in town." Nathan was a bit breathless from his run to the phone shack.

"Was anyone hurt?" Abe asked.

"*Nein.* The person at the police station didn't think so, but a *gut* portion of the construction supplies have been destroyed. She couldn't tell me any more than that."

Everyone drifted back to what they were doing before hearing the fire truck's siren. Henry sat back down at the table with Clyde and Abe and Leroy.

"A tragedy for sure," Clyde said. He glanced at Emma, who was still standing in the kitchen.

"Silas works at the site, and he says the foreman is a fair man. Certainly he doesn't need this type of trouble."

"The store could be a real blessing to our community," Henry said. "I hope this won't prevent them from finishing it."

"I'd hate for Silas to lose his job," Clyde admitted. "The money has come in handy."

"I prefer to support small businesses, but I was looking forward to its opening as well. A big discount store here in town could help everyone. Fortunately, they don't carry the types of items we sell to tourists." This from Leroy as he wiped at his beard with his napkin. "I've heard their prices are quite reasonable."

"This will put off the opening for sure." Clyde shook his head. "I wonder if it was an accident or—"

"Surely it was." Henry stabbed his fork into the raspberry pie. He didn't usually care for pies, but this was one of his favorites. There was something about tart mixed with sweet that he found particularly pleasing. "The *Englischers* are required to have insurance on their job sites."

He put the fire out of his mind, finished his pie, and then moved from table to table, talking to the members of his congregation. Usually after a funeral there were people to counsel and console, but no one seemed particularly bereft about Vernon's passing. There had been a small dustup of some sort in the kitchen. Emma had assured him everything was fine and then pushed a mug full of coffee into his hands.

Within two hours, the kitchen was cleaned, the benches loaded back into the wagon, the furniture returned to his rooms, and folks had started drifting toward their buggies. Henry was on the front porch, watching the last of his congregation drive away, when he saw a Monte Vista police car turn into his lane. Sheriff Roy Grayson pulled up close to the house and then stepped out of the cruiser, though he didn't turn off the automobile's engine.

"I need you to come with me, Henry."

"Come where?"

"To the station."

"Why?"

"Because we've arrested Sam Beiler. He's waived his right to an attorney, but he's asked that you be present during his questioning."

"Sam Beiler?"

"Yes, sir."

"Arrested for what?"

"The murder of Vernon Frey."

"That's not possible."

"We caught him at today's fire, Henry."

"Today's fire?"

"The one at the construction site. It would seem he started it as well as the fire at Vernon's place."

Henry didn't believe a word of it. He hurried

into his house and confirmed the women had taken care of turning off the stove. There was nothing for him to do but grab his hat and make his way back out to the sheriff's car.

"I could take my buggy."

"Best if you ride with me. Quicker, anyway."

They rode in silence into town. But when they turned into the police station, Henry glanced at Grayson and said, "There's been a mistake. Sam would not do such a thing."

"I hope you're right, but the evidence seems to suggest otherwise."

"What evidence?"

"It's not my investigation anymore, so I can't say. The district office is fully in charge now. We're hoping you can talk some sense into Sam. If he did this thing—and I'm not saying for sure he did because that's for a jury to decide—the court might show leniency if he confesses."

Henry would not be advising Sam to confess. Henry didn't believe him capable of such a deed. While it was true he'd had troubles lately what with the new acreage and his broken plow, those things did not push a man to arson and murder.

As he followed Grayson through the lobby and down the hall, he prayed for wisdom, and that God would clear their minds so that both he and Sam might see the way through the next few crucial hours.

Fifteen

They stopped outside a locked door that had a window in it. Grayson glanced through the glass, knocked once, and then opened the door with a key. Henry was led into a small, sparsely furnished room. A rectangular table, with two chairs on each side, made up the furnishings. The walls were painted a drab gray, and a large mirrored window was situated along one side.

Sam was handcuffed, his callused farmer's hands resting on the table in front of him. His gaze shot up when they walked into the room, but other than nodding at Henry, he showed no real reaction. Instead, he stared back down at his hands.

The arson investigator, Meg Allen, sat across the table from Sam. She stood as they walked into the room. Her bright red hair looked almost orange in the fluorescent lights, and Henry could see freckles sprinkled across her nose. She wore blue jeans, a khaki-colored button-up shirt, a simple gold chain with some sort of pendant, and a watch. She motioned for Henry to take a seat beside Sam, and Grayson took the seat beside her.

"Thank you for coming, Bishop." Her tone was formal.

Henry noticed a small recording device on the table. He nodded to the camera in the far corner of the room. "It's against our religious practices—"

"To be photographed. Yeah, I know. However, in a criminal proceeding, this is not negotiable."

Grayson nodded in agreement, and Henry decided not to push the point. The main thing was to get Sam out of the building and back home where he belonged.

"Has he been formally charged?" Henry asked.

Allen looked surprised, but then she probably didn't know about his history in Goshen. He'd learned more about the legal system than he'd ever wanted to know. And although he understood laws varied between states and even municipalities, the general way of things was the same.

"No, he hasn't. Whether he will be depends on how he answers our questions, as well as what lab results show based on evidence we gathered from his home."

"His home?"

"We have cause to believe Sam set the fire at Vernon Frey's property, as well as the one at the JSW Construction site today."

"I did not do either thing."

Henry sat back and crossed his arms. "Did you have a warrant to search his home, or rather his parents' home?"

Allen stared at Sam for a moment, as if she could will him to confess to this thing. Finally, she turned her attention back to Henry. "Based on tips we received, we were able to acquire a warrant to search the home of Abigail and Daniel Beiler. While we were in the process of that search, the fire at JSW occurred. Sam was seen running from the construction site when the fire trucks arrived."

"I wasn't running from it!" Sam's temper flared.

Henry cleared his throat and offered one short, definitive shake of his head. Sam needed to keep his emotions under control. Words said in anger would only cause him more trouble.

"I wasn't running from it," Sam said again, less forcefully. "I was running to the store across the street, to call the fire department."

"Convenient," Allen said softly.

"What were you doing at the site?" Grayson asked. "Weren't most of your friends and neighbors at Vernon's funeral?"

"They were."

"Why didn't you attend?"

Henry wondered the same thing, but he kept his expression neutral and waited for Sam's reply.

"There was no love lost between me and Vernon. That's no secret. And *ya*, I should have gone to the funeral, but I'm going to lose my fields if I don't get them cleared. If I can't clear them, I can't plant them. Our growing season is short, and I'm already behind."

So that was the reason for the cloud of despair that had surrounded Sam when Henry had visited him two days before. Henry realized he should have asked, but he'd been preoccupied with Vernon's passing and the upcoming funeral.

"All right. So you didn't attend the funeral." Allen crossed her arms and sat back. "Why were you at the construction site?"

"I need another plow, a newer one than the old thing I was trying to use when you came by, Henry. I soon figured that at the rate I was progressing, I wouldn't be done until fall, and the plow Vernon sold me was defective. I went into town to see about purchasing one."

"Did you? Purchase a plow?"

"*Nein.* The prices were too high."

"But you looked for one."

"I stopped at both the hardware store and the resale shop."

Allen scribbled something on a small pad of paper. Looking up, she asked, "Did you talk to a salesman at either place? Someone who can verify your story?"

Sam nodded. "Tall black man at the hardware store, probably in his fifties, clean shaven."

"And you went there first?"

"I did. Probably around eleven. I meant to go earlier, but I was late getting away. My *mamm* needed some work done around the house, and they were . . . they were going to the funeral."

Henry had a brief impulse to correct Sam then. If he'd only gone to the funeral, as he should have, he wouldn't be sitting here now constructing his alibi. No doubt he realized that, so Henry kept quiet.

"And the resale shop?"

"I spoke with the guy who owns the place."

"All right. Now let's talk about the construction site. Why were you there?"

"I wasn't there!" He raised his hands to his hair and attempted to push it away from his eyes. The movement reminded him that his wrists were still shackled. He stared at them a moment and dropped them back to the table.

"Surely there is no need for the handcuffs." Henry spoke softly, as if he were mildly surprised at such a thing. He wasn't, but he hoped Allen would relent, and that young Sam would relax once the cuffs were off.

Grayson glanced at Allen, who shrugged. Taking that for a yes, Grayson pulled a key from his pocket, unlocked the cuffs, and returned them to a leather pouch attached to his belt.

Sam rubbed his wrists and continued his story. "I was riding by the job site—"

"Horse and buggy?"

"No, my bicycle. I don't own a horse and buggy, though my parents do. I borrow it from time to time, but mostly I use my bike or my scooter."

"How were you going to carry a plow home on a bike?"

"They deliver."

"Go ahead."

"I'd visited both shops, realized I couldn't afford to buy from either, and was on my way home when I smelled smoke."

"You smelled smoke?"

"I did."

"I'm supposed to believe that?" Allen shook her head in mock despair. "A lot of people were on that construction site, but you were the only one who noticed the fire?"

Sam shrugged, as if it didn't matter to him what she believed.

Henry decided it was time to interject. "Sam's on the volunteer fire crew. He's taught to recognize—"

"We are aware of his association with the volunteer fire department. Unfortunately, many arsonists volunteer. They enjoy being around fires—both extinguishing and setting them."

"I did *not* set that fire." Sam pushed away from the table and began to rise from his seat.

Henry's hand on his shoulder calmed him down. Sam sank back onto his chair. "Maybe the workers were at lunch. The fire was at the back part of the site. I didn't see anyone there, so I rushed across the street to call it in."

He raised his head and leveled his gaze directly

at Sheriff Grayson. "I was hurrying back to help when a police officer arrested me. If he'd let me do that, maybe it wouldn't have spread as far as it did."

"You're admitting to calling the fire in?"

"*Ya*. Of course."

"Why wouldn't he?" Henry asked. "Calling in a fire is a good thing to do. It's the right thing to do."

"Sure it is, unless you set the fire."

"That makes no sense," Sam said.

"Neither does setting a fire at Vernon Frey's house, killing a man, and then calling it in."

Sam fell silent.

"That's what you did, Sam. Isn't it? You crept onto Vernon's property in the early morning hours of May first, set the fire, waited until it was out of control, and then you called it in to 9-1-1."

Sam had looked beaten earlier. Defeated and maybe even a tiny bit guilty. But he managed to tap into some reserve of strength or faith, or a combination of both. He sat up straighter, squared his shoulders, and spoke in a quiet, confident voice. "Okay. All right. *Ya*, I did call in that fire. I didn't tell you before because I knew how it would sound. If reporting a fire has suddenly turned into a crime, then convict me. But I tell you this and with no uncertainty—I did not kill Vernon Frey."

Sixteen

Henry requested a fifteen-minute break.

Allen shrugged. She gathered up her pad, pen, and recorder and then exited the room.

"Can I get you anything?" Grayson asked gruffly.

"Sam could use a cup of coffee or can of soda."

Sam shook his head as if none of that mattered.

"And I'll take some water."

"You got it." When he reached the door, Grayson turned and directed his next comment to Henry. "Remember what I told you in the car. If he confesses, the judge is more likely to show leniency."

"I won't confess to something I didn't do."

Grayson nodded as if he had expected that answer and left them alone.

Henry waited one minute and then two. He allowed the silence to minister to Sam's soul. He prayed for guidance and truth and wisdom and strength. Then he scooted his chair back so he was facing the boy. Sam wasn't a boy, of course. He was a man with a man's problems. But as the clock ticked toward the dinner hour, Henry thought of him as a boy. His parents would be worried. His friends and neighbors would want to know how to help. His fields were waiting.

"Quite a mess, eh?" The question was casual with a hint of amusement, and it was all Sam needed to unlock the dam of words built up inside him.

"I told you the truth, Henry. Yesterday when you stopped by, I told you the truth. However, I didn't tell you everything."

"Of course you know that withholding the truth—"

"Is the same as telling a lie. *Ya*. My pop has told me as much more than once."

"We only have a few minutes, Sam. So why don't we start with the most serious charge. Did you kill Vernon?"

"*Nein*. I did not."

"*Gut*! But you were there that night?"

"I was. As I told you before, I took the buggy to his house, returned the plow, and attempted to get my money back. I went home after arguing with him, but I couldn't sleep. I kept tossing, worrying, and the . . . the injustice of it all made me crazy."

"Probably a word you'd rather not use around Investigator Allen."

"I kept hearing his snide remarks over and over in my head." Sam was staring at the wall, reliving the events of his past that had led to the room, the table, the handcuffs. "The way he looked at me so contemptuously. He seemed . . . seemed to enjoy the game of it, pulling one over on me.

Only it wasn't a game. It was all the money I had. Mom and Pop don't have the resources to help me with the acreage."

"*Ya.* I understand."

"What Vernon had done . . . it wasn't right."

"You could have come to me. You should have."

"*Ya.* I see that now."

"What time was it when you returned to Vernon's?"

"Close to two. I rode my bike instead of hitching up the mare."

"In the middle of the night? Sam, you could have been killed."

"*Nein.* I'm always careful on the bike, and the *Englisch* vehicles . . . you can hear them a long way off."

Henry glanced at the clock. He needed to hurry the conversation along to the crux of the matter.

"What did you find when you arrived at Vernon's?"

"I smelled smoke almost as soon as I pulled into his drive, but I thought it was only from a fire he'd used to warm the house."

"You walked up to the front door?"

"I did, and that's when I noticed the glass broken from the window."

"What else did you see?"

"Flames. I ran inside, determined to find him, to save him."

"But you were angry with him."

"Not enough to watch him burn to death."

Henry glanced up, saw Investigator Allen through the small window in the door. She was talking to someone in the hall and was about to enter the room.

Sam raised his left hand to his face and wiped at the sweat beading on his forehead. "I made it upstairs, even into his room where he was lying on the bed. He was already dead. I picked him up, fireman carry and all, and started back down the stairs, but the fire had accelerated, faster than a regular fire would. I laid him back on the bed and tried to think of a way out."

"And you're sure he was dead?"

"I know how to check for a pulse. Either he'd had a heart attack or he'd died from smoke inhalation. Most folks don't know to get to the floor or to cover their mouth and nose."

"But you knew what to do."

Sam nodded. "I couldn't carry him out through the window, and I couldn't leave the way I'd come. The fire had blocked the stairs. So I left him there, on the bed, and I scrambled out onto the roof. I dropped to the ground, grabbed my bike where I'd left it next to the front porch, and hurried to the phone shack to call 9-1-1."

Henry let the confession of Sam's deeds, his sins if they were to be deemed as such, fade from the room.

"I know it was wrong."

"Which part?"

"All of it. Arguing. Lying. Leaving . . . leaving his body there."

"Sam, if what you say is true, and I have no reason to believe it isn't, then *ya*, there was sin in having an unforgiving heart, in treating Vernon as anything other than your brother in Christ—" Henry held up a hand to silence his objections. "Regardless of how you were treated, Sam. The Lord's Word is plain on this."

He waited for Sam to raise his eyes. "*Ya*, you've sinned. But Sam, the fact that you left Vernon in his home was not such a thing. His life was complete, and you did all in your power to respectfully care for him. It wasn't possible."

Sam nodded, though Henry wasn't sure he believed. Perhaps in time, he would.

"You've confessed your sins, and you can be assured of *Gotte*'s forgiveness."

Seventeen

Sheriff Grayson and Investigator Allen didn't see it the same way.

Sam was fingerprinted and booked on the charge of felony murder of Vernon Frey. There were other charges—arson, obstructing justice, and destroying evidence, but Henry wasn't concerned about those. It seemed all of the charges against Sam hinged on his one fateful decision to return to Vernon's home the early morning of May first.

Henry sat in the waiting area next to Abigail and Daniel Beiler. Sam's parents had arrived home from the funeral to find Sam gone. They learned through the Amish grapevine that their son had been arrested. As soon as Henry walked into the room, they began to pepper him with questions. Abigail wiped away tears as Daniel lapsed into Pennsylvania Dutch. They were upset. Of course they were. But they didn't believe for a second that their son was capable of such a thing.

Henry counseled with them, prayed with them, and then sent them home. They didn't need to be in the police station, Sam's brothers and sisters would be worried, and honestly, he didn't want them meeting up with Sheriff Grayson at this point. Henry still hoped to be able to talk some sense into the man.

So he sent Abigail and Daniel home after assuring them he would be by in the morning and that together they would devise a plan for how to prove Sam's innocence.

But Henry was unsure what to do next as he pushed back the memories of the trial in Goshen. That time he had been the one being fingerprinted, falsely accused, and led to a cell.

Grayson walked into the room and sat down opposite him. "You should have gone on home. There's nothing you can do here. Nothing to do until the trial begins. Sam will need legal representation. He can be appointed a public defender or—"

Henry held up his hand to stop him. "He didn't do it. If you'd heard his explanation of what happened, you would understand."

"We did hear. We heard all of it. We were on the other side of the mirror."

"You were listening to our conversation?"

"Attorney-client privilege doesn't apply here. Neither does clergy privilege. When you looked up and saw Meg about to enter the room and she backed away, it was because we suspected he was about to confess."

"But he didn't confess. Not to murder."

"He admitted he was there, and even that he handled the body. He's sugarcoating it for you, Henry. He cherry-picked what he told you. Or maybe he left out a little piece, like when he killed the man."

"*Nein.* I don't believe it."

Grayson yawned. "It doesn't matter if we believe it or not. The only thing that matters now is what a jury decides. But I'm telling you Sam Beiler had means and motive. If you factor in the evidence, the eye-witness account that places him at the scene, his own testimony, and any evidence the lab might return, I'd say there's at least a seventy percent chance of a conviction."

"Then you'll be convicting the wrong man."

"I understand your loyalty to him."

"Are you even going to check his alibi?"

"He has no alibi for the night he was at Vernon's. The only other person in the room was dead. Remember?"

"What about his alibi for the fire at the construction site?"

"Oh, that. Yeah, sure. We'll check it, but I don't see how it matters. Even if he's found not guilty of setting the fire at JSW, it doesn't absolve him of what happened at Vernon Frey's."

"Check with the salesperson at the hardware store and owner of the secondhand store. You'll see he's telling the truth, and then maybe . . . maybe you'll be motivated to look past your assumptions of guilt." Henry's temper was rising, which was a rare occurrence indeed. He stood, realized he didn't have a ride home, and decided he wouldn't ask for one.

The sheriff called after him, but Henry wasn't listening.

He needed the two-mile walk. He needed time to pray and consider what he was going to do next.

Eighteen

Breakfast was a rather big affair at the Fisher household. Three adults and four children, though Katie Ann and Silas were hardly children anymore. Regardless, they all ate heartily in the morning, and it took some planning. Emma usually made a casserole of some sort the night before, and Rachel scrambled eggs, cut up fruit, and sometimes included a side of bacon or sausage or ham. The heavenly aromas never failed to get everyone up and moving.

Emma had just set the pan of apple cinnamon French toast on the table when she heard a knock on their front door. She was surprised to look out the window and see Henry.

He ate breakfast with them—or, rather, he sat there and spoke to the grandchildren and sipped his coffee. Once the children had run off to complete various chores, the adults walked out to the front porch. Henry and Emma and Rachel sat in the rockers. Clyde opted to stand with his backside against the porch railing.

Henry explained what had happened concisely and without emotion, but he wasn't fooling her. Emma understood how devastating this turn of events was. It occasionally happened that one of their own ended up in the *Englisch* judicial system. Once there it was rare for them to find a quick or easy way out.

"You believe Sam's story?" Clyde asked.

"I do."

"There must be a way, something we can do, to prove Vernon was dead before Sam found him in his house that night."

"Maybe we don't have to do that," Emma said. "Maybe we only have to prove someone else could have done it. After all, it's not our job to catch whoever killed Vernon."

Rachel bobbed her head in agreement. "Reasonable doubt—that's what the *Englisch* call it in their court proceedings."

"I'd rather it not go that far." Emma rubbed the palm of her hand up and down the arm of her rocker. "I hate to think what it would do to Sam to have to sit in a jail cell until a trial. It's not natural for any man, but it's especially devastating for a Plain person. We're used to the sun on our faces, working with our hands, and falling into bed exhausted at night. It's our way."

Henry was staring out at the horizon, toward the sand dunes that could be seen from practically anywhere in the valley. Emma had read they were the product of years of erosion from the nearby mountains. The wind and sun and rain and snow slowly wore the mountains down, until the sand washed into the dunes.

"I understand what you're saying, Emma. I

remember well enough my time in an *Englisch* jail."

The memories fell over the four of them—dismal and heavy. It was Clyde who slapped the porch railing and grinned. Emma adored her son for his positive outlook on life. They'd yet to encounter a problem Clyde didn't believe could be fixed. "*Gotte* saw us through those times, Henry. He will see us through this."

"I'm the bishop here. I should have said that."

"Don't be so hard on yourself. You've barely slept, and you didn't eat any of Emma's fine breakfast."

Emma heard their banter. She understood that her son was trying to calm and reassure Henry, but that wasn't their primary concern. Their primary concern was to find a way to show that someone else might have killed Vernon Frey. How had the sheriff put it? Henry had explained Sheriff Grayson said Sam had "means and motive." Surely someone else might have had those as well, but if there had been any clues in Vernon's house, they'd been burned up.

"Didn't you say you'd been to see him the afternoon before he was killed?"

"*Ya.* Late in the afternoon I went by his place to see if he was okay, to see why he didn't stay to fellowship with us after the service."

"Can't you remember anything you saw there?" Rachel asked.

"Nothing useful."

"Maybe something not useful, then." Clyde crossed his arms and frowned. "Something you wouldn't think would help, but in another light, maybe could."

Henry sat forward, propped his elbows on his knees, and rubbed at his forehead. Finally he sighed, and said, "Nothing. Vernon was in a foul mood, but that wasn't unusual."

Emma suddenly had an idea. It was something they'd discussed the other night, but they never thought it would be useful in this situation. The question was, did she dare suggest it? What if it made things worse? But how was that possible? Young Sam Beiler was in jail and about to be formally charged with murder. Things didn't get much worse than that. So she pulled in a deep breath and offered a silent prayer. Then she looked directly at Henry and said, "Maybe you should draw it."

Clyde looked at her sharply, frowning and giving the distinct impression that he wanted her to drop the subject and move on.

"Why not?" She questioned her son, though he hadn't actually responded to her suggestion—at least not verbally.

Henry, for his part, was rubbing a hand up and down his jawline, staring out at the dunes.

"What harm could it possibly do?" To Emma the answer now felt right and even obvious. "It's a gift, Henry. Everything we're able to do is a gift from *Gotte*. I've heard you share as much with our congregation—our gifts are to be used to serve one another. You said that. The Bible says that."

No one interrupted her, so she pushed on. "You've also reminded us that we each have different gifts according to *Gotte*'s grace."

"Emma's right," Rachel said.

"This isn't the same thing." Henry's shoulders drooped forward, as if a great weight was pulling them down. "You know it isn't the same. You know what happened last time."

"*Ya*, I know," Emma said. "We were there, Henry, and we'll be with you through this. But what happened in Goshen wasn't your fault. And in fact, if you hadn't become involved, then that girl's killer might have never been caught. He might have gone on to hurt others. What you are able to do is a gift from *Gotte*, and forgive me for being so bold, but you're wrong to turn away from it."

"*Mamm* never was one to hold her tongue," Clyde muttered.

Henry stood, walked to the porch railing, and remained silent. Emma thought he would reject her idea, possibly even rebuke her for speaking so plainly. When he turned to face them, the expression on his face nearly broke her heart— it was so full of exhaustion and pain and fear. Yet

121

underneath all of that was the tiniest bit of hope. He was only a man, after all. He'd been given the task to watch over them. He'd been given the holy job of bishop, but he was only a man.

Finally, he nodded and said, "I'll try."

Nineteen

Henry meant what he said to Emma and her family. He would try to draw what he saw at Vernon's home the day before his death. He would, for the first time in fifteen years, indulge his *gift,* though he still wasn't sure he agreed with Emma on that definition.

First, he needed to take care of his buggy horse, and then he realized the stall needed mucking out. His buggy was also looking a bit worse for wear. He spent a good hour cleaning it thoroughly. Then he stopped by his workshop and thought about working on another one of the birdhouses he'd begun before Vernon breathed his last. This particular model was a three story, built from found lumber and some old shutters one of the local contractors tossed out when he was remodeling a home.

Henry sat down on his workbench and held the birdhouse in his hands. He particularly enjoyed the three holes placed vertically four inches apart, perhaps because he liked the thought of three bird families living together, close enough to hear the baby peeps through the walls. Or maybe it was the symbolism of the number three—Father, Son, and Holy Ghost. He often prayed as he worked, that God would use something as small as a birdhouse to touch his heart, to remind him of the joy of his salvation.

But Henry realized if he worked on the birdhouse now, he would only mess it up. Working with wood took concentration. One wrong cut, and you could ruin a piece of lumber or injure a finger. He set the birdhouse back on the table, stepped out of his workshop, and plodded over to his house. Stepping inside, he realized there was no work to do there. The women in his district had taken care of everything. They'd even left a few labeled dinners in his refrigerator, enough to last a week. He wasn't hungry, though, and it was time to stop procrastinating.

But instead of pulling out pencil and paper, he went to his rocker and picked up the family Bible. It had belonged to his father, and his father's father. The text was in German, which was as familiar and natural to him as any *Englisch* text. He thumbed through the worn pages, stopping now and then to read a passage that caught his eye.

He found the verses on talents and gifts Emma had referred to.

Each of you should use whatever gift you have received to serve others. We have different gifts, according to the grace given . . . Servants of Christ . . . entrusted with the mysteries God has revealed.

They were verses he'd read and shared with others, many times, but they did nothing to ease the trouble in his heart. There was something else he needed to read, something an unconscious part of his mind, or his soul, was yearning for. He found it in the first chapter of Philippians, verse six: "Being confident of this, that He who began a good work in you will carry it on to completion until the day of Christ Jesus."

Did he believe it? Was this promise meant even for him, at the ripe old age of sixty-four?

It had all begun so long ago, when he was a young lad of twelve. Staring out the window at the light fading across the valley, Henry could still hear the crack of the bat. He'd never actually felt the impact as the ball slammed into his head, but he had heard the gasp from those watching the game. They'd known before he did. In fact, it was weeks later, when he finally woke up in an *Englisch* hospital, that his parents told him about the blow to his head and what doctors were calling a traumatic brain injury.

Henry read the passage again. The words weren't a suggestion, but rather a commandment. A description of a fact. *Being confident of this.* There was no room for doubt or questioning. And who gave such confidence? Who gave all things? Their heavenly Father.

He bowed his head and prayed that his heart would reflect a confidence in the provision and purpose of Christ. He petitioned God to use what had begun so long ago, to use this gift, for His glory. He pleaded with God to complete the good work He had begun. He allowed the Holy Spirit to minister to his heart and his mind and his soul.

Opening his eyes, Henry was surprised to see that the sun had fled and darkness had settled across the land. He stood and turned on the lantern in the sitting room as well as the one in the kitchen. Walking to his desk, he pulled out two pencils and several sheets of the oversized paper he used when he plotted out his large garden.

It might be that he'd need a few attempts to get it right.

Or perhaps this strange ability was something that had left him, and he would be able to draw nothing more than a child's sketch.

But when he sat down and picked up a pencil, he knew neither of those things was true. He began drawing, first an outline that covered the entire sheet—the kitchen table where he and Vernon had sat and the cabinets and window beyond. Through the window, Vernon's yard, filled with a hodgepodge of items. Back inside and to the left, a doorway that looked into the sitting room.

His pencil practically flew across the page. He didn't pause to think, to try to remember, to ascertain if the details were correct. He simply allowed his hand to draw what his mind had already recorded.

He started again in the middle of the page, shading and adding even more details, working his way out to the top, the right, the left, and then the bottom edges of the sheet of paper. He added layer upon layer to the drawing, catching the slant of late sunlight through the window, the dregs of coffee in a mug, the lines of writing on a letter. No detail was more important than any other. His brain was rendering a photographic-like drawing of a specific moment in time.

He added leaves on the tree outside the window, a stack of mail on the table, a postmark stamp upon an envelope. He drew the lines on the letter, the words that weren't obscured by the stack of mail.

The entire process took place without Henry being completely aware of what he was doing. He wasn't in a trance. He knew he was sitting at the table, drawing on a piece of paper, and that his goal was to save Sam Beiler from the fate that he had once endured. But the actual drawing of the scene was as natural and unconscious as drawing the next breath.

When he'd finished, he pushed the paper away, stood, and walked to the sink. Filling a glass with water, he drank the entire thing, pulled in a deep breath, and uttered yet another prayer. Only then did he turn back to the table and study what he'd done.

His first response was that he would need to return to the police station immediately.

His second was that he did not plan on going there alone.

Twenty

Emma, Clyde, Henry, and Sheriff Grayson were crowded into a small office in the police station. Emma was painfully aware that Sam waited down the hall, probably sitting on a simple cot, no doubt inside a cell with bars. That image solidified her resolve. Somehow they would convince the sheriff to believe what they had to tell him, to show him.

Grayson offered coffee, but they all declined. It would only make Emma more jittery than she already was. Her son and the bishop seemed calm enough, but then Clyde had been a young man of twenty-five the last time. He didn't realize how quickly the legal system could turn, especially once it started off in the wrong direction. As for Henry, he seemed calmer than he had been in recent days. The bishop had found the spiritual strength to push through, and it was evident in everything from his posture to his expression.

The arson investigator, Meg Allen, appeared in the doorway. She looked as if she'd been roused from sleep. Her short red hair stuck up in the back, though plainly she'd combed through it with water in an attempt to settle the cowlick. Emma's grandson had the same problem, and somehow it made the woman seem more human to Emma—in spite of the gun she wore on her hip beneath her jacket. It was plain enough to see the outline of the holster through the thin fabric, which perhaps was the point. Was her life constantly in jeopardy because of the criminals she pursued? Emma couldn't imagine such a job, such a life, for anyone—but especially not for a young woman.

Grayson made introductions, and then he motioned to the last empty chair.

"Sorry to call you in so late, Meg."

"Not a problem. Show me what you have."

"Before we do, perhaps I should explain—"

Meg interrupted the bishop with a shake of her head and a curt, "No." As if realizing how rude and abrupt her words sounded, she added, "If you'll show me what you have, we can decide how best to proceed."

So Henry handed her the single sheet of paper.

She studied it for a full three minutes before looking up at Grayson. "You've seen this?"

"Yes. Henry brought it to me thirty minutes ago."

"You called me down here for this? For a drawing?"

"It's not merely a drawing," Clyde said.

"But it is. A quite detailed one, to be sure, but still just a drawing." Meg dropped the sheet on Grayson's desk. "Let me be clear. This is not evidence, and it will not influence the way we proceed in this case."

"Hang on, Meg. Maybe you need to listen to the bishop's story first."

Emma could tell Meg Allen wasn't used to being interrupted and told what to do. The woman clamped her mouth shut, her lips forming a tight, straight line. She sat back in her chair, stared at Henry, and waited.

If he was perturbed by her attitude, he didn't show it. But then Emma knew he'd encountered such attitudes before. No doubt he had prepared himself for this moment both emotionally and spiritually. Probably he'd spent a good amount of time in prayer since they'd spoken earlier in the day, perhaps since the night Vernon died.

"When I was twelve years old, I was playing baseball with the other children, and Atlee Stolzfus was up to bat. Atlee always had a powerful swing. He was older. Out of school already. He told me later that he'd been approached by a professional team to play for them, but after that day—the day I'm speaking of—he never picked up a bat again."

For Emma it was like being pulled back into another time, one marked by fear and uncertainty. She'd been eight when Henry's accident had occurred, old enough to question why such things happened. Old enough to worry her friend might not recover.

"I heard the crack of the bat, but I never saw the ball coming toward me. The moment of impact has always remained a blank spot in my memory. I was taken to the local hospital, where a small hole was drilled in my head to reduce the pressure from intracranial bleeding." He reached up and touched a spot on the side of his head, a scar completely covered by hair that was beginning to turn gray. "It was determined that I had a suffered a catastrophic brain injury. My *mamm* and *dat* were worried I wouldn't recover."

Henry glanced at Emma. She wanted to reach out and squeeze his hand, to assure him they were doing the right thing by sharing his history, and that they would support him regardless of the outcome. He must have sensed some of that because he nodded once and turned back to the arson investigator.

"I did recover, went home, and lived a rather normal life from that point on . . . other than this skill." He glanced at Emma again. "This gift I had. I was suddenly able to draw, in complete and accurate detail, anything I'd seen."

"Photographic memory?" Meg asked.

"Not quite. *Nein*. I couldn't tell you what I'd seen, couldn't verbalize or explain it. In that way, my memory is the same as anyone else's. Plus the doctors . . . well, they say there is no such thing as true photographic memory."

Meg sighed, put her hand on top of the sheet, and spoke in a more compassionate tone. "I appreciate your sharing this with me, Mr. Lapp, but even if I wanted to believe what you're saying, this simply isn't evidence. I can't present it in a court of law."

"*Ya*, we understand that." Emma couldn't keep quiet another second. "What we want is for you to look at it, truly look at it, and see the details there, the letter on the table and the postmark on the envelope. Plainly someone was angry enough with Vernon to write that letter, and the person who did that could be his killer."

When Meg hesitated, Grayson cleared his throat. "I checked out his story. It's called acquired savant syndrome, and it's a real thing."

"Savant syndrome? Like people who can suddenly play Mozart on the piano?"

"That's one kind. The condition presents itself in several different ways." Grayson pulled his laptop closer, searched for a moment, and then he began to read. "According to the Wisconsin Medical Society, savants can present with art and musical ability, like what you mentioned. Also calendar calculation . . ."

"What in the world is that?"

"Like you ask someone what day of the week February 3, 1645, was and they can tell you."

"Pretty useless skill if you ask me."

Grayson shrugged. "Some acquired savants have a special math skill, like a man named Daniel Tammet. He has memorized pi to 22,514 decimal places. Other savants have remarkable spatial skills. Another kind is what Henry is describing—the ability to recreate in minute detail something he has seen."

Meg shook her head, as if she didn't know how to respond.

"There's more," Clyde said. "Tell her about Goshen."

Henry nodded to Grayson, who pulled a sheet from a stack of papers and pushed it toward Meg. "That's from the court proceedings in Goshen, Indiana, fifteen years ago. A young girl, Betsy Troyer, was killed. Henry was charged for that murder when he brought one of his drawings to the police. They thought he had to be guilty to have been able to recreate such a thing and because of his knowledge of certain texts."

"We'd been to visit Betsy," Henry explained. "Her parents were worried and asked me to speak with her. When we arrived at the house, she wouldn't come downstairs, so I went up to her room, along with one of the men in my church— Emma's husband."

Grayson picked up the thread of the story. "Henry was arrested and held for trial, but before the trial commenced, one of the investigators decided to take a closer look at what Henry had drawn. His vision—or whatever you want to call it—caught an image of a text that came in on the girl's phone while they were there. Her parents claimed she had no phone. It was later discovered that they had thrown it into the pond. The officers were able to find it and submit it as evidence."

"The parents regretted trying to hide the phone." Henry shrugged his shoulders. "They didn't understand how it could lead to catching Betsy's killer."

"The cell service provider was able to provide transcripts of all her recent texts. One text was from a drifter Betsy had been seeing."

"The same text Henry had drawn," Emma explained. "His drawing is what caused the police to start looking for a phone, one her parents claimed didn't exist."

Grayson continued, "Long story short, Henry was released and the drifter, a man named Gene Wooten, was convicted of the murder. He's currently serving a life sentence."

"Those were terrible days for our community." Emma looked directly at Meg Allen. She wanted the woman to understand what Henry had sacrificed by coming to the authorities with his drawing. "Henry was held for more than three months because they wouldn't listen. And that man? Gene Wooten? He nearly killed another girl in the meantime. Henry hasn't used his gift since, but tonight he did. We're here for Sam because he did not kill Vernon. And the proof? It's on that sheet of paper if you will only look at it."

Twenty-One

Henry spent Saturday morning in his garden. He didn't have fields with crops, having purchased a small parcel of land. By the time they moved to Colorado, he'd understood that he was too old to try to farm fifty acres. But he could still raise most of the vegetables he needed in a garden, and he had his workshop.

He spent the afternoon there, finishing the birdhouse he'd studied the day before, and then working on a side table made from scraps of wood. It was the largest project in his shop, though it was only two feet tall. The top measured eighteen inches by eighteen inches, which he was fashioning from different types of wood scraps he'd picked up at the lumberyard in town. He alternated the wood, bringing to mind patchwork quilts his mother had handsewn when he was a young boy. He was thinking of that, of the feel and texture of those quilts and how they resembled the softness of the wood once it was well sanded, when there was a knock at his door.

He'd never heard the person drive up. He needed to see about purchasing one of Abe's beagle pups, which would no doubt provide an early warning system for when he had visitors.

Hurrying to the door, he was surprised to see Meg Allen waiting. She handed him an envelope. "Your original drawing. We kept a copy."

"Would you like to come in?"

She seemed surprised at the quantity and scope of projects in his workshop. "You're quite talented at woodworking."

"*Danki*."

"Have you always had this skill?"

"You're asking if it's a result of my injury. I think not. My *dat* enjoyed working with wood, though he was a farmer first and foremost. I picked up any carpentry skills I possess from him."

"I'd like to talk to you about the drawing."

Henry sat at the workbench and waited. Meg took the stool across from him, where often customers would wait as he filled out a receipt or wrote down a special order.

"I did a thorough background search on you regarding the case of Betsy Troyer and . . . your condition." She ran the palm of her hand over the worktable. "I won't say I'm a believer, Mr. Lapp, but I would like to talk to you about that drawing."

"Call me Henry, please. Do you think it might hold a clue?"

"I find the drawing . . . interesting, and at the moment I don't have any other leads."

"What about Vernon's neighbors? Not that I'm

saying they did it, but I know there were feelings of animosity between them."

"That's putting it mildly. The neighbors to the north called the police on Vernon eleven times in the last year."

"I had no idea the situation was that bad."

"They were calls about minor things—claims that he'd trespassed onto their property, complaints about the animals and items he stored there. Whatever you can imagine, they tried to use to get him in trouble. Once they even called the health department, claiming his property was a menace."

"Vernon didn't tell me any of this."

"I'm not surprised. But regardless of their past history, only two people live on the property to the north—a Mr. and Mrs. Thompson, and both have a solid alibi for the night of May first. In fact, they weren't even in town, and we've been able to corroborate that." Meg nodded to the envelope. "Which is why I'm back here, and why I'd like to discuss that."

Henry pulled out the sheet of paper, and pivoted it so it was facing Meg.

Then he walked around the table and sat on the stool beside her. Together they read the letter that had been revealed in the drawing . . . or partially revealed. Vernon's mail had been dropped on the table, on top of the letter, and it obscured nearly half of the writing, from the top left to the bottom right on a straight angle.

ined my life, and you can be sure you will pay for it.
of taxes. You wun't even fite for your counrty and
You shouln't evn be heere. When I skipted school,
truant ociffer, but yur kids are free to go about
en start high school.

or less than it was wurth. My family was
when the ol factry closed in town. Then he
like that he lost our home. I begged him
en? He died, cluching a botle of whiskey
living in a hovel. It's all becase YOU
nd decied you'd like to live in the valey.

ive those buggies out on the road. Who
s rediculous. We were drivng here
t be a man's fault if he hits a
YOU are to blame becuase you
piad for that too.

lace. Well now you wil pay.

ets hired? YOU PEOPLE do.
s. You wurk for cheep. What
insurance and more than
pposed to do when YOU

do someting about it.
You   din't   listen.
se yu'll be DEAD.
You wait nd see.

"Hard to make much sense of," Henry admitted. "Looks like gibberish."

"But the tone of it is rather bleak."

"Yes," Meg pointed to the word *DEAD*. "I'll agree with that."

They both stared at it for a moment, and then Meg asked, "You're sure you can't remember any more?"

"Doesn't work that way. I don't remember any of it, but my mind can accurately draw what it saw. It's more like recreating a photograph."

"But there is no photographic memory. You were right about that too. I checked."

"Indeed, and yet it would seem that our subconscious mind does remember more than our conscious one." Henry pointed to the corner of an envelope with a partial postage mark showing. "Can you tell where this is from?"

"Alamosa, I would imagine. We can only see the right half, but the last letters and the last numbers of the zip code match up."

"So it was mailed from there?"

"If that envelope held this letter."

"A fair assumption."

"Well, there is a whole stack of mail here."

"But most of it seems to be flyers and such."

There was one flyer announcing the special deals at the local grocer. It was amazingly detailed, and for a moment Henry found himself astounded that he had drawn such a thing.

Meg interrupted his thoughts with, "Sam Beiler was released earlier today."

Henry jerked his head up, a smile spreading across his face. "That's *wunderbaar* news!"

"We had him write out a sample text. His handwriting didn't match the letter."

"I was sure it wouldn't."

"And we checked out his alibi with the store clerks."

"I always knew you'd find he was innocent."

"He's no longer a suspect in the construction site fire. However, he's not entirely clear in the death of Vernon Frey, but we don't have enough evidence at this point to hold him."

Henry studied Meg carefully, trying to see past her professional demeanor. "But do you believe he could do such a thing?"

"It doesn't matter what I believe. It matters what I can prove."

"Perhaps it matters to me."

He didn't think she would answer, but after a moment she did. "My gut is telling me Sam isn't our guy, but I've been wrong before—and that was a costly mistake."

"You aren't wrong this time, and I'll do everything in my power to help you prove it."

Twenty-Two

He'd lost a few days, but that didn't matter.

His plan had been to spread out the destruction.

To worry them as he had been worried.

To disrupt their lives.

On one level he understood this was foolishness, that wreaking havoc on them wouldn't restore what he'd lost. That conviction occasionally rose to the top of his thoughts, but each time he pushed it away. He would remember his promise to his brother, and the anger in his heart would ignite, consuming any doubts. The worry he saw in their eyes nearly made him laugh. The way the sheriff rushed from place to place pleased him to no end. The fact that even that nosy arson investigator seemed to be at a loss helped him to sleep at night. She'd found no solid evidence.

That was the beauty of arson. It left behind few if any clues.

And he'd been careful about that. He read up on the process on the web, careful to do so on the library's computer so his search history couldn't be traced back to him. The library had a sign-in sheet, but it was easy enough to put someone else's name on the form.

The Internet search was helpful. He learned to

use only products that could easily be purchased anywhere. Another important aspect, according to the websites, was to choose a location that had plenty of material to spread a fire naturally. That way he didn't have to carry in anything more than the initial incendiary device. Vernon's house had been perfect for that. There was so much junk stacked inside and outside that, once ignited, he'd known it would burn aggressively. The same thing was true of the construction worksite. They had both deserved what happened to them. He'd crossed their names off his list with a feeling of accomplishment.

But his next location would be trickier, and he had to be careful. Revenge was all good and well, but it wasn't worth getting caught over.

Fortunately, he was smarter, craftier, and more motivated than the authorities.

So he was careful what he purchased and how he purchased it. Everyone knew mail deliveries, cell phones, and even credit card purchases could be tracked. He didn't have a credit card, so that wasn't a problem. But there was no way to track cash.

He stopped at the gas station and filled up his gas container—something people did all the time for lawnmowers and such. Only he didn't plan on mowing. What he had in mind next should get everyone talking. If he couldn't make a living, why should they be able to? He'd make a bold statement with this move. He would make them pay, as he'd promised.

And if someone was hurt? Well, that was their fault for being in his way.

Twenty-Three

Henry spent Sunday with Abe and Susan and their family.

It wasn't a church Sunday, and traditionally Amish used off Sundays for visiting family. But their community was small, and most had few relatives in the area. So they gathered in groups at various farms. Henry made sure he rotated where he spent his off Sundays. He enjoyed seeing all of his congregation, though he was closer to some than others.

"Didn't know you were interested in the pups." Abe's bushy eyebrows arched over his glasses.

"I wasn't, but either my hearing is going or my attention is. I often don't realize someone has driven down my lane until they're knocking at my door."

"Unfortunately, all I have left is the runt. She's small, but I imagine she can be as *gut* a watchdog as any of them."

They'd finished eating the lunch meal, and Henry was enjoying the walk out to the dog pen behind the barn. Susan had made her cheesy casserole, and he'd eaten two helpings of it. Now his stomach reminded him he was overly full. His belly stretched against the cloth of his shirt, and his suspenders seemed tighter.

He'd have to skip his usual evening dessert.

It felt good to be out in the sun and not thinking about arson and fire and death. "Are you still getting hate mail about running a puppy mill?"

Abe grimaced. "One or two a week from all over the country. Probably because I put something in the *Budget* about having available pups. Unfortunately, that seemed to draw attention from the wrong folks."

Henry squatted next to the dog pen to study the small beagle with giant brown eyes and long silky ears. The pen was a five feet by ten feet run, with shade over the back half, a good-sized dog house, huge water bowl, and what looked like a miniature jungle gym.

"When did you add that?"

Abe laughed. "One of the *Englischers* offered it for free if we'd haul it away. His children had outgrown it years ago, and the wife wanted to put in a butterfly garden. It was my *doschder*'s idea to put it in the dog pen. She'd read somewhere that it was *gut* exercise for them."

"You know, Abe, the reporter in town has asked me several times if she could do a feature on some of our families. Perhaps if you invited her out to let her see what you have here and do a story on the dogs, it would put an end to the letters."

"I doubt the influence of the *Monte Vista Gazette* reaches that far."

"You might be surprised. She tells me Amish

are a popular topic right now." They exchanged a knowing smile. Both had endured enough of the tourist phenomena when they lived in Goshen. It was one of the reasons they decided to move out west.

"No pictures, of course."

Henry nodded in agreement. "Though she could take some photos of the dog pen."

"This pup should grow to be about thirteen inches and weigh in at twenty to thirty pounds. She's a hunting dog, not a watchdog, but I suppose once she becomes attached to you she will protect you. It's a dog's nature."

Henry motioned for Abe to open the gate, and the beagle came charging out, tripped over her own feet, righted herself, and trundled into the bishop's legs. He bent down and picked up the pup. She had a short clean coat, a combination of black, white, and tan. And of course long, velvety ears.

"Have you named her?"

"Kids are calling her Lexi, but you can name her whatever you want. She's not exactly answering to it yet."

Henry checked her eyes, peeked into her ears, and ran a hand down her coat. He had no idea what he was looking for, but she seemed healthy enough. "I'll take her."

Abe nodded but held up a hand to refuse payment when Henry pulled out his money.

"You don't owe me anything."

"Now, Abe, we all work to make a living here. You've spent a lot of feed and attention on this dog, and I'm happy to pay for her." He pressed the money into his friend's hands. "Has she had her shots already?"

"First set. You'll need to get the boosters."

They were walking toward Henry's buggy when Abe said, "I saw one years ago—a puppy mill. Terrible thing. The smell was horrendous, and those poor animals were crammed into pens no bigger than you'd put a chicken. I hadn't been chosen to preach yet, and I don't mind telling you I had a hard time controlling my temper. I called the authorities, the *Englisch* animal control center in Goshen, but someone else had done the same and they were already sending an officer out."

"Amish?"

"Actually, an Amish man had partnered with an *Englischer*. They thought they could make a quick fortune. Neither understood how much work dogs truly are. The police shut them down and charged them both with animal cruelty."

"Animals are much like everything else on this earth—the land, the resources, even the people. All are given to us to care for and to use in service to others."

"Indeed."

Abe's two youngest—Anna and Tim—ran up

to them carrying a rather large cardboard box and a paper sack.

"*Mamm* said to bring you this." Anna handed him the cardboard box. It was bigger, but apparently lighter than whatever was in the sack. "So Lexi doesn't crawl all over your feet while you're driving."

Her brother stood beside her. "She sent some food too, since you probably won't get to town until tomorrow."

"Thank you both."

Anna reached forward and kissed the pup. "I'm going to miss her, but I can come visit, right?"

"Of course you can."

Which was all she needed to hear. Anna bounded off, her brother quick to follow once he'd placed the sack of supplies in Henry's buggy.

"I heard Sam is out of jail." Abe held the pup while Henry situated the box on the back seat.

"He is." It was the first they'd spoken of it. Henry hadn't wanted to bring it up. He didn't like to mar the peace of a Sunday, even if it wasn't a church Sunday. At the same time, he understood people needed to be reassured all was fine. Only it wasn't. Not yet.

"So do they have any idea who did it? Do they still believe Vernon was murdered?"

"*Ya.* Some, er, clues have come to light that seem to indicate so."

150

"Your drawing?" Abe grinned when Henry looked surprised. "Everyone knows about that. We all think it's a marvelous gift the Lord has given you, Henry. I'm glad you were able to use it to free Sam."

A simple way to look at things, but maybe he was right. Or so Henry thought as he put the pup into the box, climbed into his buggy, and drove toward home.

They were still left with the question of who was guilty. Henry was relieved it wasn't an Amish person—at least he didn't see how it could be. No one in their community went over to Alamosa much. Abe did now and then to check on his brother. He couldn't think of anyone else. But he still felt it was his responsibility to look after his congregation.

What if this person wasn't finished causing destruction? What if he had a vendetta against the Amish?

What could he possibly do about it?

Well, he could pray. As he had reminded people more than once, prayer wasn't a last resort. It was what they should endeavor to do first, middle, and last. God would guide them, and perhaps He would lead Meg Allen to finding the killer.

Twenty-Four

Monday morning when Meg Allen drove up, Henry wasn't caught by surprise. Not because Lexi alerted him. The dog was sound asleep in a basket on the front porch. Henry happened to be sitting there working on his Sunday sermon when he heard a car pull into his lane.

Meg nodded toward the pup, who rolled over onto her back and emitted a low whine.

"You got yourself a guard dog?"

"Something like that."

"Doesn't seem to be working."

"Give her time."

"If you have a minute, I'd like to talk to you about the investigation."

"Of course. Would you like some coffee?"

Meg sighed as she sat down in the rocker next to him. Henry thought she looked tired. He wondered if she had worked on Sunday while he'd rested. Of course she had. Law investigations didn't stop for the Sabbath. And yet perhaps if she had rested, she'd be better equipped to face whatever trials today brought. Which wasn't for him to judge one way or the other.

"I'd better not. I had three cups in town," she admitted. "Any more and I'll be orbiting."

"So what have you learned?"

"Very little." She pulled out a small notepad and studied it. "I attempted to get a subpoena for the local school records because the letter clearly indicates someone with a learning disability."

"You can do that? Get a subpoena on the weekend?"

"A subpoena can be approved anytime. We'll find a judge and wake them up if need be. Unfortunately, in this case, the judge wouldn't approve the subpoena. The academic and behavioral records of every student are sealed, and they can only be accessed by the student—if he or she is an adult—or a parent or legal guardian if they are still a minor."

"You could ask parents to let you see the records, but you wouldn't know where to start."

"Correct. Though based on the letter, I doubt this was done by someone still in school. Also, student files are periodically purged. The records might be destroyed if our perp is an older man." Meg paused and tapped the folder she'd brought. "What was your reaction on Saturday when we first looked at the letter together?"

"It was difficult to make out what was being said. The person had poor spelling and grammar."

Meg hesitated, and then she said, "I believe it was more than that. My sister is dyslexic. Do you know what that means?"

"Some children in our schools have had

problems, academically, because of dyslexia. I can't say I understand it myself. At the time, we decided to bring in a Mennonite teacher a few hours a week to work with them. They were bright children, if I remember correctly, only with some problems in the . . . " Henry mimicked writing on a piece of paper.

"Exactly. Teachers use a whole checklist to determine if a child might have dyslexic problems. I didn't remember the particulars for my sister, only that she struggled, but I thought if our perp is dyslexic, it might narrow the field of suspects. I went to the school after I left here, trying to get the records. As you know, Monte Vista is small enough that kindergarten through twelfth grade classes are all housed on the same campus. Grayson even had the head principal meet me at the main building and unlock it. The judge denied our subpoena, but I was still able to meet with the special education coordinator. She told me a dyslexic person will often exhibit certain patterns in their writing—repetition, transpositions, omissions, substitutions, and even reversal of letters."

"You found those things in the killer's letter?"

Meg frowned at the folder. "I found those characteristics in the letter, but I'm not ready to jump to the conclusion that the killer wrote it. Possibly. Then again, possibly not. My hope was that it would be a place to start, and often in an investigation that's what you need. A good solid starting place."

She pulled out the copy of Henry's drawing. It had a lined sheet of notebook paper stapled to the back. She folded back the top sheet and handed it to him. "I spent some time working on the letter, on correcting the spelling and grammar issues. I think you'll agree it makes more sense now."

ined my life, and you can be sure you will pay for it.
of taxes. You won't even fight for your country and
You shouldn't even be here. When I skipped school,
truant officer, but your kids are free to go about
en start high school.

or less than it was worth. My family was
when the old factory closed in town. Then he
like that he lost our home. I begged him
en? He died, clutching a bottle of whiskey
living in a hovel. It's all because YOU
nd decided you'd like to live in the valley.

ive those buggies out on the road. Who
s ridiculous. We were drivng here
t be a man's fault if he hits a
YOU are to blame because you
paid for that too.

lace. Well now you will pay.

ets hired? YOU PEOPLE do.
s. You work for cheap. What
insurance and more than
pposed to do when YOU

do someting about it.
You didn't listen.
se yu'll be DEAD.
You wait and see.

"*Ya*, I can see how the few letters you've changed do help. The writing makes more sense, though it's still a puzzle. The changes, though— they seem correct."

"It's only a guess . . . again, this wouldn't hold up in court, but if we can identify the writer of the letter we at least have a direction in which to take the investigation."

"The tone is decidedly negative. Hurt, even."

"Maybe it's a family vendetta. Maybe some- one's best friend went through a terrible time because of these perceived injustices. Maybe that person decided to set things right to help out someone they care about. My main concern is to identify our perp before he strikes again."

"You think that will happen?"

"It could. He has no reason to stop, unless his grudge was solely against Mr. Frey."

"If that was the case, why did he hit the construction site?"

"Precisely." Meg hesitated, and then she said, "I'd like to speak plainly, but I want to assure you I mean no disrespect to you or your congregation."

"Go on."

"In this first paragraph, our perp seems to be laying out his grievances, in particular that the Amish don't fight in wars and don't attend school past the eighth grade."

"Both are sometimes controversial aspects of our religion, at least to outsiders."

"The second paragraph seems more personal. He says *My family . . .* "

"And speaks of a factory closing." He stared down at the letter, shook his head, and then handed the letter back to her.

"I checked with Sheriff Grayson about that. A small factory in the area did close twenty years ago."

"Well before I moved here. A small community of Amish were in the area before us. They began purchasing farms . . . " Henry allowed his gaze to drift to the roof of the porch, trying to count back. "You could check records, but I believe that happened five years before we looked into the area. There was some problem, a majority of the families left, and their bishop passed. They even had to close their school and send what children remained to the *Englisch*."

"I didn't realize that ever happened. I know you prefer a parochial school."

"It's true. We do. But it's not always possible. When I volunteered to move to Monte Vista, some of the families in my congregation in Goshen decided to join me. That first year was difficult. We decided to put off reopening the schoolhouse until the next year."

"Maybe in his mind, the arrival of Amish in the valley is when the trouble began."

"You keep saying 'him.' Are we sure it couldn't be a woman?"

"The majority of arsonists are white males. Nearly sixty percent are under the age of eighteen, but those cases rarely involve murder, which is what makes me think our perp is someone older."

"So you've whittled it down to forty percent."

"Of those over eighteen, eighty percent are under the age of twenty-nine. Many have little or no education, having dropped out of school before graduating. A good percentage have prior felony arrests, and some have significant medical histories." She set the rocker in motion and stared out across Henry's yard. "They're troubled young men. In the eight years I've been an arson investigator, I've never come across a female arsonist."

She cleared her throat and brought her attention back to their case. "I believe our perp matches that profile. It's highly unlikely this person is a woman because of the statistics, plus a woman would have been more noticeable at the construction site."

"Makes sense."

She nodded toward the letter. "He mentions losing his home."

"Foreclosure?"

"I have someone working on that—getting me the names on all foreclosures that occurred in the area in the last twenty years."

Henry whistled. "Could be a long list."

"What about Vernon's place? Was it a fore-closure?"

"I couldn't say. He bought it before I arrived. Vernon was in the first group."

"We'll check the real estate records."

"If it happened so long ago, why would he be lashing out now? And your profile . . . it indicates a younger man."

"But the letter mentions his father. So I'm thinking the father might have become unemployed."

"When the factory closed."

"And then they lost the home. Let's say our perp is between twenty-five and thirty-five. He could have been a child when the home went into foreclosure."

"He blames us for moving in and buying up the homesteads."

"And he wants to get even."

Twenty-Five

"Why now?" Henry asked. "Why strike out against those around him now?"

"Sometimes these things build up." Meg studied him a moment. "Do your families play the game Jenga?"

"With the building blocks? *Ya*. Our children love that one."

"The more blocks you add, the more precarious the stack. Emotionally, people can be like that. They endure one thing and then another and another, but with each added situation the burden becomes worse until they topple, much like the Jenga blocks."

"But if he's angry with us, then it seems to me his troubles might have begun after we arrived. Perhaps he even went to school before our school-house opened, because he mentions our kids. He's angry that our young men are able to work, while he's still forced into a classroom."

"Grayson can get me a name of students brought up on truancy charges. We'll give those priority, but I'm going to work from the factory closing forward."

Henry nodded and then waved at the letter, indicating she should continue.

"We have a reference about someone drinking,

so we're pulling all DUIs, drunk and disorderly, that sort of thing."

"And this mention of buggies?"

"Could be someone who was in an accident."

"Haven't had too many of those since we moved into the valley." Henry tapped the arm of the rocker. "One terrible accident, the first year we were here, killed a father and child."

Meg sat up straighter. "That could be it. Do you know any of the details?"

"I do. I attended the trial."

"What can you tell me about it?"

"The woman who'd lost her husband and daughter was devastated, as you can imagine. The trial lasted only two days, but I was there for all of it. I didn't want her to endure such a thing alone, and she had no other family in the area. Plus, the accident happened right out there, in front of my place."

"Did you testify?"

Henry ran a thumb up and down his suspenders. "I did. I was working in my workshop when I heard the crash. I ran out to the road in time to see the *Englischer* drive away."

"Your testimony put him in jail."

"*Nein*. His blood alcohol level did that, and his prior DUIs didn't help. They didn't actually need my testimony, though it might have helped in the sentencing phase. He received life in prison. A real shame for someone that young."

161

"A real shame for the two who were killed."

"Every life is complete," Henry murmured, though he didn't suspect she would understand.

"Do you remember the name of the person convicted?"

"Shawn. Shawn Neely."

"This could be it. This could be the connection we're looking for."

"I don't see how. Shawn's in jail."

"What about his family?"

"Don't know if he had any."

"No one from his family came to the trial?"

"Not that I can recall."

Meg tapped her fingers against the chair. Finally, she turned to him and asked, "Does the wife still live here? The one whose husband and child were killed?"

"No. She moved back east as soon as the trial concluded."

Meg studied her small notepad again. She flipped through some pages until she found what she wanted and then showed it to Henry. "A half dozen traffic accidents with buggies have been reported since the first Amish family moved here. I've listed them all. I can't tell that Vernon was involved with any of them."

"*Nein*. He wasn't that I remember, though several times *Englischers* did complain to the sheriff about Vernon's driving. He had a habit of attaching a small trailer to the back of his buggy and loading up—" He almost said *junk* and paused to think of another word, but his imagination failed him. "Well, he would buy things or pick up items others had thrown away and take them out to his property. It wasn't a safe way for him to travel. I spoke to him about this, and the sheriff threatened to cite him with a ticket a couple of times."

Henry looked again at her list and pointed to one of the lines. "This was the accident that killed the two people. The other five were relatively minor in regard to human injury."

He traced his finger down the page. "In this one, the horse had to be put down, so it was rather costly. And in this one, I seem to remember the driver was cited for driving while intoxicated."

"The driver of the automobile?" Meg picked up the tablet and was flipping back through the pages. "I don't have that on my other list."

"*Nein.* The driver of the buggy was cited." At the look of surprise on her face, he said, "Never assume Plain people are perfect. We deal with the same issues as any other group, including alcoholism."

"I'll keep that in mind, which brings me to the last topic I wanted to discuss with you."

Henry waited, allowing her to order her thoughts. The pup stood, stretched, and trotted over next to them, climbing across Henry's shoes and sniffing them as if hoping a treat would appear.

"We can't be sure if this is an *Englisch* person or an Amish one. As you pointed out, it's dangerous to make assumptions. I would like you to keep your eyes open, and if you notice anyone acting suspiciously, let me know."

Henry nodded but didn't speak.

"Sheriff Grayson explained to me that at times you prefer to handle matters internally, but that's not possible in this case. This is murder. I will find the person, and when I do, we will prosecute to the full extent of the law."

"And we will cooperate," Henry assured her. "It's true that often we prefer to handle matters within the church—say, if there's a disagreement between neighbors or even within a family. We believe our faith allows us to address those problems effectively. But if this is an Amish person, then it's someone who has clearly stepped outside the faith, someone willing to kill to exact revenge. We'll cooperate. If there's anything else I can do, let me know. "

He walked her to the car, the pup following in their wake.

"One more thing. I'm holding a press conference at four this afternoon at the police station. If possible, I'd like you to be there. You won't have to speak, and I know you don't want to be in front of the cameras, but I think your presence would be helpful." She hesitated and then added, "Often in these cases, perps will show up at a press conference. They like being the center of attention. I want you to keep an eye out and let Sheriff Grayson know immediately if you see anyone who jogs a memory or looks at all suspicious."

Henry assured her he would make the press conference. As she drove back down the lane, he wondered when or if their lives would ever return to normal.

Twenty-Six

Emma was happy to accompany Henry to the press conference. Clyde had planned to attend as well, but there was a problem with the plow, and he was still working in the fields when Henry stopped by to pick her up.

As they drove toward town, they discussed the drawing, Meg's conclusions, and the situation with Sam. "Clyde plans to go over and help him with his planting tomorrow. He said Abe and Leroy would be there as well."

"That's *gut*." Henry kept his eyes on the road, even though the horse basically could find the way to town on her own. He'd always been a careful driver. "It's right that we help one another."

"I only wish we'd known of his troubles earlier."

"Perhaps he thought he could do it on his own. The youth sometimes struggle with pride."

"Oh, so it's only a problem of the *youngies*, is it?"

"I didn't say that." Henry laughed at the look she gave him. "By our age, we've usually been humbled by life, is all. The young ones are still learning."

He parked in the side lot next to the police station. It was obvious that the press conference was being held at the front of the building.

The street had been roped off, and a growing crowd milled around. Sheriff Grayson and Meg Allen were standing on the steps. Half a dozen microphones had been placed in front of them, and news reporters with their cameramen waited.

Meg looked up, saw Henry, and nodded once.

They found a place at the back of the crowd. Emma knew the last thing Henry wanted was to be filmed for a television spot.

A young officer was passing out sheets of paper. He handed one to Emma while Henry was speaking to the manager of the construction site. When Henry returned to her side, she shoved the paper into his hands. It listed contact information for the sheriff and the arson investigator, the number for a tip hotline, and a basic description of the perpetrator.

Male
Approximately 5 feet 10 inches
Age 17 or older

There may be Amish attending this press conference. We ask that you respect their wishes and not film or photograph them.

Henry grunted at the paper, folded it into quarters, and handed it back to her. Emma stuck it in her purse.

The press conference began with Sheriff

Grayson introducing himself and then summarizing the murder and arson at Vernon's and the fire at the construction site. "We have every reason to believe these two incidents are related. Our investigation indicates the person of interest described on your sheet was involved in both. Either he had knowledge of the fires beforehand and failed to warn authorities or, more likely, he was responsible for setting both blazes."

Emma must have zoned out as the sheriff explained the course the investigation had followed to date. Finally, he thanked them for coming and stepped back so Meg could speak. Emma found herself watching the crowd. Though initially she'd thought it was mostly composed of news personnel, it had grown to include quite a number of citizens, including a few from their community. Perhaps they'd been in town anyway. She waved discreetly and turned her attention back to Meg as the woman began to explain that they had a photograph of the perpetrator.

"Two of the businesses across from the construction site have security cameras. We were able to find images of the perpetrator. We know it was him based on the date, time, and also the fact that he was carrying a backpack that probably held the incendiary device. A police sketch artist has combined those photos, and you can access it on our website."

Emma noticed that several in the crowd pulled

out their cell phones and began tapping away, staring at their screen.

"Also, we'd like to announce that the merchants of Monte Vista are jointly offering a reward of five thousand dollars for information leading to the arrest and conviction of our perpetrator. Anyone with knowledge of any type should contact the tip hotline."

Emma wanted to see one of those phones. How else would she know what this person looked like? How would she protect her grandchildren if he were to show up at their home, pretending to purchase something from their vegetable stand? That was a ridiculous worry. They'd just planted their garden, so there were no vegetables to sell yet, but they did open on Saturdays and sell homemade items, such as quilts and hot pads and potted plants. They could be in danger. She needed to see that picture!

She stepped closer to an *Englisch* woman who was staring down at her phone. The woman glanced up at her, smiled, and offered to let her take a look.

Which was how Emma found herself staring at Vernon's killer.

Henry stepped closer to view the phone over her shoulder. "Could be anyone," he muttered.

"*Ya*, except he has shaggy hair."

"Which he'll no doubt cut once he realizes the picture is out."

"Still, I'd like to be able to show this to our families so people can be on alert."

"*Gut* idea. I'll ask Meg if she can print off some copies."

The arson investigator was one step ahead of him. After the reporters had finished with their questions, which were either redundant or unanswerable, Meg thanked everyone for coming and then made her way over to Henry and Emma.

Meg said hello before handing a large envelope to Henry. "Fifty copies of the photo are in there. Please pass them out to your congregation. If anyone knows anything—"

"Call the hotline," Henry said. "I saw the phone number on the information sheet."

"It's also on the back of each photo." Meg paused and then asked, "Can your people do that?"

"Place a phone call?" The retort popped out of Emma's mouth as quickly as the thought bloomed in her head. "*Ya*, I believe we could manage that."

Meg turned to appraise Emma more carefully, and Emma felt the hair on her head bristle. Fortunately, it was covered with her *kapp*, so the *Englisch* woman wouldn't notice even if her hair had stood on end.

"I only meant to confirm that each family had access to a telephone since you don't allow them in your homes."

Henry jumped in, as if afraid of how Emma might answer. "We have phone shacks within two miles of every home, and some families with businesses have one in the barn."

Satisfied with his answer, Meg asked, "Did the picture jog any memory? Anything at all? Maybe of another scene you could draw for us?"

"It doesn't work like that," Emma and Henry said simultaneously.

Henry said, "What I mean to say is no. I don't think I've ever seen this person before, or if I have, it was only in passing."

"So he's not a member of your congregation? You're sure?"

Emma felt her temper spiking again. Perhaps she should follow the doctor's advice about hormone therapy. She was as prickly as a cat caught in a water sprinkler.

"The photo doesn't reveal much about him," Henry said. "What with the ball cap pulled low and all. But he doesn't appear to be anyone we know."

Meg nodded once, assured Henry she would be in touch, and then thanked them both before trotting off in the opposite direction.

"Pushy woman," Emma said.

"Feeling a mite protective of our families, are you?"

"Maybe I am."

Henry laughed and patted her arm. "You're a *gut* woman, Emma Fisher."

She wasn't so sure about that, but she did know

if the arsonist came anywhere near her family, they would find a way to protect their own. Many people misunderstood the Amish stand on pacifism. Turning the other cheek was one thing. Allowing someone to burn down your property or hurt your loved ones was another. If they ever came across the man in Meg Allen's poster, they would find a way to restrain him. Emma would sit on the arsonist herself if need be, right up until the moment that nosy, presumptuous Meg Allen arrived to handcuff and cart the man away.

Twenty-Seven

The week passed quickly. Henry managed to visit with most of their families and assure them the *Englisch* were taking care of the arson situation. He passed out Meg's photos, but no one recognized the nondescript image.

Many Amish churches had up to three ministers, but theirs was a small congregation and had only Abe and Clyde. Henry sat on the porch Saturday morning, his Bible on his lap and Lexi playing at his feet. The mama cat in the barn had led her kittens outside. Lexi kept a close eye on them, but she had learned the hard way that mama cat would swipe if she ventured too close to her babies. The mama's protectiveness reminded Henry of Emma's reaction to the press conference. She'd confessed her uncharitable thoughts while they'd ridden home.

"I can't imagine what I'd do, Henry. But I doubt I'd turn the other cheek if someone intended to hurt my family."

"Perhaps the Scripture speaks more to our pride."

"How so?"

"Say someone slights you, speaks rudely to you in a store, or walks past without greeting you at a church meeting."

173

"Go on."

"Would you pray for the person and whatever issue in their life caused such ungraciousness, or would you vow to ignore them in turn the next time you meet?"

"So it's not about turning the other cheek when someone strikes you?"

"Maybe it is that also."

"You're not much help. I thought bishops had all the answers."

"If only that were true."

The conversation replayed in his mind as he opened his Bible and focused on Sunday's sermon. Time and again he was drawn to the Old Testament—to the testing of God's people as well as His constant care and protection of them.

Sunday morning, Henry had a simple breakfast and then dressed in a plain white shirt, black pants, and black vest. He considered adding the jacket but decided the day would be too warm. Choosing his black hat from the hooks by the back door, he said goodbye to Lexi, promising her he'd be home in a few hours. He'd rather leave the dog outside, where dogs belonged, but she didn't seem settled enough to know this was now her home. He'd come home one day to find her halfway back to Abe's. So instead, he shut her up in the mudroom. With the open window and a bowl of water, he was sure the pup would sleep most of the time he was away.

Having already hitched up his buggy, he climbed in and made his way to the Beilers'. It being Mother's Day, he spent a good part of the ride thinking of his own *mamm* and how much of a blessing she had been to him. He missed his parents still, though they'd been gone many years. The communities he'd been a part of had not celebrated Mother's Day per se, since it was a distinctly *Englisch* holiday, but children would often write a letter to their *mamm* or offer to do the dishes—little things, but they added up to show the family's appreciation.

Their home was on the small side, so he wasn't terribly surprised to see the benches had been set up in the barn.

Daniel and Sam had spent all week hard at work putting in their crops. He could see Daniel near the barn, speaking to his wife, Abigail. Sam stood at the end of the lane, ready to park the buggies and pasture the horses.

"*Gut* morning, Sam."

"Same to you, Bishop."

"Did your week improve?"

"Crops are in. Both my pop's fields and my own."

"*Wunderbaar*. Things quiet at the fire department?"

"Only emergency call we had was a grass fire on the east side of the county. The Chinook winds didn't help."

"First year we were here, we didn't know what the Chinook winds were. The blast came down through the valley, raising temperatures and melting snow. We had no idea what was happening."

"They can cause havoc, especially if one of the big ranchers is having a controlled burn when one hits."

"Well, this week the winds certainly warmed things up. I thought the roof was going to blow off my workshop. Were you able to put the grass fire out?"

"Before it reached any structures, and no one was hurt."

"*Gut* to hear." Henry clapped the young man on his shoulder. "We'll speak more after the service."

Henry was interested to hear how Sam's crops were doing, though one week would be too soon to tell. The look on young man's face as he'd left him sitting beside his unplanted fields and then his desperate confession in the holding cell had bothered Henry's conscience. It was unfortunate that Sam had become caught up in arguing with Vernon, but perhaps he had learned something from the experience.

Though it was only a few minutes past seven

in the morning, buggies were already turning into the lane.

Henry walked into the barn and whistled. The place was as clean as his own home. Abigail must have had help preparing the area, as it was spick-and-span. She couldn't have possibly done it all herself.

"Fine morning for worship," Henry said as Abigail walked inside.

"Indeed it is." She glanced toward the door, where more families were filing in, fiddled with her glasses, and then motioned in the opposite direction with her head.

Henry followed her into Daniel's office—a small room with a window, desk, woodstove, and a few chairs. There wasn't space for much else.

"Problem?" he asked.

"I thought you should know folks are worried."

"Worried?"

"About the fires."

"Ah."

"Perhaps it's not my place to say anything . . . "

"You know I value your opinion, Abigail. And I appreciate your letting me know when you're concerned."

Her right eyebrow arched over her glasses. "But I'm not. Perhaps it's because Sam works with the fire department. Who knows, but over the years I've come to see fire as merely one other destructive force in this world—like tornadoes or earthquakes or mudslides. *Gotte* will protect us from those things."

"Indeed."

"Still, a *gut* word would go a long way toward encouraging folk."

Henry nodded and reached for her hand. After squeezing it, he returned to the front of the barn. Her words mirrored his own prayers and concerns the day before. He was sure now as to who should preach the second sermon today. As for himself, he would focus on sharing his study of God's omnipotent hand through the ages.

Twenty-Eight

Henry spent the rest of the hour greeting families as they arrived. It occurred to him, not for the first time, that they had a good congregation. Sure, Leroy was a bit sullen and negative at times, but he did an excellent job distributing financial help when it was needed. Franey barely nodded when he said hello. Sundays were hard for her. Being among so many families had to serve as a nagging reminder that she would never have a family like those surrounding her. But Henry knew God had a special path for Franey Graber. He hadn't abandoned her as Alvin had.

Henry was thinking on that when he joined Abe and Clyde and Leroy. They met in Daniel's office. As they closed the door to the small room, Henry glanced out and saw Rebecca Yoder leading the women into the area where the benches had been placed. The men were already seated on the right side, and Rebecca made her way to the front of the left side. As the oldest among the women, it was her place to lead them inside, and though she walked slightly bent, with an arthritic hand clutching her cane, Henry thought he'd never seen a finer leader. Verses from Proverbs 31 popped into his mind.

She selects wool and flax and works with eager hands.

She opens her arms to the poor and extends her hands to the needy.

She is clothed with strength and dignity.

Yes, those words described Rebecca, and he was grateful she was with them.

Turning back into the room, Henry saw Clyde, Abe, and Leroy were seated, elbows on knees, eyes closed or cast down.

"It is *gut* to be gathered together, *ya*?"

Murmurs of agreement, but he could tell they were troubled.

"Two weeks ago, when we held our last service, Vernon was still among us."

"Tragedy had not yet touched our small community." Abe remained staring at the floor, his shoulders hunched.

"It is tragic, indeed."

"*Gotte* does not promise us a rose-strewn path," Leroy said.

Clyde looked up, glancing at each of the other elders before settling his gaze on Henry. "And yet we are to 'trust in the steadfast love of God forever and ever.' "

"Indeed we are. I have no doubt that recent events have taken a toll on our members. As the leaders of this church, we are each responsible for more than ensuring the physical health of our congregation. We are responsible for their spiritual health as well. We are, after all, charged with tending the flock, though of course Christ is our ultimate shepherd."

The men nodded in agreement, and some of the despair fell away from them.

"I'd like to preach the first sermon today, and I'd like for Clyde to preach the second."

All three men nodded again. They each prepared during the week to speak a good word in case they were called upon, but it was Henry's decision to make. He depended on God's guidance in that regard. This morning he felt strongly moved that Clyde would have the words of truth and encouragement their families needed to hear.

"Abe will share Scripture, and, Leroy, I would appreciate it if you would assist with closing out the service. Now, before we join the others, let's pray together."

They prayed silently for a few moments, and then Henry led them, reminding them of God's protection, His provision, His immeasurable love.

When they'd finished praying, Henry motioned toward the door.

Leroy led the way, his usual scowling expression in place. Well, every Christian wasn't blessed with a sunny disposition. Henry reminded himself that Leroy was a good man. He'd learned long ago that for Leroy life was a serious affair, a series of obstacles to carefully maneuver around.

Abe followed Leroy. He met Henry's gaze, nodded once, and stepped out into the main room of the barn.

Clyde offered him a weak smile. Though he'd been selected as one of their preachers four years ago, he still dealt with feelings of inadequacy, especially when preaching. He sometimes became tongue-tied, but their congregation was patient. God often spoke a good word through Clyde, and it was because of that Henry had chosen him to preach. Today, they needed words of comfort and truth. They needed to be reminded of their Christian duty to uphold one another. They needed to find a solid footing, and that footing would come from Scripture. He could count on Clyde to provide those things, and if the man stuttered and stumbled occasionally, then so be it. God had once used an ass to speak His word.

Henry didn't doubt for a moment that a God who could speak through a donkey could speak through him or through Clyde Fisher.

Twenty-Nine

The congregation was beginning the fourth verse of the *Loblied* when Henry, Abe, Clyde, and Leroy took their places with the men, on the right side of the room.

Thine only be the glory, O Lord,
Likeness all might and power.
That we praise Thee in our assembly
And feel grateful every hour.

It never failed to move Henry when he heard an entire community's voice raised as one, joining in worship and singing praise to God. Added to that, he was aware that every other Amish community was singing this same song at their service. Many aspects of worship varied from place to place, but the *Loblied* was one thing that united them in their faith and their worship. It spoke eloquently of God's grace and glory and might and power and presence.

Henry had doubted his ability to lead plenty of times, but he'd never doubted God's ability to watch over them. He'd been born with that certainty, born with a strong faith, his *mamm* often said. It didn't seem that way to Henry. To him, believing in God was the same as believing the sun would continue to rise. Why would he question such a thing when it had been true every day of his life?

The song ended, and Henry stepped forward.

He hadn't planned exactly what he would say. It wasn't their way to do so. They studied—sure. Each man wanted to be prepared if called on to share God's Word, but they didn't write out an outline or try to work through a specific set of talking points. Instead, they shared what God had put on their heart through prayer and Bible study.

"*Gotte* is *gut*. He was *gut* to Adam and Eve even after He cast them out of the garden. He was *gut* during the exodus from Egypt, feeding and leading the people." He easily found his rhythm, a melodic, half-sung, half-spoken manner in the Pennsylvania German dialect. It was the type of preaching he'd heard all his life. He felt the presence of his grandfather then, a bishop for more than sixty years and someone Henry had grown up listening to each Sunday.

"He established the twelve tribes of Israel and brought Abraham into the land of Canaan. Our *Gotte* hast always provided."

As he spoke, he flipped through his well-worn Bible, reading verses from it in High German.

"His promise to Joshua is the same promise He offers to you and to me. 'I will never leave you nor forsake you . . . Be strong and courageous . . . Be careful to obey all the law my servant Moses gave you; do not turn from it to the right or to the left.' "

He reminded them of Ruth and Samuel and

Ezra and Nehemiah. Sweat poured down his face, but he wiped it away and plunged into the trials of Esther and Job. "Always *Gotte* is faithful. Always He cares for His children. We can know with complete certainty that He will care for you and for me."

When he was finished, he saw many heads bowed, others nodding in agreement, and a few wiping tears from their cheeks.

Henry sat down, accepted the cup of water passed to him, and waited.

Abe stood and read from Matthew, Mark, and Luke. Promises from the lips of the Son of God. Words of truth and hope. Words to sustain them.

As one they knelt in silent prayer. The sound of a hundred and fifty men, women, and children sinking to their knees sent a ripple through Henry's soul. How he loved these people. How he prayed God's protection over them. He understood in that moment that this terrible thing that had happened could strengthen their faith and draw them together, or it could tear them apart.

Clyde had sat with his head bowed while Henry preached and Abe spoke, his Bible clutched in his right hand. Now he stood, walked to the front of the benches, and boldly began to proclaim the gospel of Christ.

He glanced around the room. Walked from the left side to the right and back again. "Paul . . . "

He stared down at his Bible, closed his eyes for

a moment, and then he began again. "Paul says . . . he says . . . 'My God will meet all your needs according to the riches of His glory in Christ Jesus.' "

With the words from the apostle, his hesitancy vanished.

"John reminds us of Christ's words. 'You did not choose me, but I chose you.' "

The group was riveted by Clyde's preaching—not that he was polished or used fancy words. No, Henry understood that it was the man's sincerity and his ability to speak to the concerns of their hearts. The members of their church connected with Clyde because his hands, like theirs, were sporting blisters from a week of plowing. And yet he stood before them, claiming the promises of God.

Christ's call to follow Him. His admonition to fear not. To be strong. To love their neighbors.

As Clyde spoke, a child would occasionally dart across the middle aisle, seeking their father's lap rather than their mother's or vice versa. Abe's wife, Susan, walked their youngest child to the side, where snacks and cups of water had been set up. Rebecca's daughter, Mary, helped her mother-in-law to the back, where she stood for a moment. No doubt her legs were cramping again.

All normal activity during a church service, but this morning few noticed. The eyes of every man, woman, and teenager were trained on Clyde, listening, drawing comfort from the promises of Scripture.

Henry could practically see the tension drain from their faces as they remembered they were in the care of the Savior.

When he was done, Clyde said, "Is it so?"

"It is," Daniel allowed.

"Have I shared the gospel correctly?"

"You have," Abe assured him.

"Then I would call for testimonies of *Gotte*'s grace and goodness among us."

Elmer Bontrager stood, pulled off his hat, and said, "My crops are in, and there's forecast of rain."

Everyone laughed, and then there were shouts of "Amen!" sprinkled throughout their midst.

"My mother remains to bless our lives," Chester Yoder said, and all eyes turned to seek out Rebecca, smile her direction, and whisper words of thanksgiving.

One after another, members stood to tell of the ways God had provided in their lives. Their words, their confessions, brought home the scriptures Abe had shared with them.

Abe stood, his Bible open in his hand. "*Gotte*'s provision stretches back into our faith's past as far as it stretches into our future. David wrote, 'Taste and see that the Lord is good; blessed is the one who takes refuge in Him.' "

Leroy heaved himself to his feet. He still didn't

smile, and for a moment Henry worried that he would contradict Clyde's message of provision—perhaps focus on the Israelites being lost for forty years. Although that was certainly true, it probably wasn't what their families needed to hear this morning.

But Leroy surprised him. "We are reminded to give no thought to what we eat or how we're clothed . . . "

Finally, they once again knelt in silent prayer, and then they stood for their closing hymns. The service had gone a little longer than usual. Having started at eight, Henry wasn't too surprised to glance at his watch and see that it was close to noon.

But it had been a good morning, a peaceful one. Henry prayed with all his heart that it was a peace that would endure and see them through the days ahead.

Thirty

Emma made sure the sandwich plates remained full as the men passed through the line, followed by the women, who were usually helping the younger children. *Youngies* brought up the rear of the line. It was good that the teens went last, as they tended to eat more than a herd of cattle. By the time the gangly boys and giggling girls began to fill their plates, the men were done—gathering up their dishes and making room at the tables for their families.

She'd been encouraged by Clyde's sermon as well as Henry's. She'd needed to hear an encouraging word. It seemed their lives had been full of trouble and toil the last two weeks. Sunday was providing a welcome respite from that. Or so she thought, until she heard an argument escalating at the *youngies'* table.

"What do you know of it?"

"I suppose I know plenty."

"You're barely Amish."

"Barely Amish?"

"You're *onkel* is *Englisch*. Isn't that so?"

"Keep him out of this."

"He could even be the one responsible for the fires."

The word *fire* had barely escaped James

Bontrager's lips when Curtis Graber launched himself across the table. Dishes went flying. Girls squealed as their drinks splashed onto their aprons, and the teens instinctively formed a circle around the two boys, who were scuffling on the floor.

Emma was slow to realize the men were gathered outside and couldn't be counted on to break up the altercation. Most of the women were now standing, trying to see what the ruckus was about. Emma skirted the table, pushed her way through the circle of children, and pulled Curtis Graber off his schoolmate.

He was sputtering, red in the face, and sporting an eye that was beginning to swell, whether from a well-landed punch or a wayward elbow, she didn't know.

"Stop it!" She had Curtis by the neck and pulled him back away from James.

James started forward, thinking he still had a chance to win the brawl, when his mother stepped into the middle and ordered him out of the building.

Emma was aware many *Englischers* thought they didn't have to deal with typical teenage behavior. Emma knew better. Though scuffles were rare, they happened, and the boy shaking with anger and standing next to her was proof of that.

Curtis's mother, Susan, reached his side and gripped his arm hard enough to pull his attention away from his foe and toward her. "Come with me, Curtis," she hissed as she marched him out of the barn's wide-open doors.

By this time, the men had caught wind of what was happening. They were walking toward the barn as Susan was marching out, Curtis still caught in her clutches. Emma glanced up in time to see Abe walk up to the boy. His expression was tight. Pained, if she had to put a word to it. He said something to the boy, who swiped at his face and hurried off in the opposite direction, toward the buggies.

Emma turned back around and saw that Grace had exited out a side door with James.

"All right, girls. Help me clean up this mess."

While they righted the tables and scooped plates and cups off the floor, no one spoke of what happened. They would, but not until their parents were out of earshot. The teens pretended they were full and scurried outside—to the ball field or the wraparound porch or the shade of a stand of cottonwood trees. Katie Ann gave her grandmother a small wave and then darted outside with her friends.

"Just when things were finally beginning to feel normal again," Rachel murmured.

Following many a *tsk-tsk*, the women sighed and finished cleaning up the remains of the luncheon. It wasn't until they, too, were seated, outside in the shade cast by the shadow of the barn, that anyone dared offer an explanation for what happened. Susan and Grace had returned and were sitting on opposite sides of the circle. Emma couldn't tell if things were okay between the two women. She knew one could become protective of a child or grandchild when something like this happened.

There was a natural inclination to place the blame on the other child. Hadn't she felt that way herself when Clyde was young? He'd once charged the baseball mound when the pitcher hit him in the forearm with a fast pitch. She'd wanted to be impartial, but she'd heard the offending boy say Clyde "needed to be knocked down a peg now and then." Even now those words scraped across her heart when she thought of them.

Children could be cruel. That was for certain. Most grew out of it when the parents offered the correct raising, a firm hand, and a compassionate heart.

The women spoke of the week's work, letters they received from relatives, and who had finished planting their family gardens. Everyone stopped talking when Abe walked up with Curtis, and Elmer with James.

"The boys have something to say to you," Abe said.

"Because they owe everyone here an apology." Elmer crossed his arms and waited.

"I'm sorry for ruining the dinner." James stared

at his shoes as he spoke. "Causing a mess, and . . . and wasting food that was intended for us to eat."

"He'll be skipping lunch for the next week to remind him food is a blessing and doesn't belong on the ground."

Abe cleared his throat, indicating it was Curtis's turn to speak.

"And I'm sorry I lost my temper. It's not in keeping with our *Ordnung*. I should have . . . I should have walked away."

"Curtis will also forgo lunch for a week." Abe scanned the circle until his gaze fell upon his wife. "Both boys will stay inside and help with the serving and the cleanup at our next luncheon."

James's mouth settled in a straight line, and Curtis's ears turned bright red.

Emma felt a moment of sympathy for them. She didn't miss her own teenage years and all the conflicting emotions that came with them. She could still remember the confusion and how a hurt could linger for much too long.

"You may go now," Abe said to the boys, who scampered away.

Abe and Elmer nodded to the women, and then they walked off to join the men.

"They're *gut* boys," Rachel offered.

"Indeed they are." Susan smiled across at Grace. "I suppose we both remember being young and unable to control our emotions."

But Grace was having none of it. "We never

lived under this type of pressure, Susan, and you know it. Back in Goshen we weren't threatened by arsonists, looking at wanted posters, and wondering who could do such a thing."

"I suppose that's true, but—"

"Of course it's true. This is unnatural is what it is, and the *youngies* are feeling the same anxiety we are."

Susan tossed a plea-for-help look toward Emma.

"Today's sermon was a nice reminder of *Gotte*'s provision and care," Emma said. "Exactly what we—and the children—needed to hear."

Grace made a sound like air going out of a buggy tire, shook her head, and finally said, "I'd best be getting home. This has worn me out, that's what it's done."

She stood, snatched up her purse, and plodded away from them toward her buggy.

"Don't let it bother you, Susan." Mary Yoder was sitting next to her mother-in-law, who nodded in agreement.

"Grace has always been an emotional sort," Rebecca said. "Give her time, and she'll calm down."

"I hope so."

"Why don't you all say it? James was speaking of Alvin. Did you hear him?" Franey stood, her hands fisted at her sides. "He said Alvin could be responsible for the fires."

"Now isn't the time to speak of private family matters," Susan cautioned.

"I will not hear his name thrown around in connection with this! I will defend him, on this, I will, whether it's Sunday or any other day of the week. Is the grace we offer one another not to extend to him? Has he stepped so far away that he is out of the reach of *Gotte*?"

Tears were tracking down her face now, and Emma felt an acute pain for the woman. How hard her life must be, and it was plain that she still cared for Alvin.

Pulling in a shaky breath, Franey straightened her back and clutched her purse to her side. "He might have abandoned me. He might have left our faith. But he would never hurt anyone. He . . . he never would."

And then she, too, fled toward the buggies.

Thirty-One

Emma's migraine must have begun when Franey stormed away from the group of women. Or maybe it was earlier, when the boys had first begun to fight. She couldn't put her finger on the exact moment, but she suddenly realized that the right side of her head had been throbbing painfully for some time.

"Are you okay?" Rachel asked.

"I think so."

"You're—" Rachel mimicked rubbing the right side of her head. "Is there anything I can do? Is it a bad one? Would you like to go home?"

Emma tried to smile through the pain. "You're a *gut doschder*," she murmured, closing her eyes and leaning against the trunk of the cotton-wood tree. She'd sought the shade and a cool breeze, hoping it would help. But it wasn't going to ease the throbbing in her head. Having had migraines since she was a young girl of ten, she understood when a bad one was pressing down on her.

"A migraine?" She jerked her head up at the sound of Henry's voice.

"Yeah, but she won't let me take her home."

"I'm right here."

"She says she doesn't want to interrupt the children's game."

"I'll take her home."

Both Emma and Rachel turned to look at him in surprise.

"What? I need to check on my pup."

"I never thought you would dote on an animal so, Henry." Emma tried to smile, but it felt like a grimace so she gave up and squeezed her eyes shut.

"I wouldn't call it doting." He took her arm gently, waited a moment while Rachel located her purse, and maneuvered her toward his buggy.

"You and Clyde stay as long as you'd like," he called back to Rachel.

Emma dreaded moving. Walking was a trial, and just the thought of riding in a bumpy buggy was enough to make her nauseated.

But Henry settled his mare into an easy trot, and the darkness of the buggy was refreshing.

"Perhaps you had too much sun."

"Maybe so."

"Terrible thing to have on Mother's Day."

She waved away his concern.

They didn't speak again until they'd pulled up in front of her house.

"Let me help you inside."

"Maybe we could sit on the porch."

"Are you sure you're up to that?"

"I think so, and the breeze is pleasant."

Henry nodded once, helped her to a rocker on the front porch, and then went inside to fetch cold drinks. He stuck his head back outside. "There's milk, water, or lemonade."

"Lemonade, please."

He returned with two glasses. Though there was no ice, the lemonade had been in the refrigerator, and the glass was cool to her touch. She rested it against her right eye.

"I hate to see you suffering."

"It's a small thing."

"Doesn't seem like a small thing when you're having a migraine."

She attempted a smile and took a sip of the lemonade. The cold, sweet, tangy drink soothed her throat. She hadn't realized how thirsty she was. She drank nearly half the glass and then set it on the table between them. Henry was rocking in his chair, watching her carefully.

"I'm fine, Henry. There's no need to worry so."

"I suppose I'll have to believe you."

"You should. I'd never lie to my bishop."

"I've been your friend longer than I've been your bishop."

Emma nodded. It was true that they'd known each other many years. She'd attended his wedding to Claire, as well as her funeral, both of which had been in the spring while the crops sprouted and the flowers bloomed.

Henry had been there when she'd married

George at the innocent age of eighteen. The four of them had been friends until Claire's death twenty years ago. Then the three of them, with Henry declaring he was an awkward third wheel. But he'd never been that. He'd been a part of their family, an integral part of their lives. And he'd arrived within the hour of hearing that she'd found her husband clutching his chest and unable to breathe. He had sat by her in the hospital, helped her through the desolate days after his death.

Theirs was a friendship that had grown stronger with each change—the birth of children, the initial move to Colorado, deaths and marriages and more births and celebrations and tragedies.

"*Danki.*"

"For bringing you home?" He waved away her gratitude. "It was no problem."

"Not for that, or not just for that. For being in my life as long as I can remember. That's a real blessing, Henry. A friendship that has endured as long as ours has."

His eyes met hers, and she felt her pulse jump—not from the migraine but from the depth of emotion in his eyes.

A hummingbird darted toward a feeder, zoomed away, and quickly returned to drink of the nectar.

"I hope you're not worried about the boys," she said.

"Curtis misses his *onkel* and feels protective toward him. That's only natural."

"What would possess James to say such a thing?"

"If I had to guess, trouble at home spiked his anger. Elmer and Grace are a fine family, but they seem to be taking the fires more personally than most. She stopped me before leaving, asked what we were doing to help the *Englischers* catch the arsonist."

"She's always been a worrier."

"Their oldest, Albert, could do that to a person. He's a *gut* lad, but always testing the boundaries of the *Ordnung*."

"Isn't he twenty?"

"And yet still finding his way as many of us were at that age."

They sat in silence, the years and memories washing over them. Her head still hurt, but the cool air and the shade from the porch helped. She never understood what caused the migraines, though she'd read the pamphlet her doctor had given her. Barometric pressure, hormonal changes, even what type of cheese she'd eaten could cause them. Today perhaps it had been the tension of the situation after the boys' scuffle. Or it could be that somewhere within her heart she, too, was worried about the arsonist.

"Did anyone speak to you about Meg Allen's flyers?"

"*Nein*. I'm not surprised. It wasn't a very *gut* picture."

"It was something, though. We know it was a man or older teen—"

"Meg already knew that."

"He's fairly thin and tallish."

"And seemed to be young."

Emma sighed. "That could describe a dozen *Englisch* men."

"Or Amish."

"You don't think—"

"I don't, but we can't ignore the possibility. We're human, Emma. Being Plain doesn't protect us from the same emotions that cause other people to struggle and sin and fall."

"I can't even imagine what would cause a person to react so. To cause him to seek to hurt another person."

"Greed, bitterness, resentment, jealousy, a personal vendetta . . ."

"Hard to envision anyone in our congregation feeling those things."

Henry watched her patiently, waiting, apparently not wanting to plant any names in her mind. He didn't have to. Her imagination was vivid enough.

"We will pray it's not one of our own," she said.

"And that whoever this person is, he has accomplished what he set out to do. The next best thing to finding the person—and I believe Meg will eventually do that—would be for him to stop and slip back into his normal life."

"I'm not sure that's possible."

"Neither am I, but for now we can hope and pray and believe that *Gotte*'s hand will stretch over our congregation and protect each person."

Thirty-Two

He waited across the street, ducked down in the brush.

From where he sat, he could barely make out the main house. Fortunately, he'd brought along a pair of binoculars he'd purchased from the pawn shop. They brought the household and its occupant into a clear, sharp focus.

His backpack lay beside him, along with the gas can.

He'd spent many nights refining his target list. He wasn't crazy. He didn't want to set blazes randomly across the area. That would be dangerous and inefficient. He felt good about tonight's plan. There would be enough combustible material to feed the fire a good long time.

The light shining from the front window finally winked out.

He glanced at his phone, tapped the screen to set the timer for two hours, and sat back to wait.

The bishop had stuck his nose where it didn't belong. In addition, the man seemed rather arrogant to him. How could one person claim to know what everyone else should and shouldn't do? Besides, if he'd done his job of leading his flock—the first time he'd heard that phrase he'd nearly doubled over laughing—Vernon Frey would have been a better person.

He sat in the darkness, counting his grievances against these people. Two other targets were on his list. He'd chosen carefully. If he'd included everyone who had treated him unfairly, the list would be long and the entire San Luis Valley would burn.

The mayor had encouraged these people to settle here.

The fire chief and sheriff had turned the case over to an outsider.

His fifth grade teacher had once called him stupid and chided him for being different.

Even the librarian looked at him as if he didn't belong in her building.

Yes, he had a long list of grievances, and he didn't need to write down the names. They were emblazoned in his head, tattooed across his heart.

But those targets in town would be harder to hit now that his picture had been circulated.

No, he would wait to even the score with those folks.

For now he would stick to the list of five and set his sights once again on a Plain household. So what if someone was hurt. It wouldn't be his fault. He had warned them with Vernon's fire and backed that up with the destruction of the construction site. They should have taken a hint.

If they were smart, they would have left the

area weeks ago. They weren't wanted here, didn't belong here, and shouldn't be buying up all the good farmland.

His memory slipped back to when he was a boy, walking through the fields with his dad. He'd been bored by the concept of raising crops even then. But he could tell it was a dream of his father's. Dreams were weaknesses. That's what his life had taught him.

So he'd been careful to never have any.

But this urge to be the one choosing, to ignite a flame that would send people scrambling, to read the write-ups and conjectures and warnings . . . all of it acted as a soothing balm on his heart. It helped him to swallow the bitter disappointment his life had become.

And it was tricky too. Any normal Joe, any of those idiots he'd gone to school with, would have been caught already.

He was smarter than they were. He had a plan, and he fully intended to carry it out.

When his phone beeped, he quickly silenced it, shouldered his backpack, and picked up the gas can. Then he hopped on his bike and began to pedal across the road.

Thirty-Three

Henry woke to the sound of Lexi barking madly. He'd taken to allowing the dog to sleep in the mudroom. She was still quite a small pup, after all. He didn't want a coyote attacking her on one of the porches or near the barn.

She normally slept quietly all night long, whining only when he turned on the battery-operated lantern on rising.

Henry rubbed at his eyes, sat up, and studied the clock next to his bed. Eleven forty. He'd been asleep nearly two hours.

Lexi's bark had become quite frantic, so Henry put on his slippers, grabbed the robe he'd laid across the end of the bed, and shuffled to the mudroom. He arrived to find the little beagle throwing herself against the back door.

He picked up a flashlight from a shelf, intending to shine it outside to find what had startled the dog so. He had no intention of opening the door. But as he switched the light on, he smelled smoke. He threw the door open, and Lexi darted out between his legs toward his workshop. Bright red flames shot up to the roof, and the entire structure groaned.

Lumber. His workshop was built of wood and contained a good supply of lumber. It was the perfect arsonist's target. He knew instantly that the shop was a complete loss. Fortunately, it sat alone across the parking area from his house. The fire wouldn't spread.

"Lexi! Here, girl."

Why would a dog run toward a fire?

He panned the beam of his flashlight across the yard, the burning structure, and toward the street. Nothing. He'd been focused on the roar of the flames, the slight wind, even the whoosh of his workshop disintegrating, but suddenly he was aware of Lexi's ferocious bark. He aimed the beam of the flashlight to the left and saw his recently planted vegetable garden, but nothing else.

Lexi's barking suddenly stopped.

His hand shook a little and the beam jerked to the right, passing over the burning workshop and a grove of trees in the distance.

Then the ray of light revealed dust, the back wheel of a bicycle, a man pedaling wildly, and Lexi, hanging on to his right pants leg with all of her might.

Henry shouted out, "You! Stop!" It sounded ridiculous even to him.

The biker kept pedaling, the dog held on, and then the sound of sirens came from down the road. As a last resort, the man pulled back his leg and kicked the little dog, who flew off into the darkness, landing with a yelp and a soft thud.

Henry ran across the yard. He stumbled, dropped the flashlight, righted himself, and looked around him in the darkness. As the fire truck pulled into his lane, the light swept across the yard, revealing the dog only a few feet from him. He ran to her, knelt down, and put a hand on her side. She was breathing heavily, but breathing.

Whoever their arsonist was, he hadn't killed her.

"*Gut* dog, Lexi. You're going to be all right." Even as the words slipped out of his mouth, he wondered if it was true. She was such a little dog to have been so brutally assaulted. Henry sat down in the dirt, and she rose, whimpered softly, and dropped something into his lap. He could see, by the strobe of the fire truck's light, that it was a small piece of fabric.

Satisfied that she'd done her best, Lexi sank into his lap and began to lick the back of his hand.

Henry struggled to his feet, clutching the piece of fabric with his left hand and cradling the dog in the crook of his right arm. He hurried toward the fire truck, where they were already spraying water on the charred remains of his workshop.

Captain Johnson was shouting orders to his men when Henry walked up.

"Complete loss, Henry. I'm sorry."

"It's only wood and projects. Nothing that can't be replaced."

"Are you okay?" Johnson studied him closely. "Say, you weren't out here when it happened, were you?"

"No. I wasn't." He explained about Lexi and described the moments leading up to the fire truck's arrival.

"Hold on. You saw him?"

"Not clearly." Henry stared down at the scrap of cloth he was holding.

"But you did see him, and that piece of fabric is from his pants."

"Lexi tore it off. I hope . . . hope she's okay. She risked her life tonight, defending me."

Johnson patted him clumsily on the shoulder. "I'm calling Meg Allen and a vet."

"At this hour?"

"Meg will want to be here, and I know Dr. Berry pretty well. She probably isn't even asleep yet."

⊷══◉══⊷

An hour later the fire crew had left, Meg was working with a crime scene technician in his lane, and Dr. Georgia Berry was examining his dog.

"Can't tell without X-rays, but I think what you have here are some bruised ribs." She gently ran her fingers along the dog's chest. "Nothing appears to be broken."

Georgia looked too young to be a veterinarian, in Henry's opinion. She had long red hair, pulled back through a baseball cap, freckles across her nose, and a kind smile. Henry liked her immediately.

"I've only had her a week. Got her so I'd hear people coming down the lane. I was hoping she would grow into the role. I never thought she'd try to catch culprits."

"Lexi is a smart girl." Georgia scratched the dog behind the ears, and then she pulled a small biscuit from the pocket of her jacket. The dog was instantly smitten with her. "Beagles are never happier than when they're following a scent. They're smart too. I think you'll be glad you have her."

"I already am."

There was a tap on his back door, and then Meg walked inside. "Do you have a minute, Bishop?"

"We're finishing up here," Doc Berry assured her. "I want Lexi to rest, no chasing arsonists, rabbits, or balls. If you notice any difficulty in breathing, weakness, or a lack of appetite, call me immediately."

"And you'll send me your bill?"

"I will." She patted him on the shoulder, gathered up her supplies, and said good night to Meg.

Once the door had closed behind her, Meg said, "We need to talk."

Thirty-Four

Meg pointed at the coffeepot on his stove. "Anything in there?"

"Left over from yesterday."

"I'll take it."

Henry turned on the burner and pulled out a single coffee mug from the cabinet. He settled for a glass of water. The last thing he needed was caffeine at this hour.

"We have only two clues—the top of a plastic gas can, which is what we think he used to ignite the building, and the swatch of fabric Lexi tore off his pants."

"No bottle? No . . . what did you call it . . . Molotov cocktail?"

"Not this time, and the fact that he's varying his methods worries me. Who knows what he has planned next." She pulled the black plastic cap out of her pocket. It was safely ensconced in a clear evidence bag. "Could this be yours?"

"*Nein.*"

"You don't have a gas can?"

"I have no reason for one, though some of our people do. If, say, they have a generator in their barn to operate their business. Even gas-powered weed eaters, but I have none of those things. How did you find it?"

"Must have fallen out of his pocket. Our perp seems to have planned this out carefully. He knew your workshop was full of shavings and wood—perfect fuel for a fire. All he had to do was bring in a gas can and surround it with some newspaper. I assume you had newspaper in your workshop?"

"*Ya*. There was a small stack next to my workbench."

"So he waits until he knows you're asleep, bikes in, puts the full gasoline can in the center of the room with newspaper bunched around it. When he sets the paper on fire, it gives him a good thirty seconds to get out, grab his bike, and leave. What he wasn't expecting was Lexi."

"She tore out after him as soon as I opened the door."

"It could be he's afraid of dogs, or maybe he was caught by surprise. Whatever the reason, he wasn't as careful. The cap fell out of his pocket. We found it in the lane."

"Will there be fingerprints?"

"Normally yes, we could lift prints from plastic, but I suspect we won't find any. Most likely he was wearing gloves. And this swatch of fabric? Looks to me like regular denim, like most blue jeans are made from."

"Which everyone wears. Even our teenagers do on occasion."

"I'm worried, Henry."

"Because?"

"Because he's targeting people in your group."

"So you think it's the same person?"

"Not much chance we'd have two arsonists in a town the size of Monte Vista."

"Should be easier to catch him, then." Henry placed sugar and cream on the table before also setting down a plate of leftover cookies.

Meg didn't even hesitate. She took one chocolate chip and one raisin and set them on the napkin in front of her. "Investigations always increase my appetite."

"You have a difficult job anytime, but especially in the middle of the night."

He checked the coffee. Satisfied it was hot enough, he filled her mug, set the burner to low, and placed the pot back on it.

"Why do you think he's targeting families in my congregation?"

"Are you in denial? First Vernon's place and now yours."

Henry didn't answer immediately. He waited for her to sip her coffee, devour one of the cookies, and pull out her notepad. Lexi was sleeping contentedly in the box of blankets he'd brought in from the mudroom.

"The construction site is decidedly *Englisch*, and yet our arsonist targeted it as well. Perhaps he doesn't like people in Monte Vista."

"Are you forgetting the letter? The details in the

letter indicated a clear desire for revenge against Amish people."

He waved away that remark.

Meg crossed her arms and sat back, studying him. "You're the one who drew it. You're the one who told me about your talent."

"Not sure I used the word *talent*."

"Do you believe the drawing was accurate?"

Henry didn't want to have this conversation. He wasn't comfortable talking about his ability to draw things he couldn't even consciously remember, but they were far past that. Meg Allen had asked him a straightforward question, and she deserved an answer.

"*Ya*, I do."

"Then he's targeting Amish families. As far as the worksite, my guess is he hit it because he lost a job or was turned down for a job. The construction manager told me a quarter of his workers are from your community."

"Building comes nearly as easily to us as farming, and the *youngies* tell me the pay is good."

"*Youngies*?"

"Teenagers. Young adults."

She considered that for a moment. "I want to have a meeting with your families."

"Not necessary. I can tell them—"

"It's not only what I want to tell your families. I also want to see their reaction. I want to give people an opportunity to come forward and speak to me. That will be easier if it's done someplace where they are comfortable and with your blessing."

"Could you not speak to only the elders?"

"Henry, why don't you want me talking to the Amish families here in Monte Vista?"

Instead of answering, he stood, fetched the coffeepot, and refilled her mug.

When he sat again, he chose his words carefully. "Much of being Amish means being separate. Our appearance and lifestyle are modest, simple. Walk into an Amish home, walk into my home, and what do you notice?"

"It looks rather like my grandparents' place. Pared down, plain . . . "

"Simple."

"Okay. I get that. I do. No television. No computers. No blaring music. There's even a subtle attraction to it." Her cell phone vibrated. She pulled it from her pocket, frowned at it, and thumbed a quick response. "But I think what you're trying to tell me is that you want to protect your people from this—"

"It's only my job to guide them. *Gotte* protects them."

"And yet one of them may be our arsonist." She pushed away the mug and crossed her arms on the table. "They may be our arsonist or know him, and even if neither of those things is true, they need to be properly warned. Now, I can go house to house and speak to each family, or you can call a general meeting and we can do it all at once. I'm giving you that option. But I'm not giving you the option of whether I talk to them. That's my job."

She was passionate about her responsibilities, that was for certain.

"When would you like to do this?"

"The sooner the better. Tomorrow, if possible."

"All right, tomorrow. Six in the evening, Leroy Kauffmann's place." He gave her directions, which she jotted down in her notebook.

"Thank you. I appreciate it." She'd made it to the mudroom door before she turned and said, "I'm sorry about your workshop."

"Temporal things."

"And yet it was important to you."

"True, but everything in that shop can be replaced."

"I'll see you tomorrow evening."

Once she was gone, he turned off the burner under the coffee and checked on his dog. Satisfied that there was nothing else he could do before sunrise, he returned to bed, but it was many hours before he managed to sleep.

Thirty-Five

"You're sure Henry's okay?" Emma's pulse had kicked into a double rhythm when Abe appeared at their door, explaining about the fire.

"*Ya*, he's fine. Says the little dog was real courageous."

"I still can't believe Henry has a dog." Clyde invited him inside, but Abe shook his head.

"I have three more houses to tell about the meeting. If you could pass it along to the neighbors on both sides of you . . . "

"Of course we will." When Abe left, Emma returned to the kitchen to help Rachel with the breakfast dishes. The boys were already out working in the field. Clyde had come to the house when he saw Abe's buggy approaching. Katie Ann, as usual, was working in the barn.

Rachel was standing in front of the sink full of dishes, reading one of the books Emma had picked up at the library.

"Careful you don't drop that in the water."

Rachel smiled, finished the paragraph she was reading, and slipped a piece of ribbon between the pages of the novel. It was a good thing the woman had apron pockets. Otherwise, she would have no place to put the books she carried everywhere.

"This one is about a young woman who travels

to Canada to teach school in 1910." Her eyes took on a faraway look as she filled the sink with soap and hot water. "Actually, their life doesn't sound so different from ours."

"Though they probably didn't have an arsonist." Clyde kissed his wife on the cheek, squeezed Emma's arm, and hurried out the back door.

"It's a bad time for this," Emma said. "Not that there's a *gut* time for such terrible things."

"Everyone's working so hard to plant the crops. Silas even read in the almanac that it's likely to be a wet summer."

The boy loved books nearly as much as his mother, though he tended toward ones that focused on farming.

"A wet summer. Are you sure Silas was talking about our San Luis Valley?"

"I know. It's hard to believe." Rachel dipped a bowl into the water, scrubbed it clean, and set it in the rinse water. "I'm a little surprised Henry would agree to such a meeting. Usually he likes to handle any interaction with the *Englisch* on his own, or quietly with those involved."

"I suspect the authorities gave him little choice." Emma picked up a dish towel. "What a tragedy about his workshop."

"We'll rebuild it for him. Didn't Abe say the men would start next week?"

"As soon as the crops are in. Maybe Thursday.

But think of all the projects he'd finished, all the hours he'd spent there working on something that—*poof*—vanished in a cloud of smoke."

"Are you worried, Emma? That the arsonist might strike here?"

"*Nein. Gotte* will take care of our family, as He always has."

Rachel bit down on her bottom lip, a habit she'd had since she was a young bride trying to learn to mind her words when she lost her temper. Emma felt a surge of affection for her daughter-in-law. It was true that she'd pull out a book if she had even a minute to spare, but she loved and cared for her family, and there were worse habits than reading.

"I know what you're thinking, Rachel Fisher. You're wondering why *Gotte* didn't take care of Vernon—"

"At least with the job site and Henry's workshop no one was hurt."

"Other than the dog."

"*Ya*, other than that, and it's sad for sure." She set a cup she hadn't quite cleaned into the rinse water, and Emma handed it back. "It's easy enough to say *Gotte* will watch over us, and I do believe that, but what about Vernon? Was *Gotte* watching over him? Was it simply his day to die?"

"Those are hard questions, and I won't pretend I know the answers."

"That's it? That's all you've got?" Now Rachel was smiling, clearly amused that Emma hadn't spouted wiser words.

"That's all I've got, but if you'd like a proverb I can quote those easily enough."

"They never made any sense to me."

"Worry ends where faith begins. How about that one?"

"That one I like."

Once they'd finished the dishes, they went outside to sow seeds into the rows of their vegetable garden. Clyde had already turned over the dirt. Long rows stretching the length of the house lay waiting.

Katie Ann joined them as they sorted through seeds and consulted the sheet where they'd drawn out what to plant where.

"Can't we just do what we did last year?" Katie Ann squinted at the drawing. "We had the green beans on this side and the tomatoes on that side. Why change it?"

"Because we learn from what we did last year. We improve on it. Remember how our tomatoes grew—"

"Large and fat."

"*Ya*, but they didn't turn red."

"We even tried putting them in a paper bag with a banana." Rachel laughed at the memory. "Seemed to be working until the boys ate the banana."

"Probably they needed less sun," Emma explained.

"Less?"

"The plants themselves like sun, but sunlight is not what makes the tomatoes ripen. Because we're at such a high elevation, we'll try moving them to partial shade . . . here, closer to the house." She pointed at a spot on the drawing. "The green beans we'll put on the far row where Clyde has set the little garden fence."

Rachel folded up the sheet and stuck it in their basket of supplies. "Which will keep the boys out while they're playing ball."

"And give the plants something to grow on."

"If you say so. Horses make complete sense to me. Plants, not so much." Katie Ann accepted a packet of seeds and made her way down the row.

"She's a *gut* girl," Emma said, watching her kneel at the end of the row.

"That she is . . . " Rachel began.

"What is it?"

"Only that I'm a bit worried about her."

"What could possibly cause you to worry about Katie Ann?"

"I saw her talking to Sam after our church service yesterday."

"He's a nice boy."

"Sam is *not* a boy," Rachel pointed out. "He's much too old for her."

Rachel pulled out two packets of green beans,

handed one to Emma, and then they both made their way to the far side of the garden. "Did you remember your sunglasses, Emma? Wouldn't want you getting a migraine."

"*Ya*. They're right here." She pulled them out of her pocket and slipped them on. "And don't think you can change the subject. Are you worried there's something besides friendship blossoming between Katie Ann and Sam?"

"I hope not."

"I've known Sam's parents all my life. They're a fine family, strong in their faith and hard workers."

"But she's only sixteen, and Sam is what . . . twenty-nine?"

"Sounds like a big age difference now, but when Katie Ann is twenty-six and Sam is thirty-nine, it won't seem like so much."

Rachel was stabbing the ground with her spade. "And what of his being on the firefighting crew? I'd rather my *doschder* not have to worry about her husband running toward a fire in the middle of the night."

"You've moved the buggy a bit before the horse."

"You can laugh, but these things happen too quickly. Before you know it, the situation is out of hand."

"There's something you're not saying."

Rachel's hand stilled over the furrow she'd

made in the row. "What if he *is* involved in what happened at Vernon's? I'm not saying he is, but what if he knew something or . . . I don't know. I'd rather Katie Ann have nothing to do with fires or arsonists or criminal investigations."

"We can't keep children from growing up, Rachel. We can't protect them from every hardship in life."

"Which doesn't stop me from wishing I could."

Emma didn't say anything for a few moments as they made their way down the row—Rachel digging the furrows, Emma dropping the seeds in and covering them up. When they'd reached the middle, Emma began to laugh.

Instead of asking, Rachel waited, an exasperated look on her face.

"I was just remembering how I worried about Clyde—marrying someone who couldn't cook, someone who was raised Mennonite and didn't understand our ways."

"There was much I didn't understand then, and I had no idea what I wanted."

"True, but it worked out, now, didn't it?"

"Sure it did."

"So all my worrying was a waste of time."

"I guess so, but only because you decided to teach me how to cook. Otherwise, he might have starved."

Thirty-Six

Henry spent the day throwing the charred remains of his workshop into a burn pile. He didn't do so alone. In fact, he was rarely alone for more than a few minutes. His congregants came as they were able—alone, in pairs, and sometimes even in small groups showing up all at once.

"We'll have this rebuilt in no time, Henry."

"You can have something a bit larger. Your business has grown, *ya*?"

"A bigger window would be nice."

Their words were encouraging, but their labor was a gift Henry realized he would not be able to repay, and he said as much to Abe.

"Actually, you have repaid it already," his elder reminded him. "You lead us well."

"I guide in ways the Lord allows me to."

"And how many homes and barns have you worked on?"

"*Ya*, it's true, but I'm learning it's easier to give help than to receive it. This is humbling, Abe. I know each man who comes here needs to be working on his crops, needs to be at home attending to his own business."

"They're here because they want to be. Accept their help with a grateful heart."

"When did you become so wise?"

"I serve under a *gut* bishop."

Henry appreciated the words of advice from his friend. It helped to lift the heaviness on his heart. That heaviness wasn't only because he'd lost his workshop and a few months' worth of work. He felt weighed down by the necessity of the sacrifice they made for one another. It seemed so unnecessary. Why would someone want to burn down his property? What was the common link between him, the job site, and Vernon?

That question plagued his mind while the site was cleared of debris, men came and went, and Lexi oversaw the entire de-construction project. Dr. Berry had suggested the little dog rest a few days, but Lexi had other ideas.

And before he knew it, the time had come to hitch up the buggy and go to Leroy's.

"Grateful you weren't hurt, girl." He patted the mare along her neck and climbed up into the buggy. He'd been undecided on whether to take Lexi with him. In the end he figured she had earned the trip. He called to her, but she was too short to climb up into the buggy. Reaching down, he managed to get a hand under her little belly. If she was suffering from the night before, she did a good job of hiding it.

The little dog rode beside him on the seat. It seemed that already, after only a few days, her one desire was to be next to him. How was it that a dog's heart so quickly settled on its owner?

He'd never given it much thought, but then again, he'd never personally owned a dog.

He reached over to scratch between her ears, and Lexi's look of complete bliss told him he'd made the right decision to bring her.

He'd thought he was arriving early, but Leroy's drive was already lined with buggies, and his yard was filled with men, women, and children milling about.

Meg and Sheriff Grayson were standing on the front porch steps.

Emma's grandson, Silas, accepted the reins of his buggy and told the bishop, "Leroy asked for you to go on inside as soon as you arrived."

Which wasn't as easy as it would seem to be.

Everyone wanted a word with him. Those who hadn't made it by his place assured him they would. Those who had, promised to come back. Henry was again filled with an enormous sense of gratitude.

He climbed the back porch steps and told Lexi to stay. She turned twice in a circle and lay where she had a good view of the door. Rather remarkable how bright the pup was, how easily she learned basic commands.

He paused a moment to look out over Leroy's vast fields. His place was easily the largest in the community, exceeding two hundred acres, and he'd heard the man intended to purchase more. Though it seemed a bit extravagant to Henry, it wasn't his place to comment on how his deacon invested his money. Perhaps he was expecting all of his sons to stay in the area, in which case the extra acreage would come in handy.

Regardless, looking out over the freshly planted fields filled Henry with a degree of calm. Yes, the fires were a terrible thing that had happened, but they were drawing together as a community, as a body of faith.

Or so he thought, until he stepped into Leroy's kitchen.

⋇═◯═⋇

One look at Leroy's expression told Henry there was trouble in the air.

"Has there been another fire?" He couldn't imagine there had, given the mood of the families outside, but perhaps they hadn't been told yet.

"*Nein*. It's not that, though it's bad enough." Leroy never was one to mince words. "There's something we'd like to speak to you about."

He was a good man. Henry knew he was always the first to find a hole in any plan. That kind of person could be handy to have in leadership. Henry would rather they anticipate problems before they became a big issue.

"Allen and Grayson arrived well before everyone else," Leroy said.

"I would have been here if I'd known."

"As soon as they told me what they want to do,

I stopped them and told them we'd discuss it no further until you arrived."

"And what do they want to do?"

Clyde took up the story. "They want to offer a reward for members of our community to turn one another in."

"Is that what they said?"

"It's apparently what they meant." Abe was scowling at a mug of coffee that was half empty. "I was here and heard their explanation. Leroy's not exaggerating."

"Repeat it back to me, word-for-word."

"They said the amount of reward money the merchants offered has been increased." Leroy crossed his arms. "When I asked why, they admitted they feel sure someone in our community knows something they haven't shared. They think the money will be an incentive. I don't like it, Henry. We have a *gut* group here, but if we begin turning on one another, that could fall apart quickly."

"You're not suggesting that anyone in our congregation would harbor a fugitive."

"Of course not."

Abe ran a thumb under his suspenders. "What Leroy is saying, and Clyde and I agree, is that this isn't the way to go about it. If someone knows something, has seen or heard something, then they are to come to you or to one of us. We keep what is happening within the church."

"Tell me how you feel about this, Clyde."

The man didn't speak right away. Instead, he stared out the window at the gathering crowd. Finally, he shrugged and admitted, "I'm not comfortable with their being here. Since you agreed to the meeting, you must have had a *gut* reason, but I'd rather deal with this internally."

Henry checked the clock above the stove. Five minutes until six. It was time to begin, but he needed to deal with his leadership first. It was important that they be in one accord, even if it meant the meeting would start a few minutes late.

"This was an internal problem when it was merely Vernon dancing along the edge of the *Ordnung*. But as soon as it became a matter of murder, we lost the privilege to handle it within the community." Henry combed his fingers through his beard, waited, and prayed that he would have the words to settle these men who genuinely cared about their congregation. "I trust that you have each prayed about this, but I think it's important that we do exactly that again . . . together. So let's do so now. Let's pray."

Henry had found the urge to share your own opinion diminished as one considered God's perspective on a topic. The four men sat together around the table and bowed their heads. He didn't lead them. In fact, no one spoke. But they each closed their eyes, and Henry silently prayed they would all bare their hearts before God. He prayed for wisdom, for God's will to be made plain, for them to have the courage and dedication to clear the path for that will.

For them to put others first.

For them to trust in God's omnipotence even in such a tragic and confusing situation as this.

He closed the prayer with one of his favorite sentiments from Paul, "Always giving thanks to God the Father for everything, in the name of our Lord Jesus Christ."

"Amen."

When he glanced up at the clock, he saw that the hands had slipped to fifteen minutes past the hour. "It would seem we're late." And without another word, he led them out to the front porch.

Thirty-Seven

The crowd around Emma was growing some-what restless by the time Henry stepped out of the house, followed by Leroy, Abe, and Clyde. The men filed to Emma's right, fanning out along the porch. Henry spoke briefly with Grayson and Meg.

The arson investigator must know a little about Plain communities, because she'd thought to print the photographs of the perpetrator, but did she truly understand them? How could she? And yet they were to place their safety in her hands. Emma didn't like it, and she was certain that those around her felt the same.

"Most of you know Sheriff Grayson." Henry's voice was calm, pleasant even. A driver passing by might have thought this was a regular May night, and that they were gathered for an evening social. "Since we moved here thirteen years ago, the sheriff has been a help to our community. I consider him a fair man, and I trust that you will listen to what he has to say with an open mind."

Grayson thanked Henry and stepped forward.

To anyone else, Henry Lapp might have looked completely at ease, but Emma noticed the lines across his forehead, the way he massaged his right hand with his left, and how his smile seemed

231

slightly forced. Only when his little dog bounded up the front steps did he smile genuinely.

"She must have heard your voice, Henry." This from one of the men at the back of the crowd.

Emma was reminded of a verse in the New Testament. *His sheep follow him because they know his voice.* The little beagle certainly knew whom to follow. As a Plain community they followed Christ, and they trusted their bishop to lead them down that path. Henry was their shepherd in more ways than one. He helped them when they were suffering heartache, sat with them when they were sick, prayed with them when they were lost. The thought helped to settle the butterflies in her stomach.

"By this time, I'm sure you all know about the fire at Henry's place," Grayson said.

A low murmur passed through the crowd, like a light breeze, tickling the hair on the back of Emma's neck.

"The reason I'm here, other than to introduce our arson investigator, is to assure you that the Monte Vista authorities are doing everything within their power to catch the person responsible. We consider your families a valuable part of our community. If you have any concerns at all, please feel free to come and speak with me tonight or stop by the station in town."

He nodded toward Meg, who stepped up front and center.

It was engrained into Plain culture that in general women did not address a crowd of men. There were no women in leadership roles, women didn't pray aloud in church, and women rarely worked outside the home. Emma understood that the larger *Englisch* culture disapproved of these things, but within their group it merely seemed normal. Contrary to what *Englischers* thought, it didn't mean women weren't valued. For Amish communities, there was no more important role than caring for the family, and that was what Amish women did.

Was their opinion important? Of course it was. And that opinion was shared openly with family and friends. Their concerns held weight in the community, if for no other reason than they were a cherished part of it. All one had to do was look over at Chester and Mary, who had brought his mother, guided her up front, and made sure she had a comfortable chair to sit in. Women counted all right, but they did not give speeches.

All those thoughts passed through Emma's mind as she watched the arson investigator scan the crowd and then begin to speak.

"Thank you, Sheriff Grayson. I appreciate everyone coming out tonight. My name is Meg Allen, and I have been assigned to this case by the county district office. I'd like to update you on the investigation, and then I'll do my best to answer any questions."

Emma had the childish urge to clap her hands over her ears. She didn't want to hear more of this. She wanted it to be over. She wanted her family to be home, where they were safe.

"We are operating under the assumption that the person who killed Vernon Frey is the same person who caused the fire at the construction site and also the same person who destroyed Bishop Lapp's workshop last night. In my fifteen years of arson investigations, I've yet to see two fire bugs working the same territory. In fact, arson is a rather rare crime, which is why I was sent here to help with the investigation."

Emma stood between Rachel and Katie Ann, waiting for Meg to get to the point. So far, she'd told them nothing new.

"It's my opinion that this person is targeting Amish homes and businesses. While the construction site isn't Amish, per se, plenty of your sons and husbands are employed there. We believe the person responsible for setting these fires is male, between the ages of seventeen and fifty, Caucasian, has a slight build, and is approximately five feet eight."

"That describes half the men in the San Luis Valley," Rachel whispered.

"It has been my experience that in every crime committed, someone has seen something. For whatever reason, people are often hesitant to step forward. Maybe you think what you saw wasn't important. Let me be the judge of that. It's my job to assess and coordinate information."

Emma noticed this comment brought a reaction in the people around her. Probably Meg Allen didn't mean it as it sounded, as if they weren't bright enough to know what was and wasn't important. If Meg noticed the response, she didn't address it.

"Maybe you would rather not become involved because you don't want to be connected in any way to these crimes. That's a natural feeling, but let me assure you that you are connected. You are involved already. Being a part of this community has involved you. I'd like you to help me stop this perpetrator before the person to your left or your right is hurt."

"*Gotte* will protect us," someone muttered.

"And we can watch out for our neighbors."

"As you watched out for Vernon Frey?" Meg didn't back down an inch. "As you watched out for your bishop?"

"His workshop will be rebuilt before you can file the proper paperwork." This from a man in the back, though Emma couldn't make out who it was.

"I appreciate how you support one another. A workshop, a barn, even a home can be rebuilt. I understand that. But people cannot be brought back from the dead, and our perpetrator has shown he's willing to kill. We can't know his motive at this point, but we do know he's dangerous." Meg scanned the crowd slowly. She waited until they had again grown quiet. "Which is why it would be very dangerous for you to try to protect someone. It would be unwise for you to think this criminal activity will stop with no more harm. I assure you, that's most certainly not the case. Once an arsonist starts down this road, the situation accelerates."

"Why would someone do such a thing?" This from Rebecca. It wasn't clear to Emma whether she'd meant the question to be heard by Meg or whether she was merely thinking aloud.

"The majority of arson crimes are motivated by profit. Someone burns down a building and collects the insurance money. That's obviously not what we have here."

"What other motive is there?" Rebecca's son asked.

"Anger. Outside of profit, anger is the most common cause of someone setting fires. Revenge is also often a factor. So what you need to ask yourself is this: Who would believe they have cause to be angry with your community? Who would want revenge?"

"Henry already gave you that list," someone called out.

Meg looked as if she might deny that, but what was the point? As far as Emma knew, everyone was aware of Henry's list, and most people understood why he had provided it.

"This has moved beyond anyone who had a vendetta against Mr. Frey. We're doing everything on our end to catch this person, but by its very nature there is little evidence left at an arson site. That's why I'm appealing to you. If you know something, come and see me. If you see something, report it. No clue is too small, and if we work together, we can catch this person."

Meg stepped back, clearly riled by the response she'd received but tapping down her frustration.

The crowd had no additional questions, so Leroy reminded them there would be a workday at Henry's the following Saturday.

Abe thanked everyone for coming, and Clyde told them cold drinks and sweets had been set up in the shade of the barn.

It was Sheriff Grayson who stepped forward and reminded them that the reward money had been increased from five to ten thousand dollars. The money would go to anyone who reported information that led to the arrest and conviction of the Monte Vista arsonist.

Thirty-Eight

Henry stayed until nearly everyone was gone. Grayson and Meg remained off to the side, talking with Leroy. Lewis Glick was helping Clyde and Rachel put up what was left of the refreshments, though twice he dropped plates Rachel had handed him. Henry wasn't sure how much help Lewis was, but he thought it best not to intervene. Abe had already left, and Emma's grandchildren were playing a game of tag in the fading light.

"That was not much fun." Emma sank onto the porch steps next to the bishop. When she slipped off her shoe to rub her foot, Lexi bounded over and began to lick her toes.

"Never seen her do that before." Henry's expression relaxed, and he snagged the dog to pull her away from Emma.

"Glad I can provide you with some entertainment."

"You always brighten my day, Emma." The confession seemed to slip from his lips unbidden, but because it was true, he didn't bother correcting himself. Instead, he moved the conversation along. "How do you think it went?"

"I think it put people on edge, even more than they were."

"Because . . . "

238

"They'd rather believe it's over. I'd rather believe it's over. Meg Allen pretty much assured us it's not."

"Forewarned is forearmed."

"What does that mean?"

"Knowledge is a weapon against your enemy. Maybe the best weapon."

Emma pulled a dog treat out of her pocket, held it up, and waited for Lexi to sit.

The dog fell over instead, showing her belly. Emma rubbed it and gave her the treat. "I can't say as we're used to having enemies."

"In some ways this world is our enemy. Doesn't the Bible say so? Peter reminded us of that very thing when he cautioned us to 'be sober-minded; be watchful. Your adversary the devil prowls around like a roaring lion, seeking someone to devour.' "

"I've heard you quote from the Bible for years, Henry—mostly verses about *Gotte*'s love and mercy."

"And there's a time for that, but we also need to be prepared."

"Forewarned."

"Indeed."

They were interrupted by Meg's arrival.

"Henry, if I could talk to you a minute . . . in private."

"You've met Emma. Anything you want to say to me, you can say to her."

239

Meg glanced from Henry to Emma and back again. Finally, she shrugged as if her preference for privacy wasn't worth a battle.

"I'd like to ask you about some of the men who were here tonight."

Henry gave her the go-ahead gesture.

She consulted her small pad of paper and said, "Sam Beiler, who works as a volunteer with the local fire department."

"You've already interrogated him."

"He was markedly agitated tonight."

"Was he now?" Henry looked to Emma for confirmation.

"I didn't see Sam. I suppose he was behind me in the crowd."

Henry returned his gaze to Meg. "You can't arrest a man for being agitated. This thing has our entire community worked up, thanks largely to your insistence of addressing them personally."

Meg didn't respond directly to that. Instead, she stared at her list. Finally she asked, "What of Abe Graber?"

Henry heard Emma's sharp intake of breath, mirroring his own surprise.

"Surely you don't believe Abe to be capable of such a thing."

"He's on your church staff?"

"We don't have a staff. We have men who were nominated by our congregation and chosen by *Gotte* to serve over us."

240

"Convenient."

Henry had spent a fair amount of time with Meg over the last two weeks. She'd always been extremely focused on her job, but he'd never seen her quite so snippy. "Abe has served competently for many years."

"He was quite adamantly against tonight's meeting."

"As was nearly every family here," Emma said.

Henry knew Emma would be calm but vocal on her opinions. It was one reason he had insisted she stay and hear what Meg had to say. As for himself, he was beginning to fear he was losing an objective perspective. When his own property had been attacked, the situation had quickly become personal.

If they were both going to have to sit and listen to Meg's foolishness, then Emma certainly had earned the right to offer her two cents' worth.

"Abe spoke to me about his doubts," Henry admitted. "He had misgivings over allowing you to speak to our families, as did all in our leadership. Each man thinks these things are best handled within the church. After we discussed it and prayed over it, they agreed with my decision to allow you to address the group."

"So you don't think he's capable of these crimes?"

"*Nein*, and why would you ask me that?"

"Because you know the men in this group

better than anyone else. Who else would I ask?" Meg shook her head in frustration. "I visited a few houses this afternoon, including Abe's."

Henry briefly wondered why Abe hadn't mentioned that, but he didn't have time to dwell on the thought. "I trust he put your mind at ease."

"No. He did not. That's why I'm asking you about him."

"Abe is a *gut* man. You're chasing rabbits now because your investigation has yielded nothing."

"My investigation is creeping along because your people won't talk to me."

"We are by nature a private group," Emma reminded her.

"Privacy won't keep you safe." She turned back to Henry. "And your guy, Abe, has family in Alamosa—where the envelope addressed to Vernon in your drawing was postmarked. That's not a possible connection I'm willing to overlook."

Without waiting for his reply, she turned and trudged off to her car.

Henry stood and reached a hand down for Emma. They walked, shoulder to shoulder, toward the last of the buggies—his, Clyde's, and Lewis Glick's.

"How's Lewis settling in?" Emma asked.

"Fair . . ."

"Except what?"

"I don't like to guess."

242

"But you're worried about him. Why is that?"

Henry shrugged. He was worried about Lewis, but he couldn't put his finger on why. So instead he said, "He still keeps to himself more than I'd like to see, but it's a hard land to adjust to, and the place he purchased . . . well, it needed quite a bit more work than he had anticipated."

They were nearly in earshot of the others.

Emma placed a hand on Henry's arm. She waited until he'd stopped before she asked, "It's a coincidence, right? That Abe's brother lives in the town postmarked on the envelope you drew."

"*If* the letter even came in that envelope. The funny thing to me? No one questions the letter's existence anymore, or that it was indeed from Alamosa. Such a small detail in a drawing."

"And yet you saw it. You remembered it, and there's no doubt it's an important clue." When he didn't answer, Emma pushed on. "I don't think Meg was saying she suspects Abe. I think she's giving you fair warning that she's about to pull in his brother, Alvin."

"Why would she do that?"

Instead of answering, Emma crossed her arms and turned away from the last of their group, toward the mountains. Together they looked out over the last of the sun's rays as they melted across the valley.

"You know Rachel is a big reader."

"*Ya.* I seem to remember she always has been."

"Sometimes she talks about the characters in her novels as if they're real people. I guess when she finishes a story, she has a longing to share it, and I have to admit . . . they are entertaining."

Henry nodded, wondering what she was getting at.

"Her books are always Christian fiction, but in some there are investigations, and sometimes . . . sometimes the investigator will leak some information or clue on purpose, to see if she can smoke out the guilty party."

"So rather than Meg revealing her suspicions about Alvin to Abe, *I'm* supposed to warn Abe, who will warn Alvin, causing him to run or do something incriminating."

Emma laughed and reached down to pick up Lexi, who was splayed belly to the dirt at Henry's feet. "Sounds like fiction, I know, but then our life . . . it seems to have taken a turn worthy of a bestseller."

Thirty-Nine

The next day passed in relative calm.

Henry spent the morning prepping for the upcoming workday.

He ordered lumber from the store in town.

Needing to burn the debris from his old workshop, he stopped by city hall to pick up the burn permit. While there, he walked over to the adjacent building to check in with Sheriff Grayson.

"Henry, I didn't expect to see you today."

"Needed a burn permit for that pile of charred wood that used to be my workshop. Then it occurred to me that I should check with you and confirm it's okay to get rid of it. Or maybe I should ask Meg?"

"I'm sure it's fine. No clues left there. As for Allen, she's been called back to the district office."

"She's given up on finding the arsonist?"

"Hardly. She'll continue working the case. Many investigations are cracked open by good, old-fashioned detective work—following threads until you find one that leads you to the perp."

"I have no idea what you're talking about."

"Lots of grunt work. She'll check computer files, records, and previous complaints in surrounding counties. Who purchased what from whom. Who benefited from the fires. Who has a background that indicates a spiral into felony murder is possible."

"She can do that from a computer?"

"That and phone calls and hitting the pavement."

Henry thought of Abe and his brother. What would she find about Alvin? What had he been involved in since he'd left the faith?

Grayson walked him to the door out of the station. "Don't be surprised if you see her back here."

"You'll keep me posted on any developments?"

"Of course."

Henry went home, burned the debris pile, directed the delivery guys on where to place the new lumber, and spent the afternoon praying and studying for Sunday's service.

He ate a light supper and then hitched up Oreo to the buggy. There were still several hours of daylight left, and Abe lived close by. He would easily make it back home before dark. Henry preferred not to be out on the road in the evening—less chance of an accident.

Lexi rode next to him on the seat.

Abe's children crowded around the buggy when he arrived.

It was Anna who hung back, worry clouding her features. "Lexi is okay? I heard the arsonist kicked her."

"Doc Berry says she's fine. Don't you worry about that."

"Why would someone do that, Henry? Why kick a little dog?" She drew on the dust covering his buggy with a single finger, a picture of stick girls and boys, and what might have been a small stick figure dog.

He thought of explaining that Lexi had been intent on stopping the arsonist, but did a child need to know that? Probably not.

He settled for, "We can't know what's in someone's heart. What we can do is pray for them."

"I guess."

"Rest assured that Lexi won't be chasing after anyone for a while. I'll see to that."

Seemingly satisfied, Anna stopped drawing and said, "Thanks, Henry." She skipped after the other children.

Abe was already standing on the front porch. "Didn't expect a visit from you tonight."

"There's something we need to talk about."

"Susan started brewing a pot of coffee when she saw you pull up, and it's decaf. Come on into the kitchen."

Henry had spent a lot of time with Abe and Susan, and not only because he was a preacher in their church. He was also a close friend. The last few years had not been easy on them. Having Franey live in their home had caused quite a bit of friction. Eventually, they'd built a small mother-in-law house for her. It was close but not attached, and it provided some degree of privacy

247

for both his family and her. From what Henry could tell, it had helped to ease the tension, though based on what had happened between the two women at Vernon's funeral luncheon, he guessed that some days were better than others.

"Meg Allen spoke to me about Alvin. She found out he lives in Alamosa, and, well, we believe Vernon received a letter from Alamosa shortly before he died."

"We know about the drawing," Susan said. "Don't look so surprised, Henry. Everyone knows about it. Your gift . . . it's an amazing thing to us."

Abe crossed his arms and scowled at the floor. "But she can't think Alvin had anything to do with this."

"What she thinks is the arsonist is someone who has a vendetta against the Amish. Viewed a certain way, Alvin could fit that description."

"My brother would never do such a thing. It's true that he fell away from the faith, but violence? *Nein.* He doesn't have it in him."

Henry accepted a mug of coffee but shook his head when Susan offered him a brownie bar. If he didn't start watching what he ate, he'd soon be dealing with health problems. The fire had reminded him of many things, including his own mortality.

"Have you spoken to him recently?"

Abe glanced at his wife, who nodded slightly.

"I go to see him, once a month."

"Franey doesn't know." Susan took a seat across from Henry, next to her husband. "We do not approve of his leaving the faith. I think it's terrible that he would divorce her, but we've learned first-hand that she isn't an easy woman to live with."

"You have provided for her since the day he left."

"Of course we have, and we'll continue to do so." Abe ran a hand up and over the top of his head. "But I won't abandon my brother. I realize that, in more traditional Plain communities, Alvin would be shunned for what he's done . . ."

Henry waited, knowing Abe was finally baring an ache he'd buried in his heart for too long.

"I think the practice of shunning is terribly harsh."

"In this instance I agree with you." Henry chose his words carefully. "However, it's important that we not be perceived as condoning such decisions. Leaving the faith and divorcing your wife can't be tolerated. Encouraging Alvin to move away from Monte Vista, and to break ties with those he knew from our community, was necessary for the *gut* of everyone."

"We tore my family apart!" Abe shook his head and made an obvious attempt to quiet his temper. "*I* tore my family apart. I agreed when we sanctioned Alvin. I'm not saying it's your fault or Leroy's. Clyde wasn't even nominated then."

"It's been many years."

"And don't misunderstand me. I'm not saying I believe in divorce. But Alvin didn't become a terrible person because of one decision. He still reads his Bible, attends church, and even volunteers on missions with MDS."

"I'm glad he's found his place within the Mennonites."

"If you think it's wrong that I visit him, Henry, then I'm sorry. I'll even confess it before our congregation on Sunday if you think that's necessary. But what I won't do is turn my back on family."

"We strive for grace and forgiveness, Abe, and while we cannot tolerate behavior in direct conflict with the *Ordnung*, I don't feel your visiting your brother once a month falls into that category." Henry finished his coffee, which was actually quite good for decaf. It would have been even better with one of the brownie bars, but he pushed that thought away.

"I would like to go and see Alvin tomorrow. I've hired a driver who will be at my place at nine in the morning. I realize this isn't the most opportune time, but if you'd like to join me—"

"I'll go," Abe said. "Our crops are in. I was planning on helping Sam, but there will be others there."

"Then it's settled."

When they walked back outside, Henry looked across at the other house and noticed Franey in the rocking chair on her porch. He raised a hand in greeting and she did the same, though she made no attempt to join them.

"She keeps to herself," Abe said. "Maybe too much."

"A wounded heart doesn't heal overnight."

"It's been years."

"The deeper the wound, the longer it can take to mend." He wished them both a good night and called to Lexi.

During the ride home, he tried to process what he'd learned.

Abe was obviously more angry about how his brother had been treated than he'd previously let on.

Furthermore, he was still in contact with Alvin.

But the idea Henry couldn't wrap his mind around was that either Abe or Alvin could be angry enough to hurt someone within their community.

Divorce and remarriage were difficult to imagine in an Amish family, though it did occasionally occur. Henry had consulted with other bishops, and he found it happened more than he was aware of. Such things were dealt with quietly, and as compassionately as possible.

But murder of one of their own by one of their own?

That was something Henry couldn't begin to fathom.

Forty

Henry had not seen Alvin Graber in the eleven years since he'd left their community. The man had certainly aged. His dark hair was now peppered with gray, and the lines around his eyes had deepened. In spite of those changes, Henry had to admit he looked better than he ever had. He appeared to be healthy, physically fit, and content. His new life agreed with him. Or so it seemed.

"I was a bit surprised, I'll admit, when Abe called. Didn't expect to ever receive a visit from you, Henry."

They were sitting in the living room. It was plainly furnished, though not as bare as an Amish home would be. There was no television or computer in sight. They might have been back in a spare bedroom or office. Some Mennonites allowed for such. The starkest difference was the pictures on the mantel—three family photographs with Alvin, his new wife, and their twin daughters, taken at different times over the years. As the girls grew, their resemblance to their mother became stronger, though Henry thought he saw a touch of their Uncle Abe in their brown eyes and plentiful freckles. As a child, Abe had been virtually covered with freckles, while Alvin had none.

"You seem to be doing well."

"*Ya*. I suppose so. I'm sorry Jessica couldn't be here. She works at the library most mornings while the girls attend school, or in a few weeks, summer camp."

"I suppose you've heard about the fires we've had in Monte Vista."

"Sure. They've been in the paper as well as on the television news."

"Do you have any idea as to who would be angry enough with our community to do such a thing?"

Alvin sat back on the couch and crossed his right leg over his left knee. "As I told Meg Allen, I don't see many Amish folk anymore. You all made sure of that."

"You've spoken with the arson investigator?"

"She came by yesterday. She even asked me if I had an alibi for the dates of the fires. I told her I didn't need an alibi since I would never do such a thing."

"And she was satisfied with that answer?"

"Hard to say. Even after eleven years, I'm still not so *gut* at reading *Englisch* women, not that we're *Englisch*, mind you, but we interact with the mainstream community more than you do."

Henry sat forward, elbows propped on knees. "We're certainly not accusing you, Alvin."

"That's a relief, since we have a history of that."

Abe attempted to stay him with a hand, but Henry said softly, "Let him speak."

"You did accuse me of plenty. Do you remember that, Henry? The night you came to my home? Franey was hysterical when I told her I couldn't stay. She had disappeared. I suspected she was at Abe's, but I had no way to know."

"It was a difficult time."

"For you? Or for Franey? Or perhaps for me as I sought a new life?"

"Perhaps for all of us."

"You accused me of not taking seriously my commitment to Christ, of stepping away from the faith, even of not caring for my family. Not caring!" He closed his eyes, visibly trying to calm himself. "If I hadn't cared about Franey I wouldn't have stayed with her as long as I did. And I tried to convince her to go to a doctor for the depression. You know that. Still, you judged me."

Henry didn't respond. He didn't think Alvin was looking for an answer to his grievances. Perhaps he only needed to share them.

"You have no idea what it's like to be told you can no longer visit your family—my own brother, my niece, my nephews. You cast me off as if I was a rotten piece of fruit. You said . . ." He shook his head, stared at the floor a moment, and then pierced Henry with his gaze. "You said my relationship with my family was broken as my relationship with the church was broken. You took a difficult situation I was going through and made it immeasurably worse."

"I'm truly sorry that you suffered."

"And that's as close to an apology as I'm likely to get." Alvin exchanged a glance with his brother. He stood, walked across to the windows, and stared outside for a moment. There was no sound except for the ticking of a clock.

Abe stared at his hands.

Henry waited.

Finally, Alvin turned back toward them. "It was many years ago. I do not carry hard feelings in my heart each day of my life. Such a burden would be too much. What is the saying *Mamm* used to quote?"

Abe smiled for the first time since they'd arrived. "To forgive heals the wound . . ."

"And to forget heals the scar. I forgive you, Henry, but it seems I have a ways to go as far as forgetting. And seeing you here . . . well, it's brought back some difficult feelings."

Henry waited a full minute. Then he said, "If I remember correctly, you did not get along well with Vernon."

"You remember correctly."

"Had you seen him recently? Did he possibly mention anyone who was particularly angry with him?"

"I have not seen him since I moved to Alamosa."

"You haven't been back to Monte Vista in all these years?"

Instead of answering, Alvin said, "I have an eleven o'clock class to teach—woodworking at the community center."

Apparently their meeting was at an end. The two brothers embraced when they reached the door.

Abe walked to the car, but Henry held back. "I am truly sorry for the pain you've been through, Alvin."

"And I'm sorry I took my anger out on you. Abe has told me you're a kind and compassionate bishop. I'm glad the community has that sort of leadership, even if it didn't extend to me."

There seemed to be nothing he could say to alleviate the hurt in Alvin's voice, so Henry nodded and wished him a good day. He walked down the drive, putting his hand on the top of Alvin's small silver Honda. It was an unexceptional car and seemed to indicate that Alvin was attempting to live as modestly as possible.

The drive home was quiet. The driver tried a few times to initiate a conversation and then finally settled for finding a news program on the radio. It wasn't until they were back at Henry's house, out of the earshot of everyone else, that he turned to Abe and said, "Tell me about Alvin's trips to Monte Vista."

Forty-One

He felt the anger building inside of him. Like heartburn it exerted a heaviness on his chest, burned his throat, and left a bitter taste in his mouth. He knew the signs. If he didn't do something to alleviate the pressure soon, he would lash out, act impulsively, and make an error.

Which was where most criminals were caught—not accounting for the building tide of emotion. He'd done a study of it, and he was determined not to fall into the same trap. He'd managed his feelings and worked his way down his list of targets, spacing the attacks a few days apart. He'd followed his plan.

But he was, after all, only human. The anger built up until he was seeing things as if through red-tinted sunglasses. And all because of the follow-up story in the newspaper. It was the last straw.

ARSON INVESTIGATION PROGRESSING

Investigator Meg Allen claims to be close to capturing the person responsible for local fires. The *Monte Vista Gazette* spoke on Tuesday with Ms. Allen. "I'd like to ask for the public's patience in this matter.

We feel certain we are making progress regarding apprehension of the person responsible for the string of fires in Monte Vista."

Ms. Allen recently returned to the county office, which she claims is not an indication that the case has gone cold. "Quite the opposite. We have several leads, not the least of which is a letter directly implicating the guilty party. It's a matter of being able to work more efficiently from the district office. Here we have the computers and manpower needed to follow every aspect of these leads from the type of paper used to the postmark on the envelope. I'll also be working closely with sketch artists, who will use the video tape from the construction site as well as eyewitness accounts we received from a few of the JSW workers. Together they can create a better composite sketch of our perpetrator than the one we have offered to date."

When pressed for details as to the contents of the letter, Allen responded with "No comment." Other sources have confirmed that the letter is thought to be from the arsonist to Vernon Frey, who was killed in the fire on May 1.

Allen reiterated that the reward money

now stands at $10,000, payable to anyone who provides information that leads to the arrest and conviction of the arsonist.

The JSW construction site suffered fire damage on May 4.

Henry Lapp's workshop was burned to the ground in the late hours of the evening on May 14.

Anyone with information should contact Crime Stoppers or phone Meg Allen directly.

He read the article again, agonizing over every word, his anger increasing with each syllable and fear causing his heart to beat wildly.

Throwing the paper onto the table, he walked to the sink, filled a glass with water, and drank the entire thing. He needed to calm down. He needed to think about what they were saying.

It was true he had sent a letter to Vernon, but he knew that couldn't be the letter Allen was referring to. Everything, absolutely everything, had been destroyed in the blaze. He'd seen it himself. She had to be bluffing.

Unless Vernon had given the letter to someone else.

The statistical odds of that were low. Vernon Frey didn't exactly have a fistful of friends. So the existence of a letter was probably a lie to provoke him into confessing.

He also didn't believe there were any eye-witnesses. He'd been careful each time. He was certain no one had seen him, and if they had? He'd already be arrested.

What he hadn't anticipated was the reward money. People would sell out their father for less.

The entire situation caused the anger in his veins to boil. He was doing everything right. His technique was perfect, and he was certain he was leaving no fingerprints at the scene—not that it would matter. His fingerprints were not in any database. He'd dropped the top to his gas can, but there were no prints on that. The gas can could hardly be traced back to him, as most families in Monte Vista had one.

"Why are you home? You should be looking for a job." His mother's voice grated on his ears.

He glanced up to see her standing in the doorway, frowning at him.

"Why don't you clean up this place? It's . . . it's . . . it's disgusting." He hated that he stuttered when he argued with her. He'd left the habit behind years ago, watching Internet videos for how to cure himself of the verbal tick. But when his mother was glowering at him, he wasn't twenty-seven years old anymore. He was eight, frightened and helpless to defend himself against her verbal and physical abuse.

"Oh, not nice enough for you? Then move out!" She pivoted and lumbered back down the hall.

Probably she was drunk already. He'd seen the bottles in the trash. No matter how little money they had, there was always enough for that. He focused on his breathing and pushed the image of his mother from his mind.

Sitting in the kitchen chair, he stared out the grimy window and forced his thoughts to calm. This situation called for reason, not unfettered emotion.

He'd killed Vernon Frey because the man was a crook and a cheat.

He'd hit the construction site because they had refused him a job.

He'd destroyed the bishop's workshop so he would suffer financially.

A headache pounded at his temple. He stood, returned to his bedroom, unlocked his closet to check his supplies, and then he made his decision. Better to release the anger, even if it meant veering away from his list. He would strike soon, within the next twenty-four hours.

One last glance at the newspaper, and then he tossed it into the trash. His next target deserved whatever happened.

Forty-Two

Clyde hitched their mare to the buggy and had it waiting when Emma was finished with the lunch dishes.

"You're sure you don't want to go?" she asked.

Rachel shook her head and smiled. They both knew she'd prefer an hour alone for some quiet time to read, and, goodness, she had earned it. They'd spent the last two days putting in the garden as the men finished planting the crops. It had been arduous work. Their skin was red turning to brown from the elbows down, around their neck, and across their cheeks.

"Bye, *Mamm*." Katie Ann kissed her mother on the cheek. "We'll be sure to stop by the library and return your books."

"I have three more on hold. Check to see if they're in."

"We will."

Emma clucked to their mare, Cinnamon, and they started off down the lane.

It was a beautiful afternoon—crisp, cool, and with a hint of rain in the air.

Clouds were building on the horizon, and with any luck they would have rain by nightfall. It would certainly help with the newly planted crops.

"I will never understand what *Mamm* sees in these books." Katie Ann was staring at a cover of a woman in a prairie dress standing beside a wagon.

"We all need our moments of rest, when we can step away from the day's troubles."

"Step away?"

"In our mind."

"Oh. When do you step away?"

"I suppose when I'm sewing or doing any type of handwork—knitting, crocheting. It relaxes me and allows me to forget about the crops and the weather and if your brother is going to be bitten by a snake when he hunts for his arrowheads."

"Whoever heard of an Amish boy who liked history? Thomas is weird."

"But girls who love horses are completely natural."

"*Ya*! They are." Katie Ann grinned at her, and they fell into a comfortable silence.

Cinnamon trotted merrily down the road. When they passed the bishop's place, both Emma and Katie Ann craned their necks to see the empty place where his workshop had been.

"Looks like he cleaned it up."

"Indeed."

"Will they be able to rebuild his workshop in one day?"

"Our men can build a large barn in one day. A

264

workshop will be no problem." Emma guided the horse to the side of the road so an automobile could pass—it was an older model, rusty in places, and sorely in need of a paint job. "How old were you when we had our last barn raising?"

"Six? Maybe?"

"There was a flurry of building when we first settled here. Less in recent years."

"I missed the one two years ago. I'd gone to spend a month with *Aenti* Rose in Pinecraft."

"After she broke her hip. Rose still mentions in letters to your mother how much she enjoyed getting to know you."

"Pinecraft is so different from here."

"How so?"

"Hotter. Sand and beach and shuffleboard courts. It's funny to see all the older folks on their bikes and scooters. And ice cream shops— they're on nearly every corner."

"Are you ready to go back?"

Katie Ann twisted her *kapp* string between her fingers. "*Nein.* I wouldn't want to leave Cinnamon or Duncan or Dakota."

"You're a big help with all the horses."

"I can't imagine not seeing them for an entire month."

"You know what they say about absence."

"I don't think my heart could grow any fonder." Katie Ann cornered herself in the buggy and studied Emma. "I'm not sure what it all means.

Why do I love them so? I even dream about horses."

"Do ya now?"

"It's not as if I can become a vet or even a vet tech."

"Well, you could become anything you want. It's just that one day you will have to decide whether to live a Plain life or an *Englisch* one."

"I would never want to move away from you all."

"And we wouldn't want you to." Emma thought of Alvin, as she always did when conversations turned to such things. It was such a sad situation. She'd always felt pity for the man.

"So why do I love horses so? What am I supposed to do with that?"

"Maybe you don't need to do anything with it, especially now. You're still young, Katie Ann."

"Young? *Mammi*, I'm sixteen. That's practically grown, and I have no idea what's next."

"*Gotte* knows what is next, so don't worry about that. He gave you a love for horses, and a real talent with them, for a reason."

For her answer, Katie Ann sighed deeply and turned to stare out the buggy window.

They stopped at the library first, arriving as the doors opened.

Emma waited for the librarian, an older woman named Betty, to fetch the books that were on hold for Rachel. Katie Ann had also asked about books that had to do with horses. Five minutes later she returned with a book by James Herriot—*All Creatures Great and Small.*

"I remember Silas reading that one."

"Silas read a book?" Katie Ann squirreled her nose in disbelief.

"He did, and he liked it. I imagine you will too."

"Mostly I don't care for reading, but *Mamm* says that's because I have to find books that appeal to my interests. When I told her I couldn't find any books about horses, at least none that I hadn't read in school, she told me to try harder."

"You'll enjoy that one," Betty assured them. "It's the story of a young veterinarian."

They both thanked the woman and then headed back out to the buggy.

"Walk or ride?" Emma asked.

"Let's walk. Cinnamon looks like she's dozing here in the shade."

Next they went to the market and purchased the items on Emma's list, returning to place the bags in the small box attached to the back of the buggy.

"Our last errand is to the newspaper." Katie Ann pulled out a map, which they'd slipped between the pages of one of Rachel's books. "I still can't believe Silas drew this."

"Your brother is *gut* at drawing."

"Like Henry?"

"Henry's drawing is a bit . . . different."

"Do you think this will bring more people to our produce stand?"

"Ours and others as well."

Katie Ann traced the route through the outskirts of Monte Vista. It passed practically every farm in their community—or at least the ones with items they wanted to sell.

Most would not have produce yet, but they'd all made things throughout the winter, and now that the summer tourists were beginning to arrive, it was a good way to direct people to their places. The map was titled *Plain & Simple Living*, which Emma thought was putting it on rather thick. It had a picture of a horse and buggy in the bottom right corner, and it showed a produce stand at the end of the lane of each farm. Most were labeled with words such as "Birdhouses," "Quilts," "Popcorn," and "Jams."

"Ours should say 'Blankets.' We sell more of your knitted baby blankets than anything else."

"But we also sell the painted gourds your father and brothers make."

"And the quilted items from *Mamm*." Rachel was not one to quilt full-sized bed quilts, but she loved making table runners and crib quilts.

"Who pays for the ad?" Katie Ann asked as they walked across to the parking lot of the newspaper office.

"Everyone pitches in." In Emma's purse was an

envelope with the cash to pay for a full summer's worth of advertising. She couldn't have imagined doing this in Goshen, where the Chamber of Commerce tended to promote the Amish shops. Amish and *Englischers* alike benefited from the Amish tourist traffic. And although they preferred their privacy, these sales provided needed money to help them through the summer until the crops could be sold.

Once they arrived in Monte Vista, they realized selling the items they made were as crucial to the family budget as the crops they grew.

They walked to the front door and Katie Ann pointed out the rusted car that had passed them on the road.

"This is what he was in a hurry for? To get to the newspaper?"

"A handful of patience is worth more than a bushel of brains."

"Do you have a proverb for everything?" Katie Ann nudged Emma's shoulder, and they both laughed as they walked toward the door.

Forty-Three

As they pushed through the front door, Emma was surprised to see Abe walking out. He nodded, said good afternoon, and then rushed past them.

"He's in a hurry too," Katie Ann remarked.

"Perhaps he's late for something."

Inside, people filled out forms and such at a counter along a wall. As she and Katie Ann got in line to place their ad, Emma noticed Lewis Glick standing there, frowning as he jotted something down on a sheet of paper. She considered speaking to him, but then the line moved forward and she thought better of it. Lewis struck her as a private person. It would embarrass him if she called out to him.

Finally, Emma and Katie Ann were third in line. She'd never imagined such a rush of people at the newspaper office. Maybe there was a deadline to have things run in the paper, and it was today.

The man working behind this counter wore wire frame glasses and looked rather harried. Emma thought she heard him say something sharp to the man he was talking to, who responded in a soft voice. As the man accepted his change and turned away, he saw Emma and stopped suddenly.

"Mrs. Fisher."

"Hello, Douglas. How are you today?"

"Okay, I suppose." He shrugged as if there was no more to say, glanced at Katie Ann, and then without another word he hurried to the door.

"Who was that?"

"Someone Sam and a few others went to school with. He was driving the car outside—the one that passed us on the road."

Katie Ann wrinkled her nose, glanced around, and lowered her voice. "How do you know him?"

"Occasionally he stops by the produce stand. And it seems that he used to live out our way, though I can hardly remember."

The person in front of them seemed to take forever.

Katie Ann stepped to the right to look at a poster advertising an upcoming horse show.

Emma tapped her foot, impatient with the delay. Suddenly, she remembered the proverb she'd shared with Katie Ann. *A handful of patience is worth more than a bushel of brains.* She resisted the urge to laugh. She thought she was a patient person, but when it came to waiting in *Englisch* lines, maybe she wasn't.

She was thinking of all the things that needed to be done before dinner, and she had just tugged her purse up on her shoulder and turned toward Katie Ann when a loud explosion filled the air. It felt as though a giant hand pushed her forward.

271

Emma stumbled, hitting her shoulder hard against the counter, but she managed to right herself.

Glass shattered. People screamed. Smoke filled the air, making it difficult to breathe or see.

Emma's sole thought was of her granddaughter. Her mind stumbled, tried to recreate what had happened, and failed. Someone coughed and pushed past her. A woman was sitting in the middle of the floor, seemingly unaware that blood was running down her face. Emma moved to help her, but an older man reached her first. He pulled her to her feet and pointed toward the back exit. Turning toward Emma, he shouted something and began waving his arms, but she couldn't hear him or understand what he was trying to tell her.

The only thought that made any sense, the one pounding at her temples, was *Find Katie Ann. Get her out of here. Take her to safety.*

Tears streaked down her face as she blinked repeatedly, coughing from the smoke.

She felt the heat of fire and heard the crackle, but she couldn't make out which direction it came from.

And what of Katie Ann? Where was she? The girl had been standing beside her.

Emma pushed to the left and then to the right. A stream of tears sprang from her eyes as the smoke thickened. "Katie Ann!" The scream was a cry straight from the depths of her heart.

But somehow the words barely sounded in her ears, which was when she realized she wasn't hearing much at all.

Someone whose shirt was torn down the front seemed to be shouting for everyone to get out of the building, waving his arms and gesturing toward the back exit.

Emma turned the other direction. She wasn't leaving. Not until she'd found her granddaughter.

Katie Ann had been looking at a poster with horses on it. Emma turned in a circle, moved to the left, and realized it was the wrong direction. Nothing was there now but ruin. Moving back to the right, to the inner wall, she spied the poster of the horses, now flapping in a breeze that shouldn't have made its way into the building.

The poster over a counter of sorts.

Pushing aside debris, she dropped to her knees, digging with her hands until she'd uncovered the cubby hole beneath the counter. Huddled there, with her hands over her head and her eyes squeezed shut, was Katie Ann.

Forty-Four

Emma drew the girl to her. She could feel her granddaughter's trembling and sense her cries, though her ears still felt as if they were clogged with cotton.

Emma pulled on Katie Ann's apron, yanking it up so that it covered her mouth and nose. When she'd done the same with hers, she half guided, half carried Katie Ann toward where the front door should have been. It was gone. All that remained was the wall's frame, fire, and smoke.

Katie Ann froze, staring at the fire. Emma wrapped her arm around the girl, using all her strength to turn them in the opposite direction. Katie Ann felt like dead weight, as if the thought of moving was too terrifying to contemplate. Emma persisted, pulling Katie Ann with one arm, and with the other pushing their way through the debris to the back door.

An *Englischer* helped her down the steps and pointed to the far side of the parking area.

Katie Ann seemed frozen, but Emma coaxed the girl on, moving them out of the smoke, skirting the front of the building, and stumbling toward the parking area.

And then Emma glanced back, and like Lot's wife, she felt rooted to the spot, incapable of moving. She could only gape at the scene in front of her.

The cars nearest the front door had been pushed back, windows shattered. Another had tipped completely on its side.

Swiveling to look in the opposite direction, toward the parking area and away from the building, she saw a collection of Amish and *Englisch*, young and old, male and female. People sat in stunned silence in a small grassy area. Some had blood trickling down their faces. Others held arms or legs that had been sliced by flying glass.

She pushed Katie Ann farther away from the building, putting her own body between the girl and any additional explosions. They'd moved toward the back of the group when Katie Ann collapsed onto the grass and Emma sank beside her.

Suddenly aware of the scream of an emergency vehicle siren, she realized her hearing had returned. "Are you okay? Katie Ann. Look at me. Are you hurt anywhere?"

Katie Ann's eyes were wide in fright or shock or both. She didn't seem able to focus on any one thing. Emma put a hand on each side of her face and forced the girl's gaze to lock with her own.

"Katie Ann. We're fine. We're safe here. Now tell me, are you hurt anywhere?"

For her answer, Katie Ann threw herself into her grandmother's arms, sobbing and shivering and babbling about the explosion and the smoke and asking if Emma had seen the woman with glass pebbled across her face. Never completing a sentence before she began another, words tumbling over one another, it seemed her thoughts were attempting to come to terms with what had happened.

Then she grew silent, huddled there in Emma's arms, trembling so hard her teeth were knocking together.

Katie Ann didn't speak. She didn't answer any of Emma's questions, and her silence frightened Emma more than her incoherent cries had.

Emergency workers began to spread out through the crowd, handing out blankets and bottles of water, moving patients who could walk to a triage center set up in the adjacent parking lot.

A middle-aged woman wearing a paramedic's vest crouched down in front of them.

"Is she hurt?"

"Not that I can tell, but she makes no sense, and she won't answer my questions."

The woman shone a small light into Katie Ann's eyes. "She's in shock."

She pointed to a grassy section adjacent to the parking area. "Help me get her to the triage site."

Though it was only thirty feet away, to Emma it seemed like miles.

The middle-aged woman handed them off to a nurse, who quickly slapped a blood pressure cuff on Katie Ann's arm. "We need to lay her down. Can you hear me, honey?"

"Her name is Katie Ann."

"Katie Ann, can you tell me how you're doing?"

Emma put her hand across Katie Ann's forehead and found her skin to be cool and clammy.

"What's wrong with her? The other woman said she's in shock."

"Her blood pressure is very low and her heartbeat is rapid." The nurse pulled a thin blanket from the tub of supplies next to them and placed it over Katie Ann, urging her to lie back in the grass and doing a cursory exam as she tucked it around her. "She doesn't seem to be bleeding anywhere, but the body can go into shock for emotional reasons as well as physical ones."

"Is that why she's shaking so?"

"Yes. Make sure you keep the blanket on her. That will help stabilize her body temperature."

"I will."

Focusing on her granddaughter, Emma said, "I'm here, Katie Ann. We're all right." Under the blanket, she squeezed the girl's hand as her heart cried out to God. *Help her, Lord. Help her. Please help her.*

The nurse raised Katie Ann's feet, placing them on top of a Styrofoam block.

"Let's give her a few minutes. I want you to stay right here beside her and call me if you notice any change in her condition."

"*Ya.*"

"What's your name?"

"Emma." She swiped at the tears running down her face. "Emma Fisher. I'm Katie Ann's grandmother."

"You're doing great, Emma. Katie Ann is going to be fine. I need to check on some other patients, but I won't go far, and I'll be back in a few minutes. Okay?"

"Okay."

Emma couldn't have said how much time passed after that. She sat with Katie Ann, keeping the blanket wrapped around her tightly, clutching her hand, and praying. The nurse returned twice to take her blood pressure. The second time, she patted Emma's arm. "She's improving. Let's give her a few more minutes. We'll send her to the hospital to be examined after we've transferred the more critically injured."

Katie Ann's eyes had been closed, though Emma didn't think she was asleep. She seemed intent to shut out the chaos around her, and who could blame her for that?

In the distance, Emma saw buggies and cars

piling up down the street. Police had blocked off the area and weren't allowing anyone through.

The blaze seemed to have been extinguished, though the firemen kept pouring water on the building. Was that Sam on the top of a ladder, holding a hose? She thought it was, and the sight calmed her.

Another ambulance arrived. When paramedics helped two men up into the back of the vehicle, Emma saw one was Lewis, holding a piece of gauze to his forehead. Next to him was Abe, with a bloody bandage wrapped around his right arm.

She wanted to call out to them but didn't dare leave Katie Ann.

Someone handed her a bottle of water, and she realized it was Douglas Rae, the young man who had passed them on the road and said hello as he was leaving the newspaper office.

"What . . . what happened, Douglas? Do you know?"

"Only that it was an explosion. Would you like another bottle of water?"

But Katie Ann's eyes were still closed.

"I don't think so."

"Is she okay?" Douglas asked.

"*Ya.* She's going to be fine. She's shook up, is all."

"Who wouldn't be? Well, I guess I better hand out the rest of these." He made his way through those who were hurt and those, like Emma, who couldn't leave while people they loved were being attended.

Emma twined her fingers with Katie Ann's and continued to pray.

Forty-Five

Henry squatted down in front of Emma.

When she glanced up, her mouth opened in a small *o*, and then she threw her arms around his neck, nearly toppling them both over. He patted her shoulder, giving her a minute to calm her emotions as he thanked God she was okay.

Finally, she sat back and wiped the tears under her eyes, which only succeeded in spreading more soot across her face. "How did you get past the barricade? I thought they had the road blocked off. What are you doing here?"

"I was in the newspaper office when it happened."

"You were? Where? I don't . . . I don't remember seeing you."

"I was meeting with a reporter in a back office."

"You're okay?"

"I'm fine. I've been checking those who are injured to see if I can be of any help."

"Oh."

"It looks as if someone has already attended to Katie Ann." Indeed, it looked as if the girl was sleeping, which when he thought about it, was rather odd given their situation. "Is she okay?"

"Shock. Some low blood pressure problem. They want to transfer her to the hospital, but they're taking the injured first."

"Sounds as if the transfer would be precautionary."

"So I should let them?"

"*Ya*, Emma. Let the doctors look at her."

"But—"

"I know you want her home. I know you want—" He waved his hand to encompass the chaotic scene before them. "I know you want to take her away from this, but it's important that she have proper medical care."

Emma nodded. "Was anyone . . . was anyone killed?"

"Not that I've heard. *Gotte* was watching over us, for sure and certain. Several people were cut up badly. One employee of the paper broke her leg when she was thrown away from the blast. The editor was being checked for a heart condition."

"Who would do this, Henry? And when is it going to stop?"

He didn't even pretend to have an answer for that.

The nurse showed up, checked on Katie Ann, and said they were ready to move her.

"I will see to your horse and buggy, Emma. Go with her."

Emma smiled her thanks and shrugged her purse over her right shoulder. For some reason

282

that motion, something about the way she did that, jogged a memory in Henry's mind. The purse was made of quilted fabric and covered in a busy pattern. It was burned in parts and covered in soot. How had she managed to keep hold of it?

They had begun moving away. Katie Ann was now on a gurney, with two paramedics transporting her. Emma was following in their wake when she turned to him and called out. "Please call Clyde."

"Of course."

"Could you . . . could you come to the hospital with him?"

"Nothing would keep me away."

The look of relief that swept her features humbled him. He had very little wisdom to offer in a situation like this. The entire community was traumatized, having been hit too often in too short a time span. They, like Katie Ann, were in a state of shock.

Nothing he could say would help in any way, but he could pray. He could sit with those who were injured and try to reassure those whose relatives had been hurt. He could lead them, not because of any innate ability within himself, but because that was the task God had given him so many years ago.

Two hours later, Henry sat next to Emma in a waiting room while Katie Ann was still being evaluated in the ER. The place was filled with people from Monte Vista, including Clyde and his family, though the hospital itself was in Alamosa. Fortunately, news reporters were barred from this area of the building, which was helpful. They sorely needed a quiet space where they could wait together for news of their loved ones.

A shared tragedy.

Englisch and Amish sitting together, waiting together, hurting together.

He saw Meg Allen the moment she peered into the room. Her gaze swept left to right and then settled on him. She was across the room and in front of them before Emma noticed the woman had arrived.

"Mrs. Fisher. I'm sorry to hear about your daughter."

"Granddaughter."

"Your granddaughter. How is she?"

"The same. Still sleeping. The doctors assured us that with rest and fluids, she should be alert soon. I've never seen anything like it."

"Shock presents in different ways for different people." Meg glanced around the room.

Some people held open magazines but didn't turn the pages. Others stared at cell phones. A few spoke in low voices.

"Henry, I need to talk to you—in private."

"I'd rather not leave Emma."

Meg studied the two of them a moment.

Nodding, she stood, walked to the nurse's station, and spoke with a person Henry thought could be in charge. Meg pointed down the hall, but the nurse shook her head. Meg reached across the counter, picked up the handset to the phone, and held it out to her. The nurse sighed—Henry could see that from where he sat—and dialed a number.

"What could she possibly want with you, Henry?"

"She thinks I know something, but I don't."

The nurse hung up the phone and nodded curtly. Meg made her way back to them. "There's a small private room down the hall for doctor-patient consults. The nurse graciously said we could use it."

Henry felt his right eyebrow—what hadn't been singed completely off—go up, and Meg smiled. Perhaps that smile did more to ease the worry in his heart than any other thing since they'd arrived.

"Mrs. Fisher—"

"Emma."

"Emma, it would be helpful if you'd join us."

Emma told Clyde where she was going in case there was news about Katie Ann, and within minutes they found themselves sitting in a small room, probably no larger than eight feet by ten, being briefed on what had happened at the *Monte Vista Gazette.*

Forty-Six

The incendiary device was placed inside the front door, which is why the front exit was blocked."

"Was anyone killed?" Emma asked.

"No. We got lucky on that count. Sixteen were injured. Of those, five received treatment on site and were released. Eleven were transferred here to the hospital. Doctors say all are expected to make a full recovery."

"Even Katie Ann."

"Yes."

A doctor had already told them that, but Emma blew out a sigh of relief, and Henry reached over to squeeze her hand.

It was good news to hear again.

"So why this private meeting?" Henry asked.

"I need you to tell me what happened."

"I wish I could, but truthfully I saw very little. I was in the back office with one of the reporters. He wanted to do a piece on the recent arson incidents and called asking me to provide the Amish perspective."

"Which you were willing to do?"

Henry shrugged. "Better they bother me than our families who are busy putting in their crops. This whole thing has been quite the disruption, as I'm sure you're aware."

Meg started to respond to that, clamped her mouth shut, and then turned to Emma.

"How much do you remember?"

"Not a lot."

"Anything might be helpful. Even the names of people you saw inside the front office."

"Let's see." Emma rubbed her forehead with the tips of her fingers. "Lewis Glick was filling out a form to my left, as I was facing the counter."

Meg pulled out her notepad and jotted something down.

"Katie Ann was to my right, of course. Oh, Douglas Rae was at the front of the line. He spoke to me as he left."

"He's Amish?"

"*Nein. Englisch.* Has lived in Monte Vista some years."

Henry nodded. "He visits our shops now and then. Quiet, but not unfriendly."

"All right. Who else?"

"Another person in line between us and the counter . . . no, two people I think. I don't know their names. And there were employees moving back and forth behind the counter. I guess you'd have a record of those."

"I do."

"Oh, and Abe Graber was there."

Meg glanced at Henry, who shrugged. He didn't believe for a second that Abe was involved in this. In fact, the man had suffered a few cuts

287

himself. No need to remind Meg of that. She would have a list of each person treated.

"He seemed to be in a hurry when he left. Said hello, but nothing more."

"Anyone else? Anything at all that you recall from the moments before the blast?"

"*Nein*. Not that I can remember. Katie Ann had seen a poster on the wall about horses, over to the right of where we were standing. She walked over to read it when . . . when the bomb went off. That's where I found her—under a counter, huddled there, unable to speak or move at all."

"All right. Thank you, Emma. Every piece of information is helpful, and I appreciate your walking back through such a traumatic time with me."

Henry thought she'd leave then, but instead she turned to him and said, "Tell me what you saw."

"Very little. The reporter had finished asking me questions. The editor stopped in and thanked me for coming. She said she would be sure I received a copy of the article. I'd stepped out of their office, walked down the hall, and was standing in the doorway to the main room when I heard what sounded like a truck backfiring—only much louder."

"That would have been the explosion."

"Glass shattered, and smoke filled the room quickly. The reporter next to me screamed. He'd been hit in a couple of places by pieces of glass."

He pointed to his right shoulder and the right side of his face. "I led him out the back exit. By then the sprinklers had come on and the place was a real madhouse."

"And what did you see once you were outside?"

"Honestly, it was so chaotic that I don't remember what I saw. It was a full thirty minutes before I stumbled on Emma and Katie Ann. I didn't realize they were there . . . " Something snagged at the back of his mind. He reached for it, but it was like trying to see a falling star someone else pointed out to you—by the time you turned your head, it was gone.

Meg reached into a messenger bag she'd been carrying and retrieved a few sheets of blank paper—a larger size like Henry used before—and three finely sharpened pencils. She sat it all on the table in front of him. "I want you to draw for me."

"Draw?"

"Do your thing, Henry. Draw what happened at the newspaper."

Forty-Seven

Part of Emma's attention was on the door, waiting for someone to come in and update her. Perhaps Clyde or Rachel would rush into the room to tell her Katie Ann was awake. She needed to hear that Katie Ann was fine. Her heart longed for the words, "She's alert and talking. She's ready to go home. She's asking for you."

Another part of her attention had been listening to Henry's account of what he'd seen and trying to square it with her own. And now, after Meg's request, Emma understood that Henry needed a few moments to make his decision.

"Some of what Henry says makes sense, but other bits don't."

"Such as?"

"I'm sure the sprinklers didn't come on that quickly. Maybe they should have, but I remember coughing from the smoke and looking around, searching the room for Katie Ann. They weren't on then."

"She could be right. My memory has never been very good."

"Your conscious memory might be prone to error," Meg admitted. "But your subconscious can accurately provide every detail. Right?"

Of course she was right. Emma knew it.

Meg Allen knew it. Henry certainly knew it.

As far as she could remember, he'd never actually drawn in front of anyone else.

Well, as far as she could remember, he'd only used his ability twice—once with the girl in Goshen and once to draw Vernon's place. But even as that thought crossed her mind, she knew it wasn't right. When he was first injured, he must have drawn more freely. Before he learned to be frightened by his strange and unaccountable gift. Only later did he make the decision to lock away that part of himself.

"Please draw what you saw in the newspaper office, Henry. It could be important. I have a feeling we're close to breaking this case open, and I want to do it before anyone else is hurt."

"You want me to draw now?" he asked.

"Yes, now. The first few hours after an incident are the most important."

"But what could I possibly have seen?"

"We can't know until you draw it."

Henry glanced at Emma, a *v* forming between his eyes. It wasn't something he wanted to do, that much was obvious. But perhaps it was something he should do.

" 'Whether you eat or drink or whatever you do, do it all for the glory of God.' " The verse jumped unbidden from Emma's heart to her lips. "This could make a difference, Henry. If we can catch this person, we can go back to our Plain life. If we don't, we're going to be constantly plagued by fear and suspicion."

"I'm not sure the last drawing really did any *gut*," Henry muttered, but he picked up the pencil, grabbed a stack of magazines to place under the paper, and began to draw.

Years earlier, when the grandchildren were young, Emma had found a book at the five and dime store. It wasn't a coloring book exactly. The pages, when you first looked at them, appeared to be blank. But if you dipped a small paint brush in water and swept it back and forth across the page, a picture emerged. The children never tired of it, and she'd had to limit them to one sheet a day or they would have gone through the entire book in an afternoon.

Watching Henry draw reminded her of that book.

He didn't so much put images on the paper, as he revealed what was there, what was in his subconscious, she supposed. What had been hidden, God made plain through the strange gift Henry had been given.

Forty-five minutes later he was finished.

No one had spoken.

Henry had drawn without stopping, without thinking. There was apparently no need for him to erase, to pause and consider, or to throw the sheet away and start over. It was a miracle, this gift, and Emma felt a sudden tenderness for her bishop, for her friend. What a thing to carry around each day. What an amazing gift. And burden—she could see how it must be that too.

Finally, he put his pencil on the table, returned the magazines to the stack, and waited.

Three drawings of photographic quality stared back at them. The first was the front room of the office before the bomb went off. The second was immediately after the explosion. And the third was the scene he must have witnessed when he exited the building.

Emma was the first to speak. "That's my purse."

She tapped drawing number one. In it, she'd turned away, turned toward Katie Ann, who was standing facing the posters. All he had caught of Emma was the back of her dress and the purse slung over her right shoulder, its paisley pattern plain even in a pencil rendering.

"Huh. I guess I did know you were there, or a part of me did."

Meg was leaning forward, studying the drawing, her nose nearly on the paper. With a sigh, she sat back, "This box. This was it."

The item she was referring to was on the floor next to the front door, as if someone had set it down and forgotten it. Wrapped in brown paper and tied with string, it looked like a package someone might prepare for mailing from home.

"How can you tell?" Emma asked.

"We know the initial flame was somewhere

293

near the front door, on the east side. If your dimensions are right, Henry, and I suspect they are, then the box is approximately the size of a shoe box. No doubt he put a timer in it."

"I'm not sure I understand," Henry said.

"Someone brought it in, acted as if they had business with the paper, and then set it by the door as they left. It was either set to go off at a preset time or it was remotely activated."

Written in bold black marker across the front of the box were the words

Monte Vista Gazette

Attention: Charles Silver

"Any idea who that is?" Emma asked Henry.

"*Ya*, he's the person I met with. The one who wrote the article about the arsonist that appeared in yesterday's paper. He'd planned a follow-up piece for next week."

"If someone had noticed the box, then they would have taken it to Mr. Silver. If that had happened while you were in his office, you'd probably both be dead."

Emma's heart thudded to a stop at those words. She'd never imagined a life without Henry Lapp. He'd been her friend, her bishop for years. Had she ever told him how much he meant to her?

Henry seemed unfazed by the revelation.

The second drawing showed the room seconds after the explosion, smoke filling the air, people scrambling for the exits, glass littering the floor.

He'd even caught flames as they were being extinguished by the sprinklers.

"So they did come on," Emma said. "I don't even remember my clothes being wet."

"They came on, *ya*. But maybe not as early as I thought. Must have taken thirty seconds or so, or those flames would have never reached that height."

Meg was staring at the third drawing. She picked it up, brought it closer to her eyes, and then held it at arm's length.

Emma's voice caught in her throat, as Henry's third and final drawing seemed to capture the reaction of those who had been caught in the explosion.

Someone helping an older man across the lawn.

A mother and children staring up at the building, eyes wide and mouths open.

People in the distance running toward the fire.

And in the far right corner, three men huddled together underneath the shade of a large elm tree—Abe Graber, Lewis Glick, and Douglas Rae.

"What can you tell me about these three?" Meg asked, tapping the sheet of paper.

"All good men," Henry assured her. "Abe is a minister in our church. You went to his house and questioned him about his brother Alvin. He and his wife have seven children."

"Lot of kids."

"Not for Amish folk," Emma reminded her. "Pretty normal for us."

"Like many Amish families, they have help from family. And his sister-in-law, Franey, is there too."

"Are they happy here in Monte Vista?"

"I suppose. Their home is in worse condition than the one they had in Goshen, but Abe seems satisfied enough."

Emma started to mention that Abe was complaining just the week before about the difficulty of the farming and the size of his home. But was that relevant? Surely not. Everyone complained now and then.

"And this man?"

"*Ya*, that's Lewis Glick. He's the newest member of our group."

"As I said, he was filling out some form when I saw him," Emma said. She picked up the first drawing and pointed to him.

"Any idea what type of form?" Meg asked.

Henry shifted uncomfortably in his seat. Emma thought he wouldn't answer. He stared at the floor a minute before raising his eyes to look at Meg.

"I can't say for sure. Lewis keeps to himself. He's the quiet sort, as many Amish men are. He hasn't been particularly happy here. Adjusting to Colorado has been difficult."

"So why did he move?"

"Same reason as most of us. Felt crowded with the growth in Lancaster. And the tourists. That sort of thing."

"All right. Tell me what you know about this man."

Both Emma and Henry knew Douglas Rae, but only by name and because he'd stopped at their homes a few times to purchase items.

"I can't tell you anything specific about him." Henry stroked his fingers through his beard.

Looking at the third drawing, there was no denying that the three men were in a heated discussion. What could have been that important? What could they have been arguing about in the middle of an explosion?

Before Emma could ask what it all meant, there was a soft knock on the door, and then Katie Ann's doctor stepped into the room.

Forty-Eight

Henry's heart thumped at the sight of Katie Ann's doctor.

"Are you Mrs. Fisher? Katie Ann's grand-mother?"

"I am."

Henry wasn't sure if she realized she had reached for his hand and was clutching it as if he were her lifeline in a storm-tossed sea.

"I'd like to have a word with you alone, please."

"Henry is family," she said, "and Ms. Allen . . . I suppose she'll receive all of the reports anyway."

The doctor hesitated, and then he stepped into the room.

"I've already told her parents this, but I know you're the one who came in with your grand-daughter. Katie Ann is awake and she's doing well."

"Praise the Lord." Emma closed her eyes, the worry and fatigue of the last several hours vanishing in an instant. "What a relief. I can't thank you enough."

The doctor smiled. Henry wondered how many times he had delivered news that was met with tears. His was a job Henry didn't covet one bit, but he was thankful to God that the man had been able to help Katie Ann. In fact, Henry didn't realize until that moment how much Katie Ann meant to him. She was more than a member of his congregation. She was like the granddaughter he'd never had.

"Her father is signing release papers now."

"She can go home?"

"Katie Ann doesn't need us anymore." He didn't have to look down at the clipboard to remember her name. Henry's opinion of the man went up another notch. "I would rather she take it easy the next forty-eight hours, though."

He was to the door when he turned and said, "Her first words on waking were about your horse—Cinnamon?"

"*Ya*. She's our buggy mare, and Katie Ann treats her like a pet."

"Quite the girl you have there."

"That she is."

The doctor left the room. Emma stood, pulling her purse over her shoulder, and Meg scooped up the drawings.

"I'm going to see her, Henry. Join us when you're done here." She practically skipped out of the room.

Meg shot him an amused look.

"What?"

"When are you going to tell her?"

"Tell her?"

"How you feel, Henry."

299

His mouth must have fallen open, and he could feel his eyebrows arch. They were starting to itch where they'd been singed.

Meg actually laughed.

"It's that obvious?"

"To anyone with eyes."

"We've been friends a long time. Her late husband was my best friend."

"How long since he died?"

"Four years. I wasn't sure . . . well, I wasn't sure it was long enough, and honestly, I've only just realized how much she means to me."

Meg's expression turned somber. "These types of situations can do that. They can cause you to reassess your feelings and bring life into a sharp, black-and-white focus. May I ask you a question?"

Henry nodded, surprised he was having such a personal conversation with an *Englisch* woman and an arson investigator to boot.

"How old are you?"

"Sixty-four."

"And Emma?"

"Sixty."

"I'm not saying you're old, because you're not. Sixty is the new forty, or so they tell us."

"In youth we learn, in age we understand."

"Yeah. That pretty much sums it up." Meg smiled as she stuffed the drawings into her messenger bag. "But don't wait too long. None of us is guaranteed tomorrow."

They walked out into the hall together. From where they stood, Henry could see into the waiting room, which was still full of families waiting to see their loved ones.

"What will you do with the drawings?" he asked.

"Follow the thread, like I would do with any type of evidence."

Now she considered his drawings evidence?

"How will you do that?"

"I'll start with background checks. There has to be a connection between our arsonist and Vernon Frey. That's where all this started, and it's the key."

"I can't imagine what the connection would be."

"Our research people are very good. If there's a connection, we'll find it. In the meantime, I'll interview the three men in your last drawing. It's bizarre for them to appear so preoccupied with something else while a building was being consumed by flames right before their eyes."

They said good night, and Henry watched her walk away.

He still didn't believe anyone in his congregation was involved in the arson events, but he had to admit that Abe, Lewis, and Douglas knew something, and perhaps, as Meg suggested, something that seemed minor would lead them to the doorstep of a killer.

Forty-Nine

It had been foolish to stay and watch the explosion, but how could he resist? The people of Monte Vista had been responsible for the disastrous course of his life. Their choices and decisions and selfishness had left him very nearly orphaned.

Besides, it had been a huge crowd. He'd hit at a good time.

The chances that anyone would figure out he was the responsible party were somewhere in the eight percent range as nearly as he could calculate. Even if surveillance tapes had survived, which he doubted, they would show nothing other than a room full of people conducting business with the local newspaper.

He didn't go directly home. Instead, he stopped by the hospital to check on folks. That was a nice touch. The arson investigator might have expected him to hang around a blaze—yes, he'd read those statistics—but she would not expect him to show up in the waiting room of a hospital. It was all he could do to keep from giggling as people speculated about who the guilty party might be. He had them all running in circles.

After he'd left the hospital, he'd grabbed a bite to eat. The chance of finding food at home was slim to none. The more his mother drank, the less she seemed to eat. One day she would disappear right before his eyes, and he couldn't say he would miss her. Yes, she was his mother, but he couldn't remember the last time she'd offered a kind word or deed. Theirs was not that type of family. Night was falling by the time he walked into his house, and she immediately began lobbing questions his way.

"Where have you been?"

"Did you find a job?"

"Where do you go all day?"

He ignored her questions and tried not to look left or right as he made his way through the living room. The place disgusted him. Memories of their last home were emblazoned on his mind. They stood in stark contrast to the room he walked through, the hall, and his pitiful excuse for a bedroom. When he opened the door, it banged into the twin bed. He shut it quickly, pulled down the shade, and collapsed on top of the mattress.

He spent the next few minutes allowing his mind to drift back over the details of the day.

Overall, he'd have to say it had been a rousing success.

But now it was time to get back on his schedule. He reached under the mattress and pulled out the sheet of paper listing his five targets. Three down and two to go. Plus bonus points for the newspaper. Time to get busy.

After all, he wasn't done exacting his revenge.

Fifty

Because of the explosion and subsequent injuries, the workday at Henry's house was postponed a week, which suited him fine. He looked forward to some time at home tending to his garden, training Lexi, and praying for his congregation. Plus, he needed to find homes for the kittens in the barn. They were growing faster than the crops in the fields.

The day after the explosion passed quickly, and he had just sat down to dinner when Lexi began to bark and turn in circles.

He glanced out the window and saw a buggy making its way down the drive. "Didn't hear them again. *Gut* thing I have you to let me know when someone's here." He scratched Lexi behind her ears and opened the door to find Elmer stepping out of his buggy.

"Elmer."

"Henry."

"Would you like to come in?"

"Best not. I have some work still to do at home."

"Oh. All right." Henry stepped out on the front porch and waited, knowing the man would get to what was on his mind eventually. Elmer was in his forties, with five children and a constantly worried expression.

"Wanted to let you know that we appreciate all you've done for us, but Grace and I believe it's time for a change."

"Change?"

"*Ya.* We heard Kentucky has a nice community." Elmer jerked his hat off his head, twirled it in his hands, and stared at it instead of meeting the gaze of his bishop.

"Kentucky?"

"Truth is, I've already talked to a real estate agent. The sign went up today."

"You're moving?"

Elmer nodded, but seemed hesitant to say more. The silence lengthened, became more uncomfortable, and then he cleared his throat and said, "I put Grace and the kids on the bus today— all except Albert, who will help me load our things into a moving van. Grace's sister moved to Marion a few years ago. Says it's *gut* farming land and that we're welcome to stay with them until we can purchase a place."

Henry moved forward, sat down on his front step, and waited.

After a few moments of silence, Elmer sat down beside him. Lexi had finished sniffing the newcomer and was attempting to catch one of the toads that lived under the porch.

"What's this about, Elmer?"

"I hardly know where to start."

"Try the first thing that comes to your mind."

305

"The last set of twins has been hard on Grace."

"No doubt five children require a lot of energy and attention, and I'm aware that your wife wasn't expecting the last set. She told me she thought her birthing years were over, but often *Gotte* has a different path for us than what we envision."

"Add to that how difficult it's been to pull in *gut* crops—"

"Last year was especially dry."

"And this year will be better. Yeah, I know. I've read the long-term forecasts too. The thing is, she misses her family."

Henry didn't interrupt. He waited, knowing that eventually Elmer would reveal the real reason for the sudden move. It was the reason he'd come—to confess to his bishop.

"The fires . . . well, they were the last straw."

"Grace is afraid?"

"She's nervous. Who wouldn't be? And yeah, I know we are to have faith, but Vernon had faith and he's dead. You had faith, and you no longer have a workshop. Abe and Lewis had faith, but now one has seven stitches and the other near a dozen."

"Having faith doesn't mean every aspect of our life will turn out fine."

Elmer stood, slapped his hat against his pant leg, and for the first time since he'd arrived looked directly at Henry. "Neither does it mean we are to live in fear. Jesus told the disciples to shake off the dust of a place where they're not welcome."

"I can see you've given this a lot of thought, and that you've spent time in *Gotte*'s Word looking for answers. I can't say as I agree with your conclusions, but I respect your decision."

"*Danki.*"

"Our congregation will keep your family in our prayers. You'll write to me once you get settled?"

"*Ya.* Of course." A look of relief passed over Elmer's face. Had he expected Henry to reprimand him? He couldn't fault the man for putting his family's safety first. And he wouldn't second-guess something Elmer had obviously spent a good amount of time agonizing over.

Henry cleared his throat and changed the subject. "Since there's no service Sunday, I'll be eating at the Fishers' place. I'm sure Emma would like you to join us."

"I'd be happy to."

"Excellent. Bring Albert, of course. Growing boys can be difficult to feed."

"I never was any use in a kitchen, and Albert is even worse. We'll be eating sandwiches until we join the family in Kentucky, which will hopefully be next week."

"I will pray that you have safe travels, sell your land here quickly, and receive a *gut* price." Henry clapped the man on the shoulder.

Elmer nodded, embarrassed, and mumbled, "We'll see you Sunday, then."

As Elmer drove away, Henry realized he needed to spend more time in prayer for his congregation. It wasn't unusual for a family to leave abruptly. Instead of arguing about a decision made by a group, often a man would say to his wife, "I heard land is inexpensive in Ohio," or "Read in the *Budget* last week that the community in Maine needs more families." It was the way things were done.

Don't agree with the use of tractors in Oklahoma? Move to Indiana.

Have strong opinions that solar energy should be allowed? Move to Pennsylvania.

Henry wasn't concerned that a family had decided to leave their fellowship. He was concerned that their reasons were driven by fear.

And beneath that lay a more disturbing question. How many would they lose? Their community was small, even after he and the others from Goshen joined those already here. It was an understood fact that a community required a minimum of ten families to be able to offer the support a community needed. If they were to fall below that, then they'd all be selling their property.

They'd be scattered to the wind.

If that was God's will, then Henry would accept

it. But in his heart, he found it hard to believe God would lead them to Monte Vista only to have their community torn apart by someone bent on destruction.

Fifty-One

"You're hovering, *Mammi*."

"I have a right, Katie Ann. I found you huddled beneath a counter as the room burned around us. Must have taken a year off my life."

They were sitting on the front porch, shelling purple hull peas Clyde had picked up at the farmer's market in town. They often resorted to purchasing fresh food shipped in from areas farther south until their own garden came in, which wouldn't happen for at least another month.

"I still don't remember any of it," Katie Ann admitted.

"Perhaps that's for the best."

"I guess, but I'm tired of hanging around the house. I want to check on the horses."

"Your brothers can do that."

"They don't brush them down as well as I do. Silas is always in a hurry. Stephen and Thomas are even worse. Half the time they become distracted and never finish."

"You care about the horses and so are very careful with their grooming. Probably it's okay for them to receive a little less attention for a day or two."

"Less attention? What if you had to sleep with tangles in your hair or walk around with a pebble caught up under your toenail?"

Rachel walked out onto the front porch, a cup of coffee in her left hand and a book in her right.

"Is my *doschder* complaining again? Surely she doesn't mind helping her grandmother." Rachel's voice was teasing, and she stopped next to Katie Ann's chair long enough to plant a kiss on top of her head.

"You all treat me like a fresh egg."

"An egg?" Rachel plopped into a rocker and set it in motion. "Are you saying we put you on the shelf in a cool place?"

"*Nein*! As if I might crack . . . get it? An egg?" Katie Ann rolled her eyes, but she also laughed, and it did Emma's heart a world of good to hear that.

"Speaking of eggs, perhaps you could go and gather today's bounty."

"I thought that was Stephen's chore."

"It was until he and his brother ended up in an egg fight earlier this week."

"How did I miss that?"

"You were in the barn. Your *dat* had them clean out the coop as a punishment, but we both agree that perhaps they'd be better mucking stalls for their morning chore."

"I'll do anything that gets me off this porch." Katie Ann dumped the last of her shelled peas into the pail and bounced out of her chair, dusting off the front of her apron as she walked toward the chickens.

"I'm not sure what other quiet things I can find for her to do," Rachel said. "She nearly drove me crazy yesterday begging to work with the horses."

"She's usually *gut* about doing any chore you give her. It's probably normal for her to be a little restless, and the horses . . . well, they seem to provide a measure of calm for her."

"That they do. I have no idea what she will do besides help me now that she's out of school, but I'm pretty sure it will be something to do with animals."

"I'm glad she doesn't seem more upset about what happened." Emma shelled another handful of peas, and then she peered over her cheater glasses at her daughter-in-law.

"I like those glasses on you," Rachel said with a smile. "A very pretty blue frame."

"On sale at the grocer. I've grown used to wearing them when I read, but I never thought I'd need them to shell peas."

"Susan has a pair in every room because she's always losing them."

"Abigail keeps hers on a chain around her neck."

Quiet settled around them as Emma shelled the peas and Rachel sipped her coffee. They'd spent the morning cleaning house for Sunday's luncheon as well as preparing most of the meal— sliced ham, fresh bread, and creamy potato salad.

The peas Emma was shelling would round out the meal nicely. Their guests always brought dessert, though Emma had told Henry not to worry about it. She didn't expect an old widower to bake a pie.

"Henry will come tomorrow?"

"Said he'd be happy to."

"That's *gut*." Rachel ran her hand across the top of her book, something with angels' wings on the front of the cover. "I worry about him."

"We all do."

"You were there when he drew the pictures for the arson investigator?"

"I was."

"What was it like? I still can't imagine being able to do such a thing, never having been taught to draw at all, and then there's the fact that years and years have passed since he did it last. Before all this started, I mean."

Emma ran her thumb over the green shell she'd yet to split open.

"It's like watching a rose bloom." She glanced up at Rachel, smiled, and resumed shelling the peas. "When you first look at a rosebud, if you hadn't seen one before, you wouldn't guess it would open up into such a beautiful flower."

"So our bishop is like a beautiful flower?"

Emma laughed with her. "He would take exception to that description. Watching Henry draw . . . it was effortless for him. There was a look of complete concentration on his face, but he never hesitated, never backed up and erased something as you and I might. It was as if he allowed a portion of his mind to take over, and it merely did what came naturally."

"Like the rose blooms—naturally."

"Effortlessly."

"Well, it's an amazing thing," Rachel said. "I personally think it's quite a gift Henry has received."

"He's uncomfortable with the skill as well as the attention it brings him."

"But without it, Sam would probably still be sitting in an *Englisch* jail. Clyde said they had enough circumstantial evidence to keep him."

"And yet he wasn't involved. I'm sure of that."

"I agree."

"It's just as hard to believe that Abe or Lewis had anything to do with it."

Emma had told Rachel and Clyde everything. She'd long ago learned that she didn't feel comfortable protecting her children from the truth. They were adults—responsible and mature. The three of them raised the children together. They couldn't make good decisions about their family if they didn't share all the information they had.

Rachel stood, walked into the house, and returned with two glasses of lemonade.

"*Danki.*" The sweet-tart taste soothed Emma's

throat as well as her nerves. Why was she on edge? It was as if she was waiting for the arsonist to pop up out of the flower bed. "Surely Abe and Lewis didn't have anything to do with the fire, but they might have seen something they don't realize was important."

"Susan said they kept Abe in that station and questioned him for more than three hours."

"I wish she had called Henry."

"There was no need, according to her. They never threatened to arrest him."

"Which is a relief."

"What about this *Englischer* you spoke of? Douglas something?"

"Rae. His name is Douglas Rae. You've seen him. He stops by our produce stand occasionally."

"Does he drive a rusty old car?"

"Same person."

"I can't imagine him doing such a thing either. Fairly quiet man. Well, honestly, he seems more like a boy. Wears those T-shirts with words across the front."

Emma nodded. "Yesterday he had one that read *Keep Calm and Log Out.*"

"What in the world does that mean?"

"I have no idea."

The laughter lightened the mood, easing some of their fears. Katie Ann returned, looking at them as if they had gone a little crazy, and perhaps they had. But it was better than the

315

worry that weighed too heavily on Emma's heart. Seeing her granddaughter huddled beneath that counter, sitting beside her in the grass as the nurse checked and rechecked her blood pressure, and waiting in the hospital had driven home the truth that they lived in dangerous times.

Until the arsonist was caught—and Emma believed he would be caught—she planned to keep a close eye on her family. All of them. She'd spend more time on her knees too, because the only person who could truly guarantee their safety was the Lord.

Fifty-Two

Though Emma had told Henry not to trouble himself with preparing a dessert for the luncheon, he'd purchased fresh strawberries in town and brought them. He also brought several cartons of ice cream.

"You spoil our children," Clyde said as he passed the ice cream to the boys and told them to put it in the freezer.

"Without opening it!" Emma called out in reminder.

Henry knew the freezer was located in the mudroom and, like their refrigerator, operated with gas. Mainly they used it to store meat. Having ice cream made for a special occasion, which was one of the reasons he liked to bring it.

Lexi bounded behind the boys, ears flopping and tail wagging.

The morning was exactly what Henry needed. He enjoyed visiting everyone in his congregation, but he was particularly at home with Emma's family. In many ways, they seemed like an extension of his own. Maybe because he and Claire had enjoyed their company so many years ago. Clyde was a young man of twenty when Claire died. Their families had been intertwined for many years, drawing strength from one another, celebrating in each other's joys, and carrying each other's burdens.

They were about to gather for the luncheon when Elmer and Albert pulled into the lane.

"I'm glad they decided to come," Emma said.

Henry nodded in agreement. "I'll admit to being a little surprised. He seemed rather hesitant when I suggested it, but it's *gut* that he's joined us."

He'd explained the situation to Clyde and Emma and Rachel. They'd all wondered if James's episode at church the week before had something to do with the impending move. Of course, at the time, they hadn't known the family was considering moving. Now Grace and the other children were already in Kentucky. How quickly things changed.

They gathered together for prayer, and Henry reminded everyone to pray for the Bontrager family during this time of change. Elmer seemed more at ease now that he'd shared the fact that they were moving.

"We're going to miss you," Clyde said. "But don't worry about your place while you're waiting for it to sell. We can keep an eye on it."

"I'm thinking of leaving Albert here."

"Alone?" Emma glanced up from the sandwich she was about to bite into.

"I'm grown enough to handle it," Albert assured her.

"Well, you can handle the fields, but we'll make sure you have plenty of meals to eat."

"That's kind of you, Emma." Elmer ducked his head, and then he glanced up, smiling. "This is a *gut* community. We'll miss the friends we've made."

"Which is why we have circle letters," Rachel said. "I've already started one to Grace and passed it on. She should receive it by the end of the week."

Elmer seemed suddenly overcome by emotion. When he looked up, tears glistened in his eyes, but he only murmured, "*Danki.*"

The rest of the meal passed pleasantly, and soon all the children—even the teenagers and Albert—had abandoned the old folks for the ball field while the adults settled in chairs on the back porch. Katie Ann carried Lexi in her arms, and Henry laughed at the image of the dog smiling up at her. Could a dog smile? He'd have said no a month ago, but his opinion of such things was changing.

The adults enjoyed another glass of lemonade and the slower pace of Sunday. They spoke of summer, news from family, and laughed at the children as they swung the bat, ran the bases, and made leaping catches. Lexi dashed from person to person as if she were a part of the game.

"It's *gut* to see them play," Emma said.

An easy silence fell between the five of

319

them—Henry, Emma, Clyde, Rachel, and Elmer.

After a few moments, Elmer leaned forward, elbows braced on his knees, and cleared his throat. Henry knew instinctively that the man was about to reveal something weighing on his heart.

"You all have been *gut* to us. Henry, I couldn't have asked for a better bishop the last thirteen years. Clyde, you preach the Word with a sincerity that is rare." He held up a hand to stave off Clyde's protests. "I understand that you struggle with confidence, but it isn't confidence that touches peoples' hearts. It's the ability to speak simply, truthfully, and kindly that causes a person to listen, and you have that."

Henry sat back and crossed his arms. "You've been a valuable part of our community, Elmer. You and your family will be missed."

"We may not be the only family missed." He wiped a hand over his face. "It's not my place to share specifically what other people have said to me privately, but you need to know others are considering a move. We're simply the first ones to act on it."

"How many families are we talking about?" Clyde asked.

"That have spoken to me personally?" Elmer stared up at the sky, and Henry noticed him touching fingers to his thumb, counting. "Seven, I think. *Ya*. Seven."

"That can't be right," Rachel protested. "We only have—"

"Twenty-two," Henry said quietly. "That's one third."

"And you're sure about this?" Clyde's right leg began to jiggle.

"*Ya.*"

"How serious are they?"

"Everyone who spoke to me has already written to family, inquiring about land or jobs."

"Yet no one has come to me." Henry felt more hurt than angry.

"I'm sure they would eventually," Emma said.

"Once they've made their decision, but by then it's too late."

"They understand how much you're dealing with right now, Henry. Or so they have said to me. No one wants to add to your burden."

"But how can I help or guide if I don't know?"

For a moment, maybe two, his answer hung in the air between them.

Clyde said, "And this is all because of the fires?"

"In some cases that's the primary reason. No one likes to feel vulnerable."

"But they haven't been, not personally." Rachel was worrying her thumbnail between her front teeth, but then she clasped both hands in her lap. "No one has threatened them personally."

"When one is in danger, we all feel unsafe."

"But no one is in danger," Rachel insisted. "Their homes aren't going to spontaneously combust, and this person, this arsonist, hasn't attacked—"

"Vernon's dead, Rachel. The job site was hit, and that's where many of our young men work. Henry, your workshop was burned to the ground. For many folks, the newspaper office was the last straw."

They were quiet until Clyde said, "I thought that . . . well, I'd hoped last Sunday's worship service helped."

"It did, I believe. The *gut* word you shared helped those who are determined to stay feel safer, more confident."

"But those who are considering leaving . . . "

"People will hear what they want and apply Scripture in a way that coincides with their plans." Henry felt a sinking sensation from his chest to the pit of his stomach. "It's a natural enough thing to do. If they were already planning on leaving, then they heard in your words assurance that *Gotte* would lead their way."

"Exactly." Elmer shook his head. He looked directly at Henry and said, "I'm sorry I didn't tell you sooner. I didn't feel I should betray their confidence, but at the same time . . . you need to know."

"*Ya*, I do, and *danki* for telling me."

Apparently convinced that it was better for the

bishop to know, Elmer rattled off the names of several families, which Henry jotted down.

"What will you do?"

"First, I'll pray as to how *Gotte* would have me handle this turn of events. Then I'll begin visiting each family individually."

Clyde was shaking his head before he finished speaking. "You don't have time to do that, Henry."

"Of course I do. I have no workshop, so I actually have plenty of time."

"I'm sorry," Elmer said. "You don't deserve this."

"Trouble isn't something we deserve." He reached out and clapped his friend on the back. "It's a part of this life. I would ask that you all pray for me, and for our community. Pray that we will know *Gotte's wille* and how we should proceed."

Fifty-Three

Emma was a little surprised Henry stayed as late as he did. Plainly, what Elmer shared had disturbed him.

Rachel was inside putting the children to bed.

Clyde was making his final walk-through in the barn, something he'd done with his father for years, and now he continued the tradition. *You'll sleep better knowing everything's bedded down for the night—animals and children.* Emma was surprised the memory of her husband's words didn't bring the usual ache. Perhaps she was healing after all. Not that her life would ever be whole again, but perhaps the shadow of grief was lifting.

She walked with Henry out to his buggy.

He lifted Lexi up, placed her in the buggy, and the dog collapsed on the seat.

"The children wore her out."

"A *gut* thing, I can assure you."

"I'm glad you have her, Henry. I've never liked the thought of your living alone."

He seemed about to answer, but instead he turned, rested his back against the side of the buggy, and stared up at the splash of stars adorning the night sky.

"This is a *gut* place, Emma. If it is *Gotte's wille*

324

that we leave, then I won't argue with that, but it is, it has been, a *gut* place."

"Let's not talk about us leaving."

"You're committed to staying?"

"Of course I am. This is my home."

"I wish more felt as you do."

"Perhaps you're reading too much into this, Henry."

"How so?"

"Communities change. You know as well as I do it's not unusual for things to shift and then settle again."

"*Ya.* When there's been a change in the *Ordnung* that is divisive." Henry frowned, as if the memory hurt him.

"I heard some of the communities in Pennsylvania lost thirty percent of their families when they voted to allow solar panels for home use, but within the year they'd gained back double that number."

"I doubt families will be flocking to the San Luis Valley, where the growing season is so short and an arsonist stalks us."

It was actually painful for Emma to hear such defeat in his voice. Maybe that was why she reached out, put her hand on his arm, and said, "Henry, we're not all leaving. You can count on my family. We're staying."

Perhaps it was owing to his being the bishop, needing to put a big distance between himself and even a hint of impropriety, but normally Henry would nod, thank her, and step away, increasing the distance between them. She'd noticed it before, especially with the widows. It had always made her smile, which was why she teased him about the women who would happily marry him. She knew how they talked. You'd think it was a badge of honor the way they went on about having an eligible bishop in their midst.

Maybe it was the stars or the comfortable day they'd spent together. Maybe it was that Henry Lapp occasionally needed encouragement like any other man, like any other person. Instead of stepping away, he covered her hand with his own. His warm fingers clasping hers sent a jolt of affection through her. Emma had never considered herself lonely. She was surrounded by family, and she'd had a good life with George.

Her life was rich and full and blessed.

She was satisfied. Wasn't she?

Standing under the Milky Way, with Henry clasping her hand, she realized her life could be more, that she didn't have to spend the rest of it alone, that God had meant for them to draw comfort from one another.

As if sensing the direction of her thoughts, Henry leaned toward her and planted a kiss on her cheek. A brotherly gesture if ever there was one. So why did her heart begin pounding as if she'd run to the barn?

He climbed into the buggy, but before he shut the door, he said, "I'd hoped to spend the rest of my days here."

"And perhaps we will. Let's not give up yet."

"You're a *gut* woman, Emma."

She stepped back, suddenly embarrassed. "Get on with you, Henry. Your pup is asleep and your horse is beginning to nod."

He flashed her a smile, and then he was gone.

Emma stood there, listening to the *clip-clop* of Oreo's hooves long after the buggy had disappeared into the darkness.

Instead of heading back inside, she walked to the pasture fence. Folding her arms across the top and resting her chin on her arms, she felt like a girl again. The breeze cooled the sweat on her neck. A night heron called to its mate. Frogs croaked and crickets chirped and a calf cried out for its mother. Emma knew she should follow her own advice, go to bed, and get some much-needed sleep.

But instead she stood at the fence, staring up at a star-spangled sky.

Fifty-Four

Henry was working in his vegetable garden when Meg pulled into his drive. She plodded past the house, never once smiling at Lexi, who danced at her feet.

"Doesn't look as if you're here to tell me you caught the arsonist."

"Not only have I not caught him, but your people are impeding my investigation."

"Why don't we go to the porch? I'll fetch us some lemonade."

"I don't have time for either of those things."

Henry stood and brushed his hands against his trousers to knock off the dirt.

"What can I do?"

"You can begin by helping me find Abe Graber."

"Find him—"

"He's not home, Henry. His wife says he's been gone since yesterday morning, but she claims she doesn't know where he is. She looked worried too. I've had a man staked out at his place, and unless he's hiding in the barn, he's not there."

"I'm sure it's a misunderstanding."

"That I want to see him? No. I made myself abundantly clear. I even assured his wife that whoever is hiding him would be arrested."

Henry didn't answer that. He couldn't imagine Susan hiding Abe. He couldn't imagine Abe hiding. There had to be some mistake.

"On top of that, Lewis Glick is now a guest of the Monte Vista Police Department."

"Why?"

"Because he refuses to answer my questions. He just sits there, staring at his hands. The man won't even ask for a lawyer, though I fully intend to provide him one. He's going to need good representation if he is charged."

"You're going to keep him?"

"I can hold him for another twenty-four hours."

"Why would you do that?"

"I'm trying to persuade him to talk to me, Henry. I need to know what he knows. I'm hoping a few hours in jail will change his mind and his attitude, but if it doesn't then I will proceed to file charges."

"Perhaps if I spoke to him—"

"Please do." Hands on her hips, Meg frowned at him. Suddenly she seemed to realize she was standing in the middle of his vegetable garden. "This is a big garden for one man."

Just when he thought she was beginning to understand their simple way of life, she said something showing that she plainly did not.

"*Ya*, but it's a long winter, and also I'd like to be able to help others when they have a need."

"My investigation is falling apart, and you're gardening."

"Someone once asked Saint Francis what he would do if he knew the world was about to end. He answered, 'I suppose I would finish hoeing this row of beans.' "

Meg shook her head, threw up her hands, and stomped away.

Henry had to hurry to catch up with her, and still she was already in the car, seat belted when he reached her side.

"No tips to the hotline?"

"Oh, we have tips all right. Hundreds of them. Unfortunately, nothing substantial."

"And the *Englischer* in the drawing? Douglas Rae?"

"His mother claims he was home during each of the fires."

It occurred to Henry that a mother would lie for her son. Meg must have read the skepticism in his eyes. "Yeah, it's weak, but it's something. I've run a background check. He has no priors and no family other than his mom. I can't find any connection between Douglas and Vernon or between Douglas and a prior DUI. Plus, he's the only person who was willing to answer my questions, which puts him at the bottom of my suspect list."

"I don't know where Abe is, but I will find out. And I'll come to town as soon as I clean up and speak with Lewis. Sometimes Amish men are hesitant to speak to *Englischers*. Especially . . . women."

If her eyes could have shot daggers, he would be lying in the lane beside her car.

"I'm not a *woman*, Henry. I'm the arson investigator for this case, and they will speak to me or stand trial for any charge I can make stick."

Fifty-Five

An hour later Henry was perched on a stool he had pulled up to the jail cell where Lewis was sitting on a simple cot. He wished they could have privacy. At least he could be grateful that the jail wasn't exactly full. An old man Henry suspected had been brought in for drinking in public was loudly snoring two cells down and to the left. A young teenage girl was picking at a tattoo in the cell to the right. She hadn't even looked up when he walked past.

Lewis didn't seem surprised, or happy, to see him.

"Meg Allen asked me to come and speak to you. See what the problem is."

Lewis glanced up, and then he returned his gaze to the floor.

"She's trying to help us, Lewis."

"We're to remain separate."

"*Ya*, I agree. Whenever it's possible I agree that is the best way, but sometimes our lives intersect by necessity. At that point we should treat *Englischers* as we would each other, with kindness and respect."

Lewis didn't answer. He scratched at his arms, jiggled his foot, and repeatedly glanced to the left and right. He seemed oblivious to the head injury he'd suffered from the newspaper explosion. Grayson told him the wound had been cleaned and freshly bandaged by a nurse who visited the jail once a day.

Henry waited, watching the clock on the wall tick past the noon hour.

Meg had left the building for a meeting. She'd given him one hour to convince Lewis to talk before she formally filed charges.

"Perhaps you could move closer so I don't have to shout across the cell."

Lewis had the grace to look embarrassed.

He stood and moved closer, dropping onto the concrete floor in front of Henry, but still he didn't meet his bishop's gaze.

"What's going on, Lewis?"

"I had nothing to do with those fires."

"And I believe you, but you need to tell Meg that. She's the investigator."

Lewis had seemed pumped up with indignation when Henry first walked up to the cell, but now he seemed deflated, like a child's balloon that had quickly lost air.

"I can't explain to her what I was doing at the paper."

"Can you explain it to me?"

Lewis shifted uncomfortably on the floor

"Whatever you say to me will be protected by what the *Englischers* call clergy privilege."

Henry remembered his first conversation with

Meg, when she'd assured him clergy privilege didn't apply. But this was different. This was a man baring his soul to his pastor, and no doubt it would be covered. Plus, Henry had no intention of sharing anything Lewis said, even if it meant he'd join the man on the other side of the bars. Unless what he said could lead to catching the arsonist. Then he would have to convince Lewis that such information needed to be shared with the authorities.

"If you don't want me to disclose it to anyone else, I won't. But you need to trust me, Lewis. You need to tell me what's weighing on your heart."

He thought the man wouldn't speak, that he would have to return to Meg and admit defeat. When Lewis at last looked up, Henry understood the full measure of his misery, and thoughts of the investigation fell away. He was a bishop, and the man on the other side of the bars was his parishioner. A person in need of help. A man with a burden.

"You know I hurt my back, in Pennsylvania, before I came here."

"*Ya*, you explained that when you first joined us."

As was customary, Henry had written to Lewis's previous bishop. Usually he would receive a letter giving a brief history of the person or family's time in the community along with any problems or ways he could minister as well as any particular talents. Henry had once learned that one of his parishioners could carve incredible scenes from the Bible into wood, which was something the man hadn't mentioned. When Henry had asked him about it, he'd taken him into his workshop to show him dozens of completed projects. Henry had set him up with a local gift shop that sold his works on consignment. The man had been worried that his talent was worldly, and that it would be prideful to share it with anyone.

Something told him Lewis wasn't hiding an unusual talent. The man looked utterly dejected. The letter Henry had received from his previous bishop had been less than three lines, little more than the date of his baptism and a small bit about his family.

"How is your back now, Lewis?"

"Tolerable if I take the pills."

"Pills?"

"OxyContin. It's the reason . . . " He licked his lips and forced himself to continue. "It's the reason I was in the newspaper office."

"I assume you're not getting these from a doctor."

"At first I was, but then they wouldn't give me any more. That's when I moved here."

"How do you purchase them?"

"I have a contact at the paper." He glanced up at Henry. "And I won't tell you his name. He's

335

helped me tremendously. I won't . . . I won't betray him."

"Tell me how the transaction works."

"I fill out a form for an ad, only I don't want an ad, of course." Lewis wrapped his arms around his stomach and grimaced. "I slip the money into the envelope and put . . . my contact's name on the outside. They call him to the counter, and then I hand him the envelope, and he hands me the package of pills."

Henry wanted to kick himself for not recognizing the signs of drug addiction. The man in front of him could be a poster child for drug withdrawal symptoms—abdominal pain, heavy sweating, anxiety, and agitation. Why hadn't he put the clues together?

Self-incrimination would have to wait, though. First he needed to get Lewis out of jail.

When Henry didn't speak, Lewis began to speak more quickly.

"It's the only way . . . the only way I can continue to work." Lewis's hands had begun to shake. "I had filled out the form and was moving to get in line when the explosion happened."

"You ran outside."

"Initially, but after I saw the fire truck and realized the sprinklers were on, I figured there wasn't any danger—"

"The building was on fire, Lewis. There was plenty of danger."

He seemed not to have heard his bishop. "I knew I had to get back inside, and find . . . find what I'd paid for."

"You tried to go back into the building."

"*Ya*, but Abe stopped me. I think he suspects something about my . . . my situation."

"Do you know where Abe is? Meg's having trouble locating him, and Susan doesn't seem to know where he's gone. She's worried."

"No. I don't know. When he stopped by my house Saturday afternoon to see how I was after the explosion, he said . . . he said something about needing to get to his brother, but I didn't know what he was talking about. I didn't know he had a brother."

Henry stood and placed his stool back against the wall.

"We'll get you out of here, Lewis. Until then, try to drink some water and lie down."

"And the oxy? Can you get me those?"

"No. I can't. But I will get you some help."

Fifty-Six

Henry found Meg sitting at Sheriff Grayson's desk, hunched over a large stack of papers.

"These are transcripts from the tips hotline." She picked up the printed sheets and fanned them, her eyebrows arched. "Useless. From what I can tell, every single one of them is useless."

"Did you sleep at all last night?"

Instead of answering, she asked, "Is Glick going to talk to me now?"

"He will."

"Progress. About time."

She popped up from the desk, but Henry reached out and stopped her.

"He's not your guy."

"I'll decide that." Her eyes narrowed. "What are you not telling me?"

"It must not go in your reports or be released to the press."

Meg's scowl deepened. She crossed her arms and perched on the edge of her chair, her foot tapping an impatient rhythm on the floor. "I'll be the one to decide that too."

"The things he told me were spoken in confidence." Before she could argue with him about clergy privilege laws, Henry pushed on. "Lewis has a drug problem. The newspaper was where he was supposed to pick up his supply. He initially ran out of the building, but when he saw that the sprinklers had come on and the firemen had arrived, he was determined to get back inside. He's a desperate man, for sure and certain."

"Drugs?"

"OxyContin."

Meg sank back against her chair. "I thought he had a shifty look. I assumed it was because he was hiding something."

"He is, but he's also suffering through the first stages of withdrawal."

Meg leaned forward, propped her elbows on the desk, and pressed her fingers against her lips.

"Next you're going to tell me Abe was trying to restrain him."

"*Ya.* Abe and the young *Englischer*, Douglas. They held him back and wouldn't let him return into the building."

"I'm going to need to talk to Abe and confirm that story."

"Abe is still missing. I checked with Susan before I came here. As she told you, she hasn't seen him since yesterday morning, and she *is* worried. She really doesn't know where he is."

"If he was simply restraining Lewis Glick, then he had nothing to hide."

"True."

"Or this could be about his brother."

"We have no reason to suspect Alvin."

"That's not good enough, Henry. We have every reason to suspect him." Her bravado collapsed. "Unfortunately, he had an ironclad alibi for each of the fires, especially the daytime ones. He was teaching and has an entire classroom of students who will vouch for him. Unless there are two arsonists, which I doubt, he's not our guy."

"Then why must you talk to Abe again? I heard you questioned him for three hours after the newspaper incident."

"Because I still think he's hiding something, and whatever it is might crack open this case."

He waited, letting her work through her options, which to Henry looked rather limited.

"I suppose you'd like me to release Glick to you?"

"He needs to be in a rehab facility. There's a good one in Del Norte."

"After I speak to him and confirm what you're saying."

He said nothing, waiting.

"Look, I trust you, Henry. And your drawings have been a help. They're practically the only clues we have. But I'm turning up nothing, and our perp isn't slowing down."

"Any luck trying to connect Vernon to something in the letter?"

"No. The land he was living on wasn't even in Vernon's name. I'm still tracking that down."

Something darted into Henry's memory and back out again.

"Other foreclosures that might have been purchased from one of our families?"

"None that I can find." She tapped her fingers against the desk. "We cross-referenced all of your congregation's names with below-market sales."

Meg reached for another stack of paper.

"There was one, the land the Bontragers own, but that was purchased from a family whose parents were aging. The children moved the mother and dad, who were in their nineties, back to live with them in California. I spoke with the woman, and I didn't detect even a hint of hard feelings. In fact, she claimed to have been quite relieved to sell the place so quickly."

Henry thought it was interesting that the Bontragers had been the first to decide to move. Apparently, Meg didn't know that, and he didn't see that it was relevant to the case. "So a dead end."

"Yes. They're all dead ends."

"If I see Abe, I will impress on him how important it is that you speak to him."

"If you see Abe, bring him into the station."

Fifty-Seven

The rehab facility in Del Norte was a joint venture operated by Mennonites and Brethren in Christ. Henry had referred someone from his congregation to their facilities twice before—once for a teen who was in trouble, and another time for a young woman who had become addicted to sleeping pills. In the case of the boy, he had returned home, adjusted well, and eventually joined an Amish community in Arkansas. The young woman had seemed to recover, only to suffer a dramatic relapse. The family had moved back to Goshen, hoping that being in a more familiar surrounding would be less stressful for her.

Henry figured Lewis's chances of recovery were fifty-fifty, which was more than he'd had back at his farm. So he felt fairly optimistic when he checked Lewis into the Helping Hands facility. The man seemed miserable. He was visibly anxious, sweating, and seemed to be suffering from hallucinations. Lewis signed the check-in papers with a shaky hand, but he wouldn't look Henry in the eyes—even when Henry reminded him that he would be back to visit after the first ten days. The facility strongly suggested family members write letters but hold off on visiting or calling until after this initial period.

Henry made sure the admissions clerk had noted the number for the phone shack nearest him. "Call me if there's anything I can do, and if no one answers, please leave a message."

He walked back out to the van, where Stuart Mills was waiting.

Stuart was an older guy who had recently retired from teaching, and he seemed to enjoy being a taxi driver for the Amish. He claimed it gave him plenty of time to read, and that the extra money came in handy.

Perhaps he was hoping to fix his truck. The paint had faded away completely on the top of the extended cab, and the upholstery on the seats had seen better days. It had no air conditioning, but then many automobiles in Colorado didn't bother with it. Because buggies didn't either, Henry barely noticed.

"Back home?" Stuart asked.

"Actually . . . " Henry studied the sky. It was only four in the afternoon, and they were nearing the summer solstice. He should have enough time. "Is your wife still at her sister's?"

"Left last Friday and plans to stay four weeks. I'm a bachelor with plenty of time on my hands for the next twenty-seven days. When she returns, the honey-do list will take over again."

"If you're not in a hurry, there is one more place

I'd like to go. May take us a while to find it."

"I have nothing on my schedule tonight."

"All right. Take Highway 160 west."

"Into the wilderness, huh?"

"Actually, we're going to South Twin Mountain."

Del Norte was surrounded by nearly four thousand acres of public land. Within that acreage a few slivers of private land remained. The area was a winter playground for *Englischers* who loved to snowmobile. In the summer, fewer tourists visited, although amateur geologists frequented the area and sportsmen came to hunt and fish. Henry had been to the South Twin only once, on a fishing trip with Abe and Alvin. It was the first year they'd moved to Colorado, and it was the only time Alvin had seemed happy. If the brothers were together and hiding, that was where they would be.

Once Stuart filled his gas tank and then left the main highway, they passed the occasional ranch house or hunting cabin. The valley stretched out around them. South Twin Mountain shimmered in the heat, and a light rain began to fall, smearing dirt across the windshield. As they drew closer to the mountain, Stuart cleared his throat and said, "I didn't realize you ever came out this way."

"Oh, *ya*. Good fishing."

Stuart glanced at him. "Is that what we're doing? Going fishing?"

"Actually, I'm looking for a friend."

"Does this have anything to do with the fires?"

Henry had always been an honest person. Integrity had been ingrained in him from a very young age. He didn't want to lie to Stuart, but he also didn't want to involve the man any more than he had to. "It could."

He thought Stuart might argue, or that he might pull out his cell phone to call the police department. But instead he said, "If this errand of yours will help end this thing, I'm all for it. I don't see how anyone with a smidgen of common sense could suspect an Amish person of burning down homes and businesses."

Henry should have let the conversation die a natural death, but instead he asked, "And why is that?"

"Never met an Amish person who held a grudge. Don't get me wrong. I understand you're not perfect. And Vernon Frey was what my folks's generation would have called a curmudgeon. But murder? Uh-uh. Whoever is doing this has a vendetta, and he wants to blame it on the Amish community. The sooner we catch him, the better things will be for your people and mine."

Three times they took the wrong side road and had to back up down the dirt track because there was no room to turn around. On the fourth try, they followed the lane for half a mile and pulled into a clearing in front of a log cabin. Parked next to the cabin was a silver Honda.

Henry asked Stuart to wait in the car.

"Waiting is not a problem." He held up a paperback book, his finger marking a place one-third through. It was thick and had Monte Vista Public Library stamped on the side. "If I reach the end, and you're still not back, I'll come looking for you."

"If you reach the end of that book, and I'm not back, call 9-1-1."

Fifty-Eight

Emma and Katie Ann worked in the garden as Rachel watched over the stew simmering on the stove and corn bread browning in the oven.

"You know she's in there reading."

"Your *mamm* is a hard worker. I believe she earns her quiet moments."

Katie Ann squirreled up her face as if she'd smelled something distasteful. "I'm glad to be out of school. I'd much rather be outside, even if we're pulling weeds."

"Pray for a *gut* harvest but continue to hoe."

"That one I understand."

Twenty minutes later they were sitting in the shade, looking out over the rows where soon green beans, tomatoes, okra, squash, and radishes would begin to sprout. And those were just the rows Emma could see from where they sat.

Katie Ann was attempting to clean dirt from under her fingernails. "I was surprised when Albert and Elmer came to lunch."

"Henry invited them, owing to the fact that Albert's mom and sisters have already moved."

"I don't want to move. I like it here."

"Glad to hear it, since we're staying."

Katie Ann flopped back into the grass, staring

up at a sky so blue Emma had to squint when she looked at it.

"Albert kissed me."

"Did he now?"

"Yup, and it wasn't my first kiss either." Katie Ann rolled over to her side, propped up on her elbow and facing her grandmother. A smile played at the corners of her mouth.

"And here I thought you were still a young girl, immune to romance."

"I might be. I'm not sure I even like kissing."

"It grows on you as you get older."

"*Mammi!*" Katie Ann dissolved into a fit of giggles.

It did Emma's heart good, seeing Katie Ann happy and carefree, without the worries and concern of adults. Childhood was such a precious time, and Katie Ann stood at the crossroads where she was slowly leaving childish things behind.

"So who was this first boy who kissed you, and why didn't I know anything about it?"

"Because I was embarrassed!"

"*Ya*, I remember being embarrassed when your grandpa kissed me by the tree at the end of our lane. I was sure the mail carrier had seen us."

"Mahlon kissed me by the swing set at school."

"Mahlon Graber?"

"We were seven. He missed my face completely and kissed my *kapp*, right over my ear."

"Did things go any better with Albert?"

"I guess? I'm not sure I know what a *gut* kiss is."

"Sometimes a kiss is just a kiss, Katie Ann."

"How will I know when it's the right kiss, like yours and *Daddi*'s?"

"Oh, I don't think anyone will have to tell you. Your heart will clench up and your knees will feel a little weak and you might have trouble catching your breath."

"Sounds like the flu."

"Feels a little like it."

"Maybe I'm not in such a hurry to experience the real thing, then."

"There's definitely no need to rush."

Emma thought the conversation was over. They sat there a few more minutes, enjoying the breeze. Realizing Rachel could probably use their help inside, she began picking up their gardening supplies.

Katie Ann dropped her spade into the basket alongside her gardening gloves. "Albert said they're going to catch him."

"The arsonist?"

"Uh-huh."

"Was he talking about the police?"

Katie Ann worried her thumbnail, exactly as Emma had seen Rachel do the day before. It was amazing what children picked up from their parents.

"I don't think so."

"Then who?"

"Not sure." Katie Ann took the basket of supplies from Emma and helped her grandmother up off the ground. They slowly walked toward the house. "But I had a feeling he was talking about our boys."

"Our boys?"

"You know, Amish boys. Girls too. Well, not exactly boys and girls, but *youngies*."

"Tell me word-for-word what he said, Katie Ann."

"That he hoped their place didn't sell too quickly." When she raised her eyes, Emma realized she was worried, that what Albert Bontrager had said, or the way he'd said it, had spooked her somehow. "He said they have a plan, and that they would catch the guy. He said he wanted to be here when it happened."

Emma had no idea what the boy could have been talking about, but she did know Henry would want to be aware of this plan. Apparently their *youngies* had grown tired of having their lives disrupted. If the adults couldn't, or wouldn't, solve the problem of the Monte Vista arsonist, then they were ready to take it into their own capable, young hands.

Fifty-Nine

"You're sure about this?" Clyde asked.

Emma had waited until after dinner to bring up the subject of the *youngies*' plan to catch the Monte Vista arsonist. Once Rachel had ushered the younger children upstairs for their baths and then returned to join the adults, she broached the subject. Emma had also insisted Silas and Katie Ann, who had first told her of the plan, remain at the table with them.

"What did you tell them?" Silas asked.

"Nothing." Katie Ann scowled at her brother. "It's stupid, anyway."

"It isn't."

"*Ya*, it is. I was at the last fire, remember?" She reached for her *kapp* strings and twisted them so hard Emma feared she'd pull them off. "I know how dangerous this person is. I still have nightmares about it!"

"I'm sorry you were hurt, but that has nothing to do with us."

Emma and Rachel exchanged a worried look. Silas was their happy, unconcerned child. He rarely argued with anyone.

Clyde held up his hand to stop the bickering between his two oldest children. "Tell me exactly what is supposed to happen."

351

Silas looked as if he might argue, and in that moment Emma saw Clyde in her grandson's face. Her son had given her and George a few years of sleepless nights, and right about when he was Silas's age. Any other time she might have laughed and said something like *turnabout is fair play,* but this wasn't a laughing matter, and what they were talking about wasn't play.

Clyde took in a big breath, closed his eyes, and Emma knew he was praying for patience. How many times had she uttered the very same prayer?

"Your sister cares about you, Silas."

"I guess."

"As do I and your mother and your grandmother. I need you to tell me the details. When were you supposed to meet?"

"Nine o'clock tonight."

"This isn't the first time," Emma said, suddenly remembering what she had thought was a squirrel scampering across the roof the night before. "You met last night too."

Silas shrugged. "I guess."

"Answer your grandmother directly and show some respect." There was a low growl in Clyde's voice, something the children rarely heard.

"*Ya,* we met last night. I crawled out my window so I wouldn't wake anyone."

"Out the window?" Rachel's voice rose like a tea kettle ready to boil.

"It's not that big a deal, *Mamm.* I can shimmy

right over to the front porch and drop down. I didn't mean to wake anyone. Sorry, *Mammi*."

Emma reached across the dining room table and squeezed his hand. He looked embarrassed and relieved at the same time.

"Where are you to meet tonight?" Clyde pressed.

"The Kline place."

"I'll be going with you."

"But you can't." Silas quickly backtracked. "What I mean is, if you go they'll know I told, and then . . . well, how can I ever look my friends in the face again?"

"You can tell when you're on the right track," Emma said gently. "It's usually uphill."

"What we're doing isn't easy." For the first time since the discussion had begun, Silas looked determined rather than afraid. "You should thank us. We're going to catch this person and make our community safe again."

"You and I will go together, and we'll put an end to this before someone is hurt."

"But—"

"This is for the *Englisch* authorities to handle."

"They haven't done such a swell job so far."

"I'm living proof of that," Katie Ann quipped.

Clyde glanced at his wife before he sat back, crossing his arms and studying his children—children who by now believed they were adults, and in one sense they were. Emma knew there was no use trying to protect them from the problems in their community, but neither did she want them directly involved.

"Obviously, the arson investigator does not share every bit of progress in her case with us or with the paper, so we can't know that." Clyde tapped the table for emphasis. "But it is her job, and I have no doubt she will do it to the best of her ability."

"What if this is outside her ability?" Silas stared at his hands and then out the window at his father's land. "You know how Amish can be. There are things no one will tell her. Things we keep to ourselves."

"We remain separate as much as possible, but we will help her investigation any way we can."

"You would, *Dat*. I believe that. But some of our people feel it's best to take matters into our own hands."

"And you won't tell me specifically what is being planned?"

"Those plans were shared with me in confidence. Do you want me to go back on my word?"

"Fine. We'll leave a little before dark, in about two hours."

Silas nodded in agreement, though he looked as if his girlfriend had just told him she wanted to court someone else. If only this could be about girls and courting—both things seventeen-year-old boys were supposed to be sneaking out in the middle of the night for. Not to catch an arsonist.

"Go do your chores. Throw some extra hay to Cinnamon. I'll meet you at the barn when it's time to go." Clyde stood, indicating the meeting was over. "And *danki* for telling us, Katie Ann."

She nodded but didn't say anything.

"Did you plan on going?"

"*Nein.* I told them I wouldn't. I don't want to have anything to do with this arsonist. But if you're going, *Dat*, then *ya*. I'd like to go too."

"All right."

"Are you sure you're up to that, Katie Ann?" Her mother stepped closer, put both hands on the girl's shoulders and waited until she looked up into her eyes.

"*Ya*, I think . . . I think maybe being there and knowing what is going to happen will help the nightmares."

Rachel nodded once. "As long as you're with your *dat*, then I suppose it will be all right."

Katie Ann fled from the room, following Silas out into the barn.

Emma stood and began stacking and clearing the dishes. "I hope he isn't too hard on her."

"They're less than a year apart and have always acted like twins," Rachel said.

"Two people, one heart."

"*Ya.* Only this time Katie Ann's fear overruled her need to go along with what Silas was planning." Clyde sat with his hands covering his face. No doubt he'd been looking forward to his bed and some rest, but instead he'd be intercepting several dozen teenagers.

"He's only a boy doing what he thought was best," Emma said. "Boys do things that seem foolish to men. Remember the time you snuck out to take that old Chevy to South Bend? Your father never could figure out what you were looking for there that you couldn't find in Goshen."

"We were stopped by a policeman when the muffler fell off in the middle of the road."

"You gave your *dat* and me our fair share of sleepless nights."

"It was one of the things I liked about you," Rachel admitted. "You were such a daring young man." She stacked the rest of the dishes and carried them to the sink.

"What I did was completely different," Clyde argued. "This could get someone killed."

"Oh, Clyde. That could happen any night. Someone driving too fast or glancing down at their phone. Every generation worries about their children. I'm sure it's been the way of things since Adam and Eve worried over Cain and Abel."

"*Ya*, and look how that turned out."

Emma smiled. At least his sense of humor was returning. She walked back to the table, wiping it down with a damp dish towel, and paused next to him long enough to say, "I'll meet you three in the barn, and don't even think about arguing with me, because I'm going too."

She thought he muttered something that sounded like, "When has arguing with you ever worked?" But if he had she decided to ignore it. She could also remember worrying about her parents. Yes, life was a circle that continued to turn whether or not they were ready for it.

Sixty

"How did you find us?" Abe asked.

Both he and Alvin were standing on the back porch. The cabin belonged to someone Abe had done some work for—clearing brush, trimming trees, that sort of thing. As far as Henry knew, Abe still helped to maintain the cabin when the owner was out of town, which would explain why they were able to visit it. The view beyond the porch was of trees and a yard leading down to a bubbling mountain stream that twisted this way and that behind the cabin. The light rain had turned into a nice downpour, obscuring the view. Twelve years ago, they had all fished there, laughing about the trout and what a promised land the San Luis Valley was. On that spring day, it had seemed to be all that and more. How had things changed so drastically?

"*Gut* place to get away," was all Henry said by way of explanation.

Alvin and Abe exchanged a look, and Abe finally motioned toward a chair.

Henry took it, waiting to see if they would speak first.

Abe sat beside him, but Alvin stood at the porch steps, as if he might need to plunge into the stream and then dash into the woods.

358

To their left the last of the evening's light was playing through the leaves. To their right, the shadow of the mountain was encroaching. Darkness overcoming light. Henry had to remind himself that, in the morning, the pattern would reverse. All they had to do was wait and trust that the light would return. Not a bad analogy for a Sunday morning sermon. But would it help Alvin to mention it now? He didn't think so.

"Do you remember when we first came here, Henry?" Alvin didn't look at the bishop when he asked the question. Instead, he stared out at the wilderness.

"I do."

Henry knew he was talking not about this cabin, but moving to Colorado.

"So much has changed since that year. Some of those changes I am grateful for—my wife, my children, my church. But if I had known how difficult the journey would be, if I had realized how much I would hurt Franey, I'm not sure I would have had the strength to leave." Now he turned to Henry and gazed directly at him. "I've never been a particularly courageous man. Hardworking and simple, as my *dat* was before me. But this thing we're caught up in, I can't even begin to understand it."

"Why don't you explain to me what's happened. Why are you here?"

Instead of answering, Alvin walked into the

house and returned with a large brown envelope, which he dropped in Henry's lap.

Alvin returned to staring out at the stream.

Abe motioned for Henry to open the envelope, which had an Alamosa postmark.

Henry found three things inside. A photograph of Alvin standing outside the JSW construction site. Another of him leaving the *Monte Vista Gazette* building. And clipped to the top of those two, a handwritten note.

> You have fourty-ate hours befor I will
>   send these to police.
> I've already called the tip hotline, so you
>   will now I'm cerious.
> I didn't tell them anything specific yet.
> Fourty-ate hours.
> You'll need $12,000—cash.
> I'll be in touch with delivry instructions.

"I recognize the handwriting."

"How . . . how is that possible?" Alvin asked.

But Abe understood. "The scene you drew from Vernon's. It included a letter, right? A letter from the arsonist."

"*Ya.*"

"And this is the same writing?"

"I'm sure of it. Plus, it has the same kinds of sentence errors and misspelled words."

"But you don't know who wrote it?"

"*Nein.* If I knew, the man would be in jail."

"I didn't do this thing, Henry." Alvin turned toward them, his eyes pleading for Henry to believe him. "I've never even visited the construction site, and I haven't been to the newspaper in the eleven years since I left."

"So these photographs aren't real."

"Of course they're not, but they look real enough. I don't understand how they can even exist."

"Neither do I, but the *Englisch* and their computers . . . they can make something look authentic."

"Not just the *Englisch*, Henry." Abe sat forward, his elbows on his knees, studying the floor of the porch with a worried expression. "I've seen our *youngies*, the ones with phones. I've seen them playing around. They can make a photograph with them standing in front of the London Bridge or Niagara Falls when they've never been to such a place."

"You're saying it could be an Amish person."

"I'm saying there's no way to know based on what we have."

Henry didn't answer immediately. It was growing dark, and his driver would be ready to return home. What could he say to persuade Alvin and Abe to go with him? How could he convince them hiding out was a bad idea? And then it hit him.

"This person never expected you to turn over twelve thousand dollars."

"But it says that I'm to—"

"I know what it says, but whether he's Amish or *Englisch*, he understands that few if any Amish men have that much money in the bank."

"What's the point, then?" Abe asked. "Did he want to taunt my brother? And why? Why single out Alvin among all the Amish—"

"I'm Mennonite."

"Among all the Amish or Mennonite in the area?"

Henry pushed away any intention of hurrying. Stuart would wait, reading his novel by flashlight if necessary, hoping something could be done to catch this person. He wouldn't want him to rush and miss something. Henry had the growing sensation they were close to solving this—if not the person's identity, then at least landing on a motive. There was something they weren't seeing. He picked up the letter and studied it again. The same misspelled words, missing words, and odd syntax jumped out at him. Next he picked up the envelope and studied it.

"This was mailed Friday."

Alvin shrugged.

"So it was mailed after the fire at the newspaper."

"*Ya.* Why does that matter?'

"In the first letter, the writer was angry, needing

to spew out some of the bitterness building in his heart and mind. Needing to let someone know his grievances." Henry tapped the letter. "There's none of that here—only a sense of urgency."

"Yeah, like it's urgent that I decide what to do before I'm arrested, and this man urgently wants his blackmail money."

Instead of answering that, Henry turned to Abe. "Why were you at the newspaper that day?"

Abe refused to meet Henry's eyes. "I was placing a sales ad."

"Sales ad?"

"Yes, Henry." Now he looked up defiantly. "An old plow, the kids' trampoline, the extra buggy horse, pretty much anything I can get cash for."

"I didn't realize your situation was so dire. Why didn't you tell me?"

"Because I should be able to support my family."

Instead of responding to that, Henry said, "The night we were all in the hospital, you weren't there."

"I was, but not for very long. They treated me and then I went straight home."

"Do you know about my meeting with Meg at the hospital?"

Abe squirmed in his seat. "*Ya.* I suppose everyone does."

"What are they saying? What is everyone saying about that meeting?"

"Only that you . . . that you drew more pictures. This time of scenes at the fire." Abe ran a thumb under his suspenders, up and down, up and down. "Some say you drew a picture of the next fire."

Henry nearly laughed. "That would be a pretty neat trick, but I don't have the gift of prophecy."

"It's only people talking. You know how these things go."

"I do. I think people were talking, especially people in the waiting room. I think word got out that I'd drawn the scenes of the fire, and this guy"—he tapped the envelope—"is spooked."

"We'd heard that, after seeing the drawing, Meg came out and spoke to a few more people. You know she took me into the station and questioned me the next day. Did she plan to speak with anyone else?"

"She did."

"And Lewis was one? Could he have done it?"

"He is not guilty of this." Henry was convinced of Lewis's innocence. The man was at the newspaper to purchase his drugs. He'd been willing to run into a burning building to get them. That kind of addiction couldn't be faked. No, Lewis Glick was innocent, but Henry didn't want to get into that now. The clock was ticking, and they needed to decide what to do next.

His thoughts turned to the other two men in the drawings he'd made—in particular, the one outside after the fire. There had been Abe, who was sitting in front of him, and Douglas, an *Englischer* who had willingly answered Meg's questions. But he couldn't limit his suspect to those three.

People were spooked by what he'd drawn, but they hadn't seen what he'd drawn. They didn't know he hadn't identified the perpetrator. No one knew exactly what was in those drawings except for him, Emma, and Meg. But there had been rumors, and rumors could grow out of control.

"Whoever is setting these fires is nervous. He heard the same things you did, that I had drawn scenes from the fire. He's worried Meg is closing in, so he needed to switch the focus of Meg's investigation somewhere else."

"To Alvin." Abe stood now, as if he expected to see the arsonist pop out of the woods.

"I knew that by running I'd look guilty, but the pictures . . . "

"I'm fairly sure Meg can have these pictures analyzed. She can prove conclusively that they've been tampered with."

"How can you know that, Henry? How can you know it for certain?"

"Simple. You weren't there, and you didn't do it."

A look of relief washed over Alvin's face at those words. Until that moment, Henry would not have guessed how much his opinion mattered to Alvin, but then he had been the man's bishop.

He'd shared meals with Alvin and Abe. Sometimes he forgot that he stood as a father figure to many in his congregation. And sons always needed the blessing of their father.

"You believe that? You believe I'm innocent?"

"I do."

Alvin drew in a big breath and sank into the chair Abe had vacated. "What should I do now? Am I supposed to sit here and wait?"

"*Nein*. You come with me. You show Meg the evidence, and you answer any of her questions. Show her you're innocent, Alvin."

"But what if—"

"Let's do the right thing here. Abe and I will be by your side the entire time." After a moment he added, "What's the alternative? You can fish only so many days before you'll be missing your family and your classroom."

"Gave up fishing years ago. Hurts my shoulder."

"There you go." Henry smiled, the anxiousness he'd been battling suddenly fading away. For once it felt as though they were on the offensive instead of playing catch-up. With the letter and the photographs, they were one step closer to catching the Monte Vista arsonist. Which might provoke him into more drastic measures, but that was a chance they would have to take.

Sixty-One

Rachel had taken some convincing, but she eventually agreed that Clyde, Silas, Katie Ann, and Emma should be the ones to attend the evening's meeting.

"We're not going to encounter the arsonist," Clyde assured her. "Only a barn full of stubborn *youngie*."

The Kline home was on the far end of their district, and the barn was a fair distance from the house, which was probably why the kids had chosen it. Driving down the lane, Emma couldn't tell that anything at all was happening, and for a moment she wondered if Silas had the time or place wrong. One glance at his face assured her that wasn't so. He looked absolutely miserable.

Instead of going directly to the barn, Clyde stopped at the house to speak with Marcus Kline, who stepped out onto his front porch. Emma could tell from their body language that Marcus didn't believe a word Clyde was saying, but he shrugged, stepped back into the house, and returned with his hat planted firmly on his head.

Clyde motioned for her, Silas, and Katie Ann to join them.

"Best to walk up on them quietly, otherwise they're likely to scatter like a bunch of rabbits."

"Still hard to believe," Marcus said. "My son's in his bed already. We spent a long day in the fields, and he went to sleep early. Said he was exhausted."

"Did you check to see if he was there?"

"I did not." Marcus was an odd-looking guy. No hair remained on the top of his head, though he had the typical Amish beard and very bushy eyebrows. He wasn't a great deal of fun to be around—usually forecasting doom about the weather or the crops or *Englischers* or the next generation. Anyone else would have shortened their name to Mark, but Marcus did not. In spite of all that, he was a hard worker, fair, and as far as Emma knew, not considering moving out of Monte Vista.

Silence fell around their little group as they neared the barn.

Marcus stopped suddenly, causing Emma to bump into Clyde, and Silas and Katie Ann to bump into her. They stood there in the dark, listening to the sound of voices inside. A beam of light escaped under the barn door.

Marcus hesitated, as if he needed a moment to accept what he was about to see.

Then he opened the door, and they all filed inside.

There was a surprising amount of light in the barn because each teen was holding a battery-operated lantern or a flashlight.

Emma sometimes forgot so many *youngies* were in their congregation. Sure, she saw them at church, and when they filed through the food line, and as they played volleyball or softball. Usually in those instances they were in smaller groups. Seeing them all together . . . well, it was eye-opening.

Watching them as they perched on bales of hay and overturned crates, and even sat on the floor, she realized how concerned they were—not for themselves but for each other. This reminded her they were good kids, of various ages, and every one of them cared about their community. Like so many generations before them, they thought they were smarter and better equipped. They'd convinced themselves they needed to step in and do something. She might be able to fault them for their arrogance, but their hearts were in the right place.

"Don't even think about running," Marcus said as he trudged to the front of the room where his son, Nathan, was standing. "You and I will talk about this later. For now you can take a seat."

The boy swallowed so hard his Adam's apple bobbed, but he sat down without another word.

"This apparently has something to do with the fires." Marcus waited, but no one spoke.

Emma remained near the door, as if she could keep anyone from escaping. She could possibly throw herself on the floor in front of someone and trip them, slow them down a little, but she couldn't actually stop any of these teenagers and young adults from running away. Silas moved to the back of the room, where he was standing next to a young girl whose name Emma couldn't remember. Katie Ann stayed at her side.

Clyde stepped forward, and after a nod from Marcus, addressed the group. "We know you're planning something, that you're trying to help. But we can't let you put yourselves in danger."

Emma was surprised no one argued with him. Maybe this would be easier than she thought.

"We'd like you to go home now, and we'll be in contact with your parents."

"You're ratting us out?" one of the boys from the back asked.

"Can't say I know what that means."

"You're going to turn us in to our parents and get us in trouble so we can't help at all."

"What I'm doing is keeping you out of harm's way."

Now one of the older boys stepped forward. It wasn't until he was standing directly in front of Clyde that Emma recognized it was Jesse Kauffmann, Leroy's oldest son.

"But you can't do that. No one can. And what we're doing? It's already started, so you can't stop that either."

"Maybe you need to explain to me exactly what you had in mind."

"I can't do that."

"You will. You'll either tell me or your father or the police."

"So that's how it's going to be?"

"It is."

Everyone started talking at once then—all of the kids, Marcus, Clyde. Even Silas was talking in an urgent voice to the girl beside him.

Clyde allowed it to continue for a moment, and then he raised his hand to get everyone's attention. He pointed at Jesse Kauffmann. "I want you to stay, as well as my son, the girl beside him . . ."

"And my son," Marcus added.

"Stay for what?" Jesse asked.

"So we can have a private conversation. The rest of you go home. Whatever you thought you were going to do tonight, forget about it. And when you get up in the morning, be honest with your parents. It's better if they hear about this from you before I speak with them."

Sixty-Two

"I'm sorry. I don't remember your name." Emma sat down on a hay bale, next to Silas and the pretty girl he'd been standing beside.

"Naomi. Naomi Miller. I only arrived from Missouri a few weeks ago. I'm staying with my *aenti*."

Emma nearly slapped her forehead. The girl was the spitting image of Abigail Beiler. She should have recognized that. "It's *gut* to have you in our community."

"It's not social time, *Mammi*." Silas kept throwing glances at his father. "I think he's upset."

"Oh, he's upset all right, but we'll work this out. We can work out anything so long as we're honest with one another."

And perhaps it was those words that dissolved the tension in the room. Clyde and Marcus pulled crates over so that they formed a tight circle. Jesse set his lantern down in the middle, and Nathan hung his on a hook near where they sat. The light was warm but not too bright. Emma thought it invited confidences to be shared. My, but she was feeling optimistic now that she saw with her own eyes that all of the children were fine.

Katie Ann sat down beside her brother.

Jesse, Nathan, and Silas.

Katie Ann and Naomi.

Even Emma could tell these were the leaders of the bunch. While everyone in the larger group had been talking, they'd looked to these five for confirmation of their fears and answers to their questions.

What was interesting was that they were so different. Jesse was built like his father, Leroy. He was small and thin and would have looked like a much younger teen if it weren't for the muscles along his forearms and the deep farmer's tan. Nathan, conversely, was built rather like a bull—stocky, with hair that wouldn't be tamed, popping out at odd angles. Beside those two, Silas looked younger, which she supposed he was. Silas was an odd combination of his father, Clyde, and Emma's husband, George. He was tall like his father, wiry like his grand-father, and he gave the distinct impression of his body not quite having caught up with the size of his feet—an eleven the last time they'd bought shoes.

The girls, in contrast, could have been sisters. Naomi and Katie Ann were both blond, though Naomi's hair had a slight tinge of red to it. They were thin with a smattering of freckles across button noses. If there were a stereotype for Amish girls, Naomi and Katie Ann were it, at least on the outside. And yet Katie Ann hoped to find a way to work with horses, and Naomi had been sent from Missouri to Colorado to live with her *aenti*. Neither fit in the pigeonhole of an Amish girl working in a bakery, which only went to prove looks could be deceiving.

"Start at the beginning," Clyde suggested.

Jesse began ticking off points on his fingers. "There have been four fires in the last three weeks. Two at Amish homes—Vernon's and Henry's. Two have been at *Englisch* establishments—JSW Construction and the newspaper."

"We're all aware." The corners of Marcus's mouth turned down as he pulled on his beard.

"We know the investigator thinks this person is targeting Amish folk, that for whatever reason he or she—"

Clyde said, "He, for certain."

"He has a vendetta against our community, our people."

"Or Amish in general," Naomi said.

Silas looked at the girl with such affection that it caused Emma's heart to ache. When had he grown up? He must have become a man while she was hanging laundry and baking pies.

"Tell me why you all decided to become involved." Clyde looked tired, but he'd always been good handling the children. In the short time since they'd entered the barn, he'd moved from correcting them for their behavior to problem solving with them.

Emma knew he'd be fair, though that didn't mean he'd agree with what they were doing.

"We became involved because the adults haven't done anything." Nathan didn't speak with a loud voice or rudely in any way, but the look he threw at his father was part pity and part frustration. "Because somebody has to."

"It's not our way, son—"

"I know that. I understand, but a *gut* third of our families are moving because of what has happened. We . . . " His hand came out to encompass those in the circle as well as those who had left. "We like it here, and we don't want to see our community torn apart, our friends scattered, because of something one man does."

"What was your plan?" Clyde asked.

"Actually, it was Naomi's idea." Katie Ann smiled at the girl, and then she added, "I'm sorry I ratted on everyone. I didn't mean to. It's only that I was worried about you."

The other teens shrugged as one.

"What was your idea, Naomi?" Emma thought she detected a bit of mischievousness in the girl's smile.

"My parents live in a Plain community in Seymour, Missouri. We have all sorts of critters there—coons, nutria, snakes, of course, and then there are the wild pigs. They can cause a lot of havoc on a farm, so we've learned to trap them. Some people release them elsewhere, or sell them, or in some cases cook them." Her nose wrinkled at this last option. "So I thought maybe we could set a trap for this person. Make him come to us."

"What sort of trap?" Clyde stretched his legs out in front of him and crossed them at the ankle.

All five of the teens glanced at each other, reached some silent consensus, and Jesse said, "He's a firebug, whoever this person is, and his targets have a lot of combustible material. Typical behavior for an arsonist."

"How would you know that?" Marcus asked, clearly baffled.

Emma thought Jesse was going to admit to having one of the smartphones that were all the rage, but he stopped himself in time and simply said, "Research."

"All right." Clyde looked more tired by the moment, but he pushed on. "You set a trap."

"Three," Katie Ann murmured.

"You set three traps. Where are they? How are they supposed to work?"

Nathan cleared his throat. Apparently, he had been in charge of implementing the plan. "We put one at the far northern end of our farms, one to the south, and another to the east. Nothing to the west, since that's where the town is, and we wouldn't want anyone to get hurt."

"Considerate of you. What exactly are these traps?"

"A large brush pile to the north," Jesse said.

"A bonfire pile to the east," Silas said.

"And the demolished barn to the south." Nathan looked almost proud but instantly became more serious when he saw the reprimand in his father's eyes.

"How is this arsonist supposed to know about these traps? What makes you think he'd even show up?"

"Oh, we're *gut* at getting word out," Naomi said.

"If I remember right, *youngies* have a grapevine all their own." Emma was thinking of her own teenage years, and how news would spread that they were meeting at a neighbor's or sneaking into town on a certain evening. Teens not only had their own language, but a way to spread information that existed all on its own, rather like an independent telephone system.

Nathan cleared his throat. "We think whoever is doing this somehow has a way of learning about things going on in our community. He had some dealings with Vernon. He also seemed to know Henry was helping the investigator, and that Henry's workshop was full of old lumber."

"And you expect him to just approach one of your traps." Clyde stood and began pacing back and forth in front of them.

"How can he resist?" Silas asked. "He likes to

burn things up. This stuff is sitting there waiting, and it's on Amish land."

"What was your plan when and if he showed?"

"To have lookouts stationed each evening at all three of the traps," Nathan explained. "Each person has . . . um . . . borrowed cell phones to call the police when our guy shows, and they only take four-hour shifts so they can still do their work the next day."

"And even if they did burn up one of the traps, so what? It wouldn't hurt anyone." Jesse shrugged. "But the police could catch him."

Silas jumped in to his friends' defense. "All we have to do is intercept him in the process and then sit on him . . . literally . . . until the authorities arrive."

"And the three spots we settled on are far enough from any homestead that no one's home would get damaged in the process." Naomi smiled, as if she'd answered a teacher's question correctly.

"Someone could get hurt, though." Katie Ann pulled her bottom lip in between her teeth. "I was in the newspaper fire, and I don't want to see . . . couldn't bear to see any of my friends go through the same thing."

Nathan ran his fingers through his hair in frustration, causing it to stick out even more. "It wouldn't be the same, though—"

"We've heard enough." Marcus walked over

to the office inside the barn and returned with a pad of paper and a pencil. He handed it to Jesse. "Write down the addresses where you put these traps."

"Naomi and Jesse, we'll take you home." Clyde returned the crate to the area where Marcus kept his supplies.

Marcus nodded toward the house and then spoke to his son, Nathan. "You can go inside. We'll speak more of this tomorrow."

Marcus agreed to speak with the parents nearest him in the morning. Clyde said he would go to see Henry first thing, and they would divide up the task of notifying the rest of the families.

It was tight when they all climbed into the buggy—Emma and Clyde in the front, Silas, Katie Ann, Naomi, and Jesse in the back. Something told her the young people didn't mind, that they were drawing solace being so close together. They were quiet, which didn't mean anything. They could be thinking of another way to catch the arsonist now that their initial plan had been foiled. They probably had developed a sign language all their own.

If there was one thing Emma was sure of, it was that *youngies* had a stubborn streak wider than the Colorado sky.

Sixty-Three

Henry arrived home well past midnight.

Earlier, he'd paid Stuart at the cabin and thanked him for his time, and then he rode to the police station with Alvin and Abe in Alvin's car. He sat through the questioning by both Meg Allen and Roy Grayson. In the end, both the investigator and sheriff agreed that the photos looked as though they had been altered with a computer program. This was after studying them with a magnifying glass and consulting with one of their technicians.

During the questioning, Alvin had admitted returning to Monte Vista regularly. Often he would meet with his brother or oldest nephew. Each time he would give a small amount of money, whatever he could spare, to his brother to help with Franey's expenses. He'd insisted that she not know where the funds came from.

"I have every reason to believe you're telling me the truth, Alvin." Meg stood. "Thank you for coming in. Thanks to all of you. We don't always get this sort of support on an investigation, and it makes a big difference. Now instead of scouring the countryside for you, we can focus on finding the real arsonist."

"I'm free to go?" Alvin's eyes widened in

disbelief. Perhaps the day's highs and lows, mostly lows, had come as too big a surprise. Maybe he was in shock, finding himself at the center of an investigation. Or it could be that he was emotionally and physically exhausted. Henry suspected it was all three.

Alvin had driven his brother Abe home first because his house was closer to town, and then he continued on to Henry's. When Henry opened the car door, Alvin stayed him with a hand.

"I want to thank you."

Henry waited, remembering that it sometimes took Alvin a few moments to find the words he was hunting for. It wasn't that he was slow, but he had a desire to say exactly what he meant.

"Today you showed grace to me. You acted . . . well, you acted much more compassionately and fairly than I would have given you credit for."

"I only dealt with you as I hope you would deal with me, given the same situation."

"*Ya*, you followed the Golden Rule. 'In everything, do to others what you would have them do to you.' I hope one day I do have the chance to return the favor."

"Only not during an arson investigation."

"*Nein*. This one is plenty to last me a lifetime."

Henry grew suddenly somber, remembering what Alvin had given up and all he had been through the last twelve years. He would never be able to agree with the reasons Alvin had felt it necessary to leave his wife and his faith and begin his life again, but he certainly understood that the man was doing his best, given the choices he'd made.

"*Gotte*'s blessings upon you, Alvin. Upon you and your family, your friends, your church, and all you hold dear."

Henry didn't glance back until he was on the porch and fitting his house key into the lock. When he turned around to watch Alvin leave, the interior of the car was still illuminated by the dome light. Henry saw Alvin wipe his eyes with the back of his hand. Alvin gave a short wave, put the car in reverse, and turned around to travel back down Henry's lane.

Lexi was ecstatic to see him. He'd been gone for more than twelve hours. Fortunately, before he'd left he had stopped by his neighbors', who had a key, and asked them to look in on the pup. Apparently they had because there were no messes in the mudroom and there was plenty of water in the dog's bowl. He walked out the back door with Lexi and stared up at the night sky as she took care of her business.

Henry focused on the stars and the coolness of the night. He smiled to himself when he remembered one of his grandfather's favorite verses, from the Psalms. " 'In his hand are the depths of the earth, and the mountain peaks belong to him.' "

Lexi stopped sniffing the porch steps and cocked her head, as if she were waiting for an explanation.

"I suppose if *Gotte* can handle all that, He can take care of one person bent on destruction."

Lexi didn't disagree.

Sixty-Four

Henry was up early, as usual, but he wasn't yet fully awake when a buggy turned down his lane. Lexi set to barking as if she could scare the intruders away with her voice. When Henry told her to "sit and hush," she gave him one reproachful look before curling up in her basket.

Five minutes later Clyde and Emma and Henry were seated around the kitchen table. Emma had poured everyone a cup of coffee and cut thick pieces of the coffee cake she'd brought. Henry savored the taste of cinnamon and brown sugar. Clyde finished his piece and shook his head when Emma offered another.

"We've come to talk to you about a serious matter. It has to do with the fires."

"I was afraid this wasn't merely a social call." Henry smiled to let them know he was kidding. Although he was still tired from the day with Lewis and Alvin and Abe, he understood their situation would only grow more taxing until Meg caught the arsonist. He'd steeled himself even as he went to bed the night before, praying for strength and wisdom and the energy to endure.

It took only a few moments for Clyde to lay out what they'd learned from the *youngies*. Emma interjected with observations now and again. When they were done, Henry poured them more coffee.

"It's a *gut* thing Katie Ann trusts you enough to be honest with you, Emma."

"*Ya.* I agree."

"And *danki*, Clyde, for handling this situation while I was away."

He gave them a brief accounting of the day before.

"What does it all mean, Henry?" Clyde looked worried and tired.

Henry needed to remember that, as they were struggling through this situation, men like Clyde still had farms to run, children to raise, and homes to care for. Life didn't stop because danger lurked around the corner.

Emma folded her napkin in half and then in half again. "Are we closer or only entangling ourselves in the chaos of this person?"

"I believe we are closer, but sometimes when you get closer to a dangerous thing . . . "

"It becomes even more dangerous." Emma's eyes met his.

"*Ya*, like a wild animal you've cornered. A person must be extra careful in such situations."

Clyde sat back and crossed his arms. "Would you like me to handle speaking to the parents?"

"The fact that you said you would probably buys us some time. The *youngies* will be on their

385

best behavior, waiting for one of us to arrive and spill the beans."

"Is that what we're going to do?" Emma asked. "Tattle on them and force them to abandon their traps?"

When Henry and Clyde stared at her, she added, "Their plan wasn't a bad one. It's only that we don't want to see our *youngies* in harm's way."

"What are you suggesting, *Mamm*?"

"She's suggesting we keep the traps." When Emma nodded, Henry almost laughed out loud. Emma Fisher never failed to surprise him.

"I agree with Emma that the plan might work. But no one does anything until I speak with Meg Allen. If she approves our doing so, or even offers to help, then we'll move forward."

"What of the parents?" Clyde asked.

"Emma, could you start something through the women in our group? Send a smoke signal or however you gals do such things."

Emma laughed out loud. "It's nothing so complicated. One person speaks to another. It's a form of communication that worked for my grandparents and their grandparents."

"Tell them of the traps and that we don't want any children involved, though we will take boys who are sixteen or older."

"To help catch an arsonist?" Clyde nearly came out of his chair, surprise raising his voice and causing his face to flush red.

"Only if Meg approves it. These boys will soon be men, Clyde. They want to help ensure the safety of our homes, and they should be a part of anything we decide to do."

"The girls aren't going to take that very well." Emma stopped Clyde's retort with a look. "Those girls have every bit as much invested in this community, and they deserve to be included."

Clyde muttered something about his mother being the first "Amish feminist," but Henry knew she had a point.

"All right. Girls and boys, but only those sixteen and up. And they can be involved only in ways we approve. We're not putting anyone inside a dilapidated barn waiting on our arsonist to show up."

Both Emma and Clyde seemed satisfied with the compromise. As they made their way back outside, Emma stopped to scratch Lexi behind her ears. "She's getting bigger."

"A little more every day. Abe warned me she was the runt, but I think she's growing nicely."

"It seems appropriate you should have the runt, Henry."

"And why is that?"

She pulled a treat out of her pocket and handed it to Lexi. "Because you are a champion of the underdog."

Henry called out to Clyde as he stood holding the buggy door open for his mother. "Come back

387

tonight after dinner. We'll meet with Leroy and Abe and decide what needs to be done."

"And you'll talk to Meg before then?"

"I'll go right away."

As Emma and Clyde made their way back down his lane, Henry hurried inside to fetch his hat. Lexi gave him the most pleading look he'd ever seen on the face of an animal, and he found himself saying, "Okay, fine. But you'll have to wait in the buggy."

Which for Lexi was apparently the best thing she'd heard so far that day.

Sixty-Five

Henry, Clyde, Abe, and Leroy met later that evening. There was no coffee cake this time. The mood was all business.

"I don't like it," Abe said. "I don't like anything about this."

"It's a *gut* plan, though." They were sitting on the front porch, their chairs pulled into a circle of sorts. Rain beat a soft rhythm against the roof, and Henry offered a silent prayer of thanksgiving for that. It would help the crops and had come at a perfect time.

Clyde jiggled his knee, tapped his fingers against the chair, and scanned left to right. He'd had more time to think about the plan and was obviously ready to tackle it head-on. "We probably should have thought of it ourselves."

"We shouldn't have thought of it," Leroy argued. "We should not be involved in this at all. It's an *Englisch* problem, not an Amish one."

"Tell Vernon that."

"You've made your point, Clyde." Henry paused a moment, hoping everyone's emotions would simmer down. "Meg decided there was no need for three locations. It's natural enough for our *youngie* to get together, and she thinks the bonfire is a perfect ruse. She will have people from her department at that location—hidden, of course. They'll be there two hours before sunset to ensure no one sees them."

"Why do we even need our *youngie*, then?" Leroy ran his thumb over a callus on his forefinger. "I don't like Jesse being involved in this at all. He thinks he's grown, but he's only twenty. He's still a pup."

Lexi yipped in her sleep, no doubt chasing rabbits like the one she'd caught after lunch. Fortunately, she'd dropped it at Henry's feet, and he'd been able to set the little thing free.

"I know it seems like they're young," Abe agreed. "But they're out of school."

"We expect them to act like adults," Clyde added. "We need to treat them like adults."

"Explain to me again what they'd need to do." Abe was plainly leaning toward Clyde's position.

Leroy continued to frown and shake his head.

While their leadership wasn't exactly a democratic process, Henry wouldn't go forward with something like this unless he had the support of each man sitting on his porch. Unity was the best policy if at all possible.

"First of all, we'd need them to spread the word, as they were planning to do. This only involves being in public—at the restaurants or stores—and talking about an upcoming meeting of young people."

"And they think the arsonist will just be hanging

around?" Leroy scoffed at the idea. "He'll happen to listen in to one of their conversations?"

"He's obviously tied into our community somehow. Chances are that, *ya*, he will hear. Outside of taking out an ad in the paper, which would look ridiculously obvious, it's our best chance."

"I see no danger in allowing the *youngie* to talk of such a thing." Abe rubbed at a muscle on the back of his neck. "Though it's not completely honest since they won't be actually meeting."

"It is honest in that they will be close to the meeting place, which will draw our arsonist in. The idea is that—for an arsonist—it's not enough to cause a fire; someone has to see it. Meg agrees this is the perfect set-up. She's surprised our *youngie* thought of it."

"Let me get this straight." Leroy shook his head in disbelief. "We have our sons and daughters out there talking about a supposed party, trying to lure this person into a trap where they will be waiting, though not too close because Meg's people will be there, and then we catch him as he sets the fire."

"Well, *ya*. I suppose that sums this up."

No one spoke for a moment, and then Leroy said, "Is this what we've come to? Because if it is, then it's as far from the plain and simple life as I can imagine being."

Henry's temper flared, and he clamped his mouth shut. The younger version of himself had learned long ago to wait for emotions to recede. When he trusted himself to speak, he said, "You bring up a *gut* point, Leroy. We don't want this type of life. We want a quiet one. We want a life set apart where we can focus on our families, hard and honest work, and following Christ's example. But we can't live a simple life as long as this arsonist is intent on causing devastation and hurting people. *Ya*, we are pacifist, and that's important to remember. However, this doesn't require us to lift a hand against another person. There's nothing at all violent or militant about it."

"Neither is it completely honest." Leroy was now leaning forward, his forearms propped against his legs, his eyes on the porch floor.

"I share Leroy's concerns," Abe admitted. "But it seems to be the only way, and I trust you, Henry. I trust that you have prayed over this and that you're sure it's the proper thing to do."

Clyde nodded in agreement. "That's *gut* enough for me."

Leroy closed his eyes.

Henry knew he didn't want to agree, but neither could he argue with what Abe said. He blew out a sigh and said, "*Ya*. All right. Put that way, I'll agree. But there's something else."

Leroy sat up straighter. "We need to speak of the families that are leaving."

"I've stopped by and visited with a few of

them." Henry thought of the list on the scrap of paper in his house. It seemed that every few days another name was added. "There are no hard feelings. They just don't want to be involved in this. They don't want to remain in a place where they're not wanted. They don't want to live where someone is actively trying to force them to leave."

"Better to go than to resist the pressure."

"Exactly, even though this pressure comes from someone who is misguided, at best."

"The reason I bring it up . . . " Leroy scanned the group, settling his gaze on Henry. "The reason I bring it up is because this will drastically reduce the amount of money we have for missions and benevolence."

"*Gotte* will provide what we need," Henry assured him.

"No doubt, but this reminds me of a leak in a dam. You put your finger in the first hole and water spurts from another spot. It continues until the dam fails, flooding everything around it."

"An unpleasant analogy, but I see your point." Henry stood, indicating the meeting was over. "Let's hope and pray the arsonist is caught before we are all carried away in the flood waters."

Sixty-Six

He was standing in line to purchase a burger behind two Amish girls. At first he didn't grasp what they were saying, but gradually he became conscious of the conversation, especially since they made no attempt to lower their voices. Girls, especially Amish ones, were oblivious to others. His pulse jumped when the taller of the two, with slightly reddish hair, mentioned the proposed bonfire.

They literally did not realize he was behind them. But then, when had an Amish girl given him more than a nod and hello? Nope. For whatever reason, he wasn't their type. He was practically invisible, which could work to his advantage.

The bonfire wouldn't happen until the weekend, and it was going to be held at a farm to the east of town. Based on their description, he knew exactly where they were talking about.

"It's too bad we have to wait until Friday."

"*Ya*, but no one could get away tonight or tomorrow. Too much work in the fields. Friday most everyone stops working a few hours early. It's the perfect time."

Maybe it was, for them. He'd promised himself

after the newspaper incident that he would stick to the list. Two more targets and he would be done. He'd started worrying about that. The fires provided something for him to plan and look forward to. What would he do once he'd finished? And would it be enough? Would they have paid the debt they owed him?

He wasn't so sure.

And the plans for a bonfire . . . well, they proved he was still not being taken seriously. He needed to show them he decided when fires would occur. He was the one in charge here.

A bonfire on Friday night.

Providence.

But he was thinking it would be much funnier if they arrived to find their bonfire a smoldering stack.

The place wouldn't be much of a challenge—no cameras to disable or security to avoid. He momentarily wondered if it might be beneath a man of his talents.

But it was sitting there—waiting.

Unless it was a trap.

The girls in front of him giggled, heads practically touching as they accepted their order from the cashier. They smiled at him shyly—smiled through him, actually—and hurried over to a table in the corner.

He asked for his order to go.

There were things to prepare if this was going

to be done correctly, and he had little time to waste. Plus, he'd need to stop by the discount store. He mentally started a shopping list, which included more fuel and a kitchen timer.

Sixty-Seven

Henry sat inside a hastily constructed deer blind with Meg.

They were positioned on the far side of the field, about fifty yards from the stack of wood where the youth were supposed to have their bonfire. The sun had dropped significantly in the last few minutes, but they were still at least an hour away from when the activities were supposed to start.

He picked up the binoculars he'd bought years ago to watch the spring migration of the sandhill cranes. Raising them to his eyes, he stared through them toward the *youngies* who were beginning to arrive in buggies, carts, and on bicycles.

Meg was fiddling with her police radio. "Group one, status report."

"Nothing here but Amish kids," the officer responded.

Group one was stationed on the opposite side of the field. They had a different vantage point and were so well hidden that Henry couldn't see them even with his binoculars.

"Group two."

"Other than the original wino we stumbled on, we've only seen the teens in our charge."

The man drinking in the dilapidated barn on the far corner of the property had been arrested and taken to the town jail, in case he wasn't who he appeared to be.

Meg clicked off her radio. "It's going to happen, Henry. I'm sure of it."

"*Ya?*"

"We can't be spotted from the highway, but we're close enough that anyone driving home would see the blaze, and that's a fairly busy road on Friday evening." She paused and added, "If there's one thing an arsonist loves, it's an audience."

"So all we have to do is sit and wait."

"Yeah. Both are things I'm not very good at if you haven't noticed."

Henry again picked up his binoculars and was focusing them on the Amish teens, who were unloading coolers, baskets of food, and blankets. Meg had made it very clear that they were to stay a safe distance from the site of the bonfire.

"Won't that look suspicious?" Silas had asked.

"No. It won't," she'd told him. "And it's non-negotiable."

Of course they wanted the youth meeting to look authentic. The teens actually seemed to be having a good time. Either they were good actors, or they'd decided to take advantage of the fine weather. Maybe it was the fact that they were actually helping in the investigation.

He was thinking of the way Meg had taken complete control of the situation and ensured their children's safety when the wood stacked for the bonfire exploded.

Flames shot into the sky. Smoke drifted toward them.

Some of the lumber was thrown several yards out from the pile, and the rest was instantly consumed.

Meg was talking into her radio as she ran toward the fire. "Keep those kids back. Lock down both exits. Stop anyone who attempts to leave."

Henry stood there, wondering if he should go after Meg or check on the youth. One look told him the *youngies* were unharmed. They were standing close together and gesturing toward the fire. Everyone seemed to be talking at once. Plainly they were fine. Meg's plan had worked. But he had to check on them personally. He'd promised each of their parents he would. So he hurried over to the group.

They were quite animated.

"It worked, Henry! He took the bait." Silas high-fived Nathan.

Katie Ann and Naomi stood close together, ignoring the boys and staring across at the fire.

He walked through the entire group, reversed directions, and made a second round. Though everyone was safe and uninjured, Henry stayed with them, talking to anyone who looked as if they needed a word of encouragement and making sure no one attempted to go out toward the fire. He was also scanning the group, confirming that each person there was in fact a member of their congregation. After another ten minutes, he was absolutely certain there wasn't a single person who didn't belong. Whoever the arsonist was, he wasn't hiding within the group of young people.

Perhaps the officers on the road had caught him.

He hurried toward Meg. She stood three feet from the smoldering pile of logs, fatigue and anger pulling at her shoulders.

"Did you catch him?"

"No."

"But . . . he set off the fire. Didn't he?"

"Yes." Meg scrubbed a hand over her face and turned to look him in the eye. "He must have used a timer."

"So he knew this was a trap?"

Meg shrugged. "He couldn't resist the target, but he didn't want to risk being caught."

"So we're no better off than we were."

"I don't know, Henry. What I do know is that this is a very resourceful person, but he's also smug. He thinks he's smarter than we are." She turned, her eyes filled with a steely resolve. "Smug people make mistakes. We will catch him, and we're going to do it soon."

Sixty-Eight

"It should have worked, Henry. You can't possibly blame yourself."

Families were pouring down Henry's lane. Jesse and Nathan were moving the buggies to the east field. Clyde stood at the building site for Henry's new workshop, directing people and supplies. The weather was beautiful, but a storm was coming. Emma knew it as surely as she knew they would have Henry's workshop finished by dark. The pressure in her head was an accurate barometer. If she could only make it through the day before the migraine took hold, she would be grateful.

"But I do blame myself. I convinced Clyde and Leroy and Abe to go along with the idea."

"We couldn't have known the arsonist would be so resourceful."

By now everyone knew the bonfire had been triggered remotely. The blaze was seen for miles, stopping cars in both directions along the highway. Fortunately, no one was hurt.

But neither had it produced additional clues or a single suspect.

"Meg says we're no further from catching the arsonist than we were before, but we're certainly no closer."

"We did our best." Emma reached out and touched his arm. "No one expects more."

The worry lines around Henry's eyes relaxed for a moment, but then he was called over to the workshop. He started that direction and then turned back toward Emma.

"I heard Clyde's workhorse was injured."

"Stepped into a hole."

"How is he?"

"He'll be fine. Now go. They're calling you."

Henry hurried away, Lexi trailing behind him, ears flopping, tail wagging.

"Is Henry going to be all right?" Rachel asked. "He seems to be taking the bonfire failure personally."

"Henry wants to protect everyone. But he needs to rest and let the *Englischers* solve this."

"It's sweet how you worry about him."

Emma glanced up in time to see a smile tugging at the corner of Rachel's mouth.

"What are you saying, *doschder*?"

"Why, nothing."

"You're sure?"

"Oh, I'm positive . . . " She glanced around to make sure no one was in earshot. "Only I do think you'd make a cute couple."

"Cute couple?"

"*Ya*. You're perfect for each other."

"Perfect?"

"Why are you repeating what I say?"

"Because I think you've lost your mind. Maybe you've read too many of those romance books."

"They're *Christian* romance."

"Well, I don't know what they are, but they're causing you to imagine things."

"The lady doth protest too much," Rachel murmured.

"What does that mean?"

"Oh. Well, it's from Shakespeare. See, in *Hamlet*, Queen Gertrude believes her husband to be dead, and so she has her eye on—"

"They need me at the food table." Emma hurried away before Rachel had a chance to say anything else, but she could have sworn she heard laughter behind her.

What had come over her daughter-in-law?

Emma pushed the question from her mind. She needed to focus on feeding the workers breakfast, lunch, and dinner. When all of the meals had been served she could go home, close the shades, and put a cool cloth across her forehead. Until then, she'd have to find a way to endure.

The morning passed quickly, with families arriving, more supplies delivered, and an unlimited stream of children underfoot.

When news crews arrived before lunch, Emma wanted to throw up her hands.

"Why are they here?" Katie Ann asked.

Susan put three more jars of peanut butter spread on the table. "I heard they're doing a follow-up story about the Monte Vista Arsonist." She put virtual quote marks around the last three words.

"I'm tired of that creep getting so much attention," Katie Ann announced quite seriously, but something about her tone and frustration caused Susan to break into laughter.

"Aren't we all, child. Aren't we all."

Naomi tucked a stray lock of hair into Katie Ann's *kapp*. The two had been as thick as ticks on a hound dog ever since the night in the Klines' barn. "Whenever we had a barn raising in Seymour, the *Englisch* would pull off the road for miles to watch and take pictures."

"This is hardly a barn," Susan reminded her. "It'll only take all day because they want to extend Henry's porch around the west side of his house as well while they're here. It will help cool the rooms inside and provide him a nice place to sit in the evening."

"It's *gut* for us to take care of our bishop," Ruth declared, marching past their table holding a pie in one hand and a cake in the other.

For some reason that started the girls to giggling again.

Emma fanned herself and glanced over at the shade on the front porch.

"Why don't you go up there and rest," Susan suggested.

"*Nein.* I'm fine."

"You're not fine. We'll call you if things get too busy. For now, rest a little."

"What's wrong with her?" Katie Ann asked as Emma walked away.

"She has one of her migraines."

"Why didn't she say something to me about it?"

"I'm sure she didn't want to worry you."

Emma wanted to turn around and assure Katie Ann she was okay, but that would take too much energy. Instead, she sought the shade and quiet of the porch. Once there, she watched the commotion taking place out toward the road as the news vehicles set up their cameras and microphones.

Meg drove into the lane, stopped, and stepped out of her car to make a statement. It must have been a short one, because after only a moment she climbed back in the car and drove toward the worksite. Emma closed her eyes for a moment. When she opened them Henry was walking Meg back to her car. She could tell, watching Henry, that Meg hadn't brought good news.

Henry told her that, after the bonfire, she'd promised to stop by and update them. She'd also cautioned Henry and said they needed to be patient. That eventually the forensics team would find something. The arsonist would make a mistake. He was only human, and eventually he'd slip up. When he did, they'd catch him. All

405

of those things should have reassured Emma, but they didn't. There was no telling what this person would do next.

"Rough week?" Abigail sat down in the chair beside her, allowing her cheater glasses to fall on their chain and hang against the front of her dress.

"*Ya*. I suppose so."

"We'll get through this, Emma. Never doubt."

They sat for a while, rocking and listening to the hammering of nails against lumber.

Making an effort to open her eyes, Emma said, "Your niece is a sweet thing. Katie Ann's quite taken with her."

"From what I've been able to see, so is Silas."

"*Ya*. I noticed that too."

"It's *gut* Naomi is here. Her family was in a . . . difficult situation." She didn't offer more, and Emma didn't push.

"I heard about Clyde's horse stepping into a hole. How is he doing?"

"Fair. Doc Berry says he sprained the tendons in his ankle joint and also scraped it up quite a bit. Clyde bought Duncan when we first moved here. He's become more of a pet than a workhorse."

"I know how that goes."

"Katie Ann wanted to stay home with him because the vet said we should apply ointment to the wound three times a day." Emma glanced over at her friend. "I convinced her that missing one application won't hurt Duncan."

406

"I'm more worried about you than the horse. Are you sure you're feeling all right?"

"*Ya.* It's only a migraine."

"Only a migraine? I knew a woman in Goshen who would take to her bed for two or three days, refusing to come out of the room at all. No doubt they were very painful. She couldn't function one bit when she had one."

"The dark helps," Emma admitted. "But the truth is that my head will ache whether I'm home in bed or here . . . and I'd rather be here."

"And we're glad to have you." Abigail sighed and stood, smoothing down her apron. "They're gathering for lunch."

"I'll come help—"

"*Nein.* You won't. I might not be able to force you home, but I can at least make sure you sit here in the cool of the porch and out of the sun."

"You're a *gut* friend, Abigail."

Instead of answering, Abigail patted her on the shoulder and scurried off to help serve the workers their luncheon.

Emma closed her eyes, prayed that the workshop would go up with no problems, and that the arsonist would stay far, far away.

Sixty-Nine

Emma's migraine only worsened as the day progressed. Susan walked up as she was holding her head firmly between her palms.

"Go home."

"We haven't begun laying out the dinner spread."

"We have many hands to help with that, Emma. Your face is as pale as the white of your apron, and I can tell from the way you're wincing that this is a bad one."

"I thought it might pass."

"And yet it hasn't. Now, let Clyde take you home."

"He's on the roof. I hate to call him down. It can wait if only I can—"

"I'll be happy to take you home."

Emma turned to see Henry had walked up and was studying them, a look of compassion covering his face. He was wearing his jacket, and that was when she realized the day had cooled. Though June had brought daytime temperatures to near seventy, the evenings could still drop into the thirties.

She didn't quite understand the way he looked at her. There was something in his gaze, something more than concern over her migraine. She felt she should have understood, but the pulsing in her head once again claimed her attention and the thought was pushed aside.

"I didn't see you."

"Because you had your eyes squeezed shut."

"She needs to go home," Susan said. "Clyde is helping with the roofing."

"It's settled, then. I promised I would go by and check on Rebecca. I can drop Emma off at home, visit Rebecca, and still be back for the evening meal."

"If you're not, Abe or Clyde or Leroy will take care of the evening prayer."

"All right. I'll do my best, but if I haven't returned by then, don't worry about me."

Emma pulled her *kapp* tighter on her head, as if it might shield her face from the cruel brightness of the sun.

"Let me help you."

His arm encircled her waist, and Emma allowed herself to be led toward his buggy.

Henry whistled once, and Lexi made a beeline toward them, trotting happily behind her master. When they reached the buggy, she sat and waited for Henry to lift her up onto the seat. The little dog scooted toward the middle of the front seat and sat waiting for the ride to commence.

"You've trained your dog."

"Indeed. Though now she thinks it's time for her to take a ride whenever I harness Oreo to the buggy."

Emma nodded, but she didn't respond. Talking hurt. Everything hurt. She was accustomed to the headaches, having endured them since she was ten years old. There was nothing to be done for them except wait them out and, during the worst ones, seek out a dark, cool place.

Once they were on the road, Henry asked, "Have you spoken to Doc Wilson about this?"

"*Ya.*" Emma leaned forward, propped her elbows on her knees, and used her hands to shield out the bright afternoon light. She focused on breathing slowly and deeply. She told herself that in a few minutes she'd be in bed, in a darkened room, and then the rolling in her stomach would settle.

"Perhaps it's time to speak to him again."

"There's medicine, but I'd rather not take it."

"Rebecca would rather not have rheumatoid arthritis, but she does. Doc's medicine has helped."

"Lecturing a sick woman?" Emma peeked at him before again covering her eyes. "Not fair, Henry."

"As your bishop, and your friend, I rather feel it's my duty."

He reached over and patted her arm. In that moment something deep inside Emma shifted, something she hadn't felt in quite a while, some stirrings of a younger, more innocent self. She recognized her loneliness for what it was.

Amazing how one could be lonely even in a crowd, even while in pain.

Her thoughts, or rather her emotions, had jumped the track all from a touch of the bishop's hand.

Foolishness. That's what it was. Perhaps because her defenses were down. During the worst of her migraines, it seemed every aspect of her body and soul became more sensitive. The smallest sounds grated on her nerves. Any scents, even those she usually loved, such as coffee or baking or flowers, were overpowering. She could actually feel the clothes against her skin, and what she normally considered soft fabric became rough and difficult to endure. And possibly the worst aspect was that her emotions became overly tender. She would cry about something she might have laughed about the day before.

Now she had interpreted her bishop's compassionate attitude as something more. She clamped her teeth together and prayed that God would strengthen her until they reached her home.

Henry seemed to understand. There was no idle chatter or attempt to convince her to go to the doctor. He didn't even call out to the horse, but gently guided her with the reins instead.

Emma focused all of her energy on taking the next breath. On overcoming the next wave of pain. Enduring until she could lie down in her

411

room, the shades pulled low, and a cool cloth on her head. She'd have the house all to herself for a few hours, and the idea of quiet and solitude gave her hope. Normally she preferred a full, active home. But not today.

Henry turned into their lane. She wondered what they must look like—a bishop, a beagle, and a widow clutching her head. Not that it mattered. No one would see them.

"Were you expecting company today?"

"What?"

"Was anyone coming by to check on the animals?"

"No. Why?"

"Barn door's open."

Emma resisted the urge to slap her forehead. It would only cause her head to ache more.

"Katie Ann," she murmured. Her tongue felt thick, her words clumsy. "Sam brought back her . . . her back. She . . . she worried Clyde's workhorse needed . . ."

She fought to ignore the pounding in her head, to make some sort of sense. "Doc Berry told her to apply ointment . . . three times a day."

Emma felt more than heard Henry's sharp intake of breath as the reins went slack in his hands.

Lexi growled low and deep in her throat.

Emma looked up and saw only a small cloud of dust coming from the side of the barn.

Henry exclaimed, "It's on fire!" He slapped the reins, causing Oreo to gallop down the lane. Lexi bared her teeth and stood up on her hind legs to better see out the front window. Emma clasped both hands to the sides of her head and prayed Henry was mistaken.

Seventy

Henry hoped he was mistaken. As he had turned into Emma's lane, he'd noticed the dust. The thought crossed his mind that it had rained the day before, only a quarter inch but enough to wet the dirt lane. And then he realized it was rising, which dust didn't tend to do, up and out like smoke from a chimney, like the fire from his own workshop. He'd slapped the reins against his horse, causing Oreo to toss her head and whinny. The ride was jarring, and the mare wasn't keen on hurrying toward a fire.

As they drew closer, Henry's heart sank. Flames were spreading, licking at the western wall of Clyde's barn.

Emma leapt out of the buggy before it stopped, screaming for Katie Ann as she ran toward the barn. Lexi scrambled down from the seat and out of the buggy, barking ferociously and darting past Emma before disappearing into the smoke.

When Emma staggered and dropped to the ground, Henry knelt beside her.

"Katie Ann," she groaned before retching violently.

"Stay here. I'll get her. Stay here and pray, Emma."

Henry hurried toward the barn, pulse racing, thoughts tumbling one over the other, and sweat already running down his back.

Lexi had taken off toward the woods. He'd find her later.

As he neared the door on the south side, one of Clyde's workhorses bolted from the barn.

Henry hopped back, stumbled on an uneven patch of ground, and lost his balance. He fell with a hard thud and pain shot up into his hip.

Scrambling back to his feet, he dashed in to find Katie Ann slapping the rump of a Percheron that towered over her. The horse was jet black, at least eighteen hands, and no doubt weighed close to two thousand pounds. Despite Katie Ann's efforts, the beast refused to move closer to the fire. As Henry ran toward them, Katie Ann scooted around and in front of the horse.

The gelding tossed its head as she reached to grasp the halter.

Eyes rolling, sweat pouring off its neck, the animal skidded left and then right, knocking into the stalls on either side.

Henry managed to grab the lead and tug hard as Katie Ann ran behind the beast and slapped its rump again. "Get out of here, Duncan!" The horse reared up once and then bolted for the door.

"The water spigot is at the northwest corner." Katie Ann didn't wait for him to respond. She'd grabbed an old blanket from the nearest horse stall, rushed over to the west wall, and began to beat at the flames.

He was supposed to be rescuing Katie Ann. He'd promised he would. But the girl was intent on saving her father's barn and had already saved his horses.

Henry nodded and ran toward the door.

The recent rains they'd had—more precipitation than any other summer since their group had moved to Monte Vista—had dampened the barn's timber. Although flames were licking at the shelves, shelves Katie Ann was even now beating with the old blanket, the wall itself had not caught on fire. Henry hurried outside, around the corner, and turned on the faucet, but as usual the water poured slowly and gently into the bucket. Then he saw the horse trough, situated a few feet away and brimming with water.

He grabbed another pail, ran to the trough, filled the pail with water, and threw it onto the outside of the wall Katie Ann was defending.

By the time he ran back to the pump, the bucket he'd left there was full.

He switched them out and ran back to the wall.

On his fourth or fifth run, Emma handed him the bucket.

"You should be—"

"Go!"

She grabbed the empty pail from him and ran back to the faucet.

Henry didn't realize the fire was out until Katie Ann stepped out of the barn, her clothes smudged with soot, *kapp* askew, hair frizzed, and frantically looking for the horses.

"They're fine. They're . . ." Henry gulped for a full breath of air. He'd sweat through his shirt so that it was dripping. His hip had begun to ache from the fall, and his arms were trembling.

But somehow he felt more alive than he had in a long time.

"They're in the west field."

Katie Ann rewarded him with a smile, then her eyes widened and she ran to Emma's side. She was beside the pump, sitting in the mud created from the many buckets of water, and cradling her head. "*Mammi!* Are you all right?"

For an answer, Emma groaned.

"It's a migraine," Henry explained. "A bad one. It's why I brought her home."

Emma didn't attempt to raise her head, but he stepped closer and heard her ask her granddaughter. "Are you . . ."

"I'm fine."

"And the barn?"

"*Gut.* Shelves will have to be rebuilt, but we saved the wall. And the horses. Thank *Gotte* we saved the horses."

Henry overturned the pail he was holding and sat on it.

Katie Ann collapsed into the dirt next to Emma

and began rubbing her grandmother's back in gentle circles. Exactly what Henry had wanted to do while they were walking toward the buggy, but then he'd felt foolish and settled for supporting her with his arm. It hurt him so to see her in pain, every bit as much as it hurt to see Clyde's barn nearly ablaze. As much as it hurt him to see the terror in Katie Ann's eyes when the horse had resisted going through the door.

He realized in that moment how much he cared for Emma and for her family. All of his congregation was dear to him, but what he felt for Emma was different. He saw that now. Saw it as clearly as the Percheron cropping grass a few yards from him.

Emma raised her head, squinted against the sun, and asked, "Lexi?"

"She ran . . . ran toward the woods." And suddenly he was remembering that other fire, in the darkness of the night, and Lexi holding on to the arsonist's leg as he attempted to pedal away.

Henry scrambled to his feet. "Whoever did this must have fled into the trees."

"Lexi went after him?" Katie Ann rose too, alarmed by the thought of the little dog being in trouble. "We'd better check on her."

Emma waved at them to go, and Henry started to.

But what if the wall of the barn was a distraction? What if their arsonist meant to set fire to the house? What if this person was watching, waiting for them to go into the woods?

What if he was looking for another person to kill?

Henry couldn't leave Emma alone. He couldn't risk any harm coming to her.

"Come with us." He helped Emma to her feet, not bothering to explain his reasoning.

With Katie Ann on one side of Emma and Henry on the other, they all walked into the woods.

Seventy-One

Emma wasn't sure exactly what she was doing under the canopy of trees behind their home, walking between Henry and Katie Ann. She was grateful for the shade. Her head still felt as if someone had driven a spike into it, but she no longer felt waves of nausea. She longed to fall to the ground, curl up, and sleep until morning.

Henry and Katie Ann had other ideas.

"Tell me what happened," Henry said to Katie Ann. "Describe exactly what happened before you saw the fire."

"Sam brought me home so I could check on Duncan. He has that place on his leg where he needs medicated ointment. Doc said three times a day, without fail, so I came home to take care of it."

"Wait." Henry stopped so suddenly that Emma kept walking for a brief second and was jerked back because one arm was linked with Henry's and the other with Katie Ann's. She bounced back like a boomerang the boys had once played with. "Sam brought you home?"

"*Ya.* Did you think I walked?"

"How long did he stay?"

"I don't know. He hung around for a little

420

while. We talked as I looked after Duncan's leg. There was nothing improper about it."

Emma had been standing there, eyes closed, pretending she was in her bed. But she heard something in her granddaughter's voice that caused her to jerk her eyes open and glance up. Katie Ann was blushing prettily. There was no doubt about it. Did she have feelings for Sam? Emma's mind flashed back on the conversation with Rachel and her worries that Katie Ann and Sam might be courting. Were they courting? Wouldn't Katie Ann have mentioned it to her?

More puzzling than those questions, Henry was now scowling mightily, and his hands were clenched so tightly that his knuckles had turned white.

"I want you to tell me everything you can remember . . . every detail . . . before Sam left."

"I had already applied the ointment on Duncan, so I replaced it on the shelf where we keep such things. Sam walked with me, back toward the front when I did that. Then we said goodbye, and I returned to the back stall. I like to give Duncan a little treat after the ointment and a *gut* brushing." She ran her fingers up and down her *kapp* string, and glanced left and right.

Emma wanted to ask why Sam would leave Katie Ann alone with an arsonist on the loose, a man dead set against their community. Why didn't he wait and take her back to the workday?

Before she could ask either of those things, Henry urged Katie Ann to continue. "What happened next?"

"Well, I was brushing Duncan, and he began to toss his head, and then I realized I smelled smoke."

Emma forced herself to meet Henry's gaze. A wiggly line was running through her vision, but it didn't diminish the look of angry determination on his face. It was an expression she wasn't accustomed to seeing on her bishop, and she knew without a doubt what he was thinking.

"*Nein*, Henry. You are wrong on this."

"Too many coincidences. It has to be."

"What are you two talking about?"

"I think . . . that is, there's a possibility . . . circumstances seem to point to the fact that Sam was involved with the fire."

"That's impossible."

"I wish it were."

Henry began walking forward, but Katie Ann remained where she was, standing next to Emma.

"I'm telling you it wasn't him. Sam wouldn't do that. He cares . . . " She quickly rephrased whatever she was about to say. "He's a *gut* man. He wouldn't do such a thing."

Henry walked back slowly, no doubt weighing his words.

The pain in Emma's head had reached a dull roar. She'd been to the ocean once when she was a young bride. This aching reminded her of the waves that kept coming, relentlessly, one after another. The thought passed through her mind that this was no ordinary migraine, that she should go and see the doctor. But that was quickly followed by the realization that Henry had insisted she come with them into the woods. Was he afraid . . . for her?

"I hope you're right, Katie Ann, but we have to look at the facts. Sam has been in the vicinity of all the fires to date. He was either seen there by someone or admits to being in the neighborhood. Now you tell me he was with you, in the barn, minutes before the fire."

"It looks bad, Henry, I know. I do understand what you're saying. But Sam wouldn't do such a thing. I know he wouldn't. He was supposed to take me back to the workday, but I convinced him I'd be fine just staying here with the horses. I didn't know—"

"If what you're saying is true, then he must have left mere minutes before the fire. He's a fireman, Katie Ann. He would recognize the signs of a fire. He'd be alert to the smell of smoke. He would have stayed to help you. But he didn't. Why?"

"I-I don't know."

Emma realized her granddaughter was close to tears by the way her words trembled.

She crossed her arms, frowned at her bishop,

and said, "I don't know the answer to that, but when we find him, we'll ask him."

She pushed past Henry, and then she turned and asked, "Why are we here in the woods? What are we looking for?"

"My dog."

"Right. Lexi. I forgot."

Henry looked directly at Emma and then reached to help her forward. Their hands touched, and warmth rushed through her as it had when they'd walked to the buggy. Perhaps her blood pressure was high, because she suddenly felt somewhat lightheaded.

"I want to keep her away from the house," Henry said in a low voice. "For a few minutes, until we're sure whoever has done this has left. Let the *Englisch* authorities catch the culprit. My goal is to keep you and Katie Ann safe. Now, can you walk a little farther?"

Emma nodded her head and focused on putting one foot in front of the other. She didn't pay attention to where they were going. The woods behind their home were on a little less than ten acres. They couldn't become lost, and if they walked north they would end up at the Kline farm. Of course, no one would be there. Everyone was still working on Henry's workshop and porch.

Katie Ann had walked ahead and was now a few yards to the north of them.

When she shouted out and dropped to the ground, Emma tried to run, stumbled, and fell against a tree. Henry hurried to help her, but she pushed him away. "Go. Go check on Katie Ann."

Seventy-Two

Henry didn't want to leave Emma leaning against the tree, but the second time she insisted he turned and trotted toward where they'd seen Katie Ann go down. He found her kneeling next to Sam.

"Sam! Talk to me. Sam, can you hear me?" She glanced up as Henry drew closer. "Help him, Henry. Please, help him."

Henry knelt beside Sam's body, directly across from Katie Ann. Sam was lying on his side and blood was oozing from a wound on his head. Sam didn't speak or even stir as Henry checked him for other injuries. He placed his fingers against the carotid artery in Sam's neck and counted the beats of his pulse against a clock in his head. "Seems a bit slow, but it's steady."

"So he's alive?"

"*Ya*, sure and certain he is."

"But he looks so pale, and he's not waking up."

"Give him a few minutes." He pulled a handkerchief out of his pocket. "Hold this against his head while I look around."

"Okay."

Henry was surprised Emma had managed to join them. She still looked pale, but she'd recovered her equilibrium. "Katie, take the bishop's handkerchief and go and wet it in the creek. Get it *gut* and cold."

She'd pulled a similar handkerchief out of her apron pocket. After folding it in half and then half again, she placed it gently against Sam's head.

"He didn't do this to himself," she said.

"*Nein*, though he could have fallen."

"Most people fall forward."

"I suppose." Henry was thinking of his own fall. When he'd lost his balance, he'd landed on his side. Even if Sam had fallen backward, there were no large rocks in the vicinity. How had he suffered the blow to his head?

"The gash is on the top of his head, but near the back. Looks to me like someone snuck up from behind and struck him."

"Who? Who would do that?"

Emma didn't hazard a guess, but she did look up and meet his gaze.

He'd been wrong. He'd jumped to a conclusion and blamed one of their own for a terrible crime. But Sam had not hit himself, and in all likelihood whoever had done so had also set the fires of the last month and had killed Vernon.

"The authorities will catch him," Emma said. "We only have to find Lexi, rouse Sam, and get everyone safely home."

Katie Ann returned with the dripping wet handkerchief.

"Now wring it out," Emma said.

After she had, Emma placed it across Sam's forehead. "Hold it for me."

She continued to apply pressure to the wound on the back of his head.

"That's a lot of blood." Henry honestly didn't know what to do. He had the feeling answers were here beneath the giant trees. And he still needed to find Lexi, but he didn't want to leave Emma and Katie Ann alone, and he was worried about Sam. How Emma could possibly guess all the things he was thinking, he had no idea, but she did.

"Head wounds bleed a lot, but this one seems to be superficial. He might have a concussion. The cold rag will probably help bring him around. In the meantime, go look for Lexi . . . and be careful."

He nodded once but didn't leave immediately. Instead, he knelt beside them and put one hand on Emma's shoulder and the other on Katie Ann's head. They made a complete circle with both women ministering to Sam. "Father, watch over these, Your children. Protect them. Send Your angels to guard them. Give us strength, compassion, and wisdom. We ask these things in the name of Christ . . . "

Three soft "Amens" rose up toward the birds singing in the trees.

Henry struggled to his feet and continued in the

direction it seemed Sam must have been going. He found Lexi after only a few minutes of searching. The little beagle was lying in the bottom of a ravine, half in and half out of the water.

She didn't raise her head when Henry squatted beside her, but her tail began to thump a happy beat. When he ran his hand up and down her side, she made a feeble attempt to lick his fingers. It was obvious that she had been kicked, possibly injuring her ribs again, and one eye was swollen from where she'd landed hard against the ground. Other than those two things, she seemed okay. She whimpered softly and laid her head back on the ground.

"It'll be all right, now." He shrugged out of his jacket, surprised he still had it on after putting out the fire and then hurrying through the woods. "This may hurt a little. Don't bite me."

But Lexi only stared up at him with large brown eyes as he moved her onto the jacket, wrapped her up, and then carried her back to Emma and Katie Ann.

He arrived as Sam was beginning to stir.

Seventy-Three

"He must have snuck up behind me." Sam pulled away from Emma and stared at the cloth she was holding as if he couldn't fathom where the blood stains had come from. He raised a hand to the back of his head and winced.

"Who?" Henry asked.

"Not sure. As I was leaving the barn, I saw him slinking off into the woods."

"Why didn't you stop to help with the fire?"

"Fire?" Sam attempted to jump up, but Emma placed a hand on his shoulder.

"It's all right. There was little damage. Katie Ann and Henry managed to put it out."

Sam shook his head. "There wasn't any fire when I left. I'm sure of it. I would have noticed or smelled it, even if it was just beginning."

"Then how—"

"I suppose he attached a timer to whatever he's using to start the fires."

"Like he did with the bonfire."

"It's not that difficult a thing to do, but it does seem to point to the fact that this is not merely a teenager messing around."

"No. I think we're well past that theory."

"Why would he hang around at all once he'd started the timer?" Emma asked.

"He probably wasn't expecting anyone to be home."

"So he knew about the workday at Henry's?" Katie Ann tilted her head to the side, as if this was a puzzle she might figure out.

"No doubt everyone in the community knew about the workday. They even broadcast it on the local news." Henry shook his head. "Which provided a perfect time for him to stage his next fire."

"Maybe he snuck up to the barn, not expecting anyone to be there. He heard Katie Ann and me, he set the timer, and then ran off into the woods. When I saw him, my only thought was that someone running away from the barn didn't seem right. Didn't seem to me that anyone should have been on the Fisher place. I knew everyone in the family was at your place, Henry."

"Why did you leave my house before the work was finished?" Henry realized his tone sounded like that of an interrogator. Perhaps he'd spent too much time around Meg. Maybe that was what came of mixing with the *Englisch*.

"Katie Ann wanted a ride home . . . " He started to say something else but snapped his jaw shut.

"So you stayed in the barn a few minutes—"

"He was helping me, and we were *talking*," Katie Ann said. "Nothing more."

"We're not worried that anything inappropriate might have happened," Emma assured her.

To Henry it seemed as if Emma's migraine was easing. He certainly hoped and prayed it had. He'd never seen her suffer so intensely from one, but perhaps he'd never paid enough attention.

"You still think he may have done it?" Katie Ann minced no words.

Sam had been staring at Lexi, but now he raised his eyes to Henry. The flicker of emotions across the lad's face shamed Henry—he read easily enough his surprise, then hurt, and finally a quiet resolve.

"*Nein*, I no longer think Sam was involved," he said to Katie Ann.

Turning his attention to Sam, he said, "When Katie Ann told me you were in the barn, I'll admit my faith in you wavered. There have been so many coincidences, and at every event you were either present or in the neighborhood."

"*Ya*, I was beginning to doubt myself, as if I might have done something I know I didn't do. And I never should have even considered leaving Katie Ann here by herself. "

"Still, it was wrong of me to suspect you. I'd like to ask your forgiveness."

Sam had been sitting on the ground, holding the cloth to his head, but at Henry's words he stood, wiped his hands on his pants, and said, "Of course I forgive you. I also respect you for caring about us and protecting our families."

"It is *Gotte* who protects us, though it would

help if He would send a postcard just now to tell us what to do next."

"We need to get Lexi to Doc Berry." Katie Ann had taken the dog from Henry's arms. Now she was stroking Lexi's velvety ears.

"*Ya*, she needs the veterinarian for sure." Henry hesitated, peered around them, and then asked Emma, "How are you doing? Is it terribly painful for you to stay outside?"

She waved away his concerns. "The worst of it was out in the sunlight. Now that we're in the shade . . . the pain remains but is manageable."

"*Gut.* I don't want you to go back to the house alone. Not yet. Not until Clyde has returned home. I don't think it's safe for any of us to be there."

"We could all go back to your place." The bleeding on Sam's head had slowed, but it hadn't stopped completely. "Send the *Englischers* out here to search."

"If he's here, he'd be gone by then." Katie Ann's voice was soft, low, and she kept her eyes focused on the dog.

Henry turned slowly in a circle, and then he stopped in front of Sam. "Do you think the person who hit you could still be here?"

"Maybe. He ran into these woods. I don't think he'd have risked coming out on the other side of this fence. The Klines keep an old bull in that pen."

"He might have run past you."

"Possibly," Sam admitted. "But wouldn't you have seen him? It sounds as if you were still at the barn when I was chasing him into these woods. You would have seen him come out, or you would have passed him when you came in."

"Makes sense. I say we look around." Henry didn't like it, but he also understood this might be a rare opportunity. He'd never wished for the *Englischers'* technology, but he could certainly use one of their cell phones right now. "If we can catch him, we can stop this destruction."

"As long as we all stay together." Emma put her hand through Katie Ann's arm. "And no longer than a half hour. We need to have the wound on Sam's head looked after, as well as the dog."

Henry walked in front, followed by Emma and Katie Ann. Sam brought up the rear of their little group.

They retraced Henry's steps to the spot where he'd found Lexi. The woods weren't that large or that dense, and he had a hard time imagining where someone could hide. They walked to the far western side, then tracked back toward the east. They were roughly in the middle and had stopped to consider which direction to go next when Lexi emitted a low, throaty growl.

They stepped closer together, forming a tight circle, then turned as one toward the outside, each looking in a different direction.

But none of them was looking up.

Douglas Rae landed on the ground in front of Emma, holding a crowbar in one hand and sporting a backpack.

Henry blinked once and then again. Douglas was the Monte Vista arsonist?

Douglas was the person who had killed Vernon Frey, burned down his workshop, and hurt innocent people at the newspaper?

His mind couldn't quite come to terms with the fact. In truth, he looked like a teenage boy. His black hair flopped in front of his eyes, and he wore a baseball cap backward. His jeans were freshly pressed, and his cargo jacket was old but clean. For some reason, the T-shirt he wore under the jacket was on inside out.

Henry knew Douglas. Most everyone in Monte Vista did. He'd won the state chess championship the first year they'd moved to Colorado, and he was a frequent visitor at their auctions and yard sales. Of course, in a small rural area, nearly everyone knew everyone else, whether they were Amish or *Englisch*.

The person in front of them was responsible for a long string of destruction and death and injury.

With a puzzled look, Douglas asked, "Why couldn't you all leave well enough alone?"

Seventy-Four

Emma nearly choked on her reply. "Well enough alone? Did you do all of this, Douglas?" When he didn't answer, she moved in front of him, hands on her hips. "You did. It's plainly written on your face. You tried to burn down my son's barn, you did burn down the bishop's workshop, and you killed Vernon Frey. You are an evil, evil man."

Douglas raised the crowbar, but Henry and Sam stepped in front of Emma, shielding her and Katie Ann from harm.

"You're pacifists, remember?" A little spittle flew from his lips, and the anger in his eyes sent a shiver down Emma's spine.

"It's true we will not harm you," Henry said. He held up both hands, palms forward. "But your reign of terror is over. We can and will identify you to the police."

"I won't let you do that."

"How are you going to stop us?"

Emma could see that Sam's hands were curled into tight fists. Katie Ann was still clutching the dog, her head swiveling back and forth between their group and Douglas Rae.

"Will you kill four more people?" Emma asked. "Will you have that on your conscience?"

"I've done nothing wrong, only what was necessary because of you people. I've done nothing except set a few things right." Douglas pushed through Henry and Sam and grabbed Emma roughly by the arm, raising the crowbar over her head. "Do as I say, or I'll bean her like I did you, Sam. You think I don't know your names? I know everything about you. I've been paying attention. You're the ones who don't understand what's happening around you."

He jerked his head to the southeast. "That way. Where the field meets the road. Let's go."

Emma met Henry's gaze. He shook his head slightly. She wanted to push this young man, to knock the crowbar from his arm. Pacifism was good and fine, but this was her granddaughter, her neighbor, and her friend. She couldn't allow them to come to harm.

But the warning in Henry's eyes changed the direction of her thoughts. Perhaps if they went with Douglas, he would take them to where he was staying. No doubt there would be plenty of evidence there. It was a bold plan, and it would only work if he thought they were cowed. People like Douglas Rae wanted control of their situation. They wanted to believe others would do whatever they said.

So Emma allowed her hand to shake slightly, and in her meekest voice she said, "*Ya*, we'll go with you, Douglas. Only don't hurt anyone."

He scowled at her, but she thought she detected a look of triumph in his eyes.

"Old man, you go first. Then Sam and the girl with the mutt. Mrs. Fisher and I will bring up the rear. Try anything crazy, and she'll be the first to go down."

He clutched her arm hard enough to leave fingerprints.

But that was nothing. Bruises would heal. She needed to find a way to keep Katie Ann safe.

It would be easy enough to fall to the ground and take Douglas Rae with her. She could scream *run* as she fell. But would they run? Would they leave her? She doubted it. No, she needed a better plan.

It took them less than ten minutes to exit the woods and cross the field. In the distance, Emma saw the barn, the door still open, and the horses cropping grass in the pasture. Little had changed and yet everything was different. They now knew who meant their community harm, who was bent on scaring them away. What they didn't know was how to stop him.

At the southeast corner of the property, Emma saw an *Englisch* automobile. It was the same rusted sedan Douglas had been driving when he passed her and Katie Ann on the road the day they saw him at the newspaper office. It had probably been parked here as they'd driven home today. They'd passed it, but with her migraine, she'd never noticed.

Douglas was right. They didn't know what was happening around them. They hadn't been paying attention. She hadn't put together all the clues that pointed to him being the arsonist.

The sun's position in the sky told her plenty of hours of daylight remained. Though she didn't wear a watch, she guessed it to be near six in the evening. Normally everyone would be coming in from the field, settling around the kitchen table, saying a silent prayer of blessing over their food.

But no one else would be coming down the road toward their home, not for several hours.

The summer days were long, and everyone at Henry's would work until eight, maybe nine that night. They'd enjoy dinner, fellowship, prayer, and the contentment of knowing they were helping one of their own. They would think Emma was in bed resting, that Katie Ann was caring for the horses, and that Sam had slipped away to work on his fields.

She'd heard Henry say he intended to visit Rebecca after seeing her home.

It would be hours before anyone would look for them.

As they approached the car, Emma kept her eyes open, scanning constantly for a way to escape. And as she did so, she prayed with all of her might that God would protect those she loved, that He would send someone to rescue them, and that Douglas would be stopped from spreading more mayhem or committing another murder.

Seventy-Five

Douglas needed a plan.

On the one hand, it was terrible that they had caught him.

Why had he run into the woods? The odds of them making the decision to follow him were extremely low, less than three percent near as he could calculate. Maybe it was because of the dog.

And who would have thought there would be a bull on the other side of that fence? He had looked like something out of a cartoon with those long, sharp horns. Douglas wasn't about to risk his life climbing into the same field as that beast. No, he wasn't a fool. So he'd waited in the woods. He'd hit the dog with the crowbar when it had first come charging at him. He had aimed for the mutt's head, but it had turned at the last second, and he'd struck it in the ribs. Another piece of bad luck. Another statistically improbable turn of events.

Sam had heard the dog yelp and come running. He was so busy watching for the beast that he'd never heard Douglas walk up behind him.

As the crowbar connected with the back of his head, the impact made a satisfying sound. "That's for ignoring me in school. And for having the perfect life while I suffered through a despicable existence."

He'd tried to befriend Sam once, back when they were in eighth grade, before he'd realized the Amish weren't about to allow the likes of him into their closed circle. The result had been swift and humiliating. Sam had barely spoken at all, murmured something about needing to help his dad, and hurried in the opposite direction. Some kids standing close by had broken into laughter, calling him a loser and telling him to just go home. That was the last time Douglas had tried to make friends with anyone. He'd learned his lesson.

He'd thought he was safe once he'd taken care of the dog and Sam, but then he'd seen the others coming closer, and he'd climbed the tree. If it wasn't for that stupid dog's growl, they never would have stopped under the tree where he was hiding on their way out.

They'd reached his old Buick when Douglas had an idea.

He fished the car keys out of his pocket, unlocked the trunk, and then thrust the keys at Sam.

"Drive."

"Me?"

"Don't act like you don't know how."

"It's been years."

"I know you can drive." Douglas almost laughed at the look on his face. "I've seen you around.

I've been watching you. We were in eighth grade together. You . . . you people had just moved here. You don't even remember, do you? You dropped out that year, but I had to stay in and deal with algebra and Shakespeare and chemistry."

"You were good in all of those subjects."

"Of course I was, but that didn't stop the football jocks from stuffing me in a locker or tripping me as I walked down the hall."

"You fought a lot."

"I defended myself. The next year was worse, but while I was spending time in the principal's office, you were already earning money. And while I was still riding a bike, you already had a car."

The memories flowed over him like a bad wind. They haunted him in his sleep and flamed his anger. By all calculations, the others should have left him alone, but they never had. The worst of it was that he ought to have been able to think of a way to make them stop since the principal apparently couldn't and his mother wouldn't.

He could still see the sneer on her face as she said, "Gotta learn to defend yourself. For all your smarts, seems you'd figure that out."

It had taken years before he'd learned to think of a way to even the score.

Douglas opened the trunk, all the time careful to hold the crowbar in a threatening gesture. Quick as a cat, he dropped the crowbar into the

443

trunk and picked up the gun he should have kept in his pocket. But he wasn't expecting to run into anyone. They were all supposed to be rebuilding Henry's workshop.

A satisfying feeling cascaded over him when he saw the fear in their eyes. A good weapon could have that effect on people and cause them to respect you and take you seriously.

A car appeared in the distance, and Douglas realized he'd taken too long. He slammed the trunk shut.

"Get in. Get in! Preacher man, you get up front with him." He opened the back door and pushed the girl onto the seat. Mrs. Fisher wouldn't meet his eyes. She dropped in beside her granddaughter and slid over to the middle of the seat. Douglas jumped in and slammed the door at the same moment Sam started the car.

"Where are we going?"

"Don't you worry about that. Follow my directions. Do what I say, and no one gets hurt." And then he had to laugh, because they all knew that wasn't true. The odds were that someone in this group was going to die.

Seventy-Six

Henry prayed as they drove toward the outskirts of Monte Vista and then took Highway 285 toward Alamosa. Of course that was where they were going. It was twice the size of Monte Vista, though still small at under ten thousand folks. More importantly, it was where the letter he'd seen at Vernon's had been postmarked, as well as the blackmail photos of Alvin. There was no doubt in his mind that Douglas had been responsible for that first fire, Vernon's death, and every fire since. The only question was why.

Henry prayed for wisdom. He prayed for their safety. He prayed for a means of escape. And he prayed for Douglas Rae's soul.

They drove through Alamosa, past adobe buildings and new hotels. He saw a sign proclaiming Alamosa as the commercial center of the San Luis Valley and "the place to work" in south-central Colorado. Douglas told Sam to pull into the left lane after they passed an exit for Adams State University. They crossed over the Rio Grande, exited the main road, and wound through an industrial district.

"Stop here," Douglas said.

The clock on the dash said the time was near seven, but there was still plenty of light. Enough to see the large, abandoned warehouse. Douglas directed Sam to park the car at the back of the building, near what must have once been a loading dock. He pocketed the car keys and motioned for everyone to get out of the car. As far as Henry could tell, no one saw them approach the back side of the building. The street was virtually deserted.

Someone had wound a metal chain through the two door handles and secured it with a padlock. Douglas pulled a key from his pocket and tossed it at Sam. He was still holding the gun on them. Henry didn't think he would use it, but he wasn't willing to take a chance that could endanger their lives.

"Put it in the lock," Douglas told Sam. "And don't try anything. I can shoot you before you hit me with that chain if that's what you're thinking."

Sam placed the key in the lock, turned it, removed the chain, and handed the entire thing to Douglas. He motioned for them to go inside first. Sam glanced back at Henry, who gave him a short nod. They needed to escape, but not if it meant one of them would be shot. God would provide a way. He would provide a safe way.

The room was cavernous, though there was little remaining in it. Perhaps it had been a supply room of some sort, or a workroom. The only windows were set high on the wall and so grimy as to let in little light.

Douglas motioned them toward a corner at the back, where he had apparently been living. A bedroll lay on the floor, next to a box of food and large jug of water. Beside the bedroll was a laptop. There was also a stack of books that looked to be high-level math texts. And past all of that was an ironing board and iron. Where had he found those, and how had he managed to get any electricity to use the laptop and iron? But then Douglas was exceedingly bright.

Was that his problem?

Henry tried to imagine always being two steps ahead of everyone around you, even your teachers and your parents. In the right atmosphere, such a gift could be cultivated and used for wonderful things. Douglas had apparently not had a good home life. Henry didn't remember those details, if he'd ever known them, but the man was living in an abandoned warehouse. How bad was home that you preferred such solitude?

Along the adjacent wall were gasoline cans, piles of old rags, and a box with the word FIREWORKS stamped on the side.

"Are you living here, Douglas?" Emma looked and sounded better.

Henry knew her migraine was still bothering her, as they never eased so quickly as that. But she was making a valiant attempt to cover her pain. Henry knew Emma Fisher well enough to understand that all of her energies were directed toward finding a safe escape for Katie Ann, for all of them. Now a look of concern covered her face, but Henry couldn't imagine that it was for Douglas.

"I do." Douglas's expression was placid enough, until he looked at Sam and Katie Ann. "I do now, because the police have been by my mother's place. It's not safe there for me anymore. That's your fault." He glowered at Sam, who met his gaze straight on but didn't attempt to argue with the man.

"That must be hard on you, not seeing your mother." Emma kept her voice soft, reasonable.

Douglas stared at her a moment, and then he shrugged, all anger apparently forgotten.

"At least I don't have to hear her hollering when I stay here. I'm able to stay clean, and"— he glanced at the ironing board—"presentable. I can wear each shirt twice if I turn it inside out. So laundry hasn't been a problem, but I still have to press them. Wrinkles . . . they're for bums."

He laughed as if he'd said something funny. "Once I figured out how to turn the electricity back on, things improved. There's even a shower in the employee locker room, and now I have hot water. I don't have to pay a cent, and the city officials will never figure it out."

He motioned for them to sit on the floor, against the wall.

He sat down, too, his back resting against a

pole support situated ten feet in front of them. He was still holding the gun, and apparently in no hurry.

"What are we waiting for, Douglas?" Henry worked to keep his voice calm, steady, and non-threatening.

"Dark." The young man's gaze met his and held a moment, and then he glanced away. His finger rested near the trigger of the gun—not on it, but close enough.

"You seem like an intelligent young man."

"Do you think so?" Douglas cocked his head much like Lexi would. Fortunately, the dog remained quiet, still bundled in Henry's jacket, still lying in Katie Ann's arms.

"You speak well, and you seem to know what you're doing—as far as working with fire."

Douglas smiled slightly. It wasn't a happy look.

"A child could follow the directions on the Internet. I'm surprised more don't."

"Did you ever want to be a fireman?"

Douglas glanced at Sam, a frown forming on his face.

"I wasn't accepted."

"Why not?"

"Didn't pass the psychological tests. I've never been good with those." He brushed his hair out of his eyes. "Any other test I could ace without half trying. But the psych ones . . . it's hard to know what they want."

"Is that what this is about? You're not being accepted into the fire and rescue program?"

He thought the young man wouldn't answer. He was staring at a spot on the wall above their heads, though his finger remained next to the trigger. "No. Not really. This is about righting wrongs. It's about retribution—at any cost. It's about a promise I made to my brother to *make them pay.*" He uttered the last words in a whisper, as if speaking to someone else. And then he closed his mouth and wouldn't say another word, though Henry tried to engage him in conversation several times.

How intelligent was Douglas? Was that the issue here?

Many geniuses had trouble finding their place in the world. Albert Einstein was believed to be mentally handicapped and was eventually expelled from school. Isaac Newton failed at running the family farm. Thomas Edison was fired from his first two jobs. Henry had studied the subject when he was a teen and struggling with his own gift. It was hard to be different. Best as he could tell, that was what it came down to. He understood the pain and loneliness in that.

What he didn't know was how to reach Douglas, how to soften his anger and assuage his hurt. He didn't even know how to get him to put down his gun. So he did what he often did when confused—he closed his eyes and began to pray.

Seventy-Seven

Time passed slowly as they waited in the warehouse.

Henry could tell Sam's anger was building. He clenched and unclenched his fists, sent scathing looks toward Douglas, and occasionally made biting remarks that, fortunately for them, Douglas ignored.

Katie Ann looked frightened and confused.

Henry glanced at Emma. When she thought no one was paying attention to her, she put her hand to her temple and rubbed vigorously. When she saw Henry watching, she jerked her hand away and slipped it into the pocket of her apron.

Henry patted her arm and scooted over to give her a little more space on the floor.

Katie Ann sat on Emma's far side, and Sam made up the other end of their sad little group.

Darkness began to fall. The small amount of light that had managed to penetrate through the grimy windows disappeared. For hours Douglas had sat, watching them, not moving, and not speaking. But now apparently enough time had passed. He stood and began pacing around the large room, apparently confident that they would continue to follow his orders. Henry had to squint to make out exactly what he was doing.

Then lights must have come on in the parking area behind the building because weak light once again filtered through the windows.

Douglas walked over to his boxes and began to paw through his supplies. He laid the gun down on a box in front of him, and said, "Don't try anything you'll regret. I can pick up that gun faster than you could get off the floor, and I won't hesitate to shoot you. They're already after me for murder, even though Vernon Frey was the impetus for his own demise."

"What did he do?" Henry asked, though he had a feeling he knew. The puzzle was coming together in his mind.

"He stole our farm, and then he ruined it." Douglas's tone was surprisingly flat, as if he were reciting something from an encyclopedia. "He bought it for thousands of dollars below the market value. What real estate agents call a disaster sale."

"That must have been painful for you to watch."

Douglas shrugged, a slight movement of shoulders beneath the cargo jacket. "How could my dad turn it down?"

"I suppose he couldn't."

"Our life was a disaster, all right."

"Not an easy thing for a young boy to see."

Douglas's head jerked up. "Don't think being sympathetic is going to help your situation.

Every tragic thing that happened to my family was because of you people."

"I'm sorry it seems that way."

"When the factory closed, my dad lost his job. For seven years he tried to make a living off the land, but he wasn't a farmer."

"Farming in the valley is a difficult thing."

"He lost the land, the house, everything. It's no surprise he started drinking or that he left, and then he died, clutching a bottle of whiskey. Everything began to unravel the day he sold our farm."

"And Vernon is the one who bought it."

"Stole it is a more accurate word."

"How old were you then?"

Douglas waved away the question. "He ruined it too. The place looks more like a dump than the dump does. Makes me sick, and it broke my mother's heart."

"Vernon moved into your home, and Sam refused to be your friend," Henry said. "What did I do? Why did you burn down my workshop?"

"You testified against my brother." The words shot across the room like arrows. "You took away the one person who cared about me, and it wasn't even his fault. Those stupid buggies are dangerous. I told him I would make you pay. I promised, and that's what I intend to do."

He swiped at his eyes with the back of his sleeve.

Glancing up at them every few seconds, he pulled out a backpack and began to fill it with supplies. Henry couldn't see everything he put in there, but he transferred quite a few items from his fireworks box, including large firework sticks, some old rags, a couple of glass bottles, and a box of matches.

Zipping the pack shut, he hoisted it to his shoulder, picked up the gun with his right hand, and grabbed a can of gasoline with the other. "I'm locking you in here."

"Why would you do that?" Sam had stayed silent and still through the entire conversation between Henry and Douglas. But now his patience had reached its limit. He made a move to stand, and Henry heard Douglas click off the safety on the gun.

"I wouldn't," Douglas said. "I'm locking you in here because I can't trust you, and I'm not finished yet."

"What does that even mean?" Katie Ann's voice shook, but she didn't look away when Douglas stepped closer.

"It means I have one more place on my list. Don't try anything." He stared at the girl a moment and then he moved in front of Sam and pointed the gun at his chest. "Don't underestimate what I'm willing to do."

"What are you doing?" Emma asked quietly.

"That's none of your business." He began

to back up, back toward the door. "The janitor comes by here every Wednesday. You won't die because you're locked in here for four days, so sit tight. Otherwise, you might be surprised by a BOOM!"

He laughed and slipped out the door. Henry could hear him weave the chain back through the outer handles. There was no doubt that he attached the lock, but Henry had to be sure. He walked across the room and rattled the door. It wouldn't open at all. So he turned back to his friends, souls God had put in his care, and said, "Time to come up with an escape plan, but first let's pray."

Seventy-Eight

In that moment Emma realized she loved Henry Lapp, and not only as her bishop and her brother in Christ. She loved him as she had loved George, and that came as a real surprise to her. Did it take a life-threatening situation to realize your true feelings for someone? Or was God using this terrible situation they were in to speak to her?

Henry's calm, steady presence eased the fear in her heart and the trouble in her soul. As they stood in a circle, heads bowed, hands clasped, Emma understood that if she made it out of this mess, it was time to start living again. She'd grieved for George long enough. They'd had a good marriage together, but it was time to embrace life. "Be open to whatever or whomever *Gotte* brings your way." That was one of the last things George had said to her, but she'd pushed it from her memory for four long years.

Now she realized she'd put her own dreams and needs on hold long enough. That wasn't God's plan for her. God's plan was to live victoriously, fully, completely.

To do that, they had to find a way out of this warehouse.

The second Henry said, "Amen," Sam bolted for the door. He rattled it, tried kicking it, and even stepped back and ran toward it, throwing his shoulder against it. But the lock held. Of course it held. It was made of metal. Sam was made of flesh and bone. Emma figured it helped Sam to burn off his anger. She patted his arm when he came back to stand beside her.

Henry had searched through the boxes and found a battery-operated lantern, which he set in the middle of the room and turned on. Light cast shadows across the concrete floor, giving the place an even more sinister feel.

Katie Ann had hurried back over to the dog. "She's the same. Still breathing, but not moving much, and rarely wakes up." She gently reached down and picked up Lexi, cradling her in the crook of her arm.

Henry was walking around the room looking up at the windows.

"Too high," Sam said.

"I agree, but we don't have to all get out. If we can get one person through that window, they could go for help."

"I'll do it," Sam said.

But Henry was already shaking his head. "You're too big to get through those windows, even if we could lift you up, which I doubt we could."

"Then who—"

But Henry was already walking over to Katie Ann.

Emma's heart lurched at the thought of her

granddaughter scrambling through a window and out into the night, searching for help, alone in the *Englisch* world. But beneath her fear, her mind understood the wisdom of what Henry was saying. It would be worse to stay and wait for Douglas to return. And she didn't believe that part about a custodian coming on Wednesdays. This place hadn't been cleaned in years.

Henry squatted down in front of Katie Ann, reached a hand out to pet Lexi, and finally raised his eyes to hers.

"Can you do this for us? Will you?"

"*Ya*, of course. I guess. But . . . what about Lexi?"

"We'll look after her."

"What if I can't find anyone?"

"A town this size has a lot of people. You find the river, and cross it at the bridge. Head toward a store or police station or even the college."

"All right. I'll try."

"Head toward lights."

"Okay."

"Don't stop unless it's someone you're sure will help you. Keep your head down and keep walking."

Katie Ann nodded, glancing once at the dog and then at Henry, Sam, and her grandmother.

"Someone will help you," Emma said.

"And we will pray. All of us will." Sam reached out and squeezed her shoulder.

"We will cover you in prayer, Katie Ann." Henry's voice was calm and confident. "*Gotte* will provide, *ya*? Do you believe that?"

"I do." Her voice was a whisper, but she gently set Lexi on the floor, still bundled in Henry's jacket, stood, and brushed off the back of her dress.

Emma stepped closer, put her arms around her granddaughter, and said, "I love you, child."

"I love you too, *Mammi*."

The idea had sounded like a good one, but it was a bit more difficult to find a way to boost Katie Ann up and out the window. The room contained nothing for them to stand on. They tried the ironing board, but it wobbled when Henry climbed on top of it. It certainly wouldn't support him when he was holding Katie Ann. Sam tried to stand on one of Douglas's boxes, but it collapsed under his weight.

"I should stand on bottom," Sam said.

"*Nein*. You're stronger than I am."

"Exactly. Put me on bottom."

"I wouldn't be able to climb on your shoulders and have the strength to pull Katie Ann up."

"We're going to crush you, Henry."

"It won't be for long. Let's try it my way first."

The first two times Sam tried climbing on Henry's shoulders, he lost his balance, probably because he was trying not to lean too heavily on his bishop. Henry put both hands on his shoulders and said, "We don't know how long he'll be gone. We need to do this, and I'm not worried about your hurting me."

Henry squatted, Sam climbed onto his shoulders, and Emma and Katie Ann, each grasping one of Henry's arms, helped him to stand.

Emma didn't think he'd be able to do it. Didn't think he would have the strength. Henry turned red in the face, but he motioned for Katie Ann to hurry.

Putting his hands in front, he laced his fingers together. Both men had their backs against the wall.

"Send her up," Sam said.

Katie Ann placed her foot into the bishop's hands.

Emma stood behind her. "On three," she said.

"One. Two."

Katie Ann bounced up on three, and Emma steadied her from behind.

Henry gasped, "Better . . . hurry."

Again they counted, and this time Katie Ann stepped up into Sam's outstretched hands.

"I can reach it!" she called down. "But it's locked."

"Try turning the . . . latch," Henry said. "Quickly!"

There was the squeak of rusty metal and then fresh air poured into the room.

"Can you fit through?" Emma asked.

"*Ya*, I think so." Katie Ann squirmed up, through, and out the window.

Sam jumped down from Henry's shoulders, and the bishop sighed in relief.

For a moment all Emma could see was the hem of Katie Ann's dress, and then the bottom of her shoes, and then nothing.

"Katie Ann?"

The girl's head popped into the window opening. "Lucky me, there's a fire escape directly outside this window."

"Thanks be to *Gotte*," Henry said. "Remember what we talked about. Walk until you find someone who will help you. Walk across the bridge and toward the lights."

Emma stepped back and craned her neck to see better. "Can you get down okay?"

The girl's head disappeared, and then she popped back into the opening and said, "*Ya*. The ladder lets down to the ground."

Henry sank to the floor.

"Are you okay?" Sam asked.

"No doubt we'll both have a stiff neck tomorrow." Henry smiled at them, and then he called out to Katie Ann.

"Take a *gut* look at the buildings around you, so you can describe it to the police."

"*Ya*, okay." Katie Ann stuck her head back through the window. "I'll hurry," she promised.

And then she was gone.

Seventy-Nine

Time passed slowly.

Emma prayed for Katie Ann. Her heart cried out to God, petitioning for the girl's safety. But eventually she ran out of words, so she sat there silently, waiting, hoping God would hear and answer the prayers she didn't know how to speak. The pain of her migraine had not abated. When Sam found a box of food, Henry brought her a bottle of water and a granola bar.

"I don't think—"

"Eat, Emma. We must keep up our strength."

"I'll try." She nibbled at the granola bar, and though it didn't have much taste, it did settle her stomach. She hadn't realized how thirsty she was until she'd guzzled nearly half the bottle.

Sam had carried the box of provisions over to where they sat in the middle of the room.

Henry turned the lantern to low.

"It'll save the batteries," he said. "It could be that we're in for a long night."

They made a small circle, the three of them. Sam had no qualms pillaging the supply box. "Missed supper," he said when he caught her looking.

Emma laughed. It sounded strange in the large, abandoned room. "You're no longer a growing boy, Sam, but I suspect you work hard and are used to a *gut* dinner."

"Mom keeps us well fed." He stared at the peanut butter crackers in his hand. "They'll be worried now. Your family, mine, and the whole community will be looking for Henry."

"They will all be looking for all of us." Henry ran both hands up and down the sides of his face. "As will Sheriff Grayson and Meg Allen."

"Tell us about Douglas." Emma peered at Sam, not sure she wanted the details, but knowing she needed to fill this time of waiting with something, some new information.

"I met him in eighth grade, the first year we were here."

"We hadn't established our parochial school yet," Henry said. He was reminded of the conversation he'd had with Meg. Everything was coming together, starting to make sense, but to think that Douglas's anger had been boiling for so long was disconcerting. "We talked of it and decided to wait until the second year."

"It was different from school in Indiana, of course. Mostly I was ready to be out."

"He was in your classes?" Emma asked.

"One, maybe two."

"And how did he . . . how did he do?"

"Well, academically. Douglas was always at the top of the class, and it didn't seem to take much effort."

"Socially?"

"Not so well. Kids made fun of him for the way he dressed, the way he talked, even the fact that he was so smart."

It seemed to Emma that Sam was lost in that memory of thirteen years ago. Henry was content to listen.

"Maybe I should have reached out and tried to be a friend to him. But Douglas Rae was not an easy person to like, and at the end of each day I was ready to get home and help Pop with the fields. I didn't exactly hang around the school. I don't even remember the time he talked about, when he tried to befriend me."

"He would come by our vegetable stand," Emma said. "Said he was buying things for his mother. It was obvious something was off, but I never guessed he would harbor such animosity toward us."

"I've testified in only one trial since we moved to Monte Vista," Henry said. "The DUI case where the driver killed Mervin and Lilly Weaver."

"That was a terrible time," Emma remembered. "I can't remember the name of the person who was found guilty."

"Shawn." Emma stared down at her hands. "Shawn Neely. I don't know why that name stuck in my head. I remember the trial and how devastated Barbara Weaver was. She moved back to Elkhart. We still write one another occasionally."

Sam crammed the last of the crackers into his mouth and took a swig of water. "Douglas said you testified against his brother."

"Doesn't make sense, does it? Rae? Neely? And I remember no family at the trial. None at all."

No one spoke after that. Emma was wondering what it would feel like, to be accused of something, found guilty of a terrible thing, and have no one to stand beside you. To be completely alone in the world. Was that how Douglas felt? If so it explained a lot, though it excused nothing he'd done. The man was still guilty of murder.

Henry reached over to check on Lexi. Satisfied that the dog was no worse, he lay back on the floor, his fingers laced together and forming something of a pillow beneath his head.

Sam moved away from their circle and sat with his back braced against the wall. "If I had acted differently, all those years ago, maybe we wouldn't be in this situation now."

"It is not your fault for failing to see the need in the boy. Douglas was plenty smart, and he had apparently learned to keep his feelings well hidden. The pain in his heart simply overrode any moral qualms he may have had. His actions resulted in Vernon's death."

"All so tragic." Emma rubbed at the muscles on the back of her neck.

"Indeed, and yet our *Gotte* is all about healing. He can restore even the likes of Douglas Rae."

"I hope he experiences any such healing from a federal prison," Sam said. "The man is a danger to those around him."

"It's true he needs to be incarcerated—to protect himself as well as others," Henry admitted. "But never doubt the reach of *Gotte*'s love and the life-changing power of it."

"I know a little about that firsthand." Emma glanced up from the granola bar she was still holding. Henry was staring at the ceiling, but Sam was watching her closely. "When George died, I thought my life was over. I was convinced all joy had been buried with his body on the hill at Leroy's place. I still miss my husband, but *Gotte* has healed the grieving places in my heart."

"Paul prayed that we would be rooted and grounded in love." Henry sat up and offered them both a weak smile. "If we are? Then we may have the power to comprehend the length and width and height and depth of His love."

Eighty

Emma would never understand how, but she must have fallen asleep when she moved to rest her back against the wall.

She woke to a commotion outside the door. Sam and Henry were already rushing across the room. Emma rubbed at her eyes and realized the migraine continued to pulse, especially on the right side of her head, but that didn't matter. All that mattered was Katie Ann. She put a hand against the wall and struggled to a standing position.

By the time she reached the others, a man's voice was hollering through the metal door. "An officer has gone to fetch a bolt cutter from the trunk of his vehicle!"

Sam cheered, Henry reached out and grabbed their hands, and Emma nearly collapsed with relief.

"Katie Ann?" she called through the door.

"I'm here, *Mammi*." The rest of what she said was garbled, but it didn't matter. What mattered was that the girl was all right and they were being rescued.

Emma thought she would never hear a more satisfying sound than the pop of the metal chain as the officer cut through it, and then the chain

467

being dragged through the handles of the door.

An older man in a police uniform opened the door, a smile wreathing his face.

Emma barely took the time to notice him. Her eyes were on the girl standing at the back of the group, waiting to make her way inside, her hands clasped together, and an expression of hope on her face.

"You're okay!" Katie Ann flew into Emma's arms.

"Of course we're okay, child. It was you we were worried about." Emma's heart beat rapidly as joy and adrenaline surged through her veins. She hadn't allowed herself to imagine what might have happened to Katie Ann, but the weight of those possibilities suddenly fled, and she felt as light as a fluffy cloud in the summer sky.

"I had to walk a long way, *Mammi*. I kept my head down, like Henry said. The few stores I passed were closed and the homes looked boarded up." Katie Ann glanced at Henry and then smiled weakly at Sam, even as she continued to clutch her grandmother's hand. "I found the bridge over the river, and then . . . and then I saw a couple walking back to the college. They helped me."

"Praise be to *Gotte*." Henry raised his hands skyward.

"They . . . they called the police on their cell phone and insisted on staying with me until someone came." Tears slipped down Katie Ann's cheeks. She swiped at them and cleared her throat, allowed herself to be pulled back into Emma's arms. "I was scared, so scared that he had come back to hurt you."

"We're fine. Better than fine, especially now that you're here."

One of the officers had radioed for an ambulance, and after the paramedics arrived, they insisted on checking everyone in their group. By the time the four of them answered the officer's questions, there was a clatter at the door. Sheriff Grayson and Meg walked in.

Meg scanned the room quickly, and then she nodded to someone behind her that it was okay to enter. Immediately, a whole group of people began pushing inside. Some carried large cameras. Others toted devices that looked like toolboxes.

Meg was directing the crime scene investigators, while Sheriff Grayson pulled Henry aside to speak with him. After a few minutes, Meg rounded them up and herded them toward the door. "I need you to go to the station with me. We'll take a statement, and also we'll need your fingerprints."

"Why?" Sam asked.

"So we can eliminate your prints from the others left in this room." A smile tugged at the corners of her mouth. "What we'll be left with—"

"Will be Douglas Rae's." Henry rubbed at his

neck, which was no doubt sore, but he looked relieved. He glanced at Emma, smiled, and turned his attention back to the arson investigator. "So you haven't caught him yet?"

"No. When Clyde returned home and found you all missing and the fire damage to the barn, he called me right away. We don't know where Douglas is at this moment, but we will find him. And when we do, we'll have plenty of evidence compiled to ensure we can keep him. The prints here should match those found at Emma's barn. Because it didn't burn, we were able to pull some good ones. We'll have a strong case."

"Once you catch him." Sam looked less convinced that things would end so easily.

A squawk sounded over Grayson's radio. He turned away from them, listening and then responding to the person. When he turned back, his expression was serious but Emma thought hopeful too.

"The volunteer fire department in Monte Vista responded to a fire at the school, main building. It has to be him. Officers are on their way."

Eighty-One

The doctor ordered Henry to observe strict bed rest for the next week. He'd badly bruised his hip when he'd fallen on the ground running into the barn, pulled a muscle in his back from holding Sam on his shoulders, and then he'd come down with a nasty cold. Abe suggested perhaps God was helping him to follow the doctor's orders.

In truth, Henry didn't mind too much. He was able to read and rest with Lexi lying at the foot of his bed. If ever a dog had earned a place indoors, the little beagle had.

Doc Berry had fixed up Lexi's wounds, including a thorough examination, stitching the cut over her eye, and x-raying and wrapping her ribs that had been badly bruised. All of the costs were paid for by the reward fund created to catch the Monte Vista Arsonist—that was the paper's name for Douglas Rae.

Henry, Sam, Katie Ann, and Emma had refused the rest of the money, suggesting that it be donated to a local charity. When that had run in the local newspaper, even more donations had come in. They lived in a giving community, and it seemed to Henry that the fires had brought them together—Amish and *Englisch* working side by side to help one another.

So it was that he didn't mind the week of bed rest too much. He was well taken care of.

The widows supplied him with plenty of food, friends tended his garden, Katie Ann cared for Oreo, and his elders took care of any needs among his congregation.

Emma and Katie Ann came every other day to check on him, clean the house, and generally kick up a fuss. Katie Ann was quick to finish anything her grandmother asked and then hurry to the barn. Henry might have thought the experience with the horses and the fire would have given her pause. After all, she could have been trampled when the Percheron panicked. She could have been killed. But if anything, Katie Ann was more interested in the horses than before.

Resting in the rocker in his sitting room, where he could watch Emma as she moved from room to room in the house, Henry tried reasoning with her to no avail. "I'm not out of bed enough for the house to get dirty."

"And yet there's all this wood dust on the floor." Through the bedroom door he saw that she spied the corner of something sticking out from under his bed, leaned down, and picked it up. She turned on Henry with a knowing look. "Sandpaper? Have you been working on your projects in bed?"

"A little. *Ya*. I suppose I have."

Emma shook the sandpaper at him and tried to

look disappointed. When he started to laugh, she said, "You're incorrigible. You know that, right?" Without waiting for an answer, she hurried into the bathroom to give the tub a good scrubbing. An hour later, his small home fairly sparkled.

When he smelled fresh coffee percolating in the kitchen, he stood and made his way to the table. Lexi followed, collapsing in a heap at his feet.

"Does she follow you everywhere?"

"*Ya*, she does. Though to be fair, I've barely left the house in a week."

"*Gut* to know you're following Doc Wilson's orders, except for working on projects while you're supposed to be resting."

"It was your son who brought me a magazine that showed different types of bookends."

"Clyde did that?"

"Sure and certain, and then Leroy brought me some nice lumber scraps. How could I resist?"

"How indeed?" Emma poured them both a cup of coffee and then set an apple crumble coffee cake on the table between them before sitting down. "One moment I'm so relieved Douglas is behind bars, and then I immediately feel guilty for wishing such a fate on someone."

"Incarceration may be the best thing for him."

"I'm not sure jail is *gut* for anyone, no matter how well deserved."

"He'll finally get the help he needs—physically, mentally, and emotionally."

"Maybe he wanted to be caught, at the end. Why else would he have hung around the school? Why the need to watch it burn?"

"I imagine his school days were a source of great distress for him, perhaps even greater than what he told us in the warehouse."

They sat quietly for a few moments, considering the fate of Douglas Rae.

Emma glanced across the room, and a smile replaced her look of consternation. "I see the widows have visited."

"They all came together, which was something new."

Emma's eyebrow rose as she cut them both a piece of coffee cake. "Strength in numbers?"

Henry laughed. He felt a delicious lightness, as if the heavy burdens he'd been carrying since the death of Vernon Frey had been lifted. He suddenly realized the time for somberness was behind them.

"Life is a gift, eh, Emma?"

"Indeed it is."

"Hard times and *gut*. During the hard times, we depend on our faith and on one another." Henry added a spoonful of sugar to his coffee and placed the spoon on the napkin sitting between them. "The *gut* times we should enjoy . . . enjoy and share with one another."

Emma listened and waited, one of the many qualities he liked about her.

"I would like to enjoy more of this life with you." Now both of her eyebrows shot up, giving her a surprised look. Well, maybe she was surprised. He should have confessed his feelings long ago. "Would you be willing to go on a buggy ride with me? That is, once Doc says it's okay to drive?"

"Are you asking to court me, Henry Lapp?"

He reached out and covered her hand with his. "We're not too old, and I care for you, Emma. Courting is an important time. We can learn more about one another."

"Learn more?" Now she tilted her head back and laughed.

Lexi whined once in her sleep, rolled over, and snuggled closer to his feet.

"I've known you nearly all my life." Emma's voice softened. "I've celebrated with you during the *gut* times—"

"And sat with me during the bad. As I have with you." He picked up his fork and sampled the coffee cake. It was moist and rich, like his life. "But do you know that I wait every year for the sandhill cranes to come through in March? I can spend hours watching them. They are majestic birds."

"Are they now?"

"They are. Do you have a favorite bird, Emma?"

"I love the hummingbirds. They remind me

of children, darting back and forth. When they appear, I know summer has come, and when they leave, I know it's time to prepare for winter."

Katie Ann banged through the back door and came in from the mudroom. "I forgot the carrots." She plucked two off the counter where Emma had left them and hurried back out.

"She seems to have recovered from her traumas."

"She's still suffering from the nightmares. I don't sleep as soundly as I did when I was younger, and I hear her. More than once I've gone in to sit by her bed." Emma turned the coffee mug so that its small chip was facing him. She ran the tip of her finger over it. "Twice now she has asked me to pray with her about Douglas."

"That's *gut*. That is exactly what we all should do."

They spoke of her family, hopes for a good harvest, and the community's growth. Most of the families had decided to stay. Henry felt confident their numbers would continue to grow and prosper in the San Luis Valley.

The remainder of the hour passed too quickly for Henry's liking. He marveled that he could be so at rest in Emma's company. Usually he refueled by being alone, but she had a bolstering presence. Yes, he realized he would be a fortunate man indeed to pass the rest of his years with Emma Fisher.

Katie Ann bounded back into the house, talking of Oreo, a nest of birds in the barn, and wild-flowers she'd spied near his pump.

She had a piece of the cake and then carried her grandmother's cleaning supplies to the buggy they'd brought.

"Surprised you didn't walk."

"I offered to go to town and pick up some books from the library for Rachel." They'd walked out onto the front porch.

When Henry looked out across the valley, he was awed at the beauty, the harvest they would enjoy, the blessings of this place.

Emma touched his arm. "I care about you as well, Henry, and I'd be happy to take a buggy ride with you."

"Excellent." He reached for her hand, squeezed it, and then he sat down in a rocker to watch as they made their way down his lane.

A burden in his heart lifted, something he didn't realize he'd been carrying around—the fear that Emma would think he was being foolish, that their time for companionship was past. But they were made for companionship—friendships, family relationships, and romantic relationships. God blessed them richly, not only with the land or what they could coax from it, but with each other.

Eighty-Two

Meg stopped by later that afternoon. Henry was sitting on the front porch, whittling a piece of wood into a turkey call. He'd learned the skill from his father, but he hadn't made one in a very long time. He rather liked the challenge of remembering what he had been taught all those years ago.

Lexi slowly left the porch to greet her. When Meg pulled a dog treat out of her pocket and handed it to the little dog, Henry started laughing.

"She seems to have won you over."

"How can I not like a dog who helped me crack a case?"

"She's brave, that is for sure and certain." He motioned to the rocker beside him, and Meg sat, releasing a deep breath and putting the rocker into motion.

"Nice place you have here, Bishop."

"*Ya*? I thought you might find it rather boring compared to your big city."

"District headquarters is only three hours from here, yet it feels like a world away." Meg scooted the rocker so she could face him while they talked. "How are you feeling?"

"Everyone's treating me like I'm old."

"You are old." A mischievous grin spread across

her face. "And this community cares about you."

"For which I'm grateful."

"I actually stopped by for a reason other than to tease you about your age. I wanted to catch you up on the case."

"The paper said Douglas would be transferred to Durango for trial."

"Actually, there's not going to be a trial. Douglas decided to plead guilty and waive the right to a trial."

"I suppose that's a good thing."

"Saves money. Saves time for all involved."

"I'm a little surprised. He didn't seem to fully understand the gravity of what he'd done."

"His exact words were, and I quote, 'The statistical odds of being found innocent are less than one percent, and I would rather not waste my time.'"

"So we won't have to testify."

"No. He will appear before a judge and be sentenced. That will take place in Durango as the paper reported. Then he'll be transferred to Englewood to serve his sentence."

"Which will be—"

"He's looking at forty-five years behind bars. Felony murder always carries that sentence. Plus, there are the charges of attempted murder, arson, and destruction of property. He'll serve those sentences concurrently. The judge may offer a possibility of parole. If so, Douglas Rae will be an old man by the time he's released."

Henry thought of what he'd told Sam and Emma while they were waiting, locked in the deserted warehouse. *Never doubt the reach of Gotte's love and the life-changing power of it.* He believed in the deepest parts of his heart that God could reach Douglas. As long as there was breath, there was hope.

"It's a relief, for sure and certain. We can put all this behind us now."

"There's one more thing." She pulled a sheet of paper from her pocket and handed it to him. "We showed Douglas the drawing you did. He remembered the letter, remembered it well enough to fill in the blanks for us."

Henry stared down at the letter. Someone had transcribed it, corrected the errors, and typed it up neatly. No doubt it would now appear in Douglas's file.

"I want to apologize to you, Henry. When you first showed me that drawing, I thought you were crazy."

Henry glanced up, surprised to see she was smiling, shaking her head, nearly laughing. "Who would believe such a thing, such an ability, was even possible? I guess there will always be things in this world to surprise us."

   Vernon Frey
   You people have ruined my life, and you can be sure you will pay for it. You

don't pay a cent of taxes. You won't even fight for your country and don't honor our flag. You shouldn't even be here. When I skipped school, I had to answer to a truant officer, but your kids are free to go about their way before they even start high school.

You bought our land for less than it was worth. My family was desperate. Dad lost his job when the old factory closed in town. Then he took to drinking, and just like that he lost our home. I begged him not to sell it, but did he listen? He died, clutching a bottle of whiskey and it is your fault. Now I'm living in a hovel. It's all because YOU PEOPLE looked on some map and decided you'd like to live in the valley.

Who do you think you are? You drive those buggies out on the road. Who is responsible if you're hit? This is ridiculous. We were driving here long before you came. How can it be a man's fault if he hits a buggy in the middle of the night? YOU are to blame because you shouldn't even be on our roads. But we paid for that too.

YOU never contributed anything to this place. Well now you will pay.

Now there's some work in town, but

who gets hired? YOU PEOPLE do. We lose a job every time you steal one from us. You work for cheap. What about the rest of us still here? We need health insurance and more than minimum wage to survive here. What are we supposed to do when YOU PEOPLE move into town?

Well, this has gone on too long and I'm going to do something about it.Time is up. I've already given you two warnings, and you didn't listen.Now you will have to. But maybe not you because you'll be DEAD. But someone will listen now. They will pay attention. You wait and see.

Henry read the letter, his heart breaking anew for Vernon, for Douglas, and for all who had been hurt by his actions.

"Word-for-word, it's the same as what you gave me." Meg sat back in the chair, once again rocking.

"This is an obvious cry for help."

"It is."

"If only Vernon had listened. If he had shared this letter the afternoon I went to visit him, he might still be alive."

Meg didn't answer that.

But God's plan was perfect for each life, and Henry realized he could trust that Vernon's life was complete. *A person's days are determined;*

you have decreed the number of his months and have set limits he cannot exceed. Henry had quoted the words from Job 14:5 at many a funeral.

Looking back over the letter, he pointed at the first paragraph. "Seems to be a reference to Sam, or perhaps all of our children who attended public school the first year we were here."

"Douglas had indeed gone to school with Sam. According to his mother, the eighth grade was a time when he was struggling with his dyslexia as well as his superior intelligence. She thought he would work it out on his own."

"Obviously that didn't happen. What about the other missing pieces? Did Vernon buy his father's land? How was the trial for Shawn Neely connected to Douglas? And why did he target the newspaper and Emma's place?"

Meg held up a hand to stop his questions. "Vernon didn't directly buy the Rae family farm, which is the reason we didn't find that connection. It was bought by Vernon's uncle, a man named Jethro Kepf, in a cash sale."

"I remember now. Someone from the original Plain community once told me Vernon's uncle, his mother's brother, was in charge of the family purse strings when Vernon's parents died. He didn't approve of Vernon's chosen profession."

"Buying and selling used items?"

"That would be the nice way to describe it. Jethro thought farming was the only honest occupation, especially for an Amish man. He agreed to purchase the home, hoping Vernon would come to his senses. At the time, Vernon would have been . . . forty-nine years old by my recollection. There was no chance he was going to take up farming."

"The title transfer showed Jethro offered well below the asking price. In desperation, Douglas's father accepted." Meg nodded at the letter. "That's a chronology of the events that led to Douglas's desperate actions. Frustration in school, the factory in town closing, losing the family farm, and then his father's drinking worsened and in time he abandoned his family. I checked the county records. He died eighteen months after selling the farm. He was drunk, clutching a bottle, actually, and stepped out into the middle of the road. The trucker who hit him didn't have a chance of stopping."

"This part about the buggy . . . "

"Douglas had no brother, but his family started taking in foster children, possibly for extra money. Shawn Neely was a few years older than Douglas, and apparently Douglas thought of him as a brother. As you know, Shawn was convicted of involuntary manslaughter for killing Mervin Weaver and his young daughter Lilly. We didn't originally find that connection because Shawn and Douglas are not technically related."

"Douglas wasn't at the trial."

"No. His mother wouldn't allow it, but since

that time Douglas has written to his brother, who's imprisoned at Englewood, and we know that he has visited twice."

"Such tragic times."

"The final straw was Douglas being turned down for a job at the construction site, which seems to be why he targeted Emma's house. Her grandson, Silas, was hired the same day Douglas was turned down. He had no experience in construction, but his mother was nagging him about getting a job."

"It would seem that with his intelligence, he would have been able to find work."

"If he'd ever made it into a collegiate environment, maybe, but our day-to-day life doesn't have much use for a genius."

"A sad statement if I ever heard one." Henry paused, his mind combing back over all that had happened. "What about the newspaper? Why did he strike there?"

"The *Monte Vista Gazette* was not a part of his original plan. He was upset about the story they had run the day before covering the fires." She stood, and Henry handed her the paper with Douglas's letter.

"I appreciate your coming by."

"Thank you. If it weren't for your drawings, we might have been looking in another direction. We might never have caught Douglas Rae."

"I can't see as they were much help, actually.

485

We didn't understand the significance of a single thing in my drawings."

"But we did. The letter was the most important clue, but the drawing of Abe, Lewis, and Douglas standing outside the burning building narrowed down our suspects."

He followed Meg as she walked to her car, opened her door, and then she turned to explain.

"We were closing in on him even before he abducted you three in the woods. Sniffing around his school records, letting it slip to the paper that we had a letter—"

"He had to have known the letter burned up in the fire."

"But there was a possibility Vernon had given it to someone. All of those things provoked him into accelerating his timeline, and when rushed, even a genius like Douglas can make a mistake."

"The school fire."

"He wanted to be sure it burned all of the school records. He stayed around a little too long, which is how we caught him at the scene."

She climbed into the car, rolled down the window, and started the engine. "That gift of yours . . . it's something, Henry."

He'd always thought of it as a curse. He could admit that to himself now, but perhaps she was right. Perhaps God had found a way to use this strange ability of his. Instead of trying to explain any of those thoughts, he simply nodded.

"If I could think of a way to use you in active investigations, I'd pester you to join my department."

"An Amish man on an arson squad? Not likely."

Lexi barked twice and they both laughed.

"Hopefully, things will quiet down around here. No offense, but I hope not to return to Monte Vista until Grayson's retirement party next year."

As Henry walked back to the porch, he realized quiet was exactly what they needed—a plain, simple, quiet life. Which was the reason they'd moved to Colorado in the first place.

Epilogue

Seven months later

Henry bundled up to walk to the end of the lane and fetch the mail.

A scant half inch of snow lay on the ground, but Lexi bounded through it as if it were three feet deep.

He opened the mailbox and retrieved three letters, one bill, and a sales ad from the discount store that had recently opened.

Stuffing the letters into the sales circular, he whistled for the dog, who fell in next to him.

They walked back to the house by way of his workshop, where he picked up the item he was working on for Emma. He would take the small box to the house and add one more coat of oil to the finish. It was the length of the letters he was holding, but much deeper. He understood how much she missed Katie Ann. The girl had decided to spend the winter with relatives in Sarasota. The entire family had agreed that the warm air and change of scenery would do her good. And it seemed to be. With each letter, Emma said she saw more of the girl's joyful spirit return. She was healing, as they all were.

He set the mail on the counter. After pouring

himself a glass of water, he scooped up the letters, put on the reading glasses Emma bought him for his birthday, and sat down at the table to study what he had.

One letter was from the bishop in Elkhart—a genealogy matter Henry was researching in anticipation of a certain spring wedding announcement. The second was a circular letter from his cousins in Ohio. He looked forward to reading it and adding his portion to the bottom, then sending it on. It was a tradition he'd always enjoyed.

He pushed those two letters and the sales ad aside, and drew the letter to him with the postmark from Englewood, Colorado. Pulling out his pocketknife, he opened the small blade, slipped the tip beneath the corner of the envelope, and slit it open.

Three pages, typed.

Douglas was indeed dyslexic, but since transferring to the federal prison in Englewood, he'd been working with a computer program that was supposed to help his writing problems. Glancing at the page, Henry decided it must be working. Not a misspelled word that he could see, which meant Douglas had gone through it several times.

Henry realized he was probably the only person receiving mail from Douglas, other than perhaps Shawn Neely, who was incarcerated in the same prison. Did they have interprison mail? Did he ever see his brother? In his first letter Douglas had admitted that his mother asked him not to write to her, that she didn't think her blood pressure could handle the stress.

The first page spoke of his routine in the prison, day-to-day minutia everyone liked to share with someone.

Henry read the lines carefully, forming a response in his mind.

It was on the second page that Douglas returned to the subject of the fires.

> I'm still amazed you were able to recreate the letter I wrote to Vernon. I looked up both *acquired* and *accidental savant* in the prison library, but there was nothing to be found on the topic. Fortunately, I'm given one hour each day on the Internet (preapproved sites only), and I was able to read a few medical journals.

Henry could picture him poring over the medical texts. In another life, Douglas's genius might have been used for good. He could have been a doctor. He could have been anything he wanted to be, anything other than a man waiting out a life sentence in federal prison.

> I take issue with the term *accidental*. What happened to you was an accident, but our

lives intersecting seems too coincidental. I'm not ready to say God intended it, though I respect your beliefs and continue to read the devotional you mailed me. But the odds of your having such an ability and your being at Vernon's at exactly the right time to see the letter I mailed seem incalculable. Perhaps it was destiny or fate, or, as you believe, the will of God.

I remember sitting in my room at my mother's house, writing that letter. Mother's television was blaring some show that was supposed to be *reality TV*. I don't believe I'm insane, but if I was, her television habits would have been reason enough to send me over the edge. I'm more than a little embarrassed about my grammatical errors in the original letter. I reconstructed it in its entirety for the arson investigator. I hope she showed it to you.

Henry noticed there was no apology for killing Vernon. Sheriff Grayson had shared that Douglas had an IQ of 150, which was higher than Thomas Edison's but slightly lower than Albert Einstein's. Unfortunately, he also had the emotional maturity of a young teen.

My psychologist says it's healthy to examine my feelings at that time, but it seems so distant—something that might have happened to another person. Frustration? Anger? Desperation, possibly. Or maybe all three. I am beginning to realize my actions were a result of many years of grievances built up—some imagined and others real.

Thank you for visiting my mother and for taking her supplies. She hasn't written to me, and the two times I called she refused to accept the charges, but I don't blame her. As my doctor here says, we are all coping the best we can, and she has lost much—her entire family, actually.

Henry had met the woman three times now. He couldn't imagine two more opposite people than Douglas and his mother.

Dr. Barrow also suggested I put my abilities to work at something pro-ductive. Through him, I was contacted by the University of California at Berkley. They have a well-respected astrophysics department, something I've never had the slightest interest in, but the math problems they send me are interesting, and perhaps I can be of some use to the program. Dr. Barrow has started me on a course to earn my bachelor's degree. The English and history are tedious, but I'm enjoying the math and science. Fortunately, I was able to test out of the first three years and am working at a level that is interesting if not particularly challenging.

Henry put his finger on the paragraph, counted, and confirmed that Douglas referred to himself no less than seven times. His entire world was himself. Perhaps it always had been.

I do hope you will continue to write me, as yours is the only news I get from the outside. I think of Monte Vista often, and the wide open spaces and mountains and flowers that bloom in the spring—things I won't see for at least forty-five years. And then only if I manage to behave myself.

Though the letter was typed, he'd signed his name, and only the *s* was backward.

Douglas most probably was a genius, but he struggled as they all did.

Henry sat staring at the three pages, thinking about the letter Douglas had written to Vernon. His mind brushed back over the night on Emma's porch, when she and Clyde and Rachel had convinced him to use his ability to help find Vernon's killer. He had resisted that ability for many years, ever since that terrible time in Goshen.

I think of Monte Vista often, and the wide open spaces and mountains and flowers that bloom in the spring—things I won't see for at least forty-five years.

Henry stood, retrieved paper and pencil from his desk, and then he sat at his kitchen table, facing the wall. He spent the next hour sketching the scene from his front porch in what he knew was exquisite detail.

There was a purpose in all things. Henry trusted that God continued to have a plan for him and for his strange talent and their small community, and he even believed God had a plan for Douglas Rae.

The drawing was good. He still couldn't understand how he was able to do such a thing, but he had to admit the details were amazingly accurate. Setting the drawing aside, he drew his tablet of lined paper closer, picked up his pen, and began to write.

Discussion Questions

1. In the prologue and chapter 5, we learn Henry Lapp has a special gift. He can reproduce anything he's seen in amazing detail, but only if he draws it. His subconscious mind remembers, but his conscious mind does not. Does this sound like a blessing or a curse to you? Why?

2. We meet Rebecca Yoder in chapter 8. She is ninety-two years old and crippled with arthritis, and yet she proclaims, "The Lord is *gut*. I'm alive." Gratitude is one of the many things we can learn from our elders. What are some other things?

3. In chapter 19, Henry searches the Scripture for verses about gifts and how every gift is to be used for others, that all gifts are an extension of God's grace. Read 1 Peter 4:10 and Romans 12:6. Name some gifts you and people in your community have. How can they be used for others?

4. When Emma sees the photo of the arsonist, she begins to plan how to protect her family. She doesn't believe self-defense to be against the Amish practice of pacifism or nonresistance, which keeps the Amish from serving in the military or suing someone in

court. Read Matthew 5:39. Do you think this verse prevents someone from defending their family?

5. Pets have a way of wiggling their way into our hearts. Lexi is supposed to be in the barn, but Henry moves her to the mudroom and then into the house. While this might not be what we'd envision from the Amish, I have met Amish families who have great affection for their pets. Why do you think it's important that Henry has taken this little dog into his care? What does it say about where he is emotionally at this time?

6. After the explosion at the newspaper, Emma's one thought is for her granddaughter. Do you think this is realistic? If you're in a life-threatening situation, can you put aside concerns about your own safety because of your love for someone else? Why or why not? Can you give any examples?

7. Meg tells Henry, "Don't wait too long. None of us is guaranteed tomorrow." Why do we sometimes wait to tell loved ones how we feel? Read 1 Corinthians 13:1-13. It's an oft-quoted passage about the character and importance of love.

8. In chapter 63, we see a final scene between Henry and Alvin, who has left his Amish faith and remarried. Henry realizes "the man was doing his best to follow God, given the

choices he'd made." Can we offer the same kind of grace to people around us? What stops us from doing so?

9. After Douglas kidnaps Henry's group, Henry understands the man in front of him must be extraordinarily smart. Henry thinks back over the geniuses he read about when searching for answers about his own unique ability. He concludes with "It was hard to be different." It is hard to be different, especially in modern American society. What can we do to help those around us who don't seem to fit in?

10. Henry's strange talent is one of the reasons they were able to catch Douglas Rae, but at the end of the story we see him using this same talent to minister to Douglas. Has he had a change of heart about this unusual ability? How might that affect his life going forward?

Glossary

Aenti: aunt
Daddi: grandfather
Dat: father
Danki: thank you
Doschder: daughter
Englischer: non-Amish person
Gotte: God
Gotte's wille: God's will
Grandkinner: grandchildren
Gut: good
Kapp: prayer covering
Loblied: hymn of praise
Mamm/Mammi: mom/grandmother
Nein: no
Onkel: uncle
Ordnung: the unwritten set of rules and
    regulations that guide everyday Amish life
Wunderbaar: wonderful
Ya: yes
Youngie/Youngies: young adult/adults

Recipes

Green Bean Casserole

½ cup margarine
3 cups milk
½ cup flour
1 ½ cups grated Velveeta cheese
6 medium potatoes, cooked and diced
1 quart green beans
3 cups diced ham

Melt margarine. Then stir in flour and add milk. Stir over low heat until thickened. Add cheese and allow to melt.

Mix potatoes, green beans, ham, and cheese sauce in casserole dish. Bake at 350° for 30 minutes.

Das Dutchman Essenhaus Raspberry Cream Pie

Two baked pie shells
1 cup water
½ cup granulated sugar
1 T. cornstarch
⅛ teaspoon salt
¼ cup water
¼ tsp. lemon juice
1 box (3½ ounces) raspberry gelatin powder
3 cups fresh raspberries
3 cups milk
½ cup cornstarch
1⅓ cups granulated sugar
⅛ tsp. salt
1 tsp. vanilla extract
3 egg yolks
1 cup milk

Raspberry Pudding
Heat 1 cup of water and sugar. Mix the cornstarch, salt, ¼ cup water, and lemon juice. Add to water and sugar mixture. Boil until mixture is clear. Add gelatin and stir to dissolve. Add raspberries and cool.

Vanilla Filling

Place 3 cups of milk in pan. Heat to scalding. Mix together cornstarch, sugar, salt, vanilla extract, egg yolks, and 1 cup of milk. Slowly blend into hot milk, stirring constantly until thick. Cool. Pour 2 cups of vanilla filling into each pie shell.

Place 2 cups of raspberry pudding on top of vanilla filling. Top with whipped cream.

Apple Cinnamon French Toast

¾ cup butter, melted
1 cup brown sugar
1 tsp. ground cinnamon
2 cans (21 ounces) apple pie filling
20 slices white bread
6 eggs
1½ cups milk
1 tsp. vanilla extract
½ cup maple syrup

Grease a 9 x 13-inch baking pan. In a small bowl, stir together the melted butter, brown sugar, and cinnamon.

Spread the brown sugar mixture into the bottom of the prepared pan. Then spread the apple pie filling evenly over the sugar mixture. Layer the bread slices on top of the filling, pressing down as you go. In a medium bowl, beat the eggs with the milk and vanilla. Slowly pour this mixture over the bread, making sure it is completely absorbed. Cover the pan with aluminum foil and refrigerate overnight.

In the morning, preheat oven to 350°. Place the covered pan into the oven and bake for 60 to 75 minutes. When done, remove from the oven and turn on the broiler. Remove the foil and drizzle maple syrup on the egg topping; broil for 2 minutes or until the syrup begins to caramelize. Remove from the oven and let stand for 10 minutes, then cut into squares. Invert the pan onto a serving tray or baking sheet so the apple filling is on top. Serve hot.

Amish Cheesy Casserole

1 package (12 ounces) wide egg noodles
1 can (10.75 ounces) condensed cream of
   chicken soup
1 lb. ground beef
1 can (10.75 ounces) condensed tomato soup
⅓ cup brown sugar
⅛ tsp. black pepper
½ tsp. salt
5 slices American cheese
5 slices cheddar cheese

Preheat the oven to 350°.

Bring a large pot of lightly salted water to a boil. Add the egg noodles and cook until tender, about 7 minutes. Drain and return to the pan. Mix in the cream of chicken soup until noodles are coated.

Crumble the ground beef into a large skillet and then brown it over medium-high heat. After draining the grease, stir in the tomato soup, brown sugar, pepper, and salt. Spread half of the beef mixture in the bottom of a greased 2½-quart casserole dish. Arrange the American cheese over the beef. Top with half of the noodles, then repeat layers, ending with the cheddar cheese on top.

Bake for 35 minutes or until cheese is browned and sauce is bubbly.

Carrot Cake

2 cups flour
2 cups sugar
1 tsp. baking soda
1 tsp. salt
1 cup cooking oil
4 eggs
3 cups grated carrots
1 tsp. cinnamon
½ stick butter
4 ounces cream cheese
½ box of confectioners' sugar
½ cup chopped nuts
milk for thinning frosting

In a large bowl, sift dry ingredients together. Beat in oil and eggs. Stir in carrots and cinnamon. Bake in 13 x 9-inch pan at 350° for 25 to 30 minutes.

Cream Cheese Frosting
Cream together butter, cream cheese, confectioner's sugar, and chopped nuts. Add enough milk to spread easily.

Amish Coffee Cake

2 cups brown sugar
2 cups flour
¾ cup shortening
1 tsp. baking soda
1 cup hot coffee
2 tsp. cinnamon
1 egg
2 tsp. vanilla

Preheat oven to 350°.

Mix together the brown sugar, flour, and shortening just until mixed; there will be lumps. Take out 1 cup of sugar and flour mixture and set aside to be used later for a crumb topping.

Dissolve the baking soda in the hot coffee and add to the remaining sugar and flour mixture. Stir in cinnamon. Add the egg and vanilla and mix quickly. Do not overmix.

Pour the batter into a rectangular baking dish and sprinkle on crumb topping. Bake at 350° for 30 minutes; turn to 325° if the top starts to get too brown.

Remove from oven and sprinkle with powdered sugar or leave plain.

Peanut Butter Spread

2 cups brown sugar
1 cup water
1 tsp. vanilla or maple flavoring (I used maple the last time I made this, but I use both regularly.)
2 cups peanut butter, plus 2 heaping tablespoons
7 ounces marshmallow crème
2 T. light corn syrup

In a saucepan combine brown sugar and water; bring to a boil. Boil for 2 minutes.

Add flavoring and stir in the peanut butter, marshmallow crème, and the corn syrup.

Mix well and let cool.

Author's Note

The first Amish families who settled in Colorado did so in the early 1900s. As of 2010, the state was home to four Amish communities, with a combined population of under 100 families. In the San Luis Valley, farming has proven to be a challenge for the Amish, as the area receives only an average of seven inches of rain annually. The growing season is approximately 90 days. Many families in the area have opened small businesses to provide an additional source of income.

Amish men do serve as volunteer firemen. In Lancaster County alone, more than 300 Plain firefighters serve on local crews. Roughly 80 percent of the Gordonville, Pennsylvania, volunteers are Amish and Mennonite.

Bryce Reed, a volunteer firefighter in West, Texas, was convicted of conspiracy to make a destructive device and attempting to obstruct justice. On December 4, 2013, he was sentenced to 21 months in federal prison. He was never charged for causing the blast that killed 15 people.

Acquired and/or accidental savant syndrome both describe a condition where dormant savant skills emerge after a brain injury or disease.

Although it is quite rare, researchers in 2010 identified 32 individuals who displayed unusual skills in one or more of five major areas: art, musical abilities, calendar calculation, arithmetic, and spatial skills. Males with savant syndrome outnumber females by roughly six to one.

About the Author

Vannetta Chapman writes inspirational fiction full of grace. She is the author of several novels, including the Plain and Simple Miracles series and Pebble Creek Amish series. Vannetta is a Carol Award winner, and she has also received more than two dozen awards from Romance Writers of America chapter groups. She was a teacher for 15 years and currently resides in the Texas Hill Country. For more information, visit her at www.VannettaChapman.com.

Books are produced in the United States using U.S.-based materials

Books are printed using a revolutionary new process called THINKtech™ that lowers energy usage by 70% and increases overall quality

Books are durable and flexible because of smythe-sewing

Paper is sourced using environmentally responsible foresting methods and the paper is acid-free

Center Point Large Print
600 Brooks Road / PO Box 1
Thorndike, ME 04986-0001 USA

(207) 568-3717

US & Canada:
1 800 929-9108
www.centerpointlargeprint.com